Highlander The Demon Lord

by

Donna Fletcher

Donna Fletcher

Copyright

Highlander The Demon Lord
All rights reserved.
Copyright © May 2018 by Donna Fletcher

Cover art
Kim Killion Group

Chapter One

Adara was not in a hurry. She took her time, her steps not slow but not rushed. The chilled air felt good especially after this morning when she had woken feeling poorly. It nipped at her cheeks, setting them aglow against her pale skin. A slight breeze stirred her blonde hair that had grown to her shoulders, her long tresses having been chopped off to just below her ears not that long ago when she had been held prisoner at...

She shook her head, not wanting to think on it and yet knowing no matter how many times someone told her she was safe, she did not believe them. She had never felt safe, secure, protected. She had lived with fear for so long that it was more her friend now than her enemy. It kept her on edge, aware, and waiting for what would happen next. Something always happened to disrupt whatever moment of peace she had ever found. So, she was always prepared to run, though now... she stopped, her hand resting at her stomach, the unease returning.

She glanced up at the darkening sky that made it seem later than mid-day and added to her unrest. Autumn was strong in the air, though it was a week before it would actually arrive, its early presence portending a frigid winter. What then did the darkening sky foretell for today? A harsh rainstorm or more?

She could hear her uncle Owen admonishing her for not taking a horse and an escort with her. She wiped at the tear that rose in her eye. She wished she had gotten more time with her uncle Owen, having known him for only a few months before he died. He had been ill, but had grown strong over the months she had spent with him. A foolish fall had claimed his life and stolen the little bit of happiness she had found with someone who seemed to truly care for her.

His death had left her the sole heir to the Clan MacVarish, but her uncle, the wise man that he had been, had left the clan's care and leadership to Lord Craven of the Clan MacCara, friend and neighbor to the Clan MacVarish. Adara could not be more pleased. Craven was a good and powerful man from what she had seen of him so far and from what his wife, Espy, had told her about him. And if she trusted anyone, it was Espy.

A sudden wind caught her in a strong hug almost as if it were arms that captured her, and it sent a shiver burrowing deep into her bones. A faint thunder rumbled in the distance and her leisurely steps turned to hurried ones. It would do her no good to be caught in a thunderstorm and if the rain persisted throughout the day, she would be stuck at the MacCara keep for the night. Not something she had planned on or would want.

Adara cherished her new home and the solitude it brought her. She preferred spending time alone, not feeling comfortable with people. It was why she tucked her hood low over her head and kept a quick pace upon entering the small village that surrounded MacCara keep.

The village seemed unsettled today, people rushing about, not a smile to be seen, and women gathering up their children and hurrying them into their cottages.

Something was wrong.

Adara continued, her steps more anxious than they had been as she made her way to Espy's healing cottage. She grew even more apprehensive when she found the door shut and no one in sight. Espy should be here by now, it being mid-day. Espy was not only wife to Craven MacCara but healer for the clan as well and an exceptional one at that.

Espy's absence proved something was definitely wrong.

Fear that something may have happened to Espy had her hurrying her steps to the keep and as she did, she realized the thunder had drawn closer. A storm was brewing and would unleash itself upon the land soon. She did not want to stay here for the night and if the thunderous storm did not sound so close, she would leave and make the nearly two hours' trek back to the MacVarish keep.

She worried her hands as she approached the keep, casting a quick glance at her right hand. Her two end fingers were badly crooked, leaving them nearly useless, a result of the torture she had suffered. A torture she would have never survived if Espy had not helped her escape. She shook away the horrifying memories that refused to let go, refused to stop reminding her that she was not safe and would never be.

"Good, she is here. Now this can be settled once and for all."

Adara looked up to see Craven MacCara standing on one of the steps to the keep. There was a reason they called him the Beast. He was larger than most men, broad with such thick muscles, Adara wondered if a sword could penetrate them. His dark eyes glinted with strength and confidence that intimidated and his handsome features stirred many a woman's heart. But the mighty Beast's heart belonged to one woman alone... his wife, Espy.

"Perhaps," Espy said, not sounding as confident as her husband as she hurried down the steps toward Adara.

Adara could tell from Espy's soft blue eyes that grew wider as she approached that she had been right. Something was wrong. For a moment, Adara was plunged back into the dark cell where she heard the terrifying screams of those being tortured. Her heart beat madly against her chest and her skin prickled with fear as it once had done when terror filled her with the prospect that the guards would come for her next.

She jumped when Espy's arms slipped around her and Adara went willingly with her as she led her up the steps, just as she had done that night Espy had helped her escape. More memories assaulted her when her eyes caught sight of the scar that had faded but lingered on Espy's right cheek. A scar she suffered for freeing Adara.

"We will set this right. He has been made aware of everything and heads are already rolling for it," Craven said. "Adara will be safe."

A terrifying fear gripped Adara so tightly that she almost doubled over if it were not for Espy's firm hold on her.

"But Adara does not have to be here for it. She has not been feeling well and I think it would be wise that she retreats to a bedchamber and rests," Espy said.

"It will take but a moment and it will serve him well to see what has been done to Adara in his name," Craven said. "I warned you he would come one day and without notice. That day is here and it is time for all to be settled."

Adara felt as if her breath had been stolen from her. It could not be. *Please, dear Lord, do not let it be him*, she silently prayed.

The pounding thunder penetrated her thoughts and made her realize that it was not thunder she had heard. It was the sound of a hundred or more horses' hooves beating upon the earth as they rode closer and closer to the village.

She cast a glance in the distance and there in the lead, approaching the village, was the man she feared the most… Warrick the Demon Lord.

"She is not feeling well. She needs rest," Espy argued.

"She will rest when this is done and she will fear no more," Craven said, leaving no room to argue his command.

"All will go well," Espy said softly, keeping her arm around Adara. "Warrick has been made aware of what his dungeon guards have done and is setting things right. This will all be over soon."

Adara remained silent, words stuck in her throat or was it the silent scream locked there that blocked all sound? It would be over soon, but not as Espy thought.

Her thoughts swirled as madly as the fallen leaves the

6

wind had scooped up off the ground to send scurrying in the air around them. Why had she not listened to herself? She would never be safe. Never.

Run. Hide.

What good would it do?

Doubt and fear froze her and so she waited, knowing fate would make the decision for her as it had done most of her life.

She watched with horror as Warrick and his warriors entered the village and drew near the keep. His warriors seemed to stretch on forever behind him. A sea of men draped in black shrouds, their hoods pulled down so low you could barely see their faces. It was as if the army of the dead approached and Adara saw that everyone there thought the same, their faces as pale as freshly fallen snow.

Or was it the Demon Lord who led them that put God-awful fear in them?

Warrick rode a beast of a black horse, his hooves pounding the earth with such force that one could feel the earth tremble. He sat the majestic animal with ease, almost as if he commanded the horse by sheer will.

He was a sight to behold. His black shirt hugged defined muscles in his arms and chest while his black plaid, thin lines of red running through it, wound snug around his narrow waist and slipped over one shoulder to fit tight against it. Black boots rode high on lean but powerfully defined legs and he wore no cloak. Some believed he was forged in the fires of hell and needed no defense against the cold. His dark hair fell in unruly waves barely skimming his shoulders. But it was the exquisiteness of his face that stole the breath and made one wonder how evil could spawn such beauty. His eyes, however, were as black as night which led most to believe he had no soul. And it was said he never smiled… not ever.

Adara eased out of Espy's arm to step behind her and Espy let her go, though reassured her with gentle words.

"You are safe. Do not worry."

Adara knew differently.

Craven approached Warrick after the mighty warrior brought his stallion to a halt and dismounted. Warrick's most trusted warrior Roark dismounted as well, though he remained standing beside his horse, his hood pushed back off his head. The warriors that stretched out behind Warrick remained lined along the main path through the village and also remained mounted.

"Do you fear war with me that you bring so many warriors to my home, my friend?" Craven asked, reaching his hand out to Warrick.

Most would not dare speak to Warrick so bluntly and dare not address him properly—Lord Warrick—since the King had bestowed a title on him, for what reason, one could only wonder.

"I see you still speak bluntly to me," Warrick said and those who could hear him shivered.

Adara was one of them. He had a deep, powerful voice that none could ignore and all obeyed. Wagging tongues insisted his voice came from the depths of hell and that he spewed fire when angered. Adara wondered if it could be so.

Warrick's hand locked around Craven's wrist and the two men gave a strong squeeze.

"Always," Craven said.

"That is why I continue to call you friend," Warrick said and it was as if a collective sigh was heard throughout the village.

Not so for Adara... her breath caught.

"My men will set up camp on the outskirts of your village. I will speak to your wife about the incident at my castle, and I heard there is another woman here who suffered injustice there as well. I will also speak with her."

"You are always welcome here, Warrick. A bedchamber will be made ready for you, though let me be clear," Craven said, a warning in his tone. "You may speak to whom you wish, but no harm comes to those under my protection."

"If I intended to harm someone here in retribution for the incident at my home, the person would already be dead. Espy will tell me what she knows and those who betrayed me will suffer greatly for it as some already have."

"Then let me show my appreciation with some good food and fine wine before I sit with you while you speak with my wife." Craven turned to Espy who was already approaching the two men.

"Welcome to our home, Lord Warrick," Espy said with a respectful nod.

"I am pleased that my friend has found a good wife, though I am not pleased that I have lost a healer. I am also not pleased that you did not make me aware of what was going on at my dungeon," Warrick said his annoyance obvious in his sharp tone.

"Would you have believed me?" Espy asked, not a bit of fear or tremble in her soft voice.

"I would have believed you enough to investigate your claim."

"That would have been too late for too many."

Warrick caught the movement on the steps and a flash of a face before the woman turned away as he responded, "We have much to discuss."

"I look forward to it," Espy said and saw that Warrick's glance had drifted beyond her. "I would like you to meet one of the women who suffered wrongly at your dungeon." She held her hand out. "Adara, come meet Lord Warrick."

Adara stiffened and the voice in her head kept screaming... *run! Run! Run!*

Craven took a step closer to his wife when he saw Warrick's whole body grow taut, as if he was ready to spring into battle.

"Adara?" Warrick said not only in question but in a way that demanded a response.

9

Craven slipped his arm around Espy's waist and eased her back against him as Warrick took a step forward.

"Adara!" Warrick repeated, a warning so sharp, so pointed that it was as if he had slipped his blade from its sheath, ready to strike if no answer was forthcoming.

Silence ruled over the village, breaths were held, and all waited for Adara to turn and face Warrick.

Indescribable fear gripped every inch of Adara, forcing her to turn and face the man who would determine her fate.

Their eyes locked and when a snarl rumbled from his lips, Adara responded instinctively… she ran.

Chapter Two

Warrick's roar sounded like a wild beast bent on devouring anything in its path. "Circle the village."

His warriors responded instantly, surrounding the village before anyone could react, except for—

"Warrick!" Craven yelled, his beastly roar powerful, though not as mighty as Warrick's.

Warrick turned a snarl so vicious on Craven that Espy grabbed her husband's arm to stop him from stepping forward.

"Not a word, Craven," Warrick warned, his arm shooting out to point an accusing finger at his friend, then turned to speak with Roark.

The two talked briefly, then Warrick walked past Craven and Espy, casting neither of them a glance, and came to a stop at the top of the steps to peer out over the village.

"Do not move. Remain as you," Roark called out as he walked a short distance from where his horse stood, forcing those near to clear a path and an even wider spot when he came to a stop, no one wanting to be in close proximity to him.

Craven brushed his wife's hand off his arm and approached Warrick.

"One word and your clan will suffer for it," Warrick warned, turning a menacing eye on his friend.

Espy hurried to her husband's side and spoke up, fearful for Adara and her husband. "Adara has suffered much at your dungeon and is frightened. She means no disrespect."

The fury on Warrick's face distorted his handsome features and had Craven once again slipping his arm around his wife's waist and tucking her against him. They both cringed when Warrick yelled out.

"Show yourself, Adara, *now*!"

"I think he knows her," Espy whispered to Craven.

Craven eased her away from Warrick as he murmured, "Then it is between them."

Espy went to argue and Craven shook his head, holding her firm.

"Adara!" Warrick shouted out again.

Still no response.

Warrick glanced over the people gathered and saw no sign of movement… no sign of Adara.

He spoke for all to hear, his voice strong, commanding, and his words threatening. "Show yourself, Adara, or I will make men, women, and children suffer for your failure to obey me."

The threat had Craven stepping forward. "Then it will be me who suffers, for you will not touch any in my clan."

The people huddled with one another, grateful their clan leader would sacrifice for them, though not sure if it would make a difference.

"One last chance, Adara!" Warrick warned with a shout, ignoring Craven's noble gesture.

When no movement was seen, Warrick gave a nod to Roark.

Roark quickly grabbed a woman from the crowd and Craven rushed to her aid only to be met by two of Warrick's warriors, their swords at his neck before he could reach for his own, forcing him to halt his steps.

"Stop!" the frantic cry called out.

"Show yourself," Warrick ordered and he watched as the crowd parted to reveal Adara.

She stopped for a moment, gathering courage before forcing her feet to move, to step forward and approach the spot where Roark stood. With every step she took, her heart pounded mightily, until she thought it would burst from her chest.

Warrick nodded and Craven and the woman were released.

Warrick ignored the nasty scowl Craven turned on him as Espy hurried to her husband's side, his attention on the petite woman who walked with the hesitancy and dreadful fear of someone approaching execution.

He did not wait for her to reach him. His long, powerful strides had him down the steps and walking toward her in the mere blink of an eye.

It took all the strength Adara had not to turn and run from him bearing down on her far too rapidly, but then she could never let another suffer because of her. She lowered her head, fighting the fear that roiled her stomach and weakened her limbs, bringing her to a stop.

The tips of his boots skimmed the hem of her garment, he stopped so close in front of her and when he remained silent for what seemed like forever, she forced herself to raise her head and look at him. He towered over her, her head reaching somewhere between his shoulder and his elbow. His angry glare was enough to send gooseflesh rushing over her and churn her already roiling stomach.

The thought had her pulling her cloak more tightly around her, the green wool garment her only shield against him.

His hand reached out so fast that Adara had no time to react. He captured her arm and propelled her toward the keep steps, his rapid strides not easy to match.

"A private room," Warrick demanded as he approached Craven.

It was Espy who stepped forward, blocking his path and bringing the mighty warrior to an abrupt halt, her husband coming up behind her with a shake of his head over his wife's foolish action.

"You will not harm her," Espy commanded, her chin going up and her hands fisting at her sides as if she was prepared to fight him.

"What I do with her is none of your concern," Warrick warned, his brow creasing between his eyes as it narrowed and deepened his scowl.

Craven stepped in front of his wife, and knowing Warrick well enough to judge this was not a time to escalate his anger, kept his voice calm when he asked, "Has Adara wronged you in some way?"

"Again, not your concern."

"Her safety—"

"Lies with me," Warrick said. "Now show me to a private room."

Craven nodded and took his wife's hand and as he led the way he whispered to her, "For once listen to me, wife, and hold your tongue."

Espy squeezed his hand, letting him know she would do as he said, sensing this was not a time to defy her husband, and certainly not a time to make things worse for Adara.

Craven went to close the door after Warrick and Adara entered his solar when Warrick's sharp words stopped him.

"No one is to listen outside the door or disturb us."

His strong command reminded Adara of the sound of the metal lock closing on the dark, small cell in his dungeon she had once occupied. She was a prisoner once again and it felt even more so now since he had yet to release his grip on her arm.

He turned his eyes on her as soon as he closed the door. "How dare you leave me."

Adara jumped at his sharp tone and instinctively tried to step away from him, but he held her firm.

Warrick yanked at her arm, bringing her close. "You will not get away from me this time."

Fear kept her silent.

"I am warning you, run from me again and you will suffer for it."

She nodded, fear continuing to hold her tongue hostage.

"You have much to answer for," he said, bringing his

face down close to hers.

His dark eyes brought back the warning she had heard time and again.

He has no soul. Do not look into his hellish black eyes or you will lose yours.

"You will do as I say, obey me without hesitation, from this day on, Adara. Do you understand?"

A wave of nausea hit her so fast and hard that a small gasp escaped her lips.

Warrick watched all color leave her face until she seemed more a ghost than alive.

Adara thought for sure she would heave there and then and was glad she had not yet eaten, but when all around her began to fade away, she realized a faint was coming upon her. And she welcomed it.

As soon as Warrick felt her body go limp, he snatched her up in his arms. He knew fear when he saw it in another, having put fear in many a man and woman. He had not meant to frighten her to the point of fainting, but it would serve a purpose. She would obey him.

He let out a yell, knowing Espy was another woman who did not know her place and would not have paid heed to his order. "Espy!"

The door flew open and Espy rushed in, Craven right behind her.

"What did you do to her?" Espy accused.

"Watch your tongue with me, woman," Warrick warned his own tongue sharp and demanding.

Espy wisely and quickly offered an apology, feeling her husband about to step forward and defend her. "Forgive me, my lord. I worry over Adara. She has been feeling poorly."

"She paled and collapsed," Warrick said.

"She needs rest."

"Show me to a bedchamber," Warrick ordered.

Espy did not hesitate, she turned and hurried out of the room.

Adara felt as if she was floating as her eyes began to flutter open and it took her a moment to realize that she was being carried up a flight of stairs. All came back to her in a flash and the name she had feared to speak fell from her lips in a whisper, "Warrick."

"You are mine. Do not forget it."

She said nothing, having no choice, never having had a choice.

The curving, stone staircase took them to the third floor where a single bedchamber awaited. A fire crackled and popped in a good-sized fireplace and the bed with its thick four posts and fresh bedding as well as numerous lighted candles placed throughout the room made it obvious that this bedchamber had been prepared for him.

Espy hurried to pull back the blanket on the bed and quick to tell Warrick, "I will see that all is well with Adara."

Warrick placed Adara on the bed and turned to Espy, a warning in his strong command. "I expect to receive word from you soon."

"Aye, my lord," Espy said with a bob of her head.

Craven gave his wife's hand a squeeze. "We will wait in the Great Hall."

Warrick gave a glance at Adara. She was beautiful, though she appeared thinner then when last he had seen her and she had been slim then. Still it did not mar her beauty, if anything it defined it. He wondered what happened to her long hair, the blonde color with a faint touch of red was shorter than when he had last seen her.

His dungeon? She was the other woman he had come to speak to. She had been in his dungeon. How had she gotten there? How much had she suffered there? Anger sparked in him. Someone would pay for this and pay dearly.

Warrick stepped away and without a word left the room, Craven closing the door behind them.

"You will tell me everything you know about her," Warrick ordered.

16

"I have not known Adara long. She is quiet and speaks little to me."

"Tell me more," Warrick said as they descended the stairs.

~~~

"You can open your eyes, he is gone," Espy said, sitting on the bed beside Adara.

Adara sighed and let her eyes drift open slowly, having come fully awake when they had entered the room, but not wanting to face what awaited her.

"Warrick arrived unexpectedly or else I would have warned you," Espy said and a frown caught at her mouth. "You know Warrick? How? He was not in residence when you were prisoner in his dungeon."

Adara's voice failed her once again. This time out of habit more than fear.

"Did you wrong him?" Espy shook her head. That could not be possible. Adara was far too fearful to cause harm to anyone.

Adara found it difficult to speak up, to explain, to defend herself. All her ten plus eight years, if she believed what she was told of her age, she had been made to hold her tongue and obey or suffer for it. She had learned at a young age that the quieter she remained, the less harm came to her, and so she had spoken up little through the years. She had retreated into the shadows as much as she could, keeping out of sight, keeping away from hands that swung at her for no reason.

Espy was the first one to ever show her any kindness, any caring, any help. She had loved hearing the stories of Espy's family and home when she had treated her wounds in the dungeon. She had said little to Espy, but it had never stopped Espy from talking to her, sharing her life, and for the first time Adara got to see that life did not have to be so

17

empty, so lonely, so unloving.

"Tell me, Adara, I will do all I can to keep you safe," Espy said softly, her hand taking hold of Adara's slim one.

Adara clung to Espy's hand, knowing this time there was nothing Espy could do to help her. "I caused Warrick no harm."

Espy released a long held sigh. "I did not believe you did. But tell me, how do you know him?"

Adara could not bring herself to tell her, though she would find out soon enough. She placed her hand on her stomach that had begun to churn once again.

"Have you eaten yet this morning?" Espy asked, reaching for a cloth that sat on the small table not far from the bed.

Adara had just enough time to sit up and grab the cloth before she retched.

Espy was quick to help her, fetching a ladle of water for her to sip since Adara had nothing in her stomach, her heaving causing more strain and discomfort than anything.

When it finally passed, Adara sat braced against the pillows, her face paler than before.

Espy wiped at Adara's face with a clean, damp cloth. "You will not be able to hide this much longer. I am surprised you hid it from me as long as you did."

Adara said nothing. What could she say?

"Craven will need to be told and he will demand to know what you will not tell me. Who got you with child, Adara?"

Chapter Three

"Adara is the sole heir to the neighboring Clan MacVarish. She did not know she was Owen MacVarish's niece, her mum and da having taken her far up into the Highlands when she was just a tiny bairn. When they died, she was passed around to various people until her identity was discovered. The nephew, Penley was his name, of a family Adara once lived with hatched a plan to try and claim the Clan MacVarish as his. His one problem was Adara, the true heir to Clan MacVarish. He had to find her and make sure no one else ever did." Craven paused, his first wife's unwilling part in it and her murder a memory he would never forget and one he did not wish to speak of. "I believe Penley paid someone to get rid of Adara and that was probably how she wound up at your dungeon."

Warrick gripped the metal tankard in his hand so hard that his knuckles turned white. It infuriated him to know that the woman he had laboriously searched for had been right under his nose and suffering unspeakable torture.

"And that was how your wife came to rescue her." Warrick raised his hand, seeing Craven ready to defend Espy. "I am not condemning Espy. She is a brave woman, though foolish at times. She should have come to me."

"As Espy pointed out… it would have been too late for too many. I do agree she can be foolish at times, but as she often reminds me, she is a healer and suffering and death are her enemies."

"And she saved Adara from death."

"She did that and more. I believe she has helped Adara gain some strength. Something the petite woman never knew she had. Adara spoke little when I first met her. She still does not talk as much as most women do," Craven said with a chuckle. "But she speaks more than she once did, though she continues to remain much to herself. She trusts little, though I cannot blame her for all she has been through." Craven paused briefly before asking, "How do you know her, Warrick?"

"A chance meeting."

Craven understood Warrick's brief response meant he would say no more on it until he was ready.

"Has she been feeling poorly or is her faint due to her fear of me?"

"Espy has mentioned that Adara has not been feeling well. She was due to visit Espy today and I would have dispatched a warrior to escort her here, but she arrived before I could send anyone."

"She came here alone?"

Craven nodded. "Adara walked from your castle to here after Espy freed her. Today's walk would be nothing compared to that."

"Which probably did not help her sour stomach," Espy said, approaching the table where the two men sat.

Warrick had caught sight of her entering the Great Hall, though had made no move to acknowledge her. He preferred people not to know how alert he was to his surroundings. He learned much that way. Besides, his thoughts had been on Adara and all she had been through since last he had seen her. What perils had she met along the way? How had she ever survived?

Craven stood and offered his hand to his wife to sit.

"That is all that troubles her?" Warrick asked after Espy took the seat beside her husband.

"Your presence does not help. It brings back unwanted memories," Espy said.

"My dungeon," Warrick said. When Espy gave a nod, he demanded more than asked, "Tell me what was done to her there—everything that was done to her."

Espy held nothing back. "Adara arrived at your dungeon with two broken fingers on her right hand. It had been too long since they had been broken so I could not straighten them. They have never healed right and are useless."

"Did she say who did this to her?" Warrick asked barely able to control the anger bubbling inside him like a cauldron about to spew over.

Espy shook her head. "She never spoke of it. The dark, confined, and disgusting odors of your cells are torture enough, and the agonizing screams added to the horror of it all. It was obvious after being taken to the torture room twice that your jailers were taking great pleasure in making her suffer and intended to get as much pleasure from it before letting her die. Another woman faced the same fate and another I feared I was too late to help. I do not know where you got such monsters but they deserve to burn in hell."

"They will pray for the fires of hell by the time I get done with them."

Warrick's dark eyes held such a cold emptiness that it ran a shiver through Espy.

"Did my jailers have their way with her?"

His voice was so frighteningly devoid of emotions, so empty, so uncaring that gooseflesh crawled along Espy's entire body. She had seen him like this before when she was his healer and it had disturbed her just as much then as it did now.

She slipped her arm around her husband's, grateful she felt loved and safe with him. "No, I managed to convince the jailers and guards that the women had an incurable disease and if they coupled with them their manhood would shrivel and decay."

"And they believed you?"

"The odorous scent from the salve I concocted and had the women use, kept the jailers and guards away, especially the ones with weak stomachs. They kept a wide berth around

21

the women."

"You should have come to me. I trusted you."

Espy shook her head, tucking herself closer against her husband. "You trust no one, least of all me. You questioned everything I did and never once spoke a kind word to me."

"Yet you stayed," Warrick challenged.

"I was needed."

"By the prisoners it would seem."

"By the innocent," Espy argued.

"Who are you to judge who is innocent?" Warrick accused.

"Who are you to ignore the innocent?"

"Watch your tongue, Espy," Warrick cautioned.

Craven raised his voice in warning. "Do not threaten my wife."

Warrick stood so suddenly the bench beneath him toppled over. "Your wife keeps her freedom because of my generosity. Do not forget that."

Espy forced herself to take a calming breath, seeing the anger raging in his eyes. It would do no good to further ignite his temper. "Forgive me, Lord Warrick. I meant no disrespect."

Craven did not think for a moment that his wife meant her apology. She said it to keep peace, to stop further problems. He only worried that Warrick would realize the same.

"I would accept your apology if I thought you meant it, Espy. But I have learned that most women say what is necessary whether they mean it or not. That you worry over your husband and clan's safety is admirable, but I would prefer the truth from you."

Craven kept a stoic posture, worried over his wife's response, but remained ready to defend her at all cost.

Espy gave Warrick what he wanted. "The truth is that I find you a soulless man with no redeeming qualities. You care for nothing—"

Warrick lunged toward her and Craven moved just as quickly, shielding his wife with his body.

"You would do well to remember that, woman," Warrick warned, his fist smashing down on the table.

"My lord, a message," Roark called out, entering the Great Hall.

Warrick nodded at him, then turned to Craven. "I will speak to Adara on my return. Make sure she remains in my bedchamber waiting for me."

Worry had Espy speaking up. "I will have Adara taken to another room, so your bedchamber is free to make use of upon your return."

"Do as I commanded, Espy. Your husband may tolerate your disobedience—I will not. And I intend to make full use of my bedchamber upon my return."

Espy tried to push past her husband as Warrick turned to walk away, but his arm refused to let her pass him. Her voice rang out, not that it was necessary with Warrick being only a few steps away.

"I will not stand by and see Adara suffer any more than she already has," Espy threatened and Warrick turned, shooting her a look that struck her with the force of a blow.

"Keep that tongue in your mouth, woman, or your husband will not even be able to save you from my wrath. And do not waste another worthless apology on me."

Craven whispered a warning to his wife. "Not another word." He stepped forward. "We worry for Adara. She is a gentle soul."

"Adara is no longer your concern," Warrick said and went to turn away.

"Adara is my concern and my responsibility, Warrick. Her uncle appointed me Chieftain of Clan MacVarish upon his death and that included watching over his niece until a time—"

"That responsibility is no longer yours."

"You cannot simply claim that," Craven said.

Warrick turned a hard, cold stare on him. "I claim what is mine."

"Explain yourself, Warrick, since you are not making sense," Craven said, his own annoyance showing.

"Have you ever known me not to make sense, Craven?"

Craven's response was instant. "No." It took a moment for everything to set in. He shook his head, finally realizing what Warrick was not saying, though trying to comprehend it. "It cannot be so."

"What?" Espy whispered from behind him, her skin alive with gooseflesh yet again, sensing something was dreadfully wrong.

"Tell her, Craven. Tell your wife that I am the new Chieftain and lord of the Clan MacVarish."

"That is utter nonsense," Espy said and gasped, her eyes going wide.

"I see you realize what your husband already has," Warrick said, his face an iron mask, but his dark eyes brilliant in what one would see as victory. "Adara is my wife!"

Chapter Four

Adara wished she was home at MacVarish keep. She could retreat to her bedchamber undisturbed, tucked safe in her bed. She shook her head. There would always be someone or something to fear. It had been like that as long as she could remember.

She got out of bed and went to the small window. The rain was just beginning to tap against it. She should leave, take her chances in the storm. Her hand went to her stomach. If it was only her that she had to worry about she would go, but she had the bairn to think of now.

A soft smile touched her lips as her fingers spread protectively over her lightly rounded stomach. Her shift and tunic covered the bump beneath, though the garments would not conceal her secret much longer. She had sworn to herself that unlike what she had suffered, she would do anything necessary to keep her child safe and she would love the bairn with all her heart.

Lightning lit the sky that had darkened considerably for it being only late afternoon and she squinted, her eyes having caught the outline of a man. Not any man... Warrick.

He stood out from all men, holding himself with the dignity and confidence seen in few others. She strained to see more clearly, the view from where she stood not very good. It appeared that he spoke with someone, a dark cloak wrapped around the figure against the rain. Or was it to hide his identity?

Warrick seemed to be listening to the small figure who barely reached his chest. After a few moments, he handed the person something and he scurried off. Warrick took a few steps, then stopped abruptly, lifting his head, his eyes settling on the window where Adara stood.

Instinct had her drawing back quickly, feeling as if she had been caught doing something wrong. A way she had felt often and obviously still did. But she had done nothing wrong, yet guilt poked at her as always.

Adara walked to the fireplace, rubbing her arms, a chill settling over her. She wrapped the soft wool blanket, draped over the chair near the corner of the hearth, around her shoulders like a shawl and let the rest fall around her as she sat. She stretched her bare feet out to the flames' warmth. Espy had removed her boots and helped her shed her stockings, insisting she rest.

How could she with Warrick here?

Adara jumped as the door flew open and was ever so grateful it was Espy, though by the look on her face—pure horror—her relief faded quickly.

"Warrick is your husband? The bairn you carry is his?" Espy shook her head. "How? When?"

How had she ever thought she could hide from this?

Espy grabbed a small stool and sat on it after placing it beside Adara's chair. "You should have told me."

Adara shook her head. "I did not want anyone to know. I did not want to believe it myself."

"How? How did this marriage come about?"

"I have often wondered that myself." Embarrassment had Adara turning her head away for a moment.

"I am not here to judge you, Adara. I am here to help in any way I can."

Adara turned, tears glistening in her dark blue eyes like stars in a night sky. "If not for you, I would have never known kindness. I appreciate you more than you know."

"As I do you. I am your friend and always will be as I always will be here for you, whenever needed." A small smile broke from Espy's lips. "And I will be there to deliver your bairn. You will not be alone."

Adara grabbed tight hold of Espy's hand. "Promise?"

"I promise. You have my word on it." Espy patted her hand that continued to cling to hers. "Now tell me how is it that you are Warrick's wife?"

"It happened so fast." Adara shook her head as if she still could not fathom it. "One day a man in a cart arrived at the farm I had been at for two years. I was told to go with him, that the family had no need for me anymore. I joined the other woman in the cart and we were taken to a keep and put to work there. I was only there two days when I was summoned to the chieftain's solar. Two men besides the chieftain were there. They were looking over documents on the desk, writing something and affixing a seal to it."

"Did you get a chance to read even a snippet of what was written?"

Adara cast her eyes down at her hands in her lap. "I cannot read."

"I will teach you."

Adara's head shot up. "You will?"

"I will," Espy assured her.

Adara continued. "I stood in the room waiting for someone to tell me what I was to do, then… Warrick entered the room. It was as if he consumed it, though it was more that he commanded it. And there was not a man there who did not quiver in fear. I sunk into the shadows, trying to conceal myself, my fear so intense. I was grabbed by the arm and forced to stand in front of Warrick. His dark eyes traveled from my head, to my feet, and up again, and he stared at me as if he were about to devour me.

"This one will do," he said.

Espy let Adara be when she turned silent and waited for her to continue.

Adara tried not to think too often of that day, but it had been impossible. It lived strong in her memory and would never leave her.

She continued with the tale as if it was just that—a tale—nothing more. But it was and the tale had yet to finish.

"Warrick stood next to me as a man said some words I barely heard, I was so intimidated with Warrick's imposing size. Then it was done, though it all still had not sunk in. I waited to be dismissed. I misunderstood when a servant appeared and I was directed to go with her. It was not until we entered the room and I asked her what my task was there and she told me.

"You are the wife of the Demon Lord. You will be made ready to receive him and consummate your vows."

Adara turned silent once more and Espy thought that was the end of it, but Adara continued.

"A tub was brought to the room. I was washed, my hair scrubbed and combed, and a white nightdress was slipped over me. And there I waited for Warrick."

This time Espy knew Adara was done, though there was one last question she had to ask. "How did you escape him?"

"I did not. He left the room the next morning and a servant entered and told me to follow her. The next thing I knew I was in a cart and—"

"You were taken to Warrick's dungeon," Espy finished.

"I figured I served whatever purpose I was meant to and he intended me dead." Her brow wrinkled. "But then I wondered after that day in the forest when Penley told us that he had tracked me down and paid to be rid of me for good, if Warrick had no hand in my disappearance."

"But after escaping his dungeon, you were not going to take a chance to find out," Espy said.

Adara nodded. "By then I had the bairn to consider. If I was wrong it would cost us both our lives. I worry even now what Warrick's plans are for me."

"From what he has said, he plans to claim the title of chieftain of the Clan MacVarish."

A shiver raced through her, though she was toasty warm from the fire burning in the hearth. "I do not think my clan will be happy about that."

"He is your husband and entitled to it. I do not see how

it can be prevented. What more concerns me is what he wants of you. Why wed a servant when he is a titled lord? Though you truly are no servant, so does that now make a difference?"

"And the bairn," Adara said in a whisper. "What will he do when he discovers I carry his child?"

Espy had no answer for her and it troubled her. She held tight to Adara's hand, letting her know she was not alone.

The door swung open with such force that it had Espy jumping in front of Adara, shielding her.

Warrick entered the room, his presence overpowering it.

"I will speak with my wife alone," he said.

"She is not feeling well. She should rest," Espy said, attempting to keep him from Adara.

"She can rest when I am done with her." He raised his hand when Espy went to further debate the matter. "Enough. You will leave us now."

"Go," Adara whispered, frightened for her friend. "Please go."

Espy turned to Adara. "I will return later and see how you feel."

"Only if I permit it," Warrick said and stepped to the side of the doorway, a signal that Espy should take her leave now.

"Later," Espy whispered to Adara and gave her hand a squeeze before walking to the door.

"Not a word," Warrick cautioned when Espy looked ready to speak and she clamped her lips tight and walked out the door, Warrick shutting it closed behind her.

"Still not feeling well?" Warrick asked, approaching Adara.

He took slow steps toward her and each one made her shiver with uncertainty. "Somewhat."

"I will give you tonight to rest. Tomorrow at first light we leave for MacVarish keep. Where we will remain until I say otherwise."

He came to a stop near her and her eyes roamed over him, remembering that night when he had stood naked in front of her. He had a body unlike others, defined with muscle and tuned with strength. And his manhood... had flourished in front of her eyes, and it had frightened her.

She was small and he was far too large. They would not fit, but they had. Almost as if they had been made for each other.

"Did you run from me?" he asked his face an expressionless mask.

"No," Adara said upset and not able to keep the quiver from her voice.

"I will have the truth," he said.

"I have no reason to lie."

"Then tell me." He folded his arms across his chest, tucking them tight, the muscles growing taut as he waited for her response.

Adara fought to find her tongue, far too accustomed to holding it rather than speaking up, but with him standing over her, glaring down as if at any moment... he moved slightly and Adara flinched jolting back against the chair.

Warrick was familiar with the reaction of someone avoiding being struck by a swift hand. Adara had to have been struck often for her to react as instinctively as she did and the thought that someone had hit his wife repeatedly stirred his anger.

He waited, saying nothing. In time, he would learn more about her, but for now he wanted to know what had happened the morning following their marriage.

Unlike speaking easily with Espy, Adara had to force the words from her mouth to respond to Warrick. "A servant entered not long after you left that morning. She told me I was to follow her." She paused a moment, fighting to quell the growing quiver in her voice. "I was grabbed and shoved into a cart and taken away to your dungeon."

"Did you assume I sent you there?" An obvious

30

suspicion and one he wanted confirmed.

"I did," she admitted with a nod, "until I learned that a nephew of a family I had lived with for quite a while had arranged the abduction for his own purpose."

"Yet doubt still lingered or you would have returned to me. Or would you?"

"I do not know you. I did not know what to think." She had her own question to ask but lacked the courage. Why would a titled man wed a mere servant?

"You are my wife, Adara, and will remain so. That is all you need to know."

His words had a ring of finality to them, but it was not enough for Adara. She needed to know the why of it. Why did he marry her? And did she have anything to fear from him? A yawn broke free instead of the questions and she raised a hand to her mouth.

"You need to rest," he said.

Adara had noticed from the moment she had met him that he spoke with authority, expecting to be obeyed without question. And he had been.

Another yawn hit her. The last few hours had taken its toll on her. The walk here, her queasy stomach, having to face a husband who was a stranger to her. It had all been too much. She could feel the fatigue, as if it had burrowed deep down inside her. She hugged the blanket more tightly around her.

Warrick reached down and scooped her up in his arms, her blonde hair brushing his face and the scent of lavender meeting his nostrils and stirring memories. He was surprised that she did not pull her head away from his chest, but let it rest there, but then she was exhausted and probably gave no thought to it. As she had done when he had woken to find her head pillowed on his chest the morning after their wedding. He had inhaled the same light floral scent of lavender on her that morning, had felt the warmth of her naked body wrapped around his, and he had forced himself to leave her side, his manhood stiff in need, and she no doubt tender from his insatiable need for her the previous night.

He placed her on the bed and pulled a blanket over her and watched her eyes flutter as she fought to keep them open, forced them to remain on him, and he wondered if she feared sleep would leave her too vulnerable in front of him.

"Sleep," he ordered and as if in surrender she closed her eyes or was she simply too tired to fight her exhaustion?

He stared down at her, watching her sleep, hearing the soft purr of breath from her lips. He had been furious when he had found her gone, assuming she had run away from him. He was more furious to have discovered that she had been taken from him, and even more angry to learn that she had suffered at his dungeon. His home. Where she should have nothing to fear, but then fear seemed ever present in her.

He stepped away from the bed and went to the fireplace. He added two logs, a chill having seeped into the stone walls from the harsh wind and rain that pounded the keep.

He had known nothing of her background, his only concern had been for her to serve a purpose, nothing more. She had been what he had wanted, a woman of no consequence, accustomed to obeying, holding her tongue, demanding nothing from him. Even her features had been of no importance, though when he first laid eyes on her with dirt marring her features, her hair streaked with grime and her garments hanging loose on her petite frame, he thought her at least passable. He had not realized the extent of her beauty until he had seen her freshly washed and clothed in a nightdress. He had not realized her hair was blonde, it had been so full of grime. Or that when the glow of the fire's light caught it, it shined a delicate red. And her pale skin had been soft, like the finest spun wool that felt more like velvet.

He snarled at his musings. He would not let this woman—his wife—get in the way of things. He wed her for a purpose and that was all. She would serve him as others did. That she was not hard to look upon was a benefit he had not expected, but was pleased to have. That she feared him would not hurt either. Obedience would then come easily for her and that was all he needed from her, to be an obedient and silent wife.

That he had had to search endlessly for her had annoyed him especially since he had thought she had run from him. But that she had been right under his nose, and he had not known it, continued to infuriate him. He would take great pleasure in seeing those responsible for her abduction suffer for it.

He would let her know that if she was a good wife, she had nothing to fear. In return, he would keep her safe.

He turned a glance at Adara. She slept soundly. She would rest well and tomorrow they would leave for MacVarish keep. Acquiring Clan MacVarish and its holdings had been a benefit he had not expected, but would add to his wealth.

Warrick walked to the bed and listened a moment to her steady breathing. "You will serve me well, wife," he said and turned, and as he walked to the door and closed it quietly behind him, a single tear slipped from Adara's one eye.

Chapter Five

Adara woke hungry, her rumbling and gurgling stomach agreeing with her. A quick glance at the window told her it was night. It was no wonder she was hungry, she had not eaten all day. She needed food as did the bairn. She ate sparingly, a habit formed from years of not having enough to eat. There had been times she had to sneak food, having been given a small piece of bread as a day's meal. And while she now had more than enough food to keep from starving, she had found that her habit of eating lightly was simply too difficult to break.

However, her bairn let her know he needed more nourishment than a handful of food a day.

She wished for the hundredth time she was home. There she could take her meal alone as she often did. She was simply not comfortable around too many people or raucous noise. She preferred solitude, but she and the bairn needed to eat.

Reluctance was obvious as Adara dallied in gathering herself together to go downstairs to the Great Hall. She smiled when she ran her fingers through her hair, clearing away the tangles for it to fall in natural waves. She was so pleased it was getting longer. By winter she would be able to braid it as she had once done. No longer would she be reminded of how she had been held down, her hair pulled and tugged as it was chopped short with a knife, the blonde tresses falling at her feet along with her tears.

Her smile faded. The horrible memories would never stop haunting her. They were branded in her mind forever just like the hot pokers that had branded her skin. The scars would never go away. They would be there always reminding her of the horror.

Her stomach rumbled, reminding her of more important things and she placed her hand there, her smile returning. "Worry not, little one, I will see you fed and keep you safe."

She slipped on her cloak, not wanting to take the chance of anyone seeing the bump beneath her garments. She could easily claim a chill, a good reason for keeping her cloak on.

With quiet steps, she left the room. If she was lucky, perhaps the evening meal was done and the Great Hall was empty. She could eat alone in the peaceful quiet.

It was a hopeful thought that vanished quickly as she got nearer to the Great Hall and was greeted with loud talk and boisterous laughter. She almost turned and ran, but the bairn needed food.

Strength.

She needed strength and it would start now. She had to enter the Great Hall no matter how much it frightened her to do so. She took a deep breath and fought the dread that was rising like a mighty wave inside her, expecting any moment for it to crash down and drown her.

"Move. Move," she whispered, commanding her feet to obey and took quick steps into the Great Hall.

Seeing Espy approach with a pleasant smile kept Adara from drowning in fear.

"I was just coming to wake you and have you join us for supper."

Adara almost backed away from Espy when her arm reached out and wrapped around hers. The healer had come to know her well and had taken hold of her, worried she would take flight. And she had been right. That was exactly what Adara wanted to do... flee. Run all the way home and never look back. She fought the overwhelming urge and walked with Espy as she guided them both past tables filled with talk that was far too loud and laughter that echoed like giant bells in Adara's ears.

"You will sit next to me," Espy whispered as she came

to a stop at the long front table that looked out over numerous trestle tables overflowing with warriors. "You are safe."

Adara wanted to believe that. After all, Espy had kept her word when she promised she would free Adara from the dungeon. But with Warrick sitting there next to Craven, Adara feared she was far from safe. In an instant, she was proven right.

"Adara will sit next to me," Warrick commanded.

Espy went to speak.

"Do not waste your breath, Espy. It was not a request." Warrick looked to Adara. "Come and sit, wife."

Adara froze, the thought of running once again filling her head, but then it had never left her. The thought sat there at the edge in warning.

"Now, *wife*."

The strong command reminded her that she had no choice. Never a choice.

Warrick stood as she approached and when he reached out to take her cloak from her shoulders, she took a quick step away from him. "I have a chill." She feared he did not believe her from the strange look in his dark eyes, but then he gave a nod.

Adara sat, her taste for food fading, but knowing she had to eat.

Espy suddenly appeared at her side, a pitcher in her hand. "This brew will, hopefully, keep your stomach from souring again." She filled Adara's tankard and left the pitcher for her.

"I am grateful," Adara said not only for the brew but for the comforting squeeze Espy gave her arm, reminding her that she was not alone.

"How long have you been feeling poorly?" Warrick asked, as Adara reached out and tore a small piece of bread from the chunk on the platter.

Adara hesitated to respond, the piece of bread poised

near her mouth, not sure if Espy had made mention of it to him. Her other hand purposely remained in her lap, making certain to keep her crooked fingers tucked away so that no one would stare or make rude remarks about them.

"Has it been that long that you do not remember?" he asked with a questioning tilt of his head when no answer was forthcoming.

She stared at him, thinking no man could have such fine features. They held the eyes captive and caused the heart to flutter. She shook head at such nonsensical thoughts. He might have fine features, but he was also known as the Demon Lord.

"A day or so," she said, finding her voice and stumbling over her words. She popped the small piece of bread into her mouth, giving her an excuse to say no more.

"You will rest tonight so you will be fit to travel tomorrow."

Sudden loud shouts at the back of the Great Hall drew both of their attention. A man was shouting in the face of another man who remained calm, not saying a word. One was Craven's man and the other Warrick's. More men stood as the shouts escalated and Ryan, Craven's most trusted and closest warrior approached the group as did Roark, the warrior Warrick depended on the most. Voices grew louder and a scuffle ensued until...

"Enough!" Warrick's thundering command echoed off the walls of the Great Hall, silencing everyone. With one snap of his hand, his warrior and Roark walked toward him.

Ryan nudged Craven's warrior to follow and kept nudging the reluctant warrior all the way to the dais.

Warriors from both sides stood, ready for battle if need be and women backed against the walls to keep far from any potential fight.

The surge of warriors rising to their feet froze Adara in fear. There were too many. How would she ever get away? How could she protect herself and her child?

Warrick rose from his chair and Adara almost cringed, the size of him overpowering and consuming her like an enormous shadow swallowing her whole. Craven rose as well and the shadow spread, leaving her no way out.

Warrick turned to Craven. "My warriors do not start fights, though they will finish them."

Craven looked to his man, Gifford, and had his answer. The man always started something when too far into his cups and one look confirmed what he suspected, Gifford was more than too far into his cups—he was drowning in them. Talking to Gifford would be futile.

"Get him out of here and see that he stays out until he sobers and behaves properly," Craven ordered Ryan.

Gifford pointed at Warrick's warrior. "I am going to kick his arse."

Before anyone could respond, Gifford threw a punch. Warrick's warrior responded instinctively, sending Gifford to the floor with one punch that was delivered so fast it was barely noticeable.

Craven's warriors looked ready to pounce and he was quick to warn, "Enough. Gifford was at fault here and got what he deserved. I will not have you show disrespect to our guests as Gifford has done."

His men settled down without question.

Warrick's warrior picked Gifford up, tossed him over his shoulder, and turned to Ryan. "Where do you want him?"

The warriors returned to their tables, talk and laughter once again erupting in the Great Hall.

Warrick turned to sit and saw that Adara's seat was empty. His eyes were quick to spot her tucked in the shadows in the corner as if somehow they would shield her.

Craven grabbed his wife by the arm when she went to rush past him to Adara. "Let them be." She looked hesitant but nodded as Warrick slowly approached Adara.

"Adara," Warrick said softly when he saw how she huddled in the shadows, her arms tight around her. She did not respond and as he got closer he saw that her eyes were wide with fright, a deep fright that trembled her body and had her hands locked tight to her arms that crossed her chest.

He kept his steps slow, not wanting to add to her fear. He had seen such fright before, from the warriors he had taken prisoner after battle, but they had good reason to fear. Adara did not. Or did she? Had her suffering been so bad that it had branded her like a hot iron, a scar that always reminds?

He moved closer. "I am here, Adara. There is nothing to fear. I will let no one harm you."

She stared at him for a few moments and he was concerned that she did not recognize him.

Her name slipped from his lips again, this time more softly, though remaining strong. "Adara."

Her eyes blinked a few times, as if coming awake, and her brow wrinkled in confusion. Her eyes suddenly popped wide and she did not wait... she ran to him. She leaned against him while keeping her cloak closed tightly in front of her and buried her face against his chest.

Warrick's arms shot around her, hugging her tight, feeling the tremble that rippled through her. He scooped her up into his arms and walked out of the Great Hall without a word or glance to anyone. His first thought was to take her to Craven's solar, but confinement was not what she needed. He turned down the passageway to the kitchen.

All activity halted when Warrick entered the busy room and he made sure to tuck Adara closer against him.

Servants stared with open mouths and disbelief as the Demon Lord made his way quickly through the kitchen and headed for the door that led outside. One servant gathered his wits and courage enough to open the door, and the Demon Lord disappeared into the night.

The chill that the rain had brought whipped at Warrick, but he paid it no mind. He spotted a bench a short distance down from the door and he went to it and sat, keeping Adara snug in his arms. The rain had stopped, though numerous gray clouds rushed across the full moon, warning the storm was not yet over.

He did not speak. He simply sat there holding her. The quiet, the warmth of his body, and the safety of his strong arms was what she needed, and it was what he gave her.

Adara sighed softly, cuddling against Warrick's gentle heat while cherishing the chilled night air that brushed her face. She was reminded of when last he held her and how by the end of the night she had wished he would never let her go. But he had. He did not truly want her. No one had ever wanted her.

She wished things could be different… vastly different. She wished by some miracle that he was a kind soul and could someday love her. But wishing did not make things happen. She should know, having made endless wishes since she was young and none had ever come true.

She stirred in his arms and reluctantly turned her head away from his warm, comfortable chest to look up at his face. For a moment, she thought she was in a dream and none of this was real since she saw a tender concern in his soulless, dark eyes, but then she realized it was the glint of the moon peeking out between the gray clouds that had tricked the eye. Or had it tricked her heart?

"Feeling better?" he asked.

She was about to nod then thought better of it. "I need to rest."

"Still feeling poorly?"

She nodded without hesitation and hoped he believed her, though doubted he did. Her fear had been obvious, there for him to see.

"Rest it is then."

She sent a silent prayer to the heavens for that, though to him she said, "I am grateful for your kindness, my lord."

"Kindness is not something I possess, Adara, and while I will not burden you with talk, it will not take much for you

40

to show me what you suffered in my dungeon."

Adara raised her right hand, relieved that was all he asked of her.

Warrick shifted her in his lap so that she sat straight up, then his hand reached out to hers, his fingers tracing along her two end fingers. The small end finger was more gnarled than the other, both looking more like curved talons than fingers. They had been broken and in more than one place and had not been allowed to heal properly. It had to have been extremely painful for her, and he intended to see the person who did this to her suffer much more pain than she had.

"Who did this to you?"

"The guard I was sold to and who brought me to your dungeon."

"How did it happen?" he asked.

"He got angry when he was given orders that I was not to be touched by any man."

"Tell me more," Warrick encouraged, when she said no more.

"I was to be auctioned to the highest bidding guard before being shared with the other guards. Another man was sent with him to make certain orders were followed."

"The other guard did not warn him not to touch you?"

"He did it when no one was looking, twisting my two fingers until," —she cringed— "I heard a snap."

"Did he leave you alone after that?" he asked, gently running his fingers over her two crooked ones. "Or do your fingers tell a different story since they look to have been broken more than once."

She cringed at the painful memory of her bones snapping. "He twisted them again a few times more before they could heal, warning if I said anything he would break more of my fingers."

Warrick showed no sign of anger, but it simmered inside him. He hoped the guard was not one of those who had perished in the fire the night of Adara's escape. He wanted personally to make the man suffer for the agony he had put her through.

"Do you recall his name?" he asked, though doubted she could ever forget it.

"Lochbar," she said in a whisper, as if she feared speaking his name.

Lochbar was not one of his guards, he was compensated for collecting those indebted to Warrick. He had, however, taken it upon himself to earn extra coin. He had also convinced two of the dungeon guards to be part of his scheme. One had died in the fire and the other was being held in a cell in a section of the dungeon that had not suffered from the fire. But Lochbar had survived, having departed before the fire. It would not take long to find him and when he did... Warrick intended to administer the punishment himself.

He wanted to know all of it, so he could make anyone else who harmed her suffer unbearably. "What was done to you once you were in the dungeon?"

"I was not there long before my escape."

"You were there long enough," he said annoyed that she avoided answering him. "Now tell me."

Adara preferred not to recall the horrible memories, they came unbidden far too often as it was and rarely ever did she speak about them. She had little choice but to do so now. "A hot iron was taken to me."

"More than once?"

She nodded.

"You will show me," he demanded.

"It would not be proper," she said.

He leaned his face close to hers. "Need I remind you that you are my wife and that I have seen and touched every inch of you?"

She was surprised that a pleasant stirring settled over her, and she whispered, "That was different."

"Naked is naked, wife, and I will see you that way many more times. It is best you grow accustomed to it."

He stunned her silent. It had not been a thought in her head that he would ever want to couple with her again. She believed their marriage was nothing more than a convenience to him and he had consummated it to seal their vows. Once done she believed he had need of her no more. It had been why she had thought she had been taken to his dungeon until she had found out differently, though even then she had not been sure. What if Warrick had gladly compensated Penley for getting rid of her? What if Penley did not know and definitely did not care where Lochbar was taking her? How did she know what was the truth?

The bairn fluttered lightly in her stomach, reminding her that he was there and his father was yet to learn of him.

What would Warrick do when he discovered she carried his child? Would he even believe the bairn his?

"Time to rest, wife. We leave at first light." He stood, keeping her in his arms and carried her into the keep and up to the bedchamber.

Adara kept silent, not knowing his intention. Did he expect her to strip naked for him? Show him her scars? Did he intend to couple with her? She continued to remain silent when he placed her on the bed.

"Rest and get well, wife. I will see you in the morning." He turned and went to the door, stopping to turn and look at her after opening it. "This is the last night you sleep alone. From tomorrow on you will share my bed."

Chapter Six

Adara thanked the heavens for the heavy rainstorm the next day, preventing Warrick from leaving MacCara keep. It was not that she did not want to return home, she did, though not just yet. The thought of being alone with Warrick sent her fears soaring. She barely knew him and was frightened of him, not a good way for a wife to be toward her husband. Though, there were those odd times—she did not understand—when she felt a closeness to him.

Here at MacCara keep she could avoid him, stay to herself, or spend some time with Espy when she was not busy at her healing cottage. Today she found herself alone, not that she minded. Solitude had become her friend. It hugged with comfort, kept her safe, and demanded nothing from her.

Like now, scrunched in a seat in an alcove on the top floor of the keep, listening to the rain pound against the shutters. Adara had partially opened one shutter to breathe in the scent of earth and rain. When she was younger, she would stand outside in a rainstorm and the let the rain soak her. It was a way of feeling clean, of feeling free if only for a short while. She would often get scolded and made to wear the soaked garments while they dried, but at least she had felt clean, the dirt and grime of weeks, if not months, washed away.

While she had been frightened half to death when the women had stripped her of her garments the night of her wedding, she had relished the scrubbing they had given her. She had never felt so clean, so fresh, and for once she had enjoyed her own scent.

"You hide?"

Adara almost fell off the window seat, Warrick's silent and sudden presence startling her, but his hand was quick to grab her and keep her from tumbling. She thought how quick his hand had been to be at her side, several times, when needed. No one had ever been so fast to help her but then there had never been anyone to help her.

"I like solitude," she said.

"Then take joy in it for now, for it is yours no longer."

She stared at him, realizing she had given little thought to how much her life would change now that her husband had found her.

"You are my wife and will see to your duties," he said, thinking that he found her more beautiful each time he looked upon her, then admonishing himself for thinking so. There was no room for such nonsensical thoughts. She was his wife, there to serve him, nothing more.

"I will see to my duties, my lord," she said with a bob of her head.

"All of them," he demanded, letting her know what he expected of her, though more wanted from her.

"Whatever you say, my lord," Adara said, avoiding his dark eyes that seemed forever cold and uncaring, though not on their wedding night. That night his eyes had been filled with passion and she had thought, wanted to believe, she had seen kindness there.

Obedience. That was what he expected and that was what she would give him.

"Why did you wed me?" Adara was shocked by her own audacity to ask such a question, but it had hovered on her lips for so long that it had spilled free of its own will.

"I was in need of a wife."

"But I am a mere servant," she said still not understanding.

"Who will serve me well."

Serve the devil.

That had been what one of the women who had helped

45

prepare her for Warrick on her wedding night had whispered. *You will serve the devil.*

But she did not feel it was the devil she had joined with that night. There was a kindness to her husband then that she had favored. This man standing in front her showed not an ounce of kindness, and fear churned in her.

She remained silent, waiting for him to leave, praying that he would, so the comfort of solitude could embrace her once again.

"Do you want me to leave, Adara?"

She could not hide the surprise that he had somehow known her thoughts.

"Your face tells me much. I would remember that since it will do you no good to lie to me," he warned.

"Why would I lie to you?"

"Have you ever lied?' he asked.

"Have you?" She caught her gasp in her throat. Whatever was the matter with her, throwing his question back at him. She was quick to try to right her wrong. "Lies left my tongue when necessary."

"It was not that you lied that mattered to me. It was that you spoke the truth about lying that mattered," he said. "I believe it would be difficult to find anyone who has not lied in their life and even more difficult to find someone who would admit it." He found he was pleased by her response and few things pleased him. "As for if I lied? When I was young, like you, lies left my tongue out of necessity, but now? I speak as I wish."

Funny, Adara thought. He did not say he did not lie, just that he spoke as he wished, which perhaps meant he still told a lie or two.

"Your fingers pain you?" he asked with a nod at her hand.

Adara looked down, not realizing she had been rubbing her two crooked fingers. "When the weather is damp, and Cyra—Espy's grandmother, a skilled healer—warned that

46

the winter's cold might bring me pain."

He approached her and she fought against the fear that warned her to shrink away from him, the breadth and strength of him alone frightening. When he went to reach for her hand, she pulled it away, pressing it against her chest.

Warrick did not take offense, knowing fear-filled memories had caused her reaction. "My touch did not harm you last night and will do no harm to you now, wife." He reached down and waited for her to place her hand in his.

Adara felt foolish for reacting as she had. He had not hurt her last night when he had touched her fingers. And he had not reached and grabbed at her fingers like Lochbar had done. She slowly stretched her hand out to him.

Warrick took her hand, gently massaging her two crooked fingers. "We will see that you have several pair of gloves to keep your hands warm this winter. I do not want you to suffer more pain."

It was difficult to keep his rage from showing when he touched her injured fingers. That his own wife had suffered endless horror in his dungeon infuriated him and the only solace he could find was the thoughts of the endless torture he would inflict on those who had made her suffer.

He curled his hand around hers. "Come, it is too cold here for you. You need the warmth of a fire, and you will have the quiet and solitude of an empty bedchamber."

That he would leave her to herself had her taking hold of his hand and making sure her other hand kept her cloak from falling open and revealing her secret. It was ever present in her mind that she needed to tell him of their bairn, but fear kept her tongue still.

She walked down the stairs, Warrick going before her on the narrow staircase and when they went to enter the bedchamber, the door opened and Espy jumped with a start.

She pressed her hand to her chest. "You gave me a fright. I am finished at the healing cottage and thought you might like to share a brew with me."

"Adara would be pleased to, since she feels chilled," Warrick said and released her hand. "I will see you later, wife." With that said, he took his leave.

Adara was used to others speaking for her, though with the last few months of speaking for herself, she found she quite preferred it. On this occasion, however, she agreed with Warrick's response.

"Come, we will go to my stitching room and enjoy the soothing warmth of a hot brew and a warm fire," Espy said, slipping her arm around Adara's. "My goodness, Warrick was right, you are chilled."

Adara realized then that she shivered, but she was not sure it was from a chill or the fear that was ever present in her.

The two women settled in the sewing room, drinking hot cider and talking of many things, but avoided speaking a word about Warrick until a comfortable silence fell between them.

Adara had not planned to say anything to Espy, but she found the need to ask. "What do you know of Warrick?"

Espy smiled softly. "Warrick allows no one to know him. Tales are told but whether true or not, no one can say for sure. It is said the King bestowed a title on him for work other warriors feared to do. Others say he got the title his chieftain father always craved."

"Who is his father?"

"Phlen MacDevlin, a far ruthless warrior than Warrick from what is told. Supposedly even the Vikings feared him."

"Siblings?" Adara asked.

Espy shook her head. "No one has claimed kinship to him. I would advise you not to pay heed to wagging tongues or tall tales. Learn for yourself what kind of man your husband is."

"But you have seen his brutality in his dungeons."

"If it is true, he did not know what went on there, then believe me, he will make those responsible suffer immeasurably for it. I think what disturbed me the most about him, while I served as his healer, was his indifference. He seemed to care for nothing or no one." She shook her head again, slowly this time, as if she could still not believe what she had seen. "And he endured pain from all types of injury without a flinch, a groan, or a complaint. I often wondered if he felt pain at all or simply had the courage to refuse to show it."

Adara hugged herself against a sudden chill.

"I wish to ask you something, Adara, though it is of an intimate nature and if you do not wish to answer it, I understand," Espy said softly, and Adara nodded. "Did Warrick treat you well when you coupled?"

Adara felt her cheeks heat.

"You need say nothing, but let me say that if your husband treated you well, caused you no harm, was unselfish, and made no unwanted demands on you, then there is more good to Warrick than he shows."

Adara took heart to Espy's words, praying it was so.

A knock sounded at the door and a servant entered.

"Sorry to disturb you, my lady, but it is Tilly's time."

"Send word I will be there shortly," Espy said and turned to Adara. "Have you attended or helped with any births?"

"I have attended three, though I did not help with the births. My chore was cleaning up afterwards."

"Then you should attend this one. It is Tilly's first and seeing it for yourself will let you know what to expect," Espy said.

Adara followed Espy through the rain that had gratefully kept to a sprinkle until they reached the cottage, then the rainstorm resumed in force.

Once in the cottage, Adara worried how she would hide her rounded stomach since she had to remove her cloak if she was to help. She was grateful when Espy provided her with a large white apron that she tied loosely around Adara.

Tilly was moaning and rubbing her enormous stomach.

Espy spoke soothingly and encouragingly to the woman.

"Adara is here to assist me," Espy said, motioning Adara out of the shadows and toward the bed.

Tilly turned a cautious eye to Espy. "She belongs to the Demon Lord. I do not want evil touching my bairn."

Though the woman whispered, Adara heard her and her words hurt. Is that how people would think of her now? Evil, simply because she was wife to the Demon Lord?

"You have seen Adara here at the Clan MacCara many times and she has shown no signs of evil."

"She speaks to no one when here and rarely looks at anyone. How are we to know if she is evil or not?" Tilly asked.

Adara never gave thought to how keeping to herself had made her appear to others. She forced herself to speak. "I am sorry if I offended you but I was raised to serve others and to hold my tongue." She did not know why Espy smiled softly at her confession, but it seemed as if her smile was one of pride for Adara and that gave her courage.

"You served others?" Tilly asked surprised.

"As long as I can remember," Adara said the weight of that time still heavy upon her.

"If you are a servant, how is it you are wed to the Demon Lord?" Tilly asked, a wince surfacing as another pain began to build.

Adara repeated Warrick's words when she had asked him the same. "He needed a wife and I was there."

"I will pray for you," Tilly said and cringed, pressing her hand to her stomach as a long, loud groan spilled out of her.

Had it been that simple? He had needed a wife and she had been there. She served the purpose, and so with the Demon Lord's need... her life had changed forever.

Adara was quick to help, feeling for the woman as she

fought to birth her bairn. She wondered if she would have such strength to fight the endless pain. But then she had survived torture, never knowing when next she would suffer pain again. At least with this, she knew there was an end to the pain.

She followed Espy's every instruction, fetching whatever she asked for, wiping Tilly's sweaty brow with a cool cloth and offering encouraging words just as Espy did.

"I am grateful," Tilly would say each time Adara wiped her brow or ran a cool, wet cloth over her face.

Adara had never known such camaraderie between women. She had seen it on occasion but had never been truly part of it, and she relished the feeling. She found herself doing all she could to comfort the woman and help her through the pain.

When the time came close for the bairn to be born, Adara grew excited, eager to see the bairn and eager for the pain to be over for Tilly.

"A few more pushes, Tilly, and your bairn will be here," Espy said and Tilly let out a scream.

~~~

Warrick was annoyed and that annoyance had grown the longer it took to discover where his wife had disappeared to. He had not given Adara permission to leave the keep. And what was she doing helping Espy birth a bairn, though on second thought he wondered if it would be good for her to see since he intended for Adara to give him many children. By attending this birth, she would be aware of what was expected of her.

It had taken speaking to several servants before he found out where she had gone. He was on his way there now. He would let her know that she was to seek his permission before leaving the keep, though he had no intentions of returning her there. He would let her continue to help—

A scream ripped through the gloomy day, bringing him to an abrupt halt. The few people braving the rain paid it no heed and Warrick realized it came from the cottage where the woman was giving birth.

Another scream had him slowing his steps to the cottage door. He knew women suffered when giving birth, but he had never heard the agonizing screams of a woman in the throes of birthing. His thoughts went immediately to Adara.

She would suffer such brutal pain. She was small. He winced when he recalled how tight she had felt when he had slipped into her on their wedding night. Not that he had winced that night, it was more a groan of intense pleasure. How would she ever endure delivering a bairn? Could it possibly be too much for her? Was there a chance he could lose her in childbirth?

When another scream sounded as if the woman was being torn in two, he turned and walked away from the cottage. He had no desire to see what was happening within. What he did intend to do was speak with Espy before he laid another hand on his wife.

~~~

Adara had seen newborns after they had been delivered from their mums, but never had she participated so closely in birthing one. Never had she felt so much a part of the deliver and, seeing Tilly take her son in her arms, a wide smile on her face, and love in her eyes, she could not help but think how it would feel to hold her own newborn bairn.

Love.

Adara would finally know love. It had been there on Tilly's face as soon as she had taken her son in her arms. It shined in her eyes, in her wide smile, in the way she hugged the bairn to her and gently kissed his tiny cheek. Adara would love her bairn and the bairn would love her. A sense of joy trickled through her and for the first time since learning she was with child she was happy.

Adara finished helping tend Tilly and when all was done, the husband sitting beside the bed, admiring his newborn son with pride, Adara and Espy slipped quietly out of the cottage.

"That was amazing," Adara said as they walked back to the keep, the rain having stopped and dusk settling over the land. "I cannot wait to hold my bairn in my arms."

"Have you told Warrick?" Espy asked, keeping her voice low.

Adara's smile faded.

"You need to tell him. Do not wait. He will question why you kept it from him," Espy urged.

Adara nodded, though fear warned her against it.

The two women entered the Great Hall to find Warrick speaking with Roark.

"Did I give you permission to leave the keep?" Warrick asked his wife. Espy went to respond and Warrick turned to her. "I was not speaking to you."

Fear for Espy had Adara speaking up. "I should have informed you that Espy asked me to attend a birth with her."

"You should have sought permission," Warrick scolded.

"Adara is your wife, not a servant," Espy reminded unable to hold her tongue.

"Must I forever remind you to watch your tongue? You had no such problem when you were my healer."

"I did not want to draw attention since I intended to free the innocent from that hideous dungeon of yours," Espy said with a defiant tilt of her chin.

Warrick went to step forward.

"Warrick!" Craven called out as he entered the room. "Need I remind you. My home. My wife."

"Your wife needs to learn her place," Warrick said a flare of his nostrils a sign his temper had yet to abate.

"My wife knows her place well... right beside me,"

Craven said and settled next to her, his arm going around her waist, his hand giving the slim curve a squeeze, and Espy smiled.

Adara watched the scene with amazement. She wished she had Espy's courage and strength to speak up to Warrick, but her limbs were trembling and her heart was pounding, and she had not even been part of the exchange between the pair. She could not imagine herself ever being brave enough, or was it foolishness that took such courage, to speak as Espy did?

There was a silent pause and Adara could see all waited on the Demon Lord.

"I respect this is your home, but make your wife aware that she has tried my patience enough," Warrick commanded and turned to his wife. "You will wait in our bedchamber."

Adara bobbed her head and without glancing at anyone hurried out of the room, anxious to be away from everyone, needing to be alone to calm the fright that raced through her.

"I will have a word with you alone in the solar, Espy," Warrick ordered.

"I go with her," Craven said.

"I mean your wife no harm. I require her skills as a healer," Warrick said.

"I go with her," Craven repeated.

"This is a private matter," Warrick said.

Before her husband could object, Espy spoke up. "I will speak to Lord Warrick alone."

Craven was ready to forbid it, the words on his lips.

Espy turned around to face him, his arm still firm around her waist and with a soft smile whispered, "Do not make me use my tongue on you, husband."

Craven grinned, his voice a whisper. "I like when you use your tongue on me, wife."

"I have not another thread of patience left," Warrick bellowed and smashed his fist down on the table.

Espy pressed her hand to her husband's chest when she

saw a spark of anger flash in his eyes. "I will see this done."

"I will wait outside the solar door," Craven said and looked to Warrick. "A distance so you may have privacy, but close enough to my wife."

Warrick turned without a word and left the room, expecting the pair to follow, and they did.

As soon as the solar door closed, Espy asked, "What ails you, my lord."

"It is not me. It is Adara," Warrick said.

"How so, my lord?" she asked careful with her words since she was not sure if this had anything to do with Adara carrying his child.

"I heard the screams of the woman who was giving birth and it made me think of Adara and when she gets with child. She is a petite woman. Will she have difficulty giving birth?"

Was that concern she heard in his voice? Could he possibly care for Adara? Or was his concern for the bairns he feared Adara might not successfully deliver?

"I have seen petite women like Adara slip their bairns out with ease and large women struggle. No one can say for sure until the time comes. But Adara is stronger than she looks and thinks. I believe she will do well."

A knock sounded at the door.

"You were not to disturb us, Craven," Warrick shouted.

"It is I, Roark. You are needed in camp. It cannot wait."

Warrick looked to Espy. "You can tell me no more?"

"There is no way to know for sure, my lord. It is a chance every woman takes when she gets with child."

He nodded, turned, and walked out the door, Craven slipping in the room after him.

"All is well?" Craven asked.

"I hope so," Espy said, though wondered.

Chapter Seven

Adara woke, her eyes wide, thinking she heard a sound. She was not sure how long she had slept, though a glance at the fire that had dwindled down to barely a flicker let her know quite a bit of time had passed.

She had not seen her husband again after he had sent her to their bedchamber yesterday. She had been relieved when she had received word that he would see her on the morrow, and more relieved that she had been allowed to have her supper alone in the room.

The noise suddenly sounded again and this time she recognized it. It was the door creaking open slowly.

Was Warrick returning? Had he changed his mind about joining her in bed? Or was someone else sneaking about? The thought had her hurrying out of bed and rushing to the fireplace to grab a log from the pile stacked nearby. She padded swiftly, though quietly across the room to stand behind the door, log tightly in hand, instinct having her ready to protect her bairn.

The door continued to open slowly and Adara's stomach churned nervously with every creak.

"Adara," came the soft whisper.

Adara sighed with relief hearing Espy's voice and stepped from behind the door, causing Espy to yelp and jump in fright and causing Adara to do the same.

With a hand to each of their chests to calm their racing hearts, the two women looked at each other and laughed.

At that moment, Adara was grateful for her friendship with Espy. She had never shared laughter with anyone, never had known the kinship of friendship, and she cherished it with all her heart.

Espy nodded at the log in Adara's hand. "Ready to protect yourself?"

Adara's hand went to her stomach. "I will keep him safe."

Espy nodded. "I believe you will do just that, though I think the log would serve better in the hearth to chase away the growing chill in this room." She reached out and took it from Adara and went to the hearth to add it and two others to the dying flames.

Adara closed the door and joined Espy by the hearth, holding her hands out to the heat of the growing flames. "What brought you here, Espy?"

"I thought you might want to freshen yourself and eat before you take your leave this morning."

"It is close to sunrise?"

"It is and since mornings have been treating you poorly, I figured you could eat a light fare and see if it sits well with you before it is time to go," Espy said.

"Thank you for thinking of me and the bairn. I appreciate it more than I can say."

Espy reached out and gave her hand a squeeze. "That is what friends do for each other."

Adara smiled softly. "I never had a friend."

Espy's brow wrinkled. "Never?"

Adara was about to shake her head and stopped. "There was a woman I got to know, at this one croft I lived at for a few years. I met her one scrub day by the stream. Her name was Maia. I assumed her a servant as well since she would bring things to scrub. I did wonder though since she was so very knowledgeable about so much, if she was not more than a servant. We would talk. She loved to talk of different places and things I never gave thought to. She made me think far beyond the mundane. To me, she was more a teacher than a friend, though I was sad when I unexpectedly was given to another family, never to see her again. So perhaps, she meant more to me than I had thought."

"I wondered how you had gained such wisdom, having been treated so poorly through the years. Maia taught you well."

Adara chuckled. "I am far from wise."

"You are wiser than you realize and I believe you will grow even wiser. Now we better hurry and get you all set to return home."

Adara turned a troubled glance on Espy. "If I am wise, why do I fear what is to come?"

"Strangely enough fear often helps. It tells us to be aware, more alert, and calls on strengths we seldom realize we have. Fear was my ally when I treated you in the dungeon and helped you escape."

"You were fearful? You did not appear fearful. To me, you were confident and courageous which helped me greatly."

"I was fearful, more fearful of failing you and Hannah than I was of being discovered, just like you were fearful of your bairn being harmed so you took up a weapon—a log—and were ready to protect your unborn child. You are stronger than you know, Adara. Hold on to your fear and let it give you courage." Espy reached out and hugged Adara tightly. "And know that we will be friends forever."

Adara wiped the few tears away from her eyes after Espy stepped away and watched as her friend did the same.

"Now some food, a quick wash, and some fresh garments I managed to find that should fit you and you will be ready for your journey home."

A bit of confidence poked at Adara, making her feel somewhat less fearful of facing what was to come, not only today but beyond as well.

In no time, Espy had heated water brought to the room and fresh garments laid on the bed in wait. The pale green shift was of the softest wool and the tunic was just as soft, though a darker green. Dark stockings waited as well, but Adara would not use them. Never having had them to keep her warm, she had grown accustomed to doing without and could not stand the confined feel of them.

Espy helped hurry her out of her garments and got busy helping her wash, the water losing its warmth fast.

Adara placed a hand to her rounded stomach. "I worry he does not grow as strong as he should. You grow larger than me yet you are not as far along as I am."

"I am not that far behind you. Do not worry. I have seen some women who barely grew round and they delivered fine bairns. Feed yourself well and your bairn will do well."

"I will eat more," Adara said determined to see her bairn grow strong.

Espy got busy helping Adara to dry, her naked body running with gooseflesh.

First light was breaking through the window as Espy hurried to the bed to grab the shift when the door burst open.

Both women stilled in fright when Warrick walked in.

His eyes settled on Adara, but not on her face, her rounded stomach. He stared for a moment, then pointed to Espy. "Leave us."

Espy went to give Adara the shift and Warrick's sharp command stopped her.

"Go now!"

Adara did not want any harm to come to her friend or the Clan MacCara because of her. She sent Espy a brief nod, letting her know she should go.

Espy wisely took her leave without saying a word.

Warrick shut the door behind her and approached Adara, his eyes on the bump in her stomach.

Adara wanted so badly to cover herself, but the threatening look in his dark eyes warned her against it. He stopped in front of her, his eyes settling on hers and it was as if she knew his thought and spoke before he could. "The bairn is yours."

"No one touched you since last I did?"

She shut her eyes, recalling the way the guards had

stripped her naked and groped at her breasts, though would not touch her below the waist, Espy having been far too convincing of what would happen to them if they did. They had, however, used the hot iron on her thighs and buttocks.

"You need to think about it?" he asked harshly.

She shook her head, not sure if it was fear or shame of what was done to her that had kept her from responding. "Your guards squeezed my breasts until I shouted with pain and—" She clamped her lips closed when she saw the fury that rushed into his eyes.

"Tell me," he ordered.

"They were too fearful to touch me intimately below my waist, Espy having told them that their manhood would shrivel and die if they did."

"They believed her without question?"

"They did after two of the guards, thinking to prove her wrong, had their way with the woman who died before Espy could free her. I do not know how Espy did it but the two guards had something happen to them that had the other guards throwing them out and not allowing them back. After that, the guards no longer touched me anywhere. Instead, they took a hot iron to me."

Adara braced herself as he drew in a deep breath and his hands fisted tightly at his sides. His fury was tangible, coming off him in heated waves.

"Show me," he demanded, a low snarl following his words.

Adara pointed to a spot near her right inner thigh. She startled when he dropped down on his haunches to see the scar the hot iron had left. She did not have to point to the other three. They were clearly visible.

She jumped when his finger brushed over the one scar lightly.

"It still pains you?" he asked.

Her brief response rushed from her mouth, "No."

"My touch disturbs you?"

She managed only one word. "Unexpected." His gentle touch was not the only thing unexpected. Her reaction was as well. A tingle stirred within her at the gentle brush of his finger and it was growing as he continued to stroke the other scars. She recognized the mounting sensation. It was the one he had stirred to life in her on their wedding night and just as she was surprised by her response that night, she was so again now.

"Are there more?"

She had hoped he would not ask and keeping her eyes straight ahead, she said, "My backside."

His hands went to her hips and he turned her around gently.

Adara thought she heard him growl low like a feral animal and she jumped once again when his finger skimmed one of the two scars on her backside. She jumped again when he sprung to his feet.

"Get dressed. We leave shortly."

His quick departure shocked her. She should be glad he left, glad that he knew of the bairn, of her scars. So why did she feel upset? Had she expected, or perhaps hoped that he would be pleased that she would give him a child? Or was it that he did not believe her? That he thought the child was not his. If that was so, what would he do to her?

~~~

Warrick stood outside the closed door for a moment, fighting to contain his raging fury, something he never had trouble with before. He had been taught since he was young to keep control of his feelings, never showing what he felt, but seeing what had been done to his wife made him raw with a fury that was difficult to contain.

He intended to find the bastards who had made her suffer horribly and make them suffer until they screamed and begged for him to let them die, but he would not let them die… yet.

"Come over here, Espy," he ordered. He had known she would not leave Adara completely. She would wait nearby and go to Adara when he finished with her. He respected her strength and her conviction to help Adara and for that he was grateful.

Espy stepped out of the darkened corner, her chin up and her shoulders back, ready to do battle if necessary.

"You were aware Adara was with child?"

"She kept it from me until recently."

"It is why she has been feeling poorly?"

"Aye," Espy said with a nod.

"There is no cause for worry?"

There was that touch of concern again in his voice, but it was difficult to tell with Warrick. He rarely showed an ounce of emotion. "A sour stomach is natural, though it is more prevalent in the early part of being with child, it can last longer or even throughout the nine months. It is nothing to worry about, though Adara should make certain to keep herself and the bairn nourished." Craven showed constant concern for her and their bairn, sometimes to the point that she would need to tell him not to worry, she and the bairn were fine. Would Warrick do the same with Adara? She spoke without thinking. "You should see that she does."

"You should mind your tongue."

She paid no heed to his words, her thoughts on Adara. "She is your wife."

"You will do well to remember that."

"She needs a gentle hand."

"Whereas you need a firm one," he snapped and held up his hand when her tongue went to challenge him again. "Enough. Tell me what you did to the two guards who had their way with one of the women prisoners when you had warned them against it."

"Norella," she said softly and shook her head. "That was her name and she had been badly abused before she arrived at your dungeon. There was little I could do for her but protect her from further suffering. I was furious when I discovered what they had done."

"How did you find out? How could you be sure it had not happened to Adara? That she kept it from you."

Her chin went up a notch. "One of the guards kept me aware of what went on at all times."

"How could you be sure he was truthful with you?" Warrick demanded.

"I was tending his ill son and the lad was improving, slowly, but improving, growing stronger. He was grateful and felt it was a way to repay me, especially when his son healed completely."

"You will tell me his name," Warrick ordered.

Espy made a demand of her own. "Why?"

"You are impossible, woman," Warrick said with a snarl to his words. "If you were not Craven's wife I would—" He shook his head at Espy or was it that he was about to answer her that so annoyed him? "I will see he is not punished along with the guilty ones."

"Torrin. His name is Torrin," Espy said quickly.

"The two guards," he reminded, having detoured from his original question.

"Poison ivy," Espy said. "I offered them each a brew that I told them might help slow the inevitable. I coated the rim of the one tankard with it. One took it, the other laughed at me. The one who laughed at me got the infected tankard. The other was spared… for the moment. I told them it would start with their lips, spread to their hands, possibly other places as well, till it finally reached their manhood. As soon as the one guard's lips broke out in hideous sores, the other came to me and sealed his fate. After that, the other guards refrained from even touching Adara and Hannah when they tortured them."

Warrick admired the healer, though he did not tell her so. "Did you journey with her after the escape?"

"No, Adara and Hannah fled, as I fought one of your guards for my freedom." She pointed to the fading scar on her face. "That is how I got this. However, Adara has told me that she and Hannah traveled together a good part of the way."

"Get my wife ready. We leave shortly," he ordered and walked past her to the stairs.

His abrupt dismissal worried Espy. "Tell me you will keep Adara safe and no harm will come to her."

He stopped and turned a glare on her for a moment, then, without saying a word, he disappeared down the stairs, leaving his silence to run a chill through Espy.

Chapter Eight

Adara sat cradled in front of Warrick on his stallion, a soft wool blanket tucked around her. That and her wool cloak kept her warm against the sharp chill and strong wind. Autumn had made itself known. Winter would not be far behind and with it the birth of the bairn.

"When will the bairn arrive?"

That he should ask what had just been her thought made her wonder if he was actually a demon lord who could see into a person's mind. Or was it her fear that brought on such foolish thoughts?

"Shortly after winter arrives." She could not help but think that he had doubts the bairn was his. Though, could she blame him? He had only her word and how did he take the word of someone he barely knew? She understood his need to question, for there were many questions she wished to ask him. Fear, however, of his answers held her tongue prisoner. There was one issue that made her anxious enough to speak up. "Espy will tend my delivery"

"We shall see," he said.

That he did not look at her but kept his eyes straight ahead made her feel as though he paid her little heed. She was where she had always been… with her fate in someone else's hands. She should have known her freedom would not last, nothing lasted.

"When did you realize you were with child?"

"Shortly after arriving here."

"Once you discovered it was not me who sent you to my dungeon, did you ever give thought of returning to me… your husband?"

"I thought many things, but the only one of importance

Donna Fletcher

was keeping the bairn safe."

"The bairn is safe now and so are you."

Am I? she wondered. Every time she had ever allowed herself to believe she was safe, something would happen to prove her wrong. She wanted to hope, dream, wish he was right. That she was finally, truly, safe, but she could not allow herself that pleasure.

First and foremost, though, there was the bairn to consider and he was reminding her of his presence by churning her stomach. She had not eaten much before leaving MacCara keep, a bit of porridge was all she had managed, and she had hoped the bairn would tolerate it and leave her in peace for the journey home. Her hope grew slimmer as her stomach's upset increased.

Warrick felt her shift in his arms and watched her face pale. "You do not feel well?"

How did he know?

You grow pale.

Espy's words reminded her of the obvious and it also had been one of the recurring signs that had aided Espy in discovering that Adara was with child.

"A bit," she said, her hand going to rest on her queasy stomach.

Warrick slipped his hand beneath the blanket and worked his way past her cloak to ease her hand off her stomach so he could caress the rounded mound. "How often does the bairn leave you feeling poorly?"

"A few times in the morning and sometimes later in the day." She bit back the sigh that almost rushed out, his touch gentle, soothing, and, to her surprise, she found her stomach calming.

"Knowing this, you walked from your keep to MacCara keep?"

Adara found herself smiling softly at his surprised rather than accusing tone. "He likes when I walk, not churning my stomach as much." This time she did not hold

66

back the tender sigh that slipped out and, without thought, she rested her head against his chest.

Warrick felt her settle comfortably against him, her body no longer tense, rigid in his arms, and it took only a few moments for her eyes to flutter closed. He stared down at her nestled there, where she belonged and where she would stay. That she was his wife and would remain so was never in question. That he had found himself feeling something for her on their wedding night was not something he had expected, though it was something he questioned after failing to dismiss it as irrational.

From all he had learned, he believed the child his. He might have questioned it if he had not seen her virgin blood on the bedding the next morning before he had taken his leave of the room. He had not expected that. Men often took liberties with some of their servants, many willing, some not, a practice he found abhorring. There was no need, ever, for a man to force himself on a woman. It only proved he was no man at all.

He had not been looking for a virgin to wed just someone who would meet his need. That Adara had been a virgin pleased him more than he had expected. But then she had pleased him more than he had ever imagined she would.

Her fright had brought out a tenderness in him that he believed had long died, not something he could say he had experienced with any woman. He would like to experience what he had felt on his wedding night again and that was a dangerous thought.

He could not, would not, allow himself to wander off course. He had a mission to accomplish and he would see it done.

Warrick startled, feeling the flutter beneath his hand and stilled, waiting to feel it again and when it came, his breath caught. That his child moved inside Adara left him overwhelmed with the sense that they both belonged to him, were a part of him, and he would do anything to keep them safe.

~~~

Adara woke just before they entered the village and was glad she did. She was worried how the clan would react to Warrick and his army of men, donned in deathly shrouds, descending upon them. The clan had been good to her and had graciously accepted her as part of them without question and with Craven having been left leader of the clan all had been well and peaceful.

That, however, was about to change.

The clan members working the fields on either side of the path to the village hurried off in fright to warn the others. A bell began to toll and by the time Warrick led his warriors into the village, the loud tolling had turned to a whimper and people were clustered in groups, children clinging to their parents and wives pressed close to their husbands. The clan displayed not a single weapon. With Adara on the horse, in Warrick's arms, perhaps they believed no harm was meant to them. Or did they wisely realize it was useless to raise a weapon against the mighty Demon Lord and his warriors?

Warrick brought his stallion to a stop in front of the keep and turned the animal around to look out over the village. "Listen well," he called out, his voicing booming throughout the village. "Adara is my wife and I am now Lord of the Clan MacVarish. You will pledge your allegiance to me or you are free to leave. There will be rules to follow and those who do not follow them will be made to suffer. I expect obedience from all. In return, you will not starve, you will always have shelter, and you will be protected. Deceive me, betray me, and you will die." He pointed to Roark who had brought his horse up alongside him. "This is Roark. He speaks for me. You will obey his every word. Tomorrow I will walk through the village and will hear any problems or concerns you have. After that you will address all concerns to Roark and he will see I am made aware of them."

A brave soul called out, "How can we be sure he will speak for us?"

Warrick's eyes went straight to the man, who attempted to shrink among the crowd. "You will learn that Roark is an honest man and far more patient than me. You would be wise to remember that." He paused a moment letting his words sink in. "Roark and some of my warriors will walk among the village and make themselves known to you. You would do well to speak with them."

That he expected absolute obedience from the clan should not surprise her, for he demanded the same from her as his wife. It seemed he expected it from everyone.

After Warrick dismounted, he reached up and, with his hands at her waist, lifted her off the horse. "You will eat and then you will rest."

It was not a request and Adara nodded.

He stepped away from her, walking a distance away with Roark and keeping his voice low so that no one would hear him. Warriors stepped forward to take the horses and lead them away, while a few warriors waited, their hoods now off their heads, their eyes intent on their surroundings, and not a single smile on any of their faces.

Adara startled when she felt a strong hand close around her arm. She did not need to look to see it was Warrick, but she did. He propelled her forward toward the keep, his intent glare focused straight ahead. She thought she caught the slightest wrinkle to his brow as if something troubled his thoughts, but it had vanished so fast she did not know if she had truly seen it at all.

She kept her eyes on his face to see if she could catch it again, an unwise move, since her foot caught on something and she stumbled.

She was up in his arms so fast her breath caught in a faint gasp.

"You need to watch your step," he scolded as he continued walking.

"You need to walk slower." She bit at her lower lip, wishing she had done so before the words had slipped out. What was wrong with her to reprimand him like that?

Warrick stopped abruptly. "Watch your tongue with me, Adara. You would not want to lose it."

He would not cut her tongue out, would he? She lowered her head, repentant and fearful. Was he truly that cruel? Memories of his dungeon flashed in her head, the horrifying screams, the stomach-turning odors, the senseless cruelty, and she had her answer.

She was wed to a monster—a demon—and there was no escape.

More memories assaulted her, though this time they were of her wedding night. How could a monster show tenderness, make her feel as if he cared, then turn cold and uncaring?

Who was this strange man she married? No answer came this time. If she wanted one, she would have to search for it.

He lowered her to her feet once inside the Great Hall and she felt a sudden relief at being home. MacVarish keep was small in comparison to MacCara keep, though to Adara it was too large. Seeing it now, however, with Warrick standing in the middle of the Great Hall, the room seemed to shrink in his presence.

The few trestle tables seemed meek in size and the dais that had seemed to overpower the room when she had first seen it, now appeared small and inadequate with Warrick there. Even the fireplace, large enough for her to step into, seemed to have shrunk in size. Nothing in the room seemed adequate enough for the Demon Lord.

Two servants hovered together in a corner, wringing their hands, their eyes wide as they waited.

Warrick ordered them forward with the snap of his

hand.

The two nearly tripped over each other in their effort to hurry and obey.

He nodded toward the hearth. "That fire is not sufficient to chase the chill from this room. See to it that the flames are kept fed at all times. Bring us food and drink."

Both women bobbed their heads and one hurried to the hearth to feed the flames with several logs while the other rushed out of the room.

Adara did not expect Warrick to join her and she certainly did not expect him to sit at a table near the hearth. She assumed he would take his rightly seat at the dais. She realized why when he spoke.

"You will be warm here."

He was concerned for her? She nodded, not knowing how else to respond.

Drink was brought out immediately, the servant setting a pitcher of ale and one of cider on the table. The young woman's hand shook as she filled a tankard with ale for Warrick and one with cider for Adara. She hurried off as soon as the task was done.

Food followed quickly, though Adara scrunched her face at the smell of the salted herring and pushed the dish away, turning her head as she did.

Warrick picked the dish up, handing it to the servant, and ordered, "Take it away." He looked to Adara. "You do not care for salted herring."

"The bairn dislikes fish," she said, scrunching her nose in distaste.

"You liked it once?"

"I did. I cooked and ate what I caught whenever the chance presented itself, since I never could count on whether I would eat on any given day."

The portrait that scene painted in his mind stirred his ire while it also had him admiring her fortitude. Life had been cruel to her, to most actually, but those who fought back survived. Adara had fought back.

Roark entered the Great Hall, though he did not approach the table. He stood waiting.

Warrick stood. "I have matters to see to. Eat and rest."

Adara watched Warrick leave the room, glad when the door closed and she finally had time alone. Something she worried she would not have much of now that her husband was here. She was about to drop the piece of cheese in her hand, having lost her appetite but thought better of it. She had eaten little and while she no longer felt hungry, the bairn might feel otherwise. She forced herself to eat the small chunk. It reminded her of the countless times she had nearly starved and the winters she feared she would freeze to death. And the endless times she felt a slap to her face, a kick to her leg, a twist to her arm. At least with Warrick she would not go hungry or cold or find herself sleeping with the animals in the barn. She would have food and shelter and a husband to keep her safe. She had to remember to hold her tongue, if she wanted to keep it. What she had to do was be an obedient wife. That also meant she would have to share a bed with him.

A yawn let her know that the journey here had tired her or perhaps it was her heavy thoughts that brought fatigue on her.

"Are you feeling unwell, my lady?"

Adara jumped startled by the unexpected voice, but smiled when she saw Langdon. He had arrived at MacVarish village not long after her. He always had a kind word or a smile for her and had always spoken with her whenever he saw her even if she had not participated in the conversation. He would carry it all on his own.

"Fatigued from the journey, Langdon," she said.

"You should rest, my lady."

"A good suggestion, Langdon." And one she had intended to do.

"My heartfelt wishes on your wedding, my lady," he

said with a bob of his head.

"Thank you, Langdon." Adara often thought he needed a good washing, though he never had an odor about him. His heavily gray hair hung loose around his face and always appeared as if it needed washing, matted at times, and grime was a favorite companion of his. But then he was a hard worker, even though he was stooped and slow with age, he did his share. He had become good friends with Burchard the kitchen gardener and often helped him, both men close in age.

"And how are you, Langdon?" she asked, though by the look of his dirt-covered hands and garments, she would say he had been busy helping Burchard in the garden and his response confirmed it.

"I am well, my lady, busy helping Burchard. "Stay well, my lady," he said and with a bob of his head took his leave.

Adara smiled. She liked the old man. In an odd way, he had filled a void her uncle's death had left. She often came upon him during her late night walks through the village after her uncle had died. He would talk with her, sometimes talking much, other times saying few words. She supposed it had been his company that brought her some solace.

She ate a bit more, then climbed the stairs to the small bedchamber she had chosen for herself. A single bed, a small side table, a chest near the door, and a fireplace to keep her warm was all she needed and more than she had ever had.

She folded her cloak to lay on the chest, slipped her tunic off, folding it and placing it on top of her cloak, fed another log to the flames, then stretched out on the bed.

No soon as she did, her thoughts drifted back to her wedding night. She had been terrified, still reeling from having wed the Demon Lord. The two women who had helped ready her to receive her husband had whispered prayers as they scrubbed her.

Adara had not been sure if they had been meant to help her or to protect the women from the Demon Lord's wife.

They had hurried out of the room as soon as they had finished and she had waited there alone for the man she did not know, who would make her his wife. She had never felt so trapped, but then she had yet to experience Warrick's dungeon.

Even though she had remained fearful, she had been relieved when Warrick finally entered the room, the waiting having been unbearable. He had said nothing to her. He went to the table where food and drink had been placed and filled two goblets with wine. He had taken one and walked over to Adara to hand her the other.

"It will help make it easier," he had said.

Adara had not argued, she drank some and though she did not favor the taste, she continued to drink it. She had noticed his hair had been damp and his garments appeared clean. He had washed and she had thought him thoughtful for doing so. Not something you would expect from a man known as the Demon Lord.

He had downed his wine and placed the empty goblet on the table, then turned and stripped off his garments to stand naked in front of her. She saw him clearly, as if he were standing there in front of her now, his body hard, his muscles taut. There was no softness to him, no kindness in his dark eyes, and even though he was across the room, she took a step back.

Adara's eyes had grown too heavy with sleep to remain open and they drifted closed, leaving the image of Warrick to fade from her mind, her wedding night once again left to memory.

~~~

The light mist made it difficult for Adara to recognize the forest. Was she lost? How had she gotten here? It was not at all familiar to her. Her hand hurried to her stomach when she felt the bairn's hard kick and she looked down, shocked to see herself so heavy with child. How had she grown so large, so fast?

She turned completely around, hoping to spot something familiar, hoping to find her way home. The light mist was thickening much too fast as she anxiously searched for a familiar sign. She saw it then, a stream where she had once fished, but that was nowhere near MacVarish land. How did she get here and how would she get home?

The sudden sounds of footfalls startled her. They were heavy and pounding the earth, running, getting closer.

"Run!" a female voice warned. "Run!"

Adara did not wait, she started running and kept running through the fog, not seeing where she was going, not knowing where she was going, only knowing she had to run, had to get away.

The earth rattled beneath her feet as the footfalls drew closer and closer. No matter how fast she ran, she could not put distance between them.

Whoever chased her would catch her. Then what?

"Run!" the voice urged again. "Run to Warrick!"

Warrick. Her husband. He would keep her safe and their bairn safe.

The footfalls were near upon her and as a hand came down on her shoulder, she screamed, "Warrick!"

~~~

Warrick no soon as sat at the table near the hearth with Roark, then food and drink was brought to them.

"My wife?' he asked the servant who filled their tankards.

"Resting in her room, my lord."

"*Her* room?" he asked his tone sharp.

The young servant began to tremble and an older servant walked over and placed a comforting hand on the young lass' shoulder.

"The lord and lady's bedchamber is being made ready. Lady Adara rests in her room two floors up." With a bob of her head, she walked away and the young servant placed the pitcher on the table and scurried off.

Warrick barely turned his head to Roark when his name echoed through the keep in a terrifying scream.

Chapter Nine

Warrick took the steps three at a time, Roark following close behind him, his blood running cold at the sound of his name being screamed repeatedly. He threw the door to the room open with such force that it broke off its top hinge.

Like a fist to the gut, relief hit Warrick when he saw his wife twisting and fighting the blanket that had entrapped her. Still, she was not only trapped in the blanket, but the dream as well and he hurried to free her of both. It was not easy, since her struggles increased as he attempted to unravel the blanket.

"I am here, Adara. You are safe," he urged as Roark hurried to help him.

It took a few moments to free her and all the time, Warrick continued to ensure her that she was safe.

"Hear me, wife, you are safe. I will let no harm come to you. You are safe."

Adara's eyes sprang open when released from the entwined blanket and seeing her husband leaning over her, she threw her arms around his neck and his name fell from her lips in a thankful whisper.

Warrick scooped her up in his arms and sat on the bed, holding her as tightly as she clung to him. "All is well. You have nothing to fear."

Adara's chest heaved, her breathing rapid, as if she had been running far too long, but then she had been. She pressed her face against her husband's chest, listening to his heart thunder. He had been running as well, running to her... to save her.

"I will never let anything happen to you," —his hand went to rest on her stomach— "or the bairn. You have my word on that."

Feeling safe at the moment, and for the first time in her life, she wanted to believe his pledge, but life had taught her differently. For now, she would allow herself a small reprieve and believe she was safe… until she was not.

~~~

Night came much too soon and with it bedtime. She had gone to her room, thinking if she fell asleep there Warrick would leave her be. But what little of hers had been there had been removed and the bed stripped. Even the fire in the hearth had been doused. She had no choice but to go to the bedchamber that she would share with her husband.

The room had belonged to her uncle and when she entered, sweet memories greeted her. She would spend early evening here with uncle Owen. They would sit in the two chairs he had arranged in front of the hearth, a fire always kept burning since the stone walls seemed to forever hold a chill as had his old bones, as he would say.

A tear fell from the corner of her eye as she recalled their talks and she realized she missed her uncle more than she thought possible.

"What is wrong? Is it the bairn?" Warrick asked, after stepping around her and seeing the tear slip down her cheek. He placed a gentle hand to her lower back while his other hand came to rest tenderly on her stomach.

His concern poked at her heart, though she tried not to think too much on it, but instead reminded herself that hopes and wishes never came her way.

"Good memories of my uncle," she said. "This was his room. We would talk here in the evenings. He would tell me about my mum when she was a young, spirited lass." She had been grateful for those talks, for she had come to know her mum that way.

"You do not remember your mum?"

"I remember nothing of her or my da."

"No siblings?" he asked.

She shook her head. "What of your family?"

Warrick patted her stomach. "You both are my family."

Having been thrown into the marriage, she had never considered that it just might give her what she had always wanted, a permanent home, a family... love. Warrick might not love her but the bairn would. Hope sprang in her that it was possible and she held tight to it.

She rested her hand over his and smiled up at him to let him know his words had pleased her.

Her innocent touch struck him like a bolt of lightning, arousing him and bringing with it the memories of the one night they had shared. A night that had haunted him, playing in his mind over and over. He wanted a taste of it again. To see if the immense pleasure had been real or if he had made it more than it had been.

He had thought often of her lips and the kisses they had shared. Light, faint kisses at first, letting her grow accustom to his lips, to his desire, and her own. He had teased hers, brushing them gently until she began to respond, with caution at first. Her timid attempts had flared his desire like a spark to kindling. That moment was branded in his memory and every time he recalled it, which was far too often, he grew aroused just as he did now. There had been no recourse for him, not until now.

He lowered his head slowly to see if she would pull away, deny him, but she did not move, though her eyes, the darkest blue he had ever seen, turned wide. He brushed his lips over hers and he felt her gasp and knew he had struck a spark in her. His lips stroked hers faintly, though unlike before she responded more quickly, her lips showing their eagerness for more.

His hand went to the back of her head, cupping it, holding it firm as his lips took possession of hers, teasing, coaxing, demanding and his loins tightened when she eagerly returned his kiss.

It was not as he remembered it. It was more, so much more.

Their tongues dueled in passionate play and as his arm closed around her, she stepped closer to him, pressed her body to his so hard that it felt like she could not get close enough, like she had missed him, had finally come home to him. Or was it he who felt that way?

He had missed her and she had welcomed him home.

The thought shocked him so badly that it had him stepping away from her abruptly. He scowled at her, a low snarl rumbling in his chest as his hands fisted at his sides, and she took a step back away from him.

He stormed past her, out the door, slamming it closed behind him.

Adara hurried to sit in the chair by the hearth, fearful her trembling legs would not support her much longer. She had no idea what happened. Had she done something wrong? She had kissed him no differently then she had on their wedding night. At least, she did not believe so.

When she realized he intended to kiss her, she felt anxious, unsure, and yet something inside her was eager for his kiss, eager to taste the pleasure his lips would bring her. But it had brought her even more than she had expected. Her heart had soared when his lips touched hers and she felt…

Tears tickled her eyes. She could not believe what she had felt and was still feeling. It could not be.

She felt as if he had welcomed her home.

~~~

Warrick stepped out into the cold night air and took several deep breaths to stop himself from roaring into the darkness and waking the entire village. He had rid himself of any feelings, that would get in his way, anything that would prevent him from succeeding. A trait owed to his father's tutelage.

He had to keep his mind clear, his insights sharp, to keep all his missions victorious. He could not let a wisp of a woman distract him. He needed his thoughts focused.

He turned his face into the wind that whipped behind him, the cold that came with it hitting him like a slap in the face. He needed it, needed reminding of what was important.

He could easily lose himself in Adara. When he was with her, kissed her, touched her, was inside her, he had felt free. Free of the horrors of battle, the pain and suffering, the stench of death. That night, it had been as if her innocence had washed away his sins and he was at peace. He could not remember the last time he had felt such contentment. He had tried to deny the impact she had had on him, but kissing her again had brought it all back and now it was not only peace she brought him, but the feeling of returning home. A place he longed for, a place he had never known.

He turned an eye on the keep. He had paid the price demanded of him, though he had done so under his terms. He had wed a woman of his choice, not a woman known to him, and not a titled one. One who was accustomed to obedience. One who would live by his rules. One he would treat well and keep safe. One that would expect nothing from him.

Why now did he want something else from the woman he had chosen?

"Something amiss, Roark?" Warrick asked, turning to see his warrior and friend step out of the night shadows. He believed his keen senses had been born of experience through the years, but he was reminded they had been born more out of necessity.

"No, all is well. I could not sleep. I miss my wife."

"I am surprised she has not taken it upon herself to venture here," Warrick said.

Roark smiled. "Callie does have a strong nature."

"More than a strong nature. I do not know how you deal

with her."

Roark laughed. "Love is blind."

"The very reason I avoid it."

"It strikes you whether you want it to or not."

"I keep an impenetrable shield."

Roark shrugged. "Is the shield any longer necessary? You have a wife, chosen for her obedience. A servant who for years obeyed without thought or question. You need not worry about love. You have what you want."

"I do have what I want. Adara knows her place and will obey me without question."

"And she is fertile, already carrying your bairn."

"You doubt the bairn is mine, Roark," Warrick challenged.

"What matters is what you believe."

"Trust and truth are difficult for me, as you know."

"Those who betrayed your trust and lied to you were known to you. You do not know Adara well enough to judge if she can be trusted or if she speaks the truth," Roark said.

"It matters not. I will not speak of important matters with her."

"If that is what you wish," Roark said.

"What I wish?" Warrick snapped. "What I wish is for what happened never to have happened. But that is not possible and now I must find the truth."

"Would it not be wiser to tell Adara before she discovers for herself?"

"Do you plan on telling her?" Warrick snapped again.

"You know I would never do such a thing," Roark assured him.

"Then who would tell her?"

Roark shook his head. "You know well enough there are those who take pleasure in other peoples' pain and would only be too glad to see the shock on Adara's face at the news. They would get even more pleasure to see her recoil from you after learning about it. Tell her before someone else does."

"Not yet," Warrick argued.

"I was there when you told her you would keep her safe, let no harm come to her. She will be harmed if she learns of this from someone else."

Warrick took a step away from Roark, angry that he had brought up the matter and angrier that he was right. "She will be harmed either way."

"It will make a difference coming from you."

Warrick laughed, not a humorous one. One more tinged with evil. "A difference? I doubt that, my friend. Though, I do not doubt that she will run from the room screaming when I tell her I killed my first wife."

Chapter Ten

Two days and Adara had barely seen her husband, not that she minded that he left her alone, especially in their bedchamber. He had not shared their bed since their arrival and it left her wondering since he had informed her that he would. It also kept her on edge at night, lying there waiting to see if he would enter the room and join her in bed. Sometimes when she woke in the middle of the night she would carefully turn to see if he was there, but she continued to find an empty spot beside her.

Had she done something wrong? Was that why he seemed to avoid her?

She shook the nagging thoughts away. What difference did it make? Warrick did as he pleased. He answered to no one. The problem was that she had had a taste of the same and she favored it. Hers days had been her own since discovering she was Owen MacVarish's niece and after having tended to others from before sunrise to after sunset since she had been young, she had cherished every one of them.

Her uncle Owen had, however, insisted she learn about the running of the clan and the keep. He told her that she knew all too well from experience that life was unpredictable, ever changing, and that some people we think we can count on to help may not always be able to.

He had been right about that. She had learned to adapt more often than she had cared to, having been sent from one family to another. She did here what she had done countless times before… adapted. She got to know the clan's people and had slowly grown comfortable around them, though conversation with them had remained limited. Many faces had become familiar to her while others she knew by name, and all would bob their head, smile, or call out a greeting to her. In the last two days, however, they seemed to avoid her. She understood why, she had brought the Demon Lord down upon them and they were fearful of the future.

It was near to mid-day and she had not seen her husband since early morning when she had caught a glance of him leaving the Great Hall. She had enjoyed a quiet meal and had retired to a small room on the first floor that had fallen to neglect after Uncle Owen's wife, Corliss, had died. He had encouraged her to use it, having had it cleaned and prepared for her, insisting his wife would be happy to know another woman got as much pleasure from it as she had.

There was where she spent many enjoyable hours stitching. Stitching had been one chore that she had enjoyed and had become proficient at. It also was the one thing that had helped her accept that she was with child.

Fear had been her first thought when she had realized, shortly after settling into MacVarish keep, that she carried the Demon Lord's bairn. She had no idea at the time what she would do. There had been no thought to return to Warrick, the idea, itself, prickling her skin with fear. She never wanted to be anywhere near that horrid dungeon again.

It was when she had sat down one day in this room with some scraps of cloth the weavers had given her and began to stitch a garment for the child that a smile had surfaced on her face. The tiny, innocent bairn growing inside was not to blame for anything, and she would protect him, care for him, love him like she had never been loved.

She felt a strong flutter, then another, and she laughed softly as she patted her stomach. "You have had enough sitting. I will work on your garment later, though I believe you will like it. It is the softest of wool, but for now we walk."

Adara stepped out of the keep to find the day overcast. It did not look nor feel like rain, but one could never tell.

The air held a chill and she was glad for her wool cloak. It would keep her and the bairn warm.

She rarely left the keep through the front doors. She preferred taking the narrow passage that led out to the kitchen. Not that she entered the kitchen. She took the door to the left, just before the entrance to the kitchen, that led outside, avoiding most everyone. She saw that Burchard was tending the kitchen garden, seeing to the last of the plants before harvest. They talked on occasion and she was pleased when he waved to her and walked toward her.

He was a man of many years, his gait slow, his fingers gnarled from endless work, and a perpetual smile framed by an abundance of wrinkles.

"All is well with you, my lady?" he asked as she approached.

Adara felt uncomfortable with the title upon first hearing it. It did not seem right. It did not fit her, and yet it had become hers upon marriage.

"I am well, Burchard and you? And where is Langdon, he does not help you today?" she asked a soft smile on her face and thinking he could use the help.

"Langdon is busy elsewhere today and I am well. I only hope I do well, my lady," he said, bobbing his head. "Many changes coming. Many."

While he continued to smile, Adara saw worry in his aged eyes and attempted to reassure him. "You have nothing to fear, Burchard."

"I hope, my lady, I do hope," he said, his bobbing head suddenly going stiff and fear replaced worry in his eyes. He turned away from her without a word and hurried back to work.

When Adara turned, she saw two of Warrick's warriors, draped in their shrouds standing there watching Burchard.

Adara did not know where the foolish courage came from, perhaps it was instinct to protect an old man, and without hesitation she approached the two warriors.

"Go about your business and leave this man alone," Adara snapped at them.

They stood there, unmoving, the hoods of their shrouds covering down to the tips of their noses, making their near faceless heads even more intimidating.

"Go away," she ordered more sternly.

"They take orders only from me."

Adara jolted as she turned at the sound of her husband's deep, commanding voice. He did not wear a shroud, yet he was more intimidating than his warriors who did. His imposing presence, the defiant tilt of his chin, the way he commanded, demanded from all those around overpowered and made one back away from him... usually.

This time Adara did not back away, she approached him, the overwhelming sense to protect the old man who brought harm to none too intense to ignore.

"Then tell them to leave, there is nothing for them here."

Warrick brought his face down close to hers. "You do not dictate to me, wife."

Adara warned herself to hold her tongue, but it was too late, words were already rushing past her lips. "Why are they here?"

"That does not concern you."

A voice inside cautioned her to stop, say no more. Be obedient as she had always been. She did not listen. "It most certainly does. This is *my* clan and I will see no one harmed."

"This clan belongs to *me* as do *you*."

Chattel. That was all she was to him. That was all she ever was to anyone.

Changes. Many changes coming.

Burchard was right. There were many changes coming and she could not stop them. She could, however, defend Burchard the best she could.

"He is an old man. He can harm none. Why do they

watch him?"

"That is not your concern," Warrick repeated, annoyed that she continued to defy him yet admired her courage as misplaced as it was.

A sudden irritation pushed past all sound reason and had her saying, "You are insufferable." Adara cringed as she saw his hand swing up and she braced herself for the blow.

She was shocked when his whole body wrapped around her, cocooning her against him as he dropped to the ground, and turning her as they went down so he would take the brunt of the fall. Then he let out a roar that she could have sworn trembled the earth.

Once they hit the ground, he rolled them to their sides, keeping her body encased in his arms and planted solidly against him.

Shouts and pounding footfalls rushed past them while others came to a stop behind Warrick, forming a line, shielding them.

From what? she wondered.

"Are you harmed?" Warrick asked, keeping her tucked against him.

"I do not believe so." Before she could ask him what happened, shouts rang out. He suddenly lifted her to her feet, keeping one arm around her waist and holding her firm.

Warrick placed his hand on her stomach, his body riddled with fury that his wife or child could have been harmed. "Are you sure? I feel no movement."

"He makes himself known only when he wants to," she said and thought how much he was like his da.

"I will send for Espy."

Adara shook her head. "It is not necessary. You shielded me well. The bairn and I are unharmed." She hoped to reassure him, but the anger mixed with worry remained in his dark eyes.

His warriors parted and Warrick turned, calling out to Roark as he approached. "Do not tell me that you failed to catch him."

"He is dead," Roark said, stopping in front of Warrick.

Catch who? Who is dead, thought Adara.

"Now we will learn nothing. Who is the fool who killed him?"

"He killed himself."

"He chose death over capture."

"The sign of an assassin."

Had she heard Roark correctly? Did he say assassin? And who was the assassin's target?

Roark summoned one of the nearby warriors and the man stepped forward and handed him two arrows.

"He got off two—"

"I heard three," Warrick interrupted.

Adara stared at the arrows. Someone had tried to kill Warrick?

Roark nodded to the warrior and he hurried off. He held up the arrows. "They were made to resemble ours."

"I am getting close and someone does not like it," Warrick said, his voice low.

"Close to what?" Adara asked unable to remain quiet any longer, feeling vulnerable not understanding what was happening.

Both men's eyes fell on Adara as if they had just realized she was there.

Warrick ignored her question and turned to Roark. "The trackers?"

"They have been sent and the men scour the area."

"Find something," Warrick ordered and with a nod Roark walked off, the warriors who had been standing nearby following him.

Questions filled Adara's head but she had no time to ask even one, Warrick rushing her inside the keep into the Great Hall.

"You will stay here until I return for you," he ordered and turned to leave her.

Donna Fletcher

Her hand shot out, grabbing his arm, her fingers locking firmly around it.

Warrick's head snapped around, his eyes settling on her hand, the strength of it gripping him tight as if she did not want to let him go. But that was not likely. More likely it was fear not favor, she held for him.

"What happened out there?" she asked, fighting the tremor she felt building inside her.

"It does not—"

Adara stepped closer to him, her grip on his arm growing tighter. "Please, Warrick, do not leave me ignorant of the truth." The tremor she was fighting claimed victory and instinctively she sought the protection of her husband's powerful arms, stepping closer and collapsing against him.

Warrick's arms went around her and scooped her up. He went and sat on a bench close to the fire, keeping her cradled in his arms. She was not unharmed. She had been left shocked and frightened by the incident, and it did not help that she would be left ignorant of the situation.

He slipped his hand beneath her cloak and rubbed and squeezed her arm, letting his strength soak in and chase her tremble away.

While her husband could still put fear in her, how was it that she had also found solace in his arms? How had it become so instinctive for her to do so? Had it been memories of the one night they had spent together where surprisingly she had found comfort and contentment in his arms, his touch, his kiss? Did she long to share that time again with him?

"I should send for Espy to be sure you and the bairn are well," he said.

Adara sighed softly. "No, I had a bit of a fright, but your arms chased that away and continue to give me and the bairn all the comfort we need."

Adara did something that no one had ever done to Warrick. She stunned him speechless. He might believe she

90

sought his arms for protection but that she sought them for comfort stunned him even more.

She raised her head off his chest. "Please tell me what goes on. Who were those arrows meant for?"

He hesitated, not wanting the evil and danger that seemed forever to haunt him touch her but keeping her completely ignorant would not help either. "Me," he finally said.

She felt as if a hand squeezed at her heart and she did not know where she got the breath to ask, "Why?"

He felt a shudder run through her and her hand hurried to rest on his arm as if in protection, both caring gestures. The thought both disturbed and pleased him. It also made him decide that while he would not tell her all of it, he would at least not leave her ignorant of the problem, since there was a strong possibility that more attempts would be made.

"What I share with you can be shared with no one," he said.

She nodded. "You have my word I will say nothing."

"I search for someone and I believe that I am getting close and that someone does not want to be found. Do not ask me who is it. That is not something I will tell you."

"Is this the first attempt someone has made to," —a shiver interrupted her words— "take your life?"

"To purposely plan to take my life, aye, that it is. There have been numerous attempts in battle but they always failed."

That death was ever his companion frightened her and she hurried to say, "You must be careful." The silent words in her head that followed surprised her. *The bairn and I need you.*

Was that heartfelt concern he heard in her voice and showed in her dark blues eyes?

Did she actually care for him?

That was not possible. She feared him too much to care and what did it matter if she did. He could not let her distract

91

him.

Where the words came from that kept spilling from Adara's lips, she did not know, either did she know what caused the pangs to her heart. "Promise me. Promise me you will be careful."

The caring in her soft, gentle voice took hold of him, chasing all sound reason away, leaving him with only one thought.

He kissed her, brief at first, a mere brush of his lips across hers, before devouring her lips with his.

Forever.

That was how it felt since he had last kissed her and why he was so hungry for her now. Still it didn't feel like enough. He needed more, wanted more, ached for it. He caught hold of his soaring thoughts and grew annoyed at his aching loins. Both had him bringing the kiss to a gentle end.

This would not do. He would bed her and be done with it, satisfy this lust for her that had been growing since their arrival here. Or had it been since their wedding night?

"Promise me," she whispered a mere breath away from his lips.

He was about to ask what promise when he recalled what she wanted from him… to be careful.

"You have my word, wife," he said and could not resist to seal his promise with a tender kiss.

"My lord."

Warrick turned his head as did Adara to see Roark standing a short distance from them.

Warrick got annoyed that he had been so engrossed with Adara that he had not heard Roark approach. That would not do. It would not do at all.

"We found something," Roark said.

Chapter Eleven

"Show me," Warrick ordered, walking around the table toward Roark.

Adara followed her husband, bumping into him when he stopped abruptly.

"Where do you think you are going?" Warrick demanded, turning to face her.

His face took on a scowl that easily intimidated and the familiar flush of fear raced through her, warning her to hold her tongue, step back, obey, as she had always done. Instead, she forced herself to say, "With you."

"Absolutely not. You will remain here at the keep until I come for you," he ordered.

"It might be advisable if you remained here as well, Warrick," Roark said and ignoring the flash of annoyance in Warrick's eyes continued explaining. "We found the dead warrior's campsite and it appears that he was not alone. It also appears as if the camp has been there for at least two perhaps three weeks."

"Well before our arrival in the area," Warrick said and Roark agreed with a nod. "But how did they know I would be here? No one knew of my plans."

Adara realized it before either of the two men did and said, "Me."

"What would you have to do with it?" Roark asked.

"Bloody hell," Warrick said, realizing what his wife meant. "Someone discovered you are my wife and knew I would eventually find you. So they camped here waiting."

Roark shook his head. "Why not simply take her and force you to come for her?"

"That would reveal their identity and give me what I

93

search for," Warrick said. "Here they would remain concealed, lay in wait, and strike." He turned to Adara. "Has anyone new joined your clan recently? Or has there been anyone who stopped and sought shelter for a night or two?"

"I do not know," Adara said and it troubled her that she did not know. She had never given thought to what her solitude could mean to her clan. She should be familiar with all that went on in the clan. Had not her uncle tried to convey that to her by having her learn the workings of the keep? A thought came to her. "Wynn might know. She oversees the running of the keep and I often thought the village as well since she knows everything about everyone." Another thought came to her. "Also Jaynce our healer might know something."

"I will speak to both," Warrick said, "but first I will take a look at this campsite."

"At least wait until your warriors have combed a sufficient area before you take the chance of leaving yourself vulnerable," Roark advised.

"Their attempt to kill me failed, which left them no recourse but to flee. It will take time for them to regroup or report to the person they are answerable to before they make another attempt. Besides, they also have left themselves vulnerable by failing. Now we know they exist and it is only a matter of time before one or all are caught, then I will have my answers."

"As you say," Roark said with a nod.

Adara slipped her small hand into Warrick's large one, lacing her fingers with his and was pleased when his instinctively closed around hers firmly. She looked up at him. "I go with you."

He gave a quick glance to her small hand encased in his and felt a kick to his gut and when he saw the plea—so aching, so tender—in her blue eyes, he felt a jab to his heart. Damn, what was it about this petite woman that caused such turmoil in him? Before he could deny her request, she spoke

94

again, softly, for his ears alone.

"Please, Warrick, I feel safer with you."

Another punch to his gut at her tender plea had him nearly cursing aloud, but he kept it contained to his thoughts as he said, "You will not leave my side and you will obey my every word."

Adara nodded. "I will."

"It is a bit of a distance," Roark said. "Do you feel up to the walk?"

Annoyed that he had not given that thought, Warrick was about to order her to remain in the keep when she smiled and laughed softly as her hand went to pat her stomach.

"The bairn loves when we walk. When I sit too long he lets me know it. That was why I was outside when this happened." She patted her stomach again. "He grew tired of me sitting and stitching."

Warrick noticed that Adara spoke with ease and at length when it came to the bairn. That she loved the child that grew inside her was unmistakable and made him feel even more protective of them both.

"If you grow tired—" Another soft spurt of laughter from Adara paused Warrick.

"He will let me know." She gave another pat to her rounded stomach.

~~~

Adara had taken brief walks in the woods, throughout her years of servitude, whenever the chance had presented itself, which had not been often, her daily chores all too grueling and all too endless to ever find time. When she did get a chance—sneaked a chance—she had often given thought to keep walking, not return to whatever hell she was living. Fear, however, had managed to keep her a prisoner and at times it still did. It was not until she learned what it was truly like to be a prisoner with no chance to sneak away for even a few minutes that she had sworn to herself after escaping the dungeon that never again would she allow herself to be held captive. If that ever happened, she would take a walk and this time keep walking.

At the moment, she had no wont to do that. She had something now that she had longed for… a home. While her husband might not love her, he had proven he would keep her safe when he had protected her and their bairn not only against the arrow meant for him, but the fall that could have harmed the bairn. No one had protected her when she was just a wee one and she would not have that happen to her child.

She glanced around. At one time, she would have been frozen with fright seeing so many of Warrick's warriors. Now she was pleased to see them. They intimidated draped in their black shrouds, but not so much now with their hoods off their heads, their faces shown. Some of the warriors followed along with them while others were busy searching the area.

Warrick would keep her safe and his warriors would keep him safe and she was glad for that. However, the thought that someone wanted her husband dead troubled her terribly.

"What troubles you?" Warrick demanded. "You wear a frown."

She looked at him. "And you wear a scowl. Why?"

"Your frown causes my scowl. Do you not feel well?"

"I feel good. The walk invigorates me."

"Then why the frown?" he demanded again.

She spoke honestly. "It troubles me that someone wants to kill you."

"Grown fond of me, have you?"

Was that a bit of humor she heard in his tone? Regardless if it was or not, she responded with a slight tilt of her head, a smile, and a touch of wit. "Do I have a choice?"

It was brief but she saw it, a slight lifting at the corners of his mouth as if he had nabbed the smile before it could surface.

"I will grant you that choice," he said, enjoying their banter.

"I am grateful for that, my lord." With a bob of her head and her smile tender. She confirmed, "I have grown fond of you."

Warrick never expected those words from her or his reaction to them. He had to pounce on the smile that rushed to his lips, catching it before it could surface, but from the way his wife's smile grew, he wondered if he had failed to stop it completely. At least she could not hear how it had set his heart to thumping rapidly against his chest.

Adara caught it again, the slight lifting at the corners of his mouth, and this time a brightness to his dark eyes she had never seen before. She made no mention of either, though it did prove that her husband was capable of smiling.

"Over here," Roark called out.

Adara felt a chill wrap around her when her husband's expression turned hard, uncaring, and she promised herself that somehow, she would get her husband accustomed to smiling until it finally became a natural thing for him to do.

The campsite had been deserted quickly and in their foolish haste things had been left behind, leaving signs of their extended stay there. Signs that three or more people had occupied the camp.

Warrick walked Adara over to a large rock, the top smooth. "You will sit here and rest until I am done."

She nodded and he assisted her to sit before walking away. She took the time to look around. There were so many warriors scouting about that there was no way they would miss anything. There were even some warriors in the trees.

She watched with interest at how thorough her husband looked over the campsite and asked questions of Roark as he pushed at the cold ashes, that had once been the camp's fire, with the tip of his boot. Every now and then he would glance her way, making sure she had remained where he left her, and she would smile at him. He did not respond, but she did not expect him to. She was thinking that if she kept smiling at him that, one time, he just might return her smile. At least, it was a start.

Adara glanced around. The area was not familiar to her. It was the opposite way of where she usually walked between MacVarish and MacCara land. This area of the woods led eventually to MacKewan land. She only knew that because of Hannah, the woman who had escaped with her. She had been glad to hear that all had went well for Hannah and she was wed to Slain MacKewan, and content.

She turned to see where her husband was when her eyes took notice of a stone on the ground not far from her. It was not a large stone. It could fit in the palm of one's hand and looked almost perfectly round and flat. She scrunched her eyes, attempting to get a better look. There appeared to be something on the stone. She had always enjoyed finding stones with designs nature had imprinted on them. She had tried to keep a few, possess something of her own, but after they had been taken from her and discarded, she had stopped gathering them. The hurt of losing the few things she had managed to get for herself, that were hers and hers alone when she had nothing else, was just too much to bear.

Now, however, it was different. She could keep what she found. Not having given thought to gathering stones with designs in so long, she grew excited to start again. Without thought, she hurried to scoop up the stone.

She dropped down and picked up the flat stone, smooth all around except for the etching in the middle. Nature had not given this stone a design, a person had. She ran her finger up the straight line and over the two triangular ones that sat atop the straight line. It resembled an arrow.

"What are you doing?"

Startled by her husband's sharp voice, she almost fell

backward, but his strong grip prevented it and had her steady on her feet in a flash.

"You were to stay where I put you," Warrick snapped.

His anger never failed to spark her fears, though she needed to remember that he had showed no signs of treating her badly. He had not raised a hand to her or kept food from her and that combined with the kindness he had shown her on their wedding night gave her confidence he would not do her harm.

"Adara," Warrick said, tempering his tone when he caught the fear that flashed in her eyes. He had not meant to frighten her, but she had frightened him when he had looked and not seen her where he had left her, not that she had gone far. But still, she had not obeyed him.

His gentler tone did much to alleviate her fears and she was quick to apologize and explain. "I am sorry. I got so excited to find a stone with a design on it that I did not think. I went to snatch it up. The stones I had collected at one time were taken from me and I was so pleased to think that I could start collecting them again and not fear them being taken away." She shook her head. "I truly am sorry, Warrick."

Her sincere confession slammed at his heart and tore at his gut. That someone had robbed her of the joy of collecting a few paltry stones infuriated him. "I have no want to take the stones from you. You may collect as many stones as you wish, but you will obey my orders."

"Aye, I will," she said and was surprised when he asked about the stone she had found.

"What design does this stone hold?"

"One I believe made by man, not nature," she said, handing it to him.

"Roark," he shouted as soon as he saw the design and the warrior hurried over.

Adara watched as Roark's eyes rounded upon seeing the stone.

"See if there are any more about," Warrick ordered.

Roark nodded and rushed out, shouting orders.

Warrick hated to do what others had done to her, but he had no choice. "I have to keep this, Adara, for now. I will help you find others."

"What is it I found?" she asked, thinking the stone just might have something to do with the man who tried to kill her husband.

Warrick hesitated at first, not wanting to involve her in it, but he wanted her to understand why he took the stone from her and only the truth could explain that.

He held the stone up, the etching facing her. "This is a rune symbol. The Vikings paint or engrave on their shields when they go into battle. It represents victory."

She shook her head. "I do not understand. The Vikings are no more a threat to the Highlands. Some have even settled in a few of the isles far north well over five years ago when Denmark conceded Orkney and Shetland to Scotland, or so I was told."

"Someone spoke to you of the Vikings? It was not a discussion you overheard?" He could understand if she overheard others speak of it, but being told? Who would have discussed such a thing with a servant?

"A woman I met by the stream where I took things to be washed. We talked of many things, Vikings one of them." She shook her head again, her mind churning. "Does this mean that whoever seeks to harm you is a Viking?"

It was the second time today that she was quick to fit pieces of the puzzle together. She possessed a sharp mind, something he had not expected, but something he admired.

"Another piece to the puzzle," he said.

She sensed that he was talking about a much larger puzzle than just who had attempted to kill him. She made no mention of it, but kept the thought tucked away.

No other stones with symbols on them were found by the time Warrick and Adara took their leave, but the search continued. Warriors followed them back to the village, Roark remaining behind to make certain a thorough search was conducted.

"I can take you to the healer if you would like," Adara offered once in the village.

"You need food and rest after that walk," Warrick said.

She almost smiled, his words filled more with concern rather than his usual commanding tone. "Her cottage is but a short distance from here and the questions will not take long. I can eat and rest afterwards."

That he gave the idea thought almost had him shaking his head. He should be sending her to the keep to eat and rest after the walk into the woods and back. Yet he did not want to part company with her. He enjoyed having her with him and the thought annoyed him.

What annoyed him even more was that the shield he kept around his heart was showing signs of decay.

"We will keep it brief," he said sternly.

"As you wish," she said, her hand reaching out to take hold of his and as he had done all day, his hand wrapped around hers holding it firm, and she realized she liked the feel of it.

Warrick thought the same. He liked when she reached out for his hand, lacing her fingers with his or simply slipping her hand in his and his closing around hers. Her hand was soft. sometimes chilled and sometimes hesitant when it slipped in his. His heat chased any chill fast enough and the strength of his hand closing around hers settled any uncertainty. Surprisingly her small hand, so snug in his, began chasing an empty, bone-cold chill that had hold of him for far too long.

The cottage they approached was small and looked in need of some repairs.

"Is your clan so free of illness that no one needs your healer?" Warrick asked, seeing no one lingering about.

"Jaynce admits herself that she is not a talented healer

and encourages everyone to wait for Cyra's visits, or if necessary to go see her."

"A new healer is necessary," Warrick said, though he doubted he would ever find one as talented as Espy or Cyra.

"I will go see that we do not disturb her," Adara said and went to hurry ahead of her husband.

Warrick did not stop her. He was aware that she hurried ahead to warn the woman of his presence, otherwise the healer might take a fright.

"Jaynce, it is Adara," she said, tapping on the door and pushing it open. She stepped inside with a smile, wanting to ease any worry the healer may have when she learned Warrick was there to speak with her. "Jaynce," she called out again concerned when she saw that the woman lay on her side in her bed, fully clothed. She hurried over to her, fearful she had taken ill and placed a hand on her shoulder.

Jaynce turned at her touch, dropping on her back, and Adara let out a scream.

Warrick bolted into the cottage, his blood running cold at his wife's horrified scream. He rushed to her side, taking her in his arms, pressing her face to his chest, shielding her from the dead woman whose eyes were spread wide, appearing as if she stared in abject horror, her throat sliced from ear to ear.

Chapter Twelve

Adara sat before the hearth in the solar with a tankard of cider clasped in her hands, her trembling gone, leaving a slight quiver in its wake. She could not get the terrible image of Jaynce out of her head. The intense terror in the woman's eyes had reminded her of her own fright each time she had been taken to the torture chamber. Terrified, always terrified, how much pain she would suffer or if she would meet death that day. Today Jaynce met death.

The question was why? The answer seemed easy. Jaynce had to have known something, seen something. But what? What could the healer have possibly seen that someone did not want known?

Warrick draped a blanket over his wife's legs, tucking it in at her waist. She had not stopped shivering since discovering the healer and he was concerned. He had whisked her away and ordered one of his men to get Roark and another to stand guard in front of the healer's cottage. The thought foremost in his mind, to get her away from the hideous scene.

He raised the tankard of hot cider, that she had yet to drink, to her lips and ordered, "Drink."

Adara held the tankard to her lips, but did not drink. The brew too hot to drink too fast and her stomach not at all eager to receive it.

Warrick dropped down in front of her. "You need to warm yourself. Drink."

"It is too hot and my stomach unwilling." With a slight shake of her head, she voiced her concerns. "What could Jaynce have seen or known that had been worth taking her life?"

There were times his wife appeared as meek as a mouse, then she would do or say something that proved otherwise, like now. Even though upset, she had the wisdom to see the obvious.

"I do not know, but I intend to find out," he said, standing. "You will stay here until I return and rest, drink the hot brew, and stay warm."

She nodded, hearing him but her thoughts were elsewhere.

Warrick saw the distraction in her eyes and leaned down, taking hold of her chin. "I mean it, wife. I best find you here in this chair when I return."

She shivered, a chill grabbing hold of her and before she could respond, he muttered something she could not make out and went to the hearth.

"Do you have a shawl?" he asked, adding a fresh log.

"I do. Uncle Owen gave me his wife's shawl." She watched him balanced on his haunches, making sure the flames caught the new log before adding another one and adjusting that one until the flames licked at it sending it ablaze.

"Where is it?" he asked, dusting his hands off when he stood.

She stared at him. He was tending to her, seeing that she kept warm, caring for her. No one had ever cared for her that way. "In my stitching room."

"I will have a servant fetch it for you," he said and walked past her to the door. "And remember to stay where you are."

Adara sighed when she heard the door click closed and reached over to place the tankard of cider on the table beside the chair, then rested her head back. She silently admonished herself for such a silly thought. He cared nothing for her. He simply did his duty as a husband.

It is your old, foolish wishes, dreams, and hopes that have you thinking this way, she silently chided herself. She had often wished that one day she would meet a man who would care for her, perhaps even love her. She had not given such a possibility thought until she had met Maia. The woman had opened possibilities to her, the hope of a better a life, one where she would be loved.

Wishes, dreams, hopes, did they ever come true?

She shook her head. Her musings would get her nowhere.

She let her eyes drift closed and was instantly assaulted by the image of Jaynce, her eyes wide, her throat—she shook the horrible scene away. She could not imagine the horror the woman must have suffered. Her brow wrinkled, thinking about when she had entered the cottage. There had been no signs of Jaynce struggling with anyone. Had someone surprised her or had the person been known to her?

Adara sat up in the chair, her thoughts gathering quickly. There had been no blood anywhere but in the bed. Jaynce had been in bed when this happened.

Adara stood and started pacing. Something was not right about the whole thing. If Jaynce had screamed, someone would have heard her, her cottage not far from other cottages. What could have happened?

She recalled Espy's caution. *Be watchful, Jaynce is a caring person but lacks the skills of a good healer. She has asked me more than once to identify a plant. One sniff is all it takes for a wise healer to know.*

Her confusing thoughts brought wrinkles to her smooth brow. What was she missing? There was something there she could not quite grasp, yet poked at her. She stopped pacing and closed her eyes and the scene came rushing back to her, only this time she did not chase the vision away. She looked around.

There had been partially eaten food on the table and two tankards. Adara hurried to the door, swinging it open, and the servant standing there jumped back. Adara did not pause, she rushed right past the startled woman, ignoring the shawl the servant held in her hand.

A swirl of wind ruffled her hair and snapped at her cloak, sending it billowing around her as she ran through the village. Wide eyes and shocked stares followed her, but she paid them no heed. Her only thought was to get to the cottage.

~~~

"Two people got past my warriors. I want to know how and why," Warrick said and continued, silencing Roark before he could speak. "No excuses will be tolerated. I want to know who failed to do their duty."

"I have never given you an excuse and I will not start now," Roark said. "I began a search of this area upon our arrival since it was not a stop included in your plan. It was a matter of time before we would have reached that campsite, which was what probably precipitated the attempt on your life. They must have been watching and realized their time was short to see the chore done. They hastened their task and when met with failure hastened their departure. As for the healer's murder, it would seem reasonable to believe the attempt on your life and the ending of hers is somehow connected."

Warrick went to agree when he caught sight of his wife running toward him, her cheeks flushed red, her blonde hair swirling madly about her head, and her cloak billowing out behind her, for all to see the bump in her stomach.

Worry rose up to jab at him and he hurried to her, catching her about the waist when he reached her. "What is wrong? Did someone try to hurt you? Is it the bairn?"

Adara kept shaking her head at every question he threw at her while she let her breathing ease.

Finally, she nodded when he said, "You disobey me again." This time he shook his head. "And you admit it."

"For a good reason," she said, her breathing having

calmed enough for her to speak.

"There is no good reason for disobeying me." He got annoyed when she nodded, disagreeing with him.

"It was imperative I speak with you."

"Something was more important than you obeying my word?"

She nodded again and took his hand. "Come. I will show you."

He followed along with her, letting her have her way… for now.

"You should see this too," Adara said when they got near Roark and he followed behind Warrick.

As she crossed the threshold into the cottage, she said a silent prayer for the healer that she would rest in peace and her killer would be caught and punished. She stopped at the table and pointed to the two tankards. "Someone was here with her."

"We saw that as well and assume it was the person who killed her," Roark said.

"But there are no signs of a struggle. Why did Jaynce not struggle? Why did she not scream for help?"

"We wondered the same," Warrick said. "You are not telling us anything we have not already surmised ourselves."

Adara stepped away from her husband, their hands parting. She pointed to the bed where Jaynce still lay. "She is in bed. Why is she in bed if someone was here? And her bed is soaked with her blood. She was killed while in bed, the bedding showing no signs of a struggle."

"You noticed all this?" Warrick asked, her astuteness continuing to surprise him. Never would he have suspected such cleverness from a servant lass.

She turned her head away from the bed. "The horrid image would not leave my head either would the endless questions."

"Several questions still remain," Roark said. "Why did she not scream or fight?"

Adara turned and pointed at the tankard and the half-eaten oat-cake on the table. "I believe she ate or drank something that made her take to her bed and left her defenseless."

Warrick picked up the oat-cake and sniffed it and did the same with the wine. "If there is something in either of them, I cannot detect it."

"Espy could," Adara said. "She told me that skilled healers could recognize a plant from its scent. Jaynce could not."

"Have Benet take both to Espy and explain the situation and see what she can tell us," Warrick directed Roark.

He nodded.

"Anything else of such great importance that could not wait and had you disobeying me, wife?" Warrick asked, folding his arms across his chest.

A reminder that she had yet to answer for her disobedience. Adara offered a quick apology. "I am sorry, Warrick, but I thought it imperative you know and besides, I feared if Jaynce had been given something then someone might accidently taste or drink of what was left."

How did he chastise her for being unselfish?

"We will discuss this later," he said.

"As you say."

"Aye, wife, you would do well to remember it is always… as I say."

Adara remained silent, thinking it was best she said no more.

"Wait outside for me," Warrick ordered.

Adara nodded and stepped outside, grateful for the chilled breeze that brushed her heated cheeks. It was the second time that day she had disobeyed her husband and the thought amazed her. How had she done that? She had always obeyed, but then if she had not she would have suffered a slap to her face or feel the whip of a stick against her arm or back.

Warrick's hands had never harmed her since meeting him, possessive at times, but tender at other times, and other times... the memory of what his hands were capable of sent a slow caressing tingle through her.

She did not know what to make of her husband, more so, she did not know what to make of how she felt toward him. Did she trust him? She had trusted others, only to be disappointed until finally she had trusted no one. She learned to keep to herself, be ever watchful, and say little.

Of late, though, while her uncle was alive, she had been saying more than she ever had. Her uncle had had much to do with that. Unlike others, he had engaged her in conversation, asked her thoughts on things, encouraged her opinion. There had been a growing sense of safety with him, though a lingering doubt that it would last had nagged at her. Nothing in her life ever lasted, except for the fear that had been her constant companion. When her uncle died, that nagging doubt had been proven right again.

Would the same happen with Warrick? Would she grow to feel safe with him only to have him disappoint her as so many others had?

"We will discuss your disobedience, wife."

Adara turned at the sternness in his voice, worried at what he would do. When he stretched out his hand, instinct had her stepping away from him.

Warrick bristled at the fear he saw flare like a flame to dry kindling in her eyes. How often had she felt the strike of a hand that instinct had her backing away from nothing more than an outstretched hand? And how often did he have to remind her that he would not harm her?

As often as necessary.

The unexpected thought had him slowly stretching his hand out to her once again. "I will not harm you, Adara."

Gone was the sternness in his voice replaced with a firmness that promised truth and had Adara stepping forward and taking his hand. His fingers closed around hers with a strength that actually comforted her.

"I am sorry for disobeying you," she apologized again.

"How often have you said that through the years?" His question met silence and he asked, "I will have the truth, Adara."

She sighed. "More than I care to remember."

"Then sorry can hold little meaning to you by now. It is nothing more than an instinctive response that is meant to placate. Therefore, it serves no purpose to me. I will not hear it spill from your lips again."

"But I truly meant—"

Warrick stopped her before she could say anymore. "No, you did not. You spoke to appease as you have done through the years. It meant nothing to you, and I will not tolerate that from my wife."

Adara bit her lip to restrain the sorry that hurried to rush out. He was right, sorry meant nothing to her, yet... "I did not mean to disobey you."

"I realize that, but I still will not tolerate disobedience. It is one rule of mine I expect everyone to obey... without exception."

Adara nodded, worrying for the first time in her life that, obedience, something that had been instinctive to her, might now be too difficult for her to tolerate and having no idea why. The thought was at once alarming and also welcoming.

As they walked back to the keep, she asked, "What punishment do you inflict on those who disobey you?"

"For you it would be days confined to your room, but for someone who enjoys solitude that is no punishment. Punishment is meant to be uncomfortable, something you never wish to experience again."

Adara could not stop the shiver that ran through her, recalling her screams when the hot irons had been used on her body.

Warrick silently cursed himself, knowing his words had

brought back memories to her that were better left undisturbed. He rushed his arm around his wife and hurried her inside the keep and into the shadows of a small alcove. He slipped his hand under her chin to take gentle hold of it. "Listen to me well, wife. I may punish you, but never ever will I have you tortured."

"Then what will my punishment be?"

"You already serve it," he said.

"How so?"

"You spend eternity with the Demon Lord."

Chapter Thirteen

Adara could not chase his words from her head.
Eternity with the Demon Lord.

That was her punishment, her fate? There was no chance of it ever being different? This was her life now, wife of the... she refused to think any other way of him or call him anything other than Warrick.

They sat at a table in the Great Hall, food and drink having been brought to them and Wynn having been summoned.

"You say Wynn oversees the running of the keep?" Warrick asked.

"She has and does well at it, though of late—" Adara's thought interrupted her words. She had noticed changes in Wynn lately.

"What of late?" Warrick pressed when she failed to continue, seeing her attention had been diverted, though pleased to see she was eating without any nudging from him. She needed to keep strong for her and the bairn.

"I think it has become too burdensome for her in her advancing years," Adara said.

"Did you plan on relieving her of this burden?"

Adara was a bit stunned by his question, and it prompted her to once again think of her duties to the clan and how she had not paid enough attention to them. She wondered if the solitude she had sought actually had been fear keeping her prisoner, keeping her from getting to know her clan, from making friends, from truly being free.

"I would speak to Wynn first," Adara suggested, not wanting Warrick to simply remove the woman from her place in the keep.

"Then see to it," he ordered.

Stunned once again, Adara stared at him. "You want me to do it?"

"You are the lady of the keep. It is your duty. See it done."

Unlike her uncle Owen who encouraged her to do things, Warrick ordered her to do so. Or was he only reminding her of her duties?

"Are you not familiar with the workings of a keep? I assume being a servant in the keep where I found you that you would have knowledge of such things."

"I was only at that keep for two days."

"How did you come to be there?" Warrick asked, something sparking in his memory.

"The family I served took me there and left me. I was told I would be a servant in the keep." Adara wondered over the scowl that rose on his face.

"How many times have you been given to another family?" Warrick asked annoyed that she had been passed around as if she mattered to no one.

Adara had thought of the small sticks she had used to keep count until finally she had simply given up and thrown the sticks in the woods one day. "I stopped counting after a while."

She turned her head to see what had caught her husband's attention, his eyes glancing over her shoulder. Wynn had entered the room and Adara wondered how he had heard the soft shuffle of her feet over their voices.

One look confirmed what Adara had thought, overseeing the keep had become too much for Wynn. The woman had been of fair height, though her stooped frame made her appear shorter. The wiry strands of gray that now dominated her hair refused to remain confined to her braid and she squinted as if she was finding it difficult to see clearly. And while her face showed signs of age, there was one thing that had not changed about her from what Adara could tell. It was her smile. No matter when Adara saw the woman, she was always smiling.

"What can I do for you, my lord," Wynn asked with a respectful bob of her head.

"I have a few questions for you."

Adara saw Wynn's hands begin to tremble.

"You have done nothing wrong, Wynn," Adara reassured her and went to stand and go comfort the old woman.

Warrick squeezed her thigh, keeping her seated. He reminded her of her place and it was not alongside Wynn.

"Do you know of any travelers seeking shelter or aid here lately?"

"One or two in the last two weeks. They sought shelter and some food before moving on, eager to leave and get home before winter sets in. There was a woman traveler who required a healer or so Jaynce told me. She did not tell me anymore than that about her, though," —she paused for a moment as if attempting to remember something— "I think Jaynce mentioned that she looked familiar to her as if perhaps she had stopped here before." A tear caught at the corner of her eye. "Is it true, my lord, that Jaynce is dead and that someone killed her?"

"Aye, it is and I will find who did it and see the person punished." He stood, seeing Roark approach. If you recall anything else that Jaynce had said to you regarding this woman, tell me or Lady Adara." He looked at Adara. "You will remain in the keep until my return." He leaned over, bringing his face close to hers. "I will have your word on that."

She smiled softly, pleased, that he chose to have her word than to command her. "You have my word, husband."

He loved her smile, it felt like a sprinkle of sunshine washing over him, chasing the gloom and he reacted without thought. He kissed her, soft and gently.

Adara returned the unexpected kiss, having thought

when he brought his face close to hers, how nice it would be to feel his lips on hers once again.

Warrick had to force himself to end the kiss, another time, another place, and that would not be so. He stood, needing to put distance between them while thinking of later tonight when they would once again share a bed. He walked around the table and turned to Wynn. "Lady Adara has something to discuss with you." Then he walked away, forcing himself to take step after step when all he wanted to do was snatch his wife up in his arms and spend the remainder of the day alone in their bedchamber.

Adara's eyes followed him and continued to linger in his wake after he was gone from the room. Her heart was beating faster and a tingle of pleasure continued to prickle her skin, not to mention the pleasure that had settled between her legs. Was it possible? Had she missed the intimacy they had shared that one night? Did she want to share it with him again?

"My lady, you wish to speak with me?"

Adara turned to Wynn, having forgotten she was there. "Sit, Wynn."

Wynn shook her head. "I will stand, my lady."

Adara understood that Wynn was far too steeped in the ways of a servant to accept such an improper invitation. But Adara was the farthest thing from a proper lady of the keep.

"If you do not sit, Wynn, then I will have to stand and I am tired. Please sit so we may talk."

Wynn hesitated and when Adara went to stand Wynn sat with a sigh that Adara was sure came from the old woman's aching bones. She knew all too well the toll it took to see chores done and Wynn had done daily chores far longer than she had.

"I fear I have not been fair to you, Wynn."

Wynn shook her head repeatedly. "No. No, my lady, you have been good to the clan. You treat us well and make no demands. You have lightened many a load for more than a few."

"Not your load, though," Adara said and watched all color drain from the old woman's face.

"It is nothing I cannot handle," Wynn assured her, gripping her hands in front of her.

Adara was surprised to see fear in the old woman's eyes, but even worse her smile had vanished. "Your chores have become too burdensome for you."

"Please, my lady, the keep is my home, the people in it my family. I do not know what I would do without it." She fought back tears, though one slipped out. "I enjoy serving you and I look forward to seeing your bairn born and serving another MacVarish."

Adara's wide-eyes betrayed her shock that the woman knew of the bairn. She had thought she had hidden it well.

"The others found out today, seeing you running through the village, your protruding stomach obvious to them. Though tongues have been busy since you isolate yourself so much, having many think you kept a secret," Wynn said. "But I knew long before that that you were with child, and I was pleased that the MacVarish family, the Clan, would carry on."

Family.

All within were family to Wynn. She had thought she had been family to those she served, but that had not been true. Family did not sell you. Toss you away. Not care what happened to you. That would not happen here in her keep, in *her family*.

"You are not going anywhere, Wynn, but you have worked much too hard for far too long. You taught me much about the running of the keep. It is time I started doing my duty and the first thing I am going to do is lighten your burden,"—Adara shook her head when Wynn went to speak— "you will need rest and have extra time to tend and play with the bairn when he is born."

Wynn's smile returned.

"Let me tell you changes I will make," Adara said and filled a tankard with cider and handed it to a startled Wynn.

~~~

Adara climbed the stairs later that evening, Warrick ready to join her when Roark appeared and let him know there was a matter that needed his immediate attention. While part of her wanted Warrick in her bed, another part feared him there. What if what had been between them that one night was something born in her hopes and dreams. What if it was not at all like she had remembered it, but was the way she had wished it would be?

What if she once again was disappointed? There was no getting free of Warrick. She was his wife and would remain so. Old fears took root once again and she thought how much better it would be if she could hide once more, tuck herself away where no one would see her, where no one would hurt her or the bairn.

She was tempted, so very tempted, but what good had hiding done her? She had exchanged one prison for another. She had escaped once with help. This time she would escape on her own. Somehow she would escape her fears. She had to for her bairn's sake.

Adara yawned as she entered the bedchamber, the warmth of the crackling fire, the large bed with its fresh bedding rolled back, candles keeping the darkness away, all welcoming her like loving arms.

She recalled the first night she had entered the room she had previously occupied when she had taken up residence here. The single bed, the small fireplace, the lone chair all seemed like a dream. She had feared she would wake and find herself back in a barn with hay for a blanket and the smell of animals heavily upon her. It took time, weeks, for her to settle in and accept that the room was hers and no one was going to take it away from her... until Warrick.

117

Never, though, had she imagined occupying her uncle's bedchamber. It had been prepared and kept in wait for Craven the new Chieftain of the Clan MacVarish and rightfully so. But no more, it now belonged to Warrick just as she did.

Adara switched out of her garments and into her soft wool shift that Espy had given her. She loved the feel of it against her skin, soft and gentle... much like Warrick's touch.

She shook her head, trying to chase away the persistent memories. She slipped into bed, pulling the blankets up around her, a chill having descended on the room even with the fire that roared in the fireplace. She thought sleep would be difficult, her endless thoughts keeping her awake, but the day had been long and Adara more tired than she had realized. Her eyes barely closed when sleep took hold, though the memories lingered.

Warrick stood naked by the fireplace, the light from the flames casting a soft glow on him. Adara was not ignorant of the male body. She had tended male babies, washed men in preparation for burial, seen men strip naked and climb into bed with their wives, but never had she seen a male body as beautifully sculpted as Warrick's.

"You are my wife, be a dutiful one and I will treat you well," Warrick said. "Choose otherwise and I will see that you regret it."

Adara nodded. What else was there for her to do? He was not asking something of her that would be difficult, having been obedient all her life. And he would treat her well if she did, if she could believe the word of the Demon Lord.

"Come here," Warrick ordered.

Adara was not sure her legs would hold her when she stepped forward, they trembled so badly. She forced herself to move, to go to her husband.

Husband.

How could it be that she had a husband and he was the infamous Demon Lord? Her stomach roiled and she feared she would retch before she reached him.

Finally, after what seemed like she had taken a hundred or more steps, she stopped in front of Warrick. She cast a silent prayer for strength and another prayer that her husband was a man of his word and he would treat her well if she obeyed him.

He rested his hand on hers where it lay at her side, though he did not take hold of it, he simply let it rest there against hers. It was not long before his warmth seeped into her chilled skin, sending a shiver racing through her and prickling her skin.

"You are safe with me. You have my word on it," he said

She wanted to believe him. She wanted to feel safe, but others had given their word and it had meant nothing. Would his word mean the same?

He raised his hand and she instinctively jumped back.

He lowered his hand. "I will not strike you. Only weak men strike women and you will find I am not a weak man. Now step close to me so I may kiss you."

She did as he said, not giving it thought, for she feared if she did, she would be a coward and turn and run. She wondered if he thought the same of her when his arm slipped around her waist, holding her firm, allowing for no escape.

Her body grew rigid when he brushed his lips across hers, but after a few times of his lips whispering across hers, tainting them with the lightest of kisses, her body lost its rigidness. It tightened again when his lips pressed firmly against hers, demanding more. Never having been kissed, but having seen others kiss, she attempted to return his kiss.

Fear rose up like a hand choking at her throat when he halted the kiss abruptly. Had she done something wrong?

He stepped back, placing his hand at her elbow and slipping it slowly down to take hold of her hand and walked her to the bed.

She went along, her legs moving, though how she did not know since they trembled as badly as before.

He stopped next to the bed and his hands went to her hips. He took hold of her shift. "Raise your arms."

His voice held a command and yet there was no harshness to it, and she did as he said and raised her arms.

He pulled the shift up and over her head, tossing it aside, then scooped her up in his arms. "I will not have you fear me in bed. After this night, our bodies will hold no secrets from each other."

~~~

Warrick stripped off his garments eager to join his wife in bed even if it was only to hold her in his arms. He would wake her, but after what she had gone through today he was relieved to see her sleeping peacefully. He did not, however, like that she wore a nightdress to bed. He had hoped she would remember what he had told her their first night together.

You will sleep naked beside me always.

He would have to remind her.

He climbed into bed carefully and was about to wrap his arm around her when she turned, snuggling against him and settling her face against his chest as if she had been waiting for him. He slipped his arms around her, having been waiting impatiently to hold her like this again, and found that she felt far more precious than he had remembered.

Her soft, even breath tickled his chest as it had done that night, as it would do for endless nights to come. He would have it no other way. He could attempt to convince himself that he had no time to spend with her. She was his wife and she must do her duty, but it was not duty he wanted from her in bed. He wanted more, no matter how much he tried to ignore it, chase it away, he wanted more from Adara than he ever wanted from a woman.

Content for the first time in what felt like forever, Warrick drifted off to sleep.

He woke suddenly sensing something was not right and not knowing how long he had slept. The dying embers in the hearth indicated a length of time had passed and a heavy darkness seemed to close in around him.

That's when he sensed it… someone was there in the room, in the darkness.

He caught the movement before the blood-curdling scream tore through the air and saw the glint of the blade before it slashed down toward Adara.

Chapter Fourteen

Warrick threw himself over his wife, his arm shooting out to deflect the blade, it catching part of his forearm as he rose out of bed and threw himself at the culprit.

Adara scrambled to sit up, her heart pounding against her chest in fright as horrific screams pierced the night and she tried to make sense of what was going on. The door suddenly burst open and she scrambled out of bed to hide in the deep shadows in the corner of the room as three of Warrick's warriors rushed in.

The screams grew louder and more terrifying, and Adara found herself back in the dungeon, waiting her turn, waiting for the suffering to begin again. This time, though, she did not wait… she ran. Out the door she went and down the stairs as if hellhounds followed on her heels. She hurried to hide at the bottom of the stairs, hearing heavy footfalls heading her way. They seemed never-ending and once they ceased, she hurried through the kitchen passageway and out the door.

Rain pelted her and the ground was mush beneath her bare feet. She slipped a couple of times, but quickly righted herself. Lightning streaked the sky, looking like boney fingers reaching out for her, and she ran faster.

"Not far now, not far," she mumbled frantically.

Her eyes widened even more than they had as she spotted the barn. She struggled to get the door open when she reached it, and close it behind her, the wind tugging at it, fighting to grab it from her hands, fighting to deny her sanctuary. She stood in the dark once she was safely inside, her chest heaving with deep breaths she was forced to take, though grateful she was familiar with the place. When she had first arrived at MacVarish keep, she had come to the barn often, the familiar scent of fresh hay and animals calming to her.

"It is me. Do not worry. You are not alone," she assured the animals. Truthfully, though, it was she who did not want to be alone, wanted something familiar and safe, something to drive away the dreadful screams that continued to echo in her head.

She knew her way, even without light to guide her to the back of the barn and the corner piled high with recently stacked hay. She hurried to bury herself into the pile, hoping it would keep her safe, chase her fear, stop the screams. But they continued and she pressed her hands to her ears, begging the heavens to make it stop.

~~~

As soon as his warriors had taken hold of the crazed woman, Warrick turned to see that his wife was unharmed. He froze when he saw the bed empty. He glanced around the room, his heart pounding viciously in his chest when he saw no sign of her. He did not bother grabbing his shirt, he reached for his plaid and quickly wrapped it around him and pulled on his boots.

All the while the woman continued to scream and fight the two warriors holding her.

"I will kill the devil. Kill devil," she screamed.

Warrick hurried to dress.

"I will kill the devil and his whore too!"

Her threat did not sit well with Warrick and he walked over to her and grabbed a handful of her hair at the top of her head and yanked her head back. "You threaten my wife, you die. Gag and secure her," he ordered his warriors.

She went to scream again and a cloth was shoved into her mouth and the two warriors who held her dragged her roughly out of the room.

Warrick met Roark just outside the bedroom door. "Adara is missing. My guess is fright forced her to flee."

"The woman's screams echoed off the stone walls just as the prisoners' screams do in your dungeon," Roark informed him.

Warrick let several oaths fly.

"Do you have any idea where she might have gone?"

"Someplace safe," Warrick muttered. "Have the men search the entire keep. I go to the barn."

"The barn?" Roark asked, turning to watch Warrick rush down the stairs without a response.

Warrick hurried through the stormy night, his cloak flapping in the wind, his only thought his wife. She had to be soaked wearing nothing but her thin nightdress. He pushed the barn door open and stepped in, the vicious wind almost tearing the door out of his hand, as he closed it, and his concern for his wife and their unborn child grew.

He stood in the darkness, rainwater dripping off his cloak to puddle at his boots. His eyes needed no adjusting to the dark and he quickly glanced around.

Seeing and hearing nothing, he called out softly, "Adara."

He heard the rustle then.

Hay.

She had sought something familiar to comfort her, chase her fright. He only wished it had been him she had turned to.

"Adara," he called out gently again, not wanting to frighten her any more than she already was, and again he was met with the rustle of hay. "I will keep you safe, Adara."

He thought he heard her speak, but it was too low to be sure he had heard anything. He turned back and fetched the lantern, striking a flame to the candle inside it, then hurried his steps to the back of the barn, knowing exactly where she was… in the pile of hay that had been stored for the animals.

Warrick stopped when he saw her, his stomach twisting

and his heart feeling as if it was being ripped from his chest. Never would he forget the sight of her buried to her chin in hay, her hair covered with it and her dark blue eyes so wide with fright she reminded him of an animal cornered by its foe, waiting for death.

He wanted to leap forward and scoop her out of there and into his arms, but she was far too frightened for him to make such a foolish move.

"Not safe," she whispered, shaking her head, the straw in her hair falling down around her face.

He had been taught to harden his feelings until he had none. There had been no room for a caring heart. At that moment, however, he felt as if his heart shattered.

"You are safe," he attempted to reassure her.

"Not safe," she repeated. "Never safe."

"You are safe with me."

Fear widened her eyes further. "No. No. The screams. The dungeon. The pain."

He was going to destroy that damn dungeon when he returned home and he was going to make those who had harmed her suffer more than the fires of hell.

"That is no more, Adara. You are safe now. Safe with me. I will let no harm befall you. You have my word, wife. I will protect you always." Her eyes lost some of their fright and he kept reassuring her, repeating his words. "You are safe. You have nothing to fear. I will protect you always."

"*Always*," she whispered as if it was a secret.

"Always," he reaffirmed and stretched his hand out to her. "Let me take you home where you will be safe."

"*Home?*" she asked as if she did not understand.

"Our home, Adara, yours and mine. Where you will *always be safe*. I will make sure of it."

Fear began to fade from her eyes and when she shifted beneath the hay as if she was about to emerge from her safety nest, the barn doors flew open and Roark and several of his warriors rushed in.

Adara screamed and jumped out of the pile of hay and into Warrick's arms, her slender arms clamping tight around his neck. "Do not let them take me. Please, Warrick, please do not let them take me."

Warrick circled her waist with one arm, locking it firmly around her and held up his other to stop his men's approach. "They will not take you. No one will take you from me." He yanked his cloak off and draped it around her, then lifted her into his arms, tucking her tight against him.

Adara kept her arms snug around his neck, burying her face in the crook of it, and whispering, "Never leave me, Warrick. Please never leave me."

"Never will I leave you," he promised, pressing his cheek to her temple. "Never!"

~~~

Adara jolted up in bed.

"I am right here, Adara, I'm not going anywhere," Warrick said from where he was by the hearth. "The fire needed tending."

He was naked, only this time it was not a dream and his body was just as she had remembered it, beautifully sculpted, then she realized she was naked as well. She grabbed the edge of the blanket and yanked it up to cover her breasts.

Warrick walked over to the bed and tugged at the blanket, though not enough to slip it from her grip. "I have seen all of you, wife. There is no need to hide from me."

She cringed when he said hide, memories of last night rushing back at her. "You must think me a coward."

"You are anything but a coward, wife," he said. "We all fear at times in our life."

"You knew fear?" she asked.

Warrick joined her in bed, under the blanket, tucking her up against him as he braced himself against the thick headboard and settled the warm wool blanket over them both, allowing her to keep her breasts covered more for his sanity than hers.

"I did when I was very young."

"Tell me," she said and cuddled against him as she had done after he had returned with her to the room last night and seen to her care before placing her in bed and taking her in his arms. Remarkably to her, a definite place of comfort.

"My father was known as a ruthless warrior, his skills far surpassing anyone. He expected his son to be the same. He started teaching me at a young age. I believe I was five years when he took me into the woods and left me there for the night to survive. He was shocked when I found my way home before morning and furious that I was crying. He beat me and took me back to the woods again and told me not to come home until the sun had risen a third time."

Adara could not hide the shock in her voice. "He left you two days in the woods alone?"

"He did, though I did not return home until the fourth sunrise."

"Why? Were you hurt?"

"No, I did not want to return home to my father. I did not want to leave what I had found there."

"What did you find?"

"Freedom from my father."

Adara had wished often for a da who loved her. Strange that Warrick had one and yet from what he was telling her, the man had not been a da at all.

"What of your mum?" she asked, wondering where the woman had been while all this had gone on.

"She cared naught for me. She was as cold and heartless as my father. I often wondered how they ever begot me since neither showed an ounce of feeling for the other." He shook his head. "I remembered thinking that if my father discovered I favored the woods, he would never let me return, so I lied to him. I told him I had gotten lost and that was why it had taken me longer to get home. I told him I never wanted to go back. He made certain to continue to send me regularly into the woods. It was there I learned to detect sound and sharpen my sight whether it be darkness or light."

"Your father never found out?"

"He found out too late. By then, I had already become a more proficient and powerful warrior than him. He died as he would have wanted to... in battle."

Adara's hand went beneath the blanket to rest protectively on her stomach.

Warrick's hand disappeared beneath the blanket as well, coming to rest on top of hers. "Worry not. I have no plans to do the same to my son, though I will teach him to be a skilled warrior."

As if the bairn agreed, he moved beneath their hands.

"He is a strong one," Warrick said with pride.

Adara smiled. "Or she is."

"My daughter will also be taught to be a skilled warrior."

"I am glad," Adara said. "I do not want her to have my fears."

He did not like seeing the sadness in her eyes. "You know well of fears and for good reason, wife, and will teach our daughter or son the wisdom of them."

"What wisdom can there be in fear?"

"Much. The woods taught me that and you will learn as well."

Adara did not quite understand what he meant, but in time she hoped she would.

"Who is the woman who injured you?" she asked, pointing to the cloth wrapped around his left forearm and sprinkled with blood. When her senses had returned last night she had been relieved to learn that his wound had been minor. He had deflected the blade enough that it had not cut him deeply.

"I will find out today when I speak with her."

"You will be careful," Adara said, her worry making it sound more like a command, and she thought she caught a slight lift to the corners of his mouth. Had he almost smiled?

"Aye, wife, as you wish."

"I wish you to stay safe," she said, this time her voice was soft and gentle.

"I will keep us both," —he slipped his hand beneath hers and caressed her stomach— "all three of us safe." He moved his hand off her stomach and brought it up to tilt her chin up, and he did what he had been aching to do. He kissed her.

There was no hesitancy for Adara, she returned the kiss, was hungry for it, had been since... the last time he had kissed her.

It was a gentle kiss, a soothing one, an introduction of things to come and Adara relished the sensations it caused to race through her.

When his lips left hers abruptly, Adara was about to protest, but he hurried out of bed and she almost scrambled after him and demand he not leave her. Something had changed for her last night. Crazy as it seemed, her heart had let her know that she was safe with Warrick, truly safe.

"You need to know something, wife," he said, turning around to face her.

Her eyes turned wide at the sight of his swelled manhood.

"I want you. I ache to be inside you, as your eyes can see proof of that. Rest and be well," he urged as he slipped on his shirt, "for I will not wait another night to join with you. It has already been too long." He hurried to wrap his plaid around him, then hurried into his boots, needing to get away from her as fast as possible before he did not bother to wait until tonight.

Adara stared at the door after he left, wishing she had had the courage to say what ached to spill from her lips.

Why wait until tonight?

~~~

Warrick forced his thoughts away from Adara, she occupied them far too much, even more so now that he had found her. Never had he allowed someone to consume his thoughts as Adara did. His time alone in the woods had taught him the wisdom of keeping his head clear, his thoughts focused. He had learned the senselessness of wasting his thoughts on his father.

However, he was finding it difficult to do the same with Adara and had since meeting her. He could not stop thinking about her. She snuck her way into his thoughts no matter how hard he tried to keep her out. He even found himself almost smiling twice now at something she had said or done. He could not remember the last time he smiled.

Smiles were not something his father had encouraged and since smiles were never seen, or exchanged in his home, they disappeared completely from his life. When something is gone that long, never used, it can be forgotten. It had simply become his way not to smile.

Until Adara.

Warrick shook his head. Trying again to shake his wife from his thoughts. He had not intended to wed again. Not after his last disastrous match, but circumstances changed and he found himself in need of a wife, quickly, and one of his own choosing.

Having given thought to it, he was grateful he had found Adara, though it had been by sheer accident. Or perhaps fate had planned it well.

He entered the Great Hall and spotting Wynn, directing a servant, he summoned her with a snap of his hand. Her slow gait disturbed him. Her chore was too burdensome for her age. He had thought his wife would do what was necessary, but it seemed she had not.

"Has Adara spoken to you concerning your chores here?" he asked.

Wynn bobbed her head. "She has, my lord. She has ordered me to find two lassies to help me, and she has chosen to resume all the duties of the lady of the keep. She has plans to talk with Emona, the cook today, and she has also ordered stock to be taken of the meat house and the last of the harvest." Tears shined in her eyes. "Chieftain Owen was wise in having her learn the workings of the keep. He felt in time she would find her strength and do well here. He was right."

"That is good to know, Wynn. See that my wife gets her morning meal," Warrick ordered, wishing he had gotten a chance to meet Owen MacVarish. He had done right by Adara when no one else had, except Espy, and he wished he could thank the old man, but then he would by keeping his niece safe.

Wynn bobbed her head again and smiled. "I have her meal ready and waiting. I will see she gets it right away and that she has food throughout the day so that she keeps strong for her and the bairn."

"You do your chore well, Wynn. That is commendable."

"It is no chore, my lord, to take care of family."

Now he understood the reason for his wife keeping Wynn in her position. She was family. Something Adara never had and now that she did, she refused to lose.

Please never leave me.

His wife's words from last night rang strong in his head and his response remained strong in his heart.

Never.

They were family now and he would see that they remained so. The thought almost had him smiling.

Warrick sat to eat, Roark joining him a few moments later.

Roark knew what Warrick waited to hear and wasted no

time in telling him. "The gag was removed when the woman calmed. She now sits mumbling to herself. She has eaten and drunk the brew given to her. From what the guards observed, they believe she had not eaten in some time."

"I have my doubts she is the one who murdered the healer," Warrick said, dusting his hands of bread crumbs. "The woman does not seem to be of right mind and it would take right mind to do what was done to the healer."

"I agree. The two attacks may not be connected at all."

"Is this crazed woman simply that, demented, or does she want me dead for a reason? That is something we need to know. I will speak to her."

"If you learn nothing?"

"I will decide her fate when the time comes. Has Benet returned from speaking with Espy?"

Roark nodded. "He has and he told me that Espy got upset when she sniffed the wine. She said it contained the devil's cherry. She demanded to know who drank the wine and died." He scratched his head in thought. "If the wine would have killed the healer, then why slice her throat?"

"If the healer had died from the poison in the wine, it would have been assumed she died naturally. Either someone wanted it known that she was murdered or two people were out to kill her."

"Then why not just cut her throat? Why poison her?"

"That is a good question."

"Benet also said that Craven had to stop his wife from coming here. She insisted she wanted to make certain that Adara was all right. She calmed some, though remained upset, when she learned that the healer had died. Benet did not tell her that she had been murdered. One other thing, word has spread about the crazed woman and many now believe she is the one responsible for their healer's death and are restless to see her executed."

"It is time they learn that I, and I alone, determine a prisoner's fate. Has the post been erected in the middle of the village?"

"It has," Roark said.

"Bring the woman there and gather the clan. It is time for them to meet the Demon Lord."

Chapter Fifteen

Adara entered the Great Hall and surprisingly found it empty, though the quiet was a blessing. She supposed all were busy with their daily chores. Still, though, some of Warrick's warriors could usually be found there at different times throughout the day.

Her suspicions and concerns grew when she entered the kitchen and found it empty. The cauldron bubbled with delicious scents, turnips and onions sat partially chopped on the cutting board, and a couple of cats had snuck in to scavenge the basket of scraps near the open door, running out when they saw Adara.

Where had everyone gone? It was as if everyone had deserted the keep.

She stepped outside and listened, hearing nothing, she walked around the side of the keep and came to an abrupt stop when, in the not far distance, she saw a crowd had gathered. Adara had spent time walking through the village upon her arrival here, getting to know the paths, and making her own so she could avoid people in case she found it necessary to take her leave quickly. Though she never made use of that knowledge, it eased her worries to know it was there if need be. It helped her now, since she could make her way to see what was about without being seen.

She maneuvered her way around the cottages, keeping a good distance from the crowd. She found a spot beside one of them where the lower portion of the tree trunk looked as if it was attached to the side of the cottage. She could watch without being noticed. Besides, everyone was too busy chatting and pointing to where two of Warrick's warriors stood to either side of the post, buried deep in the dirt, its flesh appearing freshly stripped of its bark.

A sudden hush descended over the crowd and they began moving, spreading out to the sides, making room for someone's approach. Adara saw some people shudder and some women step behind their husbands, turning their heads, not wanting to look. She did not need to see who caused such fear, she knew. And when her husband came into view, she shuddered as well.

The sight of him could easily put fear in people, his confident gait, his regal bearing, his dark garments, and while his features were the finest many had ever seen and could easily draw a woman's eyes, it was his dark eyes, cold and ruthless, not a speck of caring in them that frighten deep down to the bone. At that moment, one could see why he was called the Demon Lord.

Adara shuddered again and shook her head. He had treated her well last night. He could not be the demon everyone thought him to be. As she watched, she began to wonder if she could be wrong.

"Secure her to the post," Warrick ordered and the crazed woman was braced against the post, her arms kept straight at her sides and a rope tied, several times, around her upper arms between her shoulders and elbows. Another rope was wound around her legs from just above her knees to a short distance below them. The last rope went around her ankles, though only twice. Her face hung down, her long gray hair falling like a cloak around it.

"I want each and every one of you to take a good look at her and tell me if you know her or if she looks familiar to you."

One of Warrick's warriors yanked her head up by her hair for all to see her face.

When all did not glance her way, Warrick commanded with a harsh yell, "Look at her!"

All eyes turned on the woman.

Adara did not have a view of the woman's face. She

could only see her from the side and that revealed little.

When not one person spoke up or stepped forward, Warrick continued. "She will remain tied here until I say otherwise. You are not to speak with her, feed her, offer her a drink, touch her, or throw anything at her. You will see what happens to someone who takes arms up against me. Another post will be placed beside her for anyone who dares go against my word."

Adara shuddered again, thinking what the woman would suffer left without food or drink and to the elements. How long could she possibly last? Was it his intention to leave her to die slowly for having attempted to kill him? A harsh punishment, but then it had been a harsh crime.

The woman had done the unthinkable and she would pay for her misdeed, but Adara wished the woman would not be made to endure such suffering. There had to be another way.

Adara turned away, not able to watch anymore and feeling guilty that she worried over the woman when she had attempted to take her husband's life. She hugged herself, a chill wrapping around her. Her fault since she wore no cloak, not having planned to step outside the keep. She should not offer an ounce of sympathy to the woman for what she had done and yet she could not help it. Fear had been her constant companion along with suffering. Both, all too often, paid her a visit and lingered far too long. She wished neither on anyone.

She jumped when a cloak was flung around her and she was lifted off her feet and, for a moment, fear pierced her like a hot iron.

"It is me, Adara, you are safe," Warrick said as soon as her body turned rigid in his arms. He got annoyed at himself for not alerting her to his presence, not thinking that dread had yet to leave her. As soon as her limbs turned limp, he cradled her in his arms. "Do not leave the keep without my permission."

"The keep was empty."

Her fear still lingered. He could tell by her brief response, almost as if she feared to speak.

"So your curiosity got the best of you?" he asked.

"Aye."

He entered the keep and took her to her solar as she referred to it, though only to herself. She had not known that he knew the whereabouts of this room. There had been no reason for him to be there. But having heard the story of his time in the woods, she realized he had learned to make himself aware of his surroundings.

Had she not done the same with each new place she had been sent to? She had learned to stay quiet, listen, observe, and come to know who and what to avoid, when to hide, and when to fear the most.

Warrick placed her in the one of the two chairs that faced the fireplace in the small room. A low flame flickered in it and he was quick to add logs.

Adara stood, slipping his cloak off her to return to him, but he placed it back on her shoulders.

"The room holds a chill." You will keep it on."

"You need—"

"I have another. I want you and our bairn warm and comfortable. Do what you will here. I have matters to see to."

"The woman—"

"Worry not about her."

She shook her head. "She will suffer—"

"She deserves to."

"Has she told you anything?"

"She either mumbles incoherently or remains silent."

"She obviously has a troubled mind. Can nothing be done for her?"

A glare rose in his dark eyes. "Shall I free her so she can attempt to kill the devil and his wife again?"

Adara cringed at him referring to himself as the devil

and quickly rested her hand to his chest. "No, I want no harm to come to you, and you are no devil."

He covered her hand with his, wanting to keep it there against his chest, over his heart that beat a bit faster at her touch. "Most, if not all, would not agree with you, but that matters not. It is one thing to threaten me, but a deadly mistake when she threatens you. That I will not tolerate. She can rot on that post as far as I am concerned, and all will see their fate if they dare take up arms against me and mine." He moved his hand off hers to rest on her stomach. "I told you I would keep you both safe, and I will." He kissed her lightly on the lips. "I will return later."

"I have not seen the woman. Should I not look upon her as well?" she asked, his words like a safety net wrapping around her.

"I will take you when I return. Do not go on your own," he warned.

"As you say," she said and surprised herself when she went up on her toes to brush her lips across his.

"I like when you kiss me, wife," he said and brought his thumb to trace over her lips. "I have missed the taste of you and think often of our night together."

Her mouth dropped open in surprise and she gasped lightly when his thumb slipped in her mouth and was shocked when her tongue instinctively licked at it. But it was the familiar deep rumbling moan that came from her husband that sent a tingle rushing through her to settle moistly between her legs. She remembered that moan, relished it, for she had learned on her wedding night what it meant.

He desired her.

Warrick stepped back, taking hold of her shoulders as if steadying himself. "Tonight, wife."

He rushed out of the room too fast to hear Adara's words.

"Why wait?"

She sighed and all but collapsed in the chair. That her husband desired her surprised her, though not as much as her own growing desire did. Knowing that he had not ordered her taken to his dungeon and his fury over discovering what had happened to her had helped her to see him differently and begin to change her thoughts about him. Though mostly, it was the way he had protected her, kept her safe since his arrival a week or more ago that had done more to sway her thoughts. That he continued to reassure her that he would keep her safe and show it in his actions as he had done last night, shielding her from the mad woman's blade and shielding her from her own fears, had helped her to trust his word.

She feared trusting too much, memories reminding her to be careful. There had been those she had trusted only to find they were not trustworthy. She could think of only one person she trusted completely... Espy. She owed Espy her life and she was forever grateful to her. Espy also proved time and again her trustworthy nature. Then there had been Uncle Owen. She had begun to trust him. If only they had had more time together, she was sure she would have wound up trusting him completely.

Now there was Warrick. She wanted to trust him, not hesitate to do so, but life had taught her that trust took time and was earned. Time would tell with Warrick, and she would have to be careful since her heart thought differently.

Trust. Trust, it said to her. *And maybe just maybe love would follow.*

Adara shook her head at the foolish thought. Warrick would never love her. Desire her perhaps, but love? Was he even capable of it?

Was she? She knew so little of it.

She smiled, thinking of the day she had asked Maia about love and how it felt.

"Love is tricky, she had said, "It pulls at the heart and tricks the mind. But when it truly strikes there is nothing you would not do to keep it safe."

Adara had ached to know more, ached to know love, and had not stopped asking questions.

"Enough," Maia had said, though continued explaining. "Love is different. The love a mother has for her bairn is unconditional. It is born of the heart and of all the months she carries the child, feeling it grow inside her and giving it the precious gift of life."

"All mums instinctively love their bairns?" Adara had asked, thinking how her uncle Owen had told her how much her mum had loved her. Though, he had spoken of how he had wanted his sister, her mum, to stay with him or at least leave Adara with him while she went north with her husband. He had felt it would not be safe for Adara, and he had been right.

"Most all do," Maia had said. "There are some that care naught but for themselves, but those are few."

"And love for a husband?" Adara had asked.

"That love is the tricky. It is the one that pulls at the heart and tricks the mind. Your heart tells you that you love this man and would do anything for him. Do anything to be with him."

Adara had gotten upset. "How horrible. How then do you know love is true?"

"That is an age-old question yet to be answered, though some insist you know when it happens. Tricks, though, tricks. You must be ever vigilant."

Adara often recalled their conversation, hoping one day she would make use of it. She wondered if that day was now.

~~~

Roark walked with Warrick to the keep. "I thought we would find something by now, but it is as if the others have vanished."

"Send warriors to the nearby clans to see if any

strangers have stopped there lately," Warrick ordered. "Also send word to Slain as to what has happened and have him keep a watchful eye and report anything unusual to me. Do the same as well with Craven."

Roark nodded.

Warrick stopped before entering the keep. "You always speak your mind to me, Roark. What troubles you so much that it has you holding your tongue."

"How long before we return home?" Roark asked without hesitation.

"A question you have never asked me before when we have been away. Explain," Warrick ordered.

Roark was blunt. "I miss my wife." He rubbed the back of his neck. "I have been away far too much these last few months and I wonder if Callie will even remember me."

"Or do you wonder if she will find another man while you are gone?"

"Never would Callie do that to me as I would not do it to her."

"Not even to appease the need that aches at you?" Warrick challenged.

"I have not seen you appeasing that need with another woman since you wed." Roark snapped and shook his head. "Forgive—'

"Do not bother to apologize. We both seem to be in need of our women. Since I have no immediate plans of leaving here, send for Callie and have her be informed of what goes on at home. Though, I believe the woman will know more than those in charge while in my absence."

Roark grinned from ear to ear. "She will at that, and I am grateful for this, my lord." He turned to hurry off to see it done.

"Roark."

He stopped and turned.

"Never snap at me like that again."

"Aye, my lord," Roark said with a respectful bob of his

head, his smile gone.

Warrick entered the keep. It was quiet. Everyone busy with their chores. The same with the village. Everyone was busy with daily chores and those Warrick had added. He wanted the village in good shape for winter since he did not plan on leaving here before then.

He had made no mention of it to Roark, but it was the reason he had him send for Callie. He did not want the man to face the winter without his wife. His own wife was the reason they would be remaining here through the winter. He wanted Espy to attend Adara's delivery as much as Adara wanted her to. He would trust no one else.

He had not told Adara that yet, but he would soon since he did not want her to worry.

He went to climb the stairs to fetch his wife and met her coming down.

She smiled when she saw him. He loved her smile. It made him want to smile, but he always caught his smile, stopping it. A habit he found hard to break.

He reached his hand out to her and she hurried to take it, her small hand disappearing in his as it closed firmly around hers.

"Where were you going?" he asked.

"To get a hot brew."

"Have the servants not seen to your needs that you must come fetch it yourself?"

Adara made no move to take another step when they reached the bottom of the stairs.

Warrick raised a brow at her.

"I ask for your patience, husband. I have served others as long as I can remember. I am accustomed to serving myself. It will take time for me to accept I no longer need to do that."

He was pleased she offered an explanation and annoyed that he expected far too much of her far too fast. "Patience is not one of my virtues, but you deserve that from me for what you have been through. I will try and, if I falter, you will remind me."

Adara smiled again, delighted with his response. "I will do that, husband, and I am grateful for your attempt at patience."

Warrick leaned down and whispered, "This is our secret or else others will expect the same of me."

She caught the slight, almost unnoticeable curve at the corners of his mouth. He was being humorous and someday—someday—he would let a smile free.

She returned his whisper, "I will keep your secret."

"I trust that you will."

She forced a wider smile, to hide her surprise at his words. Did he actually trust her?

"We will have a brew and then I will take you to see the crazed woman."

"I would prefer to see her first and possibly walk through the village afterwards?" she asked and chuckled softly as her hand moved to rest on her stomach. "Otherwise the bairn will protest."

"We will walk," he said, keeping her hand firm in his as they left the keep.

Adara's stomach clenched as they approached the post where the woman was tied. Villagers kept their distance from the woman as they went about their chores and Adara did not blame them. Warrick had been true to his word and another post had been pounded into the earth next to the woman for anyone who dared to defy him.

The woman's head hung even lower than when Adara had seen her last. Her chin nearly touched her chest and her gray hair hung like a veil around her head, concealing her face completely.

Adara placed her hand to her stomach, not to calm the bairn who remained quiet, but hoping to ease the clench that grew tauter. It was a familiar sensation that came upon her often and sometimes had her wishing she could run and hide.

She wished it would go away and trouble her no more.

"Stand here," Warrick said, keeping her a safe distance away but close enough for her to see the woman's face. He went and, grabbing a handful of hair at the top of her head, yanked it up.

Adara could not stop her heart from going out to the woman. Age had stolen her beauty or perhaps adversities had been the culprit. Whatever it had been, it appeared to have defeated her.

She was about to look away when the woman opened her eyes. Pale green with a touch of yellow like the catkins that appear on the trees at the first sign of spring.

Adara took a step closer. Could it be? Was it possible? It had been what? Five or more years?

The woman barely opened her eyes, though upon seeing Adara, they turned wide and, unable to speak, she mouthed, *Adara.*

"Maia!" Adara cried out and rushed forward.

Chapter Sixteen

"Free her. Free her now!" Adara cried out and rushed forward.

Warrick let go of the woman's hair and stepped in front of her, preventing Adara from reaching the woman. He grabbed her arm when she went to step around him. "You do not make demands of me, wife."

Villagers stopped and stared, their eyes wide, having heard Adara's outburst and feared for her safety.

"Go about your chores," Warrick yelled out, casting a scowl on those around them and the people scurried off, whispering prayers for the petite woman who had been good to them upon their chieftain's death.

Adara caught sight of Langdon, looking reluctant to leave, as he took slow steps away from the scene. He shook his head and his eyes seemed to plead with her not to defy her husband. They were worried. They were all worried for her.

"We will discuss this in the keep," Warrick said and, keeping his grip tight on her arm, went to walk away.

"No. No," Adara cried out, paying no mind to the warnings sent her way, her fingers digging at his where they dug into her arm. A futile attempt, his strength far superior to hers, but still she tried. "You must free her now. She is my friend."

"She is no friend when she attempts to kill you," Warrick said and began to drag her away.

Adara grabbed at his arm while trying to dig her feet into the soil to stop him from taking her away. "She must be sick. She needs help."

"She needs and deserves to be punished." He gave her

arm a yank and she fell forward against him. "You will calm now, wife, and walk with me to the keep to discuss this or, I promise you, you will regret your actions."

His harsh tone alone warned her to obey him, and she did.

Adara realized her mistake as she hurried her steps to keep up with his powerful strides. She had defied her husband in front of the clan. Would he make her suffer for it? Would he have her tied to the other post?

As soon as he closed the door to his solar, she did what she was accustomed to doing. "Forgive my foolish outburst, my lord."

His hand still firm on her arm, Warrick lowered his face close to hers. "Remember what I warned you, that things repeated often through the years mean little or nothing after a while. I will have nothing but the truth from your lips."

Truth. Did she dare speak it? Did she have a choice? "It was a foolish outburst."

He released her arm then and stepped away from her. "But you are not sorry for making it?"

Truth. She had to keep her words truthful. "I regret how I spoke to you, but not what I said. I do want my friend set free."

"She tried to take your life and still you think she is your friend?" he asked annoyed at her actions, yet amazed at her courage in having dared to speak to him as she had done. And more impressed that she kept to the truth after he had warned her. Was his trust important to her? Or did she play a game as many women did?

"She must not have known it was me. I have not seen her in years. I did not recognize her at first as she did me. Please, Warrick, imprison her if you must, but please, please remove her from the post and let her at least have some food."

Warrick knew all too well the consequences of granting his wife's plea. It would show him as weak and that was something he was not. "My word is law and I will not change it."

"Give her a chance, please," Adara begged. "I am sure she will speak to me if given the chance."

"You will speak to her with me there beside you and with her remaining secured to the post," he said, not taking a chance that the woman would harm his wife. "Tell me how you know her."

"She is the woman who told me about the Vikings. I met her in the woods one day. She was there cleaning garments in the stream. She talked to me of many things. She taught me much. She showed me friendship, kindness, neither of which I had known."

Warrick walked over to her. "I will not release her and risk harm to you and I will not rescind my command."

"Please let me speak to her now and see if there is something she may say that will change your mind," Adara pleaded.

"You can speak to her if you wish with me present, but I will not have you hope only to be disappointed. She will pay for her foolish actions."

A swell of fear rose up in Adara for her friend and what she would suffer. Or how she, herself, could watch such suffering and do nothing to help her.

Warrick reached out, his hand going to rest on her shoulder. "You are upset, perhaps you should wait to—"

"No. No," Adara said, shaking her head and stepping away from him. "I must speak to her now."

Warrick was not happy that she backed away, avoiding his touch. He was about to deny her, but he was wise enough to know it would be more prudent to let her speak with the woman now and be done with it. Once she saw that the woman made no sense and was a threat to her own and their child's safety, she would accept his command. Not that she needed to accept or approve, better she understood that his word was law and nothing would change that. But he felt that he had made that clear and she would argue no more.

They walked once again out of the keep, though this time, she hurried a few steps ahead of him instead of walking alongside him, holding his hand. He grew annoyed, having come to favor her hand in his.

"You will keep a safe distance," Warrick ordered when his wife rushed toward the woman.

Adara slowed her steps and warned herself to follow his word or risk not being able to speak to Maia at all. She stopped a short distance in front of her and called out to the woman.

"Maia. Maia, it is me, Adara."

The woman's head lifted and joy sparked in her eyes for a moment before fading to fear. "Run. Run and hide. Do not let him get you."

"I am safe, Maia. There is no need to worry over me."

Warrick came to stand behind her and Maia's eyes bulged at the sight of him.

"Run from the devil and his whore."

Adara cringed. "I am his wife, Maia, and he treats me well."

Maia let lose a sorrowful whine that echoed through the village, shivering people where they stood and had Roark and several of Warrick's warriors rushing toward him and stopping abruptly when he raised his hand.

"Noooo. Noooo. It cannot be," Maia continued to whine.

"All is good, Maia. I am safe," Adara said, trying to reassure the woman.

"No!" she shouted so suddenly and with such venom that Warrick stepped in front of his wife, shielding her.

"Never safe!" Maia screamed. "Never. Never. Never."

Warrick turned and with an arm around his wife, forced her to step away.

"You did not listen. I failed. Run!" she screeched. "Run before it is too—"

With a signal from Warrick, a cloth was shoved into the woman's mouth while his hand remained firm on his wife, guiding her away and into the keep. He sat her at the table near the hearth in the Great Hall and ordered a hot brew brought for her.

Adara had felt the pain of losing Maia those many years ago when she had been abruptly sent to live with another family never to see her again. She felt even more pain now seeing what had become of her friend and losing her all over again.

"I do not understand what happened to her," Adara said, her words meant more for herself than her husband, though he responded.

"Sometimes things cannot be explained no matter how much we want them to make sense." He placed the tankard the servant handed to him in his wife's hands. "Drink."

She sat it down. "My stomach will not tolerate it." She looked up at him, standing beside her. "Perhaps Espy could help her."

Warrick gently brushed a strand of blonde hair off her face and behind her ear. "I know it troubles you to see her like that, but she is crazed and a danger to you. There is nothing that can be done."

Adara did not want to believe it, but she knew any further discussion with her husband on the matter would prove futile, and perhaps it would.

Roark entered the Great Hall and Warrick left her side to go speak with him and so went the remainder of the day. Roark and warriors coming and going, speaking with Warrick, following his command until Adara found the noise and busyness too much.

She stood and turned to see Warrick's eyes on her. "I go to rest."

He nodded and she climbed the stairs slowly, her limbs feeling much too heavy, but then this matter with Maia rested heavily on her shoulders. Something about it made no sense.

You did not listen.

What had Maia meant that Adara had not listened and what had Maia failed at? Or was it simply the ramblings of a crazed woman?

Adara dropped down on the bed after entering the room, the last few troubling hours having worn her out. Sleep quickly took hold of her and she was glad for it, her mind needing as much rest as her body.

A crack of thunder, sounding as if it had split the room in two, woke her and ran a chill through her. A storm was brewing. She turned with a stretch and noticed the fire in the hearth had dwindled. She burrowed herself beneath the warmth of the blankets. The servants should have checked on the fires in all the rooms by now. She wondered what had kept them.

Reluctantly, she slipped out of bed and shivered when her bare feet touched the cold floor and she hurried to add logs to the fire. She was quick to get her shoes on and smooth the few wrinkles out of her garments as best she could. She ran her bone comb through her hair with haste and took the stairs down with just as much haste.

The Great Hall was alive with noise and activity, though no one sat at the tables to eat. Warriors waited in groups, weapons strapped to their backs, and at their sides, as if ready for battle.

Adara stared in horror. Could they truly be facing battle? She searched the room for her husband and when she could not find him, her heart began to beat a bit faster and that feeling of dread that she felt far too often began to poke at her. She hurried her glance around the room again. He would not be difficult to spot, his height taller than most, so why could she not find him. Her heartbeat quickened even more and the sudden fright to flee hit her. As she turned to run, she spotted him, entering the room, his eyes instantly falling on hers as if he knew exactly where she was. He did not hesitate. He took quick steps toward her while she remained where she was, the noise in the room deafening and her limbs frozen.

When he got close his arms reached out for her and she rushed into them, locking her slim arms around him as far as they would go and squeezing him with all the strength she could muster.

"You are safe," Warrick said, knowing that was what she needed to hear, having seen the fright in her wide eyes.

Aye, she was now that she was in his arms, but she did not say that, she could not find her voice. She nodded instead.

"There has been an altercation between two nearby clans. One has pledged allegiance to me, and I must go and see the clan protected."

The thought of him leaving upset her, not that it made sense to her. She had done fine without him before. There was no reason she would not do so again, so why was she upset with the prospect of his absence?

Safe.

He kept her safe.

"I leave more than enough warriors behind to protect you and I do not think it will take more than a day or two to see the matter settled."

That should have relieved any worries she had, but it did not. "Roark cannot go in your stead?" she asked, her voice returning and her fright still a flutter in her stomach.

"He comes with me to all battles, though I hope it will not come to that. I expect to persuade the other clan to pledge allegiance to me as well and stop the frequent feuding among the two clans. There is no need for worry. You will be safe." He would repeat that again and again for as long as she needed to hear it.

"You will be careful."

"Is that an order?" he asked a slight tease in his voice.

Adara surprised herself with a quick kiss to her

husband's lips and her own playful response, "It is and you will obey it."

"Or what?" he asked and she thought she heard a rumble of laughter almost break free.

A shout from Roark had Warrick turning and seeing Roark's frantic summons, he looked to his wife. "I must go. You are safe. I will return soon." He brought his lips down on hers and kissed her as if he feared he would never see her again, lingering, making sure to commit her taste to memory, which was not difficult since he could never forget it, never wanted to.

Then he was gone, leaving her staring after him.

She sent him her response on a whisper, though it would never reach him. "Or you will shatter my heart."

Love is tricky. It pulls at the heart and tricks the mind.

Maia's words struck her unexpectedly. Could that have been what she had meant when she had said you did not listen?

But she was not in love with Warrick. Then why had she believed he would shatter her heart if he did not stay safe and return to her? Was she losing her heart to him? Or had she already lost it to him on their wedding night? That night lived long in her memory and so had the thought that that was what love must feel like.

Thinking on it now, had her mind played tricks on her? Had she ached so badly to be loved that she had believed what she and Warrick had shared was love? She was Warrick's wife and he was her husband. She had a duty to him as he did to her. He had fulfilled his duty that night making certain their vows were consummated. And it was his duty to keep her safe. He did not love her and she should not be foolish and let the tugs at her heart trick her with unwise thoughts, hopes or dreams. She had wasted enough years on such things.

The Great Hall emptied out fast and Adara trailed behind the exiting warriors to peek past the door and watch her husband mount and lead his warriors out of the village. Try as she might, she could not stop the pang of pain in her heart at his departure.

"Come sup and warm yourself by the fire, my lady," Wynn said from behind her. "A storm brews, bringing a cold wind with it."

Adara closed the door, turned, and followed Wynn to the table by the hearth. It was while she was eating, her mind still on her husband that a disturbing thought invaded her musings.

How would Maia ever survive the storm?

Adara's appetite deserted her. How could she sit here in the warmth and safety of the keep while Maia went hungry and battled the storm that would soon descend on them? Should she help the woman? If she went against her husband's word, would he tie her to the post as he had threatened to do to anyone who helped Maia? And was Maia more a threat to her than the possible consequences she would suffer if she helped the woman?

Too upset to eat anymore, Adara went to her solar, hoping to keep her thoughts busy with her stitching. Unfortunately, the continued thunder and lightning kept Maia ever present in her thoughts.

The rain had yet to start when Adara slipped into bed with prayers for her friend and fear of what her husband might do if she dared to help Maia.

She was woken once again by a sharp crack of thunder and a splash of rain upon the window. This time there was no hesitation, no questioning her decision. Too many times through the years, she had wished someone would help her out of her dire situation. No one ever did. She could not do the same to Maia, no matter how fearful she was of the consequences.

Adara hurried to dress, making sure to don extra garments to protect against the rain. With it being late into the night, no one was about. She was able to gather food in a sack in the kitchen and she took one of the cloaks that hung by the door. Last, she grabbed a knife, a big one, and headed out the door to free Maia.

Chapter Seventeen

Adara kept the hood of her cloak tucked low over her head as she moved amongst the shadows of the night. The rain was not falling heavily, but in time it would and she needed to free Maia before it did. She made sure to look for signs of any of Warrick's warriors. They lurked about and could not always be spotted and she worried that her husband left more guards on duty in his absence.

She halted her steps when she spotted a dark shadow slip past Maia. With the guard having just been there, it gave her time to free the woman and hurry her away before he returned again, if he returned at all. If she was lucky, it might have been his last patrol for the night.

Not wasting a minute, Adara rushed to Maia.

"Maia, it is me, Adara. I have come to free you," Adara whispered, taking the knife to the rope.

The woman did not respond and thinking she might be too late to help the woman, Adara placed her hand beneath Maia's chin and lifted her head and kept repeating her name softly while she continued to cut at the rope.

Finally, her name fell in a whisper from Maia's lips, "Adara."

"Aye, it is me. I will have you free soon."

Maia struggled to say, "Go. Save yourself."

"Not without you." Adara thanked the heavens that the rope was old and it took less time than she thought it would. What she had not counted on was Maia's weakened state. The hours she had been strapped to the post had left her limbs numb and made it difficult for her to walk.

"Lean on me," Adara encouraged, slipping her shoulder under Maia's arm and her limp arm around her neck.

The slim woman did not argue, she leaned against Adara.

With strength born of determination, much as it had the night Espy had freed her from Warrick's dungeon, Adara started walking, keeping to the shadows. It seemed like forever until they reached the outskirts of the village, having made sure to avoid the area where Warrick's warriors had camped. Shortly after, the rain grew heavy, slowing their pace, but Adara kept going.

Distance. They needed distance from the village. With each step, Adara expected to hear the tolling of the bell that alerted the village to a problem. Gratefully, it did not sound.

She had to keep going before Maia's escape was discovered and before anyone realized she was gone. She did not know what her defiance of Warrick's orders would cost her, but at the moment she did not care. She had to see to Maia, make sure she was well and safe, and she knew exactly where she would take her.

The rain continued, light at times, heavy at others, and as much as the rain made travel more difficult, it also benefitted them. It made tracking more difficult.

No sun rose with daylight only a cloudy sky and more rain. Maia's escape would have been discovered by now and no doubt the guards would have gone to her bedchamber to make sure she was safe. She wondered what Warrick's warriors would do when they could not find her. What would they think? That someone freed Maia and then came for her. Would they even consider the possibility that she was the one who freed Maia? No doubt they would send word to Warrick. They would be too fearful not to.

The more she thought on what she had done, the more she questioned her decision. But then the thought of Maia dying slowly day after day and her not doing a thing to help her was something she believed she would have never been able to live with. So her thoughts warred as she journeyed on.

Finally, too exhausted to take another step, Adara stopped and settled them both under a large, old pine tree, it's branches heavy with growth and spreading wide. A perfect shelter for them and far enough off the well-traveled path for anyone to find them.

Maia's body sagged with fatigue and Adara worried the woman had no strength left to continue.

"We do not have far to go," Adara encouraged.

Maia opened her eyes. "I cannot take another step."

"We can rest only briefly. We must keep moving."

Adara took some cheese and bread from the sack and gave it to Maia and took some for herself as well. They ate in silence, both too tired to speak as they ate.

"Does my mind play tricks on me or did you tell me that you are wed to the devil?" Maia asked, after finishing the food.

"I am Warrick's wife and he is no devil."

"He is the devil," Maia hissed as if Adara should be ashamed for believing otherwise.

Adara could not believe the flare of hatred in the woman's eyes or the strength of it in her voice. She did not recall ever hearing such venom spew from the woman when she had known her. Doubt grew, gooseflesh running along her arms as fear began to rise in her. Had she made a foolish decision in defending the woman against her husband?

"At least you got away from him," Maia said with a bitterness that confused Adara.

"Why do you hate Warrick so much?" Adara asked, fearful that she had left Warrick vulnerable by freeing Maia. And what of her bairn? She had promised herself over and over that she would keep her bairn safe and look what she had done. She had placed the woman's life above her bairn.

"He is an evil, evil man and needs to die."

Adara stared at the woman as if she were a stranger, dread rising up in her. The woman had once been good to her or so she thought. Had she been so eager for friendship that she had given thought to nothing else?

A memory stirred of Maia gathering plants near the bank of the stream and dropping them into a basket. Why had she not remembered that? Did the woman know enough to have possibly harmed Jaynce?

Adara had to ask. "Did you kill Jaynce?"

"No."

Adara let the breath free she was holding.

"Another in our group did."

Adara's next breath lodged in her throat and had fear once again prickling her skin. She had made a mistake. A dreadful mistake.

"You will join us. You can tell us much about the devil," Maia said as if it had already been decided.

Adara stood, leaning down to snatch up the sack.

"You carry the devil's spawn," Maia said, pointing to Adara's stomach that appeared more rounded than it was since she was bent over.

Adara quickly straightened, her hand going protectively to her stomach and as she did she caught Maia's glance going to the knife, laying a hand's length away from her.

Everything happened so fast Adara had no time to think only react.

Maia went for the knife, bringing it up swiftly and swinging it toward Adara. She jumped back, but not before swinging the sack she held with as much force as possible and knocking the knife out of Maia's hand. She scrambled to retrieve it and Adara did not wait, she swung the sack again, catching Maia in the jaw and knocking her backward, but losing her balance as she did and scrambling to stop herself form falling. By then Maia had gotten hold of the knife again, only this time she got to her feet and looked ready to charge at Adara.

"I thought you were my friend," Adara said, having trusted only to once again be disappointed. Only this time her ignorance could wind up costing her and her child's life.

Maia shook her head. "You were an ignorant lass who needed to grow wise, though if I had known your fate, I would have killed you then."

At that moment, a courage born of fear rose in Adara. She had made a horrible mistake but she would not let her foolishness harm her bairn or her husband. She would fight for both.

"I thought the lessons I had taught you would help you grow, strengthen you to survive, make you wise enough to ask questions, particularly why you were sent from family to family. There had to be a reason for it, even I could see that. You accept your fate far too easily, but then you lack the courage to do otherwise."

Adara had no idea what she was talking about. Besides, she trusted nothing the woman said. She was far more evil than she claimed Warrick to be. She may have lacked courage before, but now she would do anything to protect her unborn bairn.

"A waste of life." Maia shrugged, wincing from the pain in her limbs. "I must say, though, my interest in you has served me well. I thought for sure I would rot to death on the devil's post, but once I saw it was you, I knew I had a chance to escape. You are too kind for your own good."

Adara never felt more the fool. She had trusted again only this time she had trusted the wrong person. She should have trusted the devil.

Maia chuckled. "Your empty life will have you do anything to fill it... even bear the devil's spawn. Better you die now and not release another demon on this earth." She raised the knife. "I will make it swift, since the time I had spent with you at least made my time here a bit more bearable. You listened to all my stories, though in the end another reason to kill you."

Maia lunged at Adara and once again she swung the sack. This time, however, Maia expected it and dodged her swing while bringing her other hand around to yanked the sack away from Adara.

"Nothing left to defend yourself with," Maia said with a sense of victory close at hand.

Instinct took hold, though more so Espy's words before freeing her from the dungeon.

Do not let fear freeze you. Use anything you can to defend yourself, and never ever surrender.

"I think I will cut the bairn from you and let Warrick know before he dies if it was a son I took from him." Maia grinned, then pounced like an animal on its prey.

No weapon at hand, Adara did the first thing that came to mind. She whipped off her cloak and threw it over Maia and hurried around her to pull it tight. She raised her foot and gave a sharp, forceful kick to the back of Maia knees and sent her crashing forward to land with a snap on the ground.

She scrambled to get the knife away from the woman, pulling the cloak off her. But Maia didn't move and her arms lay tucked beneath her. Adara hurried to get a large rock and, gripping it in her two hands, she made ready to bring it down if necessary. With a hard nudge of her foot, she turned Maia over.

Maia stared up at her, blood dribbling from the corner of her mouth, the knife protruding from her chest.

She struggled to speak. "Devil,"—she gasped for breath— "will kill you." She gasped again, then coughed. "Like he did to his," —breath failing her she fought to say— "first wife."

Adara stumbled back, the rock falling out of her hands.

It could not be. She was lying, putting doubt in her mind about her husband, trying to make her fear him, loathe him, hate him as much as she did.

Adara glared at the lifeless woman, she had believed her friend. A fool. Looking at the woman now, her eyes as full of hatred as they had been when she had spoken her last words, she realized how much of a fool she had been.

Thunder rumbled overhead, causing Adara to jump. She looked up at the darkening sky. Rain was coming again and she was still soaked from last night. She had to get dry, had to rest, had to keep the bairn safe. Something she should have thought of before foolishly defying her husband.

Kill you like he did his first wife.

Adara pressed her hands to her ears, trying desperately to stop the dead woman's words from tolling like a never-ending bell in her head. She lied. She had to have lied.

Do not let fear freeze you.

She was grateful for Espy's voice and she scrambled to her feet. She had to reach shelter before the rain started again. She had to get warm, keep the bairn warm and safe. She took off, hurrying her footsteps toward safety.

It was after she had walked for a while that she realized she had left the sack of what was left of the food behind. It did not matter. She was not far from her destination. She would find food there and shelter, and a healing hand.

Adara walked with determination and caution, and attempted to keep fear at bay, but it poked and nagged at her. What would Warrick do to her when he discovered she had betrayed him? That she had put not only him in danger but herself and their bairn. No excuse, no apology would do. She was wrong.

But what of him? Had he been married before he wed her? Had he killed his wife? Should she fear that he would kill her? Her heart ached. She had begun to trust him, to believe that he would keep her safe. But if he had been wed before and he had killed his wife, how did she trust him not to do the same to her?

Her thoughts were so heavy on her mind that she did not realize it had begun to rain. She kept walking, kept thinking, kept wondering what now would happen to her.

When she thought her legs could carry her no more, she stepped out of the woods and spotted the cottage. Each step she took toward it seemed more laborious than the previous one and it felt as if it seemed like forever before she reached the door and tapped on it.

The door sprung open and upon seeing Cyra, Espy's grandmother who had been so kind to her, Adara burst into tears, collapsing against the woman.

Adara clung to Cyra as the woman helped her into the cottage. There was a comfort in Cyra's arms that she did not want to leave, at least not just yet.

"It is all right, Adara," Cyra said soothingly.

Adara felt Cyra's hand on hers, lifting it. She winced when she saw the blood covering it and how it had cramped from keeping it fisted tightly for so long.

"Slowly, my dear," Cyra said, her hand remaining on Adara's.

Cyra helped her ease her fingers open. "We need to get you out of these wet clothes."

Adara nodded at the wisdom of her words, feeling a chill begin to rush through her. Reluctantly, she stepped away from the woman and gave a cautious glance around, realizing too late that Cyra might not be alone.

"Innis is not here. He is on an errand for me. He will not return until tomorrow."

Adara felt a sense of relief, glad she was alone with Cyra. Not that she did not like Innis. He was a wonderful man, a physician and friend to Espy. He had fallen in love with Cyra when he had come to visit Espy, and they now resided together in Cyra's cottage.

Cyra worked quickly in getting Adara out of her soaked garments. Her strength had not diminished for a woman of fifty plus years nor had her nimbleness. Her long, slim fingers had not gnarled like some healers did over the years and her lovely face had far less wrinkles and lines than women younger than her.

Adara stood as Cyra dried her body and wrung the water from her hair. She shivered when a soft wool nightdress fell over her head and down her body and she quickly hugged herself, the warmth of the fine wool chasing the shivers.

"You will get in bed, under the warm blankets, while I prepare a brew for you, but first," —Cyra placed her hand on Adara's stomach— "No pain or discomfort?"

Choked with tears she fought not to spill, Adara shook her head. The thought of the damage she could have caused her child over her rash actions, had guilt once again weighing heavily upon her.

"Into bed with you, so you may get warm and gather your strength, then we will talk," Cyra said, helping Adara into bed and plumping the pillows behind her back so she could rest comfortably against them.

"I did a foolish thing," Adara said, unable to stop the tears from rolling down her face.

Cyra sat on the edge of the bed and took Adara's hand. "Please, tell me you did not use that knife on Warrick."

Adara shook her head and words began pouring from her mouth as she explained everything that had happened, except the part about Warrick killing his first wife.

"I thought she was my friend," Adara finished, wiping at the tears that kept trickling out along with her words. "I was wrong to defy my husband."

"You did what you thought was right for a friend and in a way you helped your husband. He would never have known that she was part of a group that intended to see him dead. What you need to do now is to recall everything Maia has ever told you. But that is better left for when after you rest."

Adara nodded and nibbled at the corner of her mouth.

"Something else bothers you," Cyra said.

Adara did not know what to do. Did she speak to Cyra about what Maia had told her about Warrick? A thought had her stop nibbling at the corner of her mouth. Could Cyra possibly know if it was true? Did she take the chance and ask her?

"Do not let what Maia did cause you to distrust others. You have true friends now. They will not hurt or betray you like Maia did."

Adara sighed, shut her eyes a moment, praying she did the right thing confiding in Cyra and said, "Maia told me that Warrick killed his first wife." That Cyra did not show shock told Adara that the woman knew something.

"Whether truth or a tale I could not say, but there is talk that Warrick killed a woman he had had just taken as his wife. Some say he killed her on their wedding night."

Adara stared in disbelief. "Why?"

"That is the mystery of it. Some believe she failed to please him. Others say the demon in him made him do it. Still others believe she got what she deserved for marrying the devil himself. I do not know Warrick so I cannot say nor will I judge him."

"Does Espy know of this?"

"If she does, she never confessed it to me."

"She is my friend. Surely, she would have told me if she knew," Adara said, not wanting to believe Espy would keep such an important thing from her.

"How would that have helped you if she did? You were already wed and had survived your wedding night. What good would it have done to tell you a tale that might very well be false, nothing more than vicious gossip? And why did you not trust Espy enough to tell her you were with child and that you were wed to Warrick?"

"Fear," Adara said on a sigh. "Always fear. It haunts me like a shadow. I cannot seem to go anyplace without it."

"It did not stop you from freeing Maia."

"More the better for me if it had."

Cyra shook her head. "Not so. You did not let fear stop you from doing something you felt strongly about… saving a friend. And you did not let fear prevent you from saving yourself and your child. You do not think Espy feared when she helped you escape from Warrick's dungeon? Or feared even more what would happen if he had caught her? She did what she believed was right. Sometimes our decisions are wise, sometimes foolish, learning from them is the most important."

"I fear what my husband will do when he learns what I did and I do not believe an apology will suffice."

"There is time to think on that, to think on the husband you have come to know. What you and the bairn need now is food and rest."

Adara paid heed to Cyra's words. She ate what food Cyra prepared for her and drank the hot brew that warmed her and when her eyes grew heavy she slipped down in the bed, pulling the blanket up to her chin and turning on her side, she fell asleep.

Adara trembled in fear waiting for her husband to enter their bedchamber. She wished he would hurry. The wait was unbearable as were thoughts of the night that lay ahead.

The door creaked opened and she took a step back as Warrick entered the room. He stood silent for a moment, then crossed the room where food and drink had been left. He filled two goblets with wine and walked over to her handing her one.

It will help make the night easier," he said.

She took the goblet and drank and, though she did not favor the taste, she continued to drink it. She saw that his hair was damp and his garments clean. He had been thoughtful to wash, not something you would expect from the Demon Lord.

When he finished his wine, he turned and removed his boots, setting them aside, then he pushed the slip of plaid that crossed his chest off his shoulder and freed his shirt to pull over his head and toss on a chair. His hands went to his waist and he began to unwrap his plaid, letting it fall to floor when he finished.

He stood naked in front of her, his body hard, not a bulge or roll on him and his muscles taut. There was no

*softness to him, no kindness in his dark eyes, and even
though he was across the room, she took a step back away
from him.*

*He did not take a step toward her when he commanded,
"Remove your garments, wife."*

Chapter Eighteen

Fear kept her frozen, her limbs far too heavy to move. She warned herself to do as he said, yet she could not make her body obey. He walked toward her and still she could not move, could not run from him. But where was there for her to go? She was his wife and he had every right to... movement suddenly returned to her, her limbs trembling.

His arm went around her waist before she could crumble to the floor. "I will not harm you."

Did he mean that? Or like so many others did his tongue lie?

As if he read her thoughts, he said, "I am a man of my word, wife, obey me and you have nothing to fear. Defy me and you will regret it."

She had no wont to defy him. She was accustomed to being obedient. It would be no chore to obey, at least she hoped it would not be.

He took a step away from her, his arm falling from around her waist slowly, making sure she remained steady on her feet. Then he took hold of her nightdress at both sides of her hips and pulled it up and over her head.

Instinct to protect herself, feeble as it was, had her swinging her arm across her breasts to cover them as best she could and her other hand cupped between her legs.

"It will do you no good to hide from me. I intend to see all of you, touch all of you, and kiss all of you. By the end of the night, we will have come to know each other well." He brushed her arm away from her breasts and moved her hand away to reveal the triangle of blonde hair between her legs.

As he did, she watched his manhood grow before her eyes and she wondered how he would ever fit inside her without causing her pain.

His hand came up to brush over her lips. "You are more petite than I am accustomed to, and far more beautiful than the grime on your face allowed anyone to see."

Grime had been something she had discovered that kept men at a distance, especially if there was a repugnant odor along with it. It was the men whose odor was just as repugnant that had concerned her at times, though she had managed to avoid them.

Warrick was the first to see her freshly cleaned and the first to ever think her beautiful, and it stirred her heart a bit.

He ran his hand along her cheek and down along the side of her neck. "You are softer than I imagined." His hand slipped beneath her long blonde hair to rest at the back of her neck. He gave it a squeeze and Adara almost sighed at how good it felt.

When he did it again, she shut her eyes for a moment, feeling the tautness in her neck fade. Her eyes flew open when she felt him step closer to her, their naked bodies brushing against each other.

His hand took firm hold of her neck, keeping it from moving as he dropped his head down and captured her lips with his.

Having never been kissed, she did not know what to do, but it did not matter since he did. His lips seemed to tease her to respond and she found herself doing just that, greeting his lips with timid kisses, and he greedily accepting them as if he could not get enough.

When his tongue darted in her mouth, she almost pulled away from him, but his hand at her neck held her firm. Her tongue soon welcomed him as her lips had done, shyly, but he did not retreat, not get annoyed at her naïveté. He continued to kiss her as if he enjoyed every moment of it.

His hand fell away from her neck as his lips left hers and for a moment she felt a pang of disappointment. She startled when he scooped her up in his arms and carried her to the bed, freshly dressed for their wedding night. He placed her down on it and slipped in beside her.

"We will be done with this, wife, our vows sealed, and you will do your duty as expected."

She nodded, all too familiar with doing what was expected of her. She spread her legs, having seen women do that for their husbands, though there were those who got on their knees, but she was already on her back, so she remained there.

It would be over and done soon. All she had to do was lie there and let him have his way.

He climbed over her, bracing his hands to either side of her and resting his large, hard manhood between her legs.

Soon. Very soon, it would be over, she kept telling herself, then he did the unexpected. He brought his mouth down to suckle at her one nipple and it awakened a flood of dormant sensations in her that all but stole her breath. Never had she thought that what a husband and wife shared could feel so wonderful. As his mouth continued to administer to her breasts, it spurred tingles over her flesh, firing a passion she had kept hidden from when it had first come to light. Now that it had finally been released, she worried if she would ever be able to keep it hidden again.

He rubbed his manhood between her legs, against the small nub and she moaned as bursts of pleasure rippled through her. Unconsciously, she thrust her hips up to press hard against his manhood, wanting to feel more of the intense pleasure it brought her.

"Open your mouth," he demanded and she obeyed.

His tongue shot in and hers eagerly sparred with his while his lips took possession of hers and fueled the passion mounting rapidly within them.

He tore his mouth away from hers after a few moments, his breath as laborious as hers.

"Spread your legs wider," he ordered and once again she obeyed.

When she felt his manhood breech her opening, she grew eager to feel him inside her, a surprising thought, but then she wanted this over and done. Did she not?

She felt herself stretch as he made his way inside her and as he went deeper, she found she enjoyed the feel of him and wanted more. He gave it to her, driving in and out of her, going deeper and deeper with each thrust, and she gripped his arms tight.

When he finally plunged the whole way in, she cried out, not from the prick of pain, but from the overwhelming sensation that took hold of her and refused to let go.

"Please do not stop," she begged to her astonishment when he slowed his thrusts and he complied, plunging harder and harder inside her until she cried out from the pleasure that took hold of her and shivered her down to her soul. She squeezed tight, wanting to get every last bit she could from his manhood and seconds later she heard him groan and not realizing she had closed her eyes, she opened them to see him throw back his head and groan aloud over and over and over again until he shuddered and collapsed against her.

It was not long before he rolled off her to lie beside her. They both laid still, their breathing hard, though his harder than hers. Her wifely duty to her husband had not been as bad as she had thought it would be. She would not mind the task, though she was glad it was over and done for the night, or so she told herself, fearing that perhaps she enjoyed it more than she should have.

But it was far from over and fear was not something she would feel that night.

It was barely an hour later when he turned in bed and began to touch her. He started with her breasts, circling her nipple, teasing it with his fingers, then with his teeth and lips.

Adara was not certain what he was doing. Had they not consummated their vows already? Why was he touching her intimately again? Not that she minded, she enjoyed his touch and while it surprised her, it also brought relief, for she would not dread when he came to her bed.

Warrick kissed her gently. "I find I favor you, wife. It will not be a chore bedding you."

He did not expect a response since he kissed her before she could tell him she felt the same. It was a demanding kiss and she responded with a demand of her own.

This time her hands went of their own accord to explore him. She caressed his back, smooth and hard, and along his arms defined with taut muscles.

He slipped his arm around her waist to take her with him as he turned on his side so that they lay face to face, giving her access to more of his body, and she took it. She let her hand drift down along his stomach until her fingers slipped into the dark curly hair that surrounded his shaft. She wanted to touch it, but she was not sure if that was acceptable.

His hand took hold of hers and placed it on it. "You are free to touch, explore, taste all of me if you wish."

She explored with her hand, the thought of tasting him there strange to her. His manhood was soft against the palm of her hand as she caressed it and she found she quite enjoyed touching him. She even gently took the sac that rested beneath his manhood in her hand to feel and explore and she thought she heard him moan. His hard manhood drew her touch once again and she gripped it hard, taking possession of it as if she was laying claim to it, that it belonged to her and her alone, and she caressed it once again.

He felt silky to the touch, yet hard and strong as his manhood swelled with her demanding caresses and that caused her own body to grow wet with need. She looked up at her husband and his dark eyes were heated with such potent desire that she let out a small gasp.

He reached down, grabbed her beneath her arms,

pulled her up and under him, and entered her with a single thrust that had her crying out and coiling her hands firmly around his arms. Their bodies soon found a familiar rhythm and they moved as one, faster and faster, harder and harder.

"Do not stop, please, Warrick do not stop," Adara said, through gasping breaths as she felt her body ready to explode with pleasure. And she did, over and over again, and like before she squeezed as hard as she could on her husband's shaft buried deep inside her and a deep roar burst from him that echoed throughout the room.

Neither could move afterwards, their breathing so labored, their hearts pounding viciously against their chests. Warrick finally slipped off her, taking her hand in his as he lay next to her.

Adara squeezed his hand, her small one feeling so good in his, almost cherished, something she had never felt before.

After a while, he took her in his arms, drawing her against him. "You belong here and here is where you will stay."

Aye, she would stay, for finally she had found a kind soul.

They slept, but she woke a few hours later hungry, having eaten little due to her fear of what she thought the night would hold for her. She slipped out of bed and went to the table to take a piece of cheese and bread and when that did little to appease her hunger, she took a chunk of meat. She was on her fourth piece of cheese when she jumped as an arm wrapped around her.

"Coupling makes you hungry, wife?" he asked, kissing along her neck and shoulder.

A ripple of pleasure raced down her arm and along her whole body.

"I will see that food is kept in our bedchamber at night for you."

Adara found herself speechless. She had gone hungry more nights than not. To think she would not go hungry again brought a tear to her eye.

Warrick rested his warm hands at her waist, turned her around in his arms, and seeing the tear wiped at it with his thumb. "Why the tear?"

She coughed lightly, clearing her throat of the lump that had lodged there. "I am pleased to have such a kind husband."

"Kind I am not, wife, but you will be safe with me."

Safe. Something she had felt little of through the years and the thought that he would see her safe had her placing a kiss on his lips in thanks. Or had kisses along her neck sparked her desire for him?

"Your lips make me hungry," Warrick said.

Adara held what was left of the piece of cheese up to his mouth.

Warrick raised his hand and took it from her to toss on the table. "That is not what I am hungry for."

Adara's mouth dropped open with a soft, oh *that never made it past her lips, Warrick capturing it with his mouth as he claimed hers. It was not a gentle kiss, it demanded and Adara responded, her arms going up around his neck as his hands grabbed her buttocks and hoisted her up against him, forcing her legs to wrap around him.*

He tore his mouth away from hers, resting his brow to hers as he walked to the bed, his hands tight on her buttocks. "I cannot get enough of you."

She felt the same, but did not have the courage to tell him so.

He brought her bottom down to rest on the edge of the bed and spread her legs, holding them firm just below the back of her knees and stepping between them. He hoisted her legs high enough to fit his manhood at her opening that had grown wet and began to throb.

She cried out when he entered her.

"You are sore," he said and began to withdraw from her.

"No. No. Please I want you inside me," she begged, not knowing if it was right or wrong for her to do so, only knowing her need for him was great.

"I do not wish to cause you pain," he said, though had not retreated any further.

"You cause me more pain if you leave me," she said, not believing she had the courage to admit that to him, but then her desire for him was far beyond anything she could control. It was not only that he felt good inside her that had ignited that passion, it was also that he cared enough not to hurt her that fired it even more.

At that moment, he cared for her and that meant the world to her.

"Then I will not leave you, wife," he said and slipped deeper into her.

His rhythm was gentle until Adara began to thrust her bottom up harder and harder against him, forcing him to respond in kind and he did, taking control. Moans mingled with her repeated insistence that Warrick not stop filled the room as the two joined together as one.

They exploded simultaneously in a blinding climax, Adara squeezing, clinging, forcing every last burst and ripple of satisfaction out of the both of them.

Finally, Warrick dropped down over her, bracing himself on his hands to either side of her head as he hovered over her.

With her husband's face planted nearly on top of hers and the last bit of pleasure fading away and fear presently not haunting her, she smiled, kissed his lips lightly, and said, *"I like you, husband."*

"And I you, wife," he whispered and brushed his lips across hers.

He lifted her and laid her gently on the bed. Lying beside her, he took her in his arms and Adara rested her head on his chest.

Was it possible? Could she have finally found a home

with this man, someone who was kind and gentle with her and cared that she suffered no pain?

She fought sleep, afraid she would wake and find it nothing more than a dream, until exhaustion took hold.

When she stretched herself awake hours later, she smiled, finding she was in the same room. It was not a dream after all. Only she was alone, her husband nowhere to be seen.

The door rushed opened and her husband entered, fully dressed, and in his hand he held a dagger.

He will kill you like he did his first wife. The words echoed in her head and Adara screamed.

"It was a nightmare, nothing more than a nightmare, and to be expected after what you have been through," Cyra consoled, having sat on the bed and taken Adara in her arms to comfort her.

Not all of it had been a nightmare and Adara's heart ached for what had been real, her wedding night with Warrick.

Adara fell asleep again and woke to whispers and, still heavy with sleep, her eyes fluttered open, her vision yet to clear. She managed to see Cyra standing there speaking to someone, a man... Innis no doubt.

Adara thought she heard Cyra say, "Espy. Only Espy."

Exhaustion forced her eyes closed and she drifted back to sleep.

Adara woke to a delicious scent of freshly baked bread and stretched herself awake, grimacing as she did, her legs and arms crying out in protest. Her hand went immediately to her rounded stomach and when she felt the bairn move, she sighed with relief.

"Worry not about him. He is safe inside you. Those muscles in your arms and legs, however, were pushed to their limit yesterday," Cyra said.

With a soft groan as she moved, Adara sat up in bed. "I slept through the entire day yesterday?"

"You did and it was what you needed."

"Has there been any word?" Adara asked, fear poking at her as to what she might hear.

"Nothing yet, but then your husband's warriors may have chosen to search for you on their own in hopes of finding you before sending word to your husband."

Adara shook her head. "They would never keep such news from Warrick."

"Come and eat and do not worry about that now. There is time for that later," Cyra urged.

Adara ate a good meal, finding herself, or perhaps it was the bairn, hungrier than she had thought. Or it could have been the pleasant conversation that she and Cyra shared. Whatever it had been, she was grateful for it.

With her garments dry, Adara dressed and slipped on her cloak to join Cyra outside while she tended her garden.

"Let me help," Adara offered, picking up a hoe.

"Your arms are sore," Cyra reminded.

"I cannot sit idle."

"Then join me. The ground needs preparing for winter."

Adara smiled and got to work freeing a patch of soil of what was left of the few plants that had been harvested.

"You do well with your injured hand," Cyra said.

Adara nodded, giving a quick glance to her crooked fingers. "It took some getting used to and some days the two fingers pain me, but I have learned to manage."

"The winter may prove a challenge for you, the cold disturbing the crooked bones. I will prepare a salve for you that may help."

"That is kind of you, Cyra,"

"I am a healer, I do what I can for those in need, but you, Adara, are like family now and I will do anything I can to help you."

Adara choked back tears. She had cried enough and tears never did her any good. "It is good to have family."

"That it is," Cyra agreed and they continued to work

together.

It was not long after that Adara stopped to stretch her back out and spotted a rider approach. The horse seemed large, even though it was in the distance, and he was traveling at a fast speed.

Adara stepped back, suddenly fearful of who it might be on such a mighty animal.

"It is Espy," Cyra said, resting a gentle hand on Adara's shoulder. "I sent word to her that you were here."

Adara smiled with relief and joy that she would see her friend and laid the hoe aside to go greet her.

Espy hugged Adara after dismounting and leaving, Trumble, her stallion to graze nearby.

"You are well?" Espy asked, wrapping her arm around Adara's and acknowledging her grandmother with a nod before walking off with the petite woman.

"And you?" Adara asked looking to Espy's rounded stomach that appeared to have grown larger since she had last seen her.

Espy grinned. "I grow bigger by the day and I have months to go yet."

Adara patted her stomach not nearly as large as Espy's yet further along than Espy. "I stay small."

"Be grateful," Espy said with a laugh, "and do not worry. Some women grow large in the last couple of months and those who remain small deliver the same, some even give birth to larger bairns than the women who round considerably."

"I worry too much," Adara confessed.

"You have had reason to."

"I have even more reason now." Adara released a sigh and along with it some of her worry. "I did something foolish."

"Tell me," Espy encouraged.

Adara told her all even the part about Warrick killing his first wife.

Espy walked over to a bench under a tree whose branches were almost devoid of leaves and sat along with Adara. "First, let me tell you that I have made more than one similar mistake."

Adara's brow scrunched in question. "What do you mean?"

"What I tell you, you must promise me you will not share."

"I promise," Adara said, pleased that Espy would trust her enough to confide a secret.

"I freed far more prisoners than only you and Hannah and from many different dungeons."

Adara's eyes showed her surprise, growing large.

"I never believed anyone should suffer torture or a brutal death, then I learned of things that people had done, horrible, dreadful things, that deserved far more than a quick, easy death. The first time I inadvertently released one such person, I was tortured for days by thoughts of what pain and suffering he would bring to others. Fortunately, he was captured before he could harm anyone and I promised myself to never let that happen again." Espy shook her head. "But it did happen again, by accident, only this time with dire circumstances. I almost stopped freeing the innocent because of it. After that, I was even more cautious, guilt heavy upon me for the two innocent people would had died."

Adara did not know what to say. Espy's courage and unselfishness had come with a tremendous burden.

"I tell you this because we can never know for sure what we do is right. We can only follow what we believe and you believed Maia was your friend and that you had to help her. You did what was right to you and in the end you did what was right for your husband and bairn... you protected them."

"It could have ended differently," Adara said, her own words of what might have been, frightening her.

"But it did not and there is no point thinking what if. It

does not help, believe me, I know. Espy squeezed Adara's hand. "As far as Warrick killing his first wife? There was talk that he had wed and that he killed his wife. But there were so many different tales about what had happened that it was difficult to know if any of it was true or simply a tale made up to frighten. Only the brave dared speak of it and few were too fearful to listen. Some say his enemies concocted the tale, others believe he released the devil that night."

Both women shivered.

"I do not know the truth and so I held my tongue, not wanting to burden you with false tales and fill you with more fear."

Adara squeezed Espy's hand this time. "I understand. You did what you thought best for me."

"Aye, and I always will. Now you will return to MacCara keep with me and wait for your husband there."

Adara shook her head. "I appreciate that, Espy, but no. I will not bring my burden down on you again. I will stay with Cyra until he comes for me." She shook her finger when Espy went to speak. "I need to do this for myself. I need to find my courage and face my husband."

"I will wait with you."

"No, Espy. You will go home. I will do this on my own."

Tears gathered in Espy's eyes and she hugged Adara tight. "You have grown strong. I am proud of you."

Adara stared speechless, shocked by the praise Espy heaped upon her.

"Do not look so surprised," Espy said with a chuckle. "The day you fled Warrick's dungeon is the day your courage began to grow."

"You gave me strength and I am forever grateful for it," Adara said and the two women hugged again.

"How about a nice hot brew before I return home?" Espy suggested and Adara nodded happy to spend more time with Espy before she took her leave.

They stood and looked to the cottage where they saw Cyra standing in the open doorway, her hand above her eyes as she stared in the distance.

Adara felt a chill of fear rush over her as she turned knowing what she might see. It was Craven with a small troop of men and she breathed a sigh of relief.

The two women waited together by the cottage while Cyra returned to her garden to work.

"What are you doing here, Adara?" Craven asked, after bringing his horse to a stop in front of the two women.

"I will explain," Espy said.

"You have much to explain, wife, riding off on your own while our bairn grows in your stomach," Craven scolded.

"I think I know what is good and not good for our bairn, husband," Espy said, summoning Trumble to her side.

Craven was quick to dismount and assist his wife to mount Trumble, but before he did, Espy took hold of his face and kissed him. "I am glad to see you, husband."

"Do not think you can use sweet words on me to avoid the tongue-lashing you deserve," Craven warned.

Espy pressed her cheek to his and whispered, "I can think of a far better thing to do with my tongue, husband."

"Then it is best we return home so you can show me." Craven could not stop a smile from surfacing as he hoisted her up on her stallion.

"I will visit soon, so we can share that brew," Espy said and Adara nodded and waved as Espy took her leave.

They had not gone far when Craven turned to his wife with a shake of his head and said, "Damn, Espy, you distracted me from getting an answer from Adara."

"I will tell all when we get home," Espy said.

"After you show me what better thing it is that you can do with your tongue," Craven said and they both grinned.

Adara wondered why Craven was shaking his head as

he looked to his wife and smiled. Whatever it was Espy would handle it well. She always did.

Adara enjoyed a pleasant meal with Cyra, having expected Innis to join them, but Cyra informed her that Innis was delayed and would not return for another day or so. She wondered over that and thought perhaps Cyra asked Innis to stay away while Adara was there. Or did she fear what may happen when Warrick came for her?

The thought had her saying, "I think I will return home tomorrow and wait for my husband's return there."

"You still ache from your walk. It is better that you wait here for him," Cyra advised.

"I do not want any harm brought down on you or Innis."

"We have done nothing. Warrick will not hurt us," Cyra said, attempting to assure her.

"Then it is your concern what he may do to me that makes you want me to remain here?" Adara asked.

"You are more perceptive than you know," Cyra said with a smile.

Adara returned the smile. "I will leave tomorrow, Cyra."

"As you wish, but you promise me you will take your time and rest now and again."

"That I can promise you."

Cyra refused to let Adara sleep on the floor, insisting she needed a comfortable and good night's sleep for her walk tomorrow.

"My old bones will not mind another night on the floor," Cyra said.

Adara gave up arguing and took the bed, falling asleep as soon as her head rested on the pillow.

A crack of thunder woke her with a start, her eyes springing open to see a man standing beside the bed, still as can be, water dripping from his hair and face, and a scowl that would frighten the devil himself.

It was Warrick.

Chapter Nineteen

"Get out of bed *now*," Warrick ordered and without looking swung his arm out to the side, pointing his finger at Cyra as she got to her feet. "Not a word from you."

"Cyra helped me," Adara said, worried for the woman, as she struggled with the covers to obey her husband.

"I do not care. She will hold her tongue," he said and stepped forward to rip the blankets off the bed.

Adara stood, a quiver to her limbs. She had thought she had seen her husband angry, but she was wrong.

Warrick grabbed hold of her wrist and yanked her against him. "You not only disobeyed me, you wronged me."

A shiver of fear ran through her along with a chill from her husband's soaked garments. "I am truly sorry."

"An apology will not suffice." He turned to Cyra. "Some of my men need tending, go see to them and do not return here until given permission." His finger shot out again when Cyra went to speak. "Not a word, woman."

The warning was clear. Cyra gathered her healing basket and her cloak from the peg and cast a gentle smile to Adara, in an effort to offer what little comfort she could to her before leaving the cottage.

Warrick released his wife's wrist with a slight shove and he turned away from her to go to the hearth. He breathed deeply, fighting to control the burning anger inside him. His fury had mounted with each pounding of his horse's hooves as he had made his way here. When he had received word that Adara was missing along with Maia, he had feared the worse. Then he learned more and everything he had been told pointed to the fact that his wife had freed the prisoner.

She had betrayed him.

Was there no woman he could trust?

He turned to face her, his anger so close to the surface, he feared he would do something he would regret. He had thought he had found a woman that he could trust, a woman he could possibly... he turned away from her again. He had been a fool to even allow the thought to enter his head that there was a chance he would find love with Adara. His father had warned him against it, pounded it into his head to never, ever let the ignorant notion of love enter his mind. It distracted and caused more problems than it was worth.

He had let his shield down and had never realized it, but no more.

Adara stared at her husband's back, her heart feeling as if it were shattering into a million pieces. The anger she had seen in her husband's dark eyes frightened her, but it was the unexpected hurt that she had seen there that tore at her heart.

Her limbs trembled as she approached him and her hand quivered as she placed it gently on his shoulder. She forced herself not to jump back when he yanked his shoulder away from her touch. She could not blame him. He was right. She had wronged him and she was not sure what to do to make it right, if she even could. But she had to try.

"I was wrong, Warrick, so very wrong for not trusting you."

He turned with a sharp snap. "You betrayed me."

A sharp jab to Adara's heart had her cringing in pain. "I did and I was wrong, though I thought I was right at the time."

"It does not matter what you thought. I gave you an order and I trusted you to obey it."

"And I should have."

"But you did not."

Adara shook her head. "There is no excuse for my foolishness that will suffice. I believed I was helping an innocent woman as Espy had helped me."

184

Warrick grabbed her arm. "Innocent or not, does not matter. You went against my word and that I will not tolerate."

Fear trembled Adara this time, for she knew all too well what punishment awaited those who went against the Demon Lord's word. Why had she not given more consideration to the consequences of her actions before she had freed Maia?

Fool. She could not remind herself often enough of it.

"You will tell me where you parted ways with Maia so that my men can go find her," he ordered sternly.

Adara explained where to find her and when she finished said, "She will be there."

Warrick shook his head and let go of her arm. "You are a fool if you believe that."

"I am a fool for believing her, but I know she will be there, for she is dead. I killed her." Adara shook her head. "She was not innocent. She was not a friend. She used me and no words will ever make up the wrong I have done to you, husband." She lowered her head. "Though, I hope you will let me try."

Her confession shocked him and thoughts of what happened between the two women for Adara to take Maia's life left him impatient to know the details. But first… he rested his hand beneath her chin and raised her head. The fear, sorrow, and tears that glistened there tore at his heart and he warned himself to step away from her or he would take her in his arms and forgive her there and then. And that was not possible. He could not forgive her. She deserved to be punished for betraying him just like anyone who betrayed him would be, and harshly.

But she was his wife and she carried his child, and she had killed the woman who had intended him harm, intended her and their bairn harm. She had defended her family.

Warrick took her in his arms, easing her tight against him, feeling her rounded stomach press into him, feeling her quiver with fear, and feeling her body heave with tears.

"I am sorry, so, so sorry, husband," she mumbled against his chest while tears rained down her cheeks. "I am a fool, such a fool."

Warrick felt like someone ripped his heart out of his chest. If anything, this was his fault. His wife was an innocent, having known little kindness, if any at all in her life, and along comes a woman who shows her some. Of course, she would think her a friend and trust her word. And was that not what bothered him the most? That she chose to trust the woman over him?

He cupped her chin, raising it so that she was forced to look up at him. "What matters at the moment is that no harm has come to you and the bairn."

Adara shuddered in his arms.

Warrick mumbled an oath and stepped away from her. "I have soaked your nightdress and chilled you with my wet garments. You need to get dry."

Her voice quivered, proving his words. "You must get dry as well." Her hands went to his plaid and began to unwrap it, but between her trembling hands and the wet wool it made it difficult.

Warrick brushed her hands away and began tugging at the plaid himself. "See to yourself."

The chill had grown worse, Adara feeling it nearly down to her bones and unable to stop from trembling as her hands struggled to remove her garment.

With his movements quick, Warrick was out of his garments and boots by the time Adara shed her nightdress. He stared at her, taking in the changes in her body from only a couple of days ago. Her breasts were larger, growing heavy with milk for their child, and her nipples slightly darker, her waist still curved at her sides, though her hips held more of a curve, and her protruding stomach was rounder. She was more beautiful than he had remembered.

Adara felt the chill melt away as her husband's eyes seemed to devour every inch of her and seeing him there naked in front of her, his manhood stirring to life just as she felt her own body stir gave her the courage to step closer to him and rising on her toes to reach up and kiss him.

He grabbed her arms, holding her still, before her lips could touch his. "Is this how you hope to redeem yourself by offering me your body when it is mine to take whenever I please?"

That he should think that upset her. That she could understand why he would think that upset her even more. She took a step away from him, his hands falling away from her, and she turned her back to him to hide the tears that rose in her eyes.

"Adara."

"Aye, husband," she said softly, fighting the tears, not wanting to cry again, but finding it difficult.

"Look at me," he commanded.

She would rather refuse, but that definitely was not an option. She blinked back the tears lingering in her eyes and hoped he would think her wet cheeks were from her previous tears as she turned around to face him, and she kept her chin up trying hard not to appear defeated.

"Why do you want to couple with me now?" he asked his dark eyes still heated with desire.

She shook her head. "I do not want to couple."

Her response almost deflated his arousal and his own response was filled with anger. "So to repent, you sacrifice yourself?"

She shook her head again and feeling she had been more foolish than she had ever been decided to continue being foolish and speak what she felt. "No, husband, I do not repent, or sacrifice myself, or want to couple with you. What I want is to make love as we did on our wedding night. I ache to share that extraordinary feeling again with you, to feel like you cherished me... to feel that you could—possibly—love me."

Shock froze Warrick, but only for a moment, then he

187

went to her, scooped her up in his arms and carried her to the bed.

He took her in his arms after pulling the blanket over them, her body chilled, though not for long. Her lips reached out to his as he brought them to her mouth, pleased she was as eager to kiss him as he was to kiss her.

He loved the taste of her. It had lingered in his heart and mind from when he had first kissed her and he simply could not get enough of her. He had been hooked from that very first time and now he could not do without her.

He jumped when her hand settled around his manhood and he recalled how much she had enjoyed touching him on their wedding night. That she continued to feel the same caused him to swell in her hand as did the way she possessively stroked him. It felt as if she laid claim to him. That no one else could have him. That he was hers and hers alone and the thought stirred something deep inside him and grew him even harder.

He pulled his mouth away from hers, resting his brow to hers. "I will not last long if you continue to touch me like that."

Her brow scrunched. "We did it more than once on our wedding night. Can we not do that now? I saw when Cyra left that it was still night. We have time,"—she paused as if hit by a sudden thought— "unless you do not wish—"

"I will always wish to make love to you," he said and slipped over her.

Make love.

Adara smiled, hearing those words and spread her legs welcoming him home.

"Wrap your legs around me," he urged, and she did. He groaned as he entered her. "Good Lord, you are so wet for me."

"I want you inside me so very badly," she whispered and raised her hips urging him deeper inside her.

He groaned again as he sank deeper and deeper, loving

the feel of her slick, tight sheath, realizing how much he had missed the feel of her, and he let her know it. "I have missed being inside you, feeling you wrap around me, squeezing me tight."

That he had missed her, thought about her, pleased her beyond belief and she let him know with a tight squeeze, and he groaned again.

He slipped his hand between their bodies to tease her little nub that already throbbed with desire and with only a couple of strokes had her groans filling the cottage.

"Warrick," she sighed, though it sounded more like she begged.

It was not long before they moved as one, building toward a climax that would shatter them both in a million shards of pleasure before bringing them back together again.

Warrick caught his wife's roar of pleasure with his lips as she climaxed beneath him and when he followed shortly afterwards, it was a clap of thunder that muffled his roar.

Warrick made sure not to remain collapsed on his wife, conscious of the bairn growing inside her. He rolled off her onto his side and wanting her as close as he could get her, lifted her to lay against him. He was more than pleased when she draped her arm over his waist, her leg over his, and rested her head on his chest, snuggling ever closer around him.

She was where she belonged, would always belong... in his arms.

"Is morning far off?" she asked when her breathing calmed.

"A few hours."

She looked up at him. "Good we have time to make love once or twice more." Was that a smile she saw? She could not be sure, the fire the only light in the room.

"You cannot get enough of me, wife?" he asked, having failed to catch the smile that rushed to his mouth, though he stifled it soon after. He could not let that happen again. It was enough his petite, wisp of a wife had blasted past the shield to his heart and firmly ensconced herself there.

"I fear I will never get enough of you husband, but it is one fear I do not mind having." She rested her head on his chest again only this time she positioned it so she could look at him as they spoke, hoping to catch him smile.

"You have more courage than fear, Adara, or you would have never released Maia."

"That was foolishness not courage."

"Courage and foolishness often go hand in hand. Tell me what happened."

With every word, from taking the food and the knife from the kitchen to cutting the woman free, guilt weighed more heavily on Adara.

"My warriors will be changing the way they patrol," Warrick said annoyed they had failed to catch his wife, but admiring her strategy.

"It was when we stopped to rest and she had continued to tell me how evil you were that I realized the mistake I had made."

"You do not think me evil?" he asked, wondering how she could think any other way.

"No, I do not think you are evil," she said, running her finger along his cheek and over his lips, and smiled. "Tenacious and confident definitely. Impatient and demanding, absolutely. Kind and caring, I believe so."

There it was again, the lifting at the corners of his mouth, even more so this time than the last… an almost smile. She said nothing about it, but she was determined to see a wide smile light his face.

Warrick had to catch another smile and it annoyed him, more so that the smiles were trying to escape more frequently and the Demon Lord simply did not smile.

"Did she admit she killed Jaynce?" he asked, forcing his wife to continue explaining.

"That was the odd thing. She claimed she did not kill

her, but she admitted someone else in her group did."

"Group?"

Adara nodded. "That was what she said—group—and that I was to join them and tell them all I knew about the devil, though once she saw I carried your child everything changed."

Warrick hugged her closer, feeling the shiver that raced through her and tucked the blanket more tightly around them.

"She accused me of carrying the devil's spawn and if she had known my fate, she would have killed me when she had first met me. She also told me that she would make my death swift since I made her time here bearable." She blinked back a tear. "She intended to cut our bairn out of me in hopes it was a son and you would know she took his life."

Rage rose up in Warrick and he wished he had been the one to kill the woman, for having put his wife through such torment.

"How did you manage to take her life?" he asked, wanting to make sure the woman was dead and would no longer be of any harm to his family.

"I remembered what Espy had told me about fear, to never let fear freeze me, to do what I had to do to survive, her words to me before she freed me from your dungeon. The words that helped me survive my journey here."

"It would seem I owe Espy much."

"I can say with confidence and not a bit of foolishness that Espy is a good friend."

"That we agree on," he said. "Now tell anything else Maia may have said that might help me discover why she attempted to kill me and my family."

Adara wrinkled her brow. "There were a few things she told me that did not quite make sense. She told me that it was not only that I carried your bairn that I needed to die, but because of all the stories she told me." She shook her head slowly. "She also did not understand why I never questioned being moved from family to family so often. I do not know why she would say that. I simply was not wanted."

Her words stabbed at his heart. He imagined her a small bairn settled in with a family she thought loved her only to be uprooted and given to another family who did the same thing to her. Until finally, she came to believe no one wanted her.

He wanted her and he intended to keep her... forever.

He did give pause to Maia's words and it caused him to worry. If Adara had been moved from family to family often, then there might be a reason for it. The one reason that seemed the most likely would be that someone was attempting to keep her hidden, but why? If so, could that mean she was in danger?

Adara yawned and stretched her body against his.

"You need to sleep. We leave shortly after first light. I need to return to the two clans that are far too close to warring."

Adara had forgotten about that and felt even more guilt for what she had done. "Your warriors can escort me home if you need to leave."

"No," he said with a resounding finality. "I will see you safely home where you will stay put."

"I know my word probably does not mean much to you now, but I will do as you say."

"I believe you will," Warrick said and was pleased to see Adara smile and shocked when she slipped her body over his.

"If you are to leave me for a few days, then I think you should see me well satisfied."

Warrick almost smiled again, but caught himself, especially when his wife wiggled herself over him, teasing his manhood to life, not that it took much for him to grow hard. He wondered where the timid, fearful woman he had wed had gone to, but then she had not been timid on their wedding night, a bit hesitant at first but not as the night went on. She had seemed eager and it had led him to believe that she was no virgin, though he thought he had felt a bit of resistance at one point after entering her, but she had thrust her hips up and the barrier he thought he felt had disappeared. The blood on the sheets the next morning confirmed what he had suspected. She had been a virgin.

As much as he would have loved for her to ride him, he could see that fatigue haunted her and by the way she tried not to wince when she moved her arms or stretched her legs, he would guess her muscles were sore from her fight with Maia and the walk here.

He reached out, his hand going to her waist, and lifted her off him in one easy swoop and placed her beneath him on the bed, then slipped over her.

"This will be a quick one, *mo ghaol,* though I would prefer otherwise. You need rest."

My love. He called her my love. No one had ever mentioned the word love to her, not ever.

She threw her arms around his neck and kissed him from the depths of her heart. It was enough to set them both on fire and it was quick as Warrick said it would be, but not because she needed rest, but because they both grew far too excited to make it last any length of time.

~~~

"Time to get up, wife," Warrick said.

Adara mumbled and turned to snuggle next to her husband's warm body only to find he was not there in bed with her. She sat up abruptly and was disappointed to see him standing near the fireplace almost fully dressed.

"I need to get the men ready to leave and you need to dress and eat before we go. I will send Cyra to help you."

"You snuck out of bed."

The disappointment on her face touched his heart. She wanted him there beside her and that made a world of difference to Warrick.

"I did. If I had not done so we would be late taking our leave this morning."

Adara was about to agree with him when her stomach roiled terribly and her face turned ghostly white. She jumped out of bed and headed for the bucket Cyra kept in the corner.

Warrick saw her need and hurried to fetch it for her, forcing her with a slight yank of her arm to sit on the chair, and held the bucket in front of her. There was nothing in her stomach to discard and she dry heaved.

When she finished, Warrick soaked a cloth in a bucket of water and hunched down in front of her to wipe her face, his own stomach knotting and roiling for what she had gone through.

"I thought this had past," he said, her face far too pale to his liking.

"It comes and goes. I have spoken to Cyra and she tells me the same as Espy. It may stay with me the whole time or suddenly disappear. I hope it suddenly disappears. Cyra did give me a brew that helped some."

"I will go fetch her so she can prepare it for you." He went to stand and she reached out to grab his arm. He hunched down again. "You are feeling ill again?"

She shook her head. "I want you to help me into my nightdress. I do not want to be sitting here naked when Cyra enters."

"I like you as you are, but then your naked body is for my eyes alone," he said and kissed her cheek before standing and fetching her nightdress and helping her into it. He kissed her check again before he went to the door.

"Warrick," she said and he stopped and turned, worry on his face that she might be ill again. But she had worry of her own. "Fear has already started to grow in me and will worsen if I must wait to be told my punishment for disobeying you. Please tell me now, what I must suffer, and rightfully so, then fear will not haunt me endlessly." At least she hoped it would not, but then that would depend on the punishment.

Warrick stared at her, saying not a word. She wondered if he had yet to decide her punishment, though she hoped otherwise. She needed to know so that she could prepare herself, though she wondered if she already knew it. He had told all in the village that if anyone helped Maia they would join her on the other stake.

His silence fell heavy around her and she wished he would speak.

Warrick turned and opened the door and Adara thought he would leave without telling her, then he turned back, his dark eyes settling on her blue ones.

"You have suffered enough in my dungeon and now carrying my bairn, I will see you suffer no more. But make no mistake, Adara, I will not feel the same if you betray me again."

He walked out of the cottage and stood outside, staring in the distance. He had rules for all that were meant to be obeyed. His wife had deserved to be punished, but every time he felt the scars his guards had left upon her soft flesh or felt her crooked fingers brush over him, he was reminded of all she had wrongly suffered. And he could not bring himself to make her suffer even more. She was naïve in many ways and such innocence brought with it mistakes. He had promised her he would keep her safe and that even meant keeping her safe from herself.

One of his warriors approached him.

"The search has begun," the warrior said.

Warrick nodded and the warrior took his leave. He had seen on Adara's face, heard in her quivering voice that she barely could believe that she had killed Maia.

The problem… no body had been found.

Chapter Twenty

"Do you believe me?" Adara asked shocked to learn that Maia's body had not been found. How could that be? She did not understand. She had thought the woman dead. While the news surprised her what disturbed her the most was that Warrick might not believe her. "I speak the truth."

"No blood. No sign of an altercation was found," Warrick said.

"I do not understand." Adara shook her head. "How could that be?"

"Two explanations. Her friends found her and took her, leaving nothing behind to show they had been there or you freed her to go her way and told a tale to protect yourself." He felt her sink with a tremble against him and he closed his strong arms tighter around her as he directed his horse toward home.

Adara fell silent as she had done through the years when accused of a falsehood. She had learned it had mattered little to plead her innocence, people believed what they wanted to believe. But this was her husband and it mattered to her what he believed. Silence would do her no good this time.

She looked into his dark eyes. "I admit I am a fool for what I did, but I am no liar, Warrick."

A tremble continued to run through her, but it was one born of the courage it had taken her to defend herself, and he was pleased that she had chosen strength over fear.

"I agree, wife, you can be foolish, but you are no liar," Warrick said.

His response brought a smile of relief to her face and eased her quiver.

"I believe her cohorts were probably on your trail and came across her and since they took her body, it leads me to believe she may still have been alive."

Adara shook her head again. "She was bleeding from her mouth, the knife was deep in her chest, she could barely speak." She continued shaking her head.

"It was good you did not wait to make sure she was dead. You would have been caught and it would be your body discovered there."

A shudder ran through Adara and she cuddled closer against her husband.

"Sometimes wounds appear worse than they are and some that appear minor turn deadly. Maia may be alive or she may not be, but we do know that there is a group of people out to see us harm and I expect you to pay heed to that warning, take no chances, and obey my word." When he was met with silence from Adara, he said, "You need to think on that?"

"What if—"

"There are no what ifs, wife."

Adara hurried to speak before he could stop her. "What if you are in need of help?"

"You think to come to my rescue?" His tone not only betrayed his shock, but so did his wide eyes.

"Of course, you are my husband."

She was doing what she felt would be her duty, nothing more. Why did he want more from her?

"I need no rescue, no protecting. You will not put yourself in harm's way for me," he ordered.

Adara could not hold her words back. "I cannot give my word on that."

Warrick looked ready to unleash his anger on her when one of his warriors approached.

"A message from Roark."

Warrick nodded for the warrior to continue.

"You are needed immediately. It cannot wait."

"Send Benet to me," Warrick ordered and when the warrior rode off, he looked to his wife. "My warriors will see you home safely. You are gaining courage, wife, use it wisely." He kissed her gently. Then motioned to nearby warriors.

Everything happened so fast, Adara barely had a chance to kiss her husband's cheek and whisper, "Stay safe, husband." Before she found herself lifted off his horse and placed on a horse with one of Warrick's older warriors.

"My wife is in your care, Benet, see her home safe," Warrick ordered.

"You have no worries my lord, my lady will be safe," Benet assured him.

Adara did not get a chance to watch her husband ride off. Benet turned away from Warrick and rode off with ten of Warrick's warriors following along with them. As the distance grew between her and her husband, so did the ache in her heart. She missed him already.

~~~

Six days. It had been six days since Adara returned to MacVarish keep and six days since Warrick had been gone. He sent word through a messenger, letting her know that his return home would be delayed. He offered no explanation, but she assumed the matter between the two clans was what kept him. Each day she had gone outside and stood in the front of the keep and looked to the distance, hoping to see him leading his warriors home.

She had continued to miss him. How much she missed him stunned her. There seemed to be this ache in her that she simply could not console. Somehow Warrick had become a part of her and she felt a piece of herself missing since he was not there. His absence had her giving thought to the prospect that she had lost her heart to him and was falling in love with him. But how could she know for sure when love was so foreign to her?

She shook her head at her jumbled thoughts. If love was this confusing, how could anyone know if they were truly in love? There was only one thing left for her to do. She would surrender her misgivings to her heart and fate, and leave it in their hands.

Warrick had made no mention of her staying put before he left and she had not expected him to. He was not a man to repeat his warnings and she was not foolish enough to make the same mistake again. Though, she had noticed that wherever she went a guard seemed to be in close proximity. At first, she had worried that he did not trust her and that would be her own fault for what she had done. However, the more thought she had given it the more she had realized he was protecting her should Maia and her crew attempt to harm her.

The only order he had left her with was for her to think on her time with Maia and see what stories she could recall. She had pulled as many as she could from memory and thought on them, eager to share them with her husband upon his return.

She also had found her thoughts occupied with what Maia had said about Adara's frequent moves. She still could not fathom what the woman had tried to imply. No one wanted her, so she was given to someone else. She remembered crying when she had first been given to another family. And Aubrey did as well, the young lass she had believed was her sister. To find out she had not been, that she had had no family, hurt even now after all this time. Having thought it had been something she had done that had caused her to be given away, she had worked extra hard at the next home. But it had never been a home and she had not been there long. So she had gone from place to place, no one wanting her.

She smiled and placed her hand on her stomach. Now she had a home and soon a family.

He killed his first wife.

A shiver ran through her and her smile faded. She did not want to believe Maia or the tales, but she also did not want to be foolish. Somehow she could not fathom Warrick doing such a thing. Though, what if he had? Could there be good reason for it? She wanted to find out what she could about Warrick's wife's death. But if no one spoke of it as Espy had said, then how could she learn anything about it? She debated asking Warrick, but fear held her tongue. Whether it was fear of what she would learn or how he would react, she was not certain, but it was enough for her to say nothing.

Something did happen during Warrick's absence that she had not expected. She found that solitude did not hold the appeal it once did. She preferred being with others, talking with them, learning more things about the running of the keep, and even digging in the kitchen garden's soil and discussing future plantings with Emona the cook.

She had discovered that being with others, two or three people at the most, kept her fear at a distance. Any more would trigger her fear, not that it still did not rush over her unexpectedly at times, but somehow she had gained the courage to force it to retreat.

Her growing ease had an added benefit. The clan greeted her with more smiles and the women stopped to speak with her, ask her how she was feeling and how the bairn was doing. And they shared encouraging stories of delivering their own bairns.

She had been pleased when Langdon once again joined her on her walks through the village, just before dusk. He shared funny stories of when he was young and a hardy lad and often had her laughing. She found herself sharing a few stories of her own and he brought tears to her eyes when after learning of her rock collection being taken away from her, he gave her a rock with a design, given by nature, on it one day. They were not easy to find and that he had purposely searched for it for her had warmed her heart. She had hugged him and it had brought tears to his eyes.

For the first time since her arrival here, she felt it truly was her home, that she truly had a family, and she was more determined than ever to see to her duties and well-being of the clan.

A strong chill in the air made it feel more like winter than autumn and with that chill holding the last few days, Adara had made sure to take stock of the food supplies. She had been happy to see how well Emona had stocked the keep for the coming winter. The storage sheds also overflowed with salted and dried meats as well as various root plants.

She smiled on her way back to the keep. With the sheds and the keep stocked so well, it could mean only one thing… Warrick planned on remaining here throughout the winter. She was glad of that, since she would have no other but Espy deliver her bairn.

Adara went straight to the fire burning in the large fireplace, in the Great Hall, to warm herself, holding her hands out to the heat before rubbing them together.

Warrick would warm her.

Memories of their night at Cyra's brought heat to her cheeks. That was the other thing she missed, making love with her husband. Truth be told, she wondered if she liked it more than she should. What was it that Maia had said to her one day? She did not recall the manner in how the subject had come up only the words that had stuck with her.

Do not be prudish with your husband in bed. Enjoy it as much as he does and you will know pleasure. The women of my birth home are just as strong as the men.

She had not been prudish with Warrick, to her astonishment. She had allowed herself to enjoy him and she had known indescribable pleasure. One thing Maia had been right about.

Adara dropped her arms to her sides and stared at the flames as if they had suddenly revealed something to her as

Maia's words repeated in her head.

The women of my birth home.

Scotland was not Maia's native home. Where had she been born?

Adara tucked the information away, reminding herself to tell Warrick about it.

"A hot brew to warm you, my lady."

Adara jumped with a start, her hand going to her chest as she turned to Wynn.

"Forgive me, my lady. I did not mean to startle you," Wynn said.

"Busy thoughts keep my mind far too occupied," Adara said and gratefully accepted the tankard Wynn handed to her.

"Your mum was often lost in her thoughts."

"You knew my mum?" Adara asked, wondering why this was the first she had heard of it. But would it have been different had she not kept so much to herself? She had barely spoken to anyone upon her arrival here and she certainly had not encouraged anyone to speak with her. And look what locking herself away had done to her.

A sadness filled Wynn's aged eyes. "Your mum spent three weeks here before taking her leave."

"I did not know that. Uncle Owen made no mention of the length of her stay here."

"Your uncle did everything he could to discourage her from taking you to the wilds of the far north. He believed it no place for a young bairn, which was why he begged your mum to leave you with him. At least until she got settled and could see for herself you would be safe." Wynn gave a slight shake of her head. "Your mum would not be parted from you. She was courageous and fierce in protecting you."

Like I am with my bairn, Adara thought, her hand patting her stomach.

"Uncle Owen spoke about my mum, his sister, who he loved dearly, but he did not say much about my da. Can you tell me anything about him?" Adara asked, curious about the father she had never met.

"He was a quiet man, a crofter, and protective of your mum."

"Why would a crofter go so far north in the Highlands?" Adara asked, like her uncle Owen, she never truly understood why her parents had chosen to settle there. A crofter would know it was not good farming land and there was an emptiness to the area that only the hardy could endure. She also could not help but wonder how different life would have been if her parents had not made that choice.

"I would not know, my lady," Wynn said, "but it is good you have come home and have a husband who will look after you as your da did with your mum. I will get you more brew." She turned and walked off.

Adara wondered over her rushed words and her hasty departure. It was as if she was reluctant to discuss it any further. She gave a slight shake of her head. Why had she never considered that the servants would know more about her mum and da, then her uncle Owen did? She knew from experience that most believed servants had no ears or eyes and certainly no tongue, but often they knew more about the family than the family itself. Adara had a feeling that Wynn might know more than she was saying.

Her suspicions were confirmed when a servant returned with the brew and not Wynn. Did Wynn think Adara would ask more questions about her parents and so she avoided returning to the Great Hall? Why, though, would Wynn be reluctant to speak about Adara's parents?

Could Wynn know a secret about her parents?

She would discuss this with Warrick when he returned. Or should she? Warrick would demand Wynn tell him all she knew of Adara's parents. What if Adara was wrong as she had been with Maia? Her suspicions could cause Wynn harm. She would hold her tongue on this until she learned more.

The bairn moved inside her and she smiled as she patted

her stomach. "We have not walked enough?" As if he heard her, he moved again. "We will go see how the kitchen garden comes along, then we rest." The bairn moved again as if agreeing and Adara laughed softly.

~~~

Another week passed and Adara was beginning to wonder if Warrick would ever return. In that time, she had questioned Wynn now and again about her mum. Simple questions, ones that would not frighten her off. What color eyes did her mum have? Was she petite like me?

Those questions were always answered with a smile. "You are a mirror image of your mum. One look and your uncle Owen knew you were his sister's daughter."

Wynn was, however, brief in her response when Adara asked, "Was my mum fearful like me?"

"We all fear something."

If that was so, what had her mum feared and why?

Adara kept herself busy and made a point of talking to people. She was pleasantly surprised to know that the clan did think well of her and was concerned for her well-being. The one question she was repeatedly asked was if Warrick would take up permanent residence here at MacVarish keep. She was honest with them and told them she did not know, that he had made no mention of it. The question itself always raised fear in her. The thought of returning to Warrick's castle and the dungeons beneath where she had suffered frightened her beyond belief. She would much rather remain at MacVarish keep and close to her friend Espy.

"My lady."

Adara turned to see Langdon approach her. He was smiling and held something in his hand.

"Burchard and I found this while we cleared the earth to extend the kitchen garden as you requested." He held a stone out to her.

Adara took it. It was a triangle shape, cleaned of all dirt and imprinted on it was what looked like an insect of sorts. "This is wonderful, Langdon. I am going to have to dig with you and Burchard one day."

"We can dig. You can watch, my lady."

"I will not be deprived of the fun of finding more stones to add to the two you have generously found for me," she said with a smile.

"It is fun. I find myself looking more closely at stones now, in hopes of finding ones with designs on them."

"Then I will join you in the hunt," Adara said with a sense of excitement.

"As you wish, my lady," Langdon said with a nod. "A sharp chill fills the air. You should seek the warmth of the keep."

"My thoughts exactly and thank you for the gift," she said and tucked it in the cuff of her sleeve for safe keeping. She gave Langdon a smile and a wave as they parted ways and she kept a tempered pace to the keep.

She was not alarmed when the bell tolled once, announcing an expected arrival. She had learned from wagging tongues that a troop from one of the warring clans would arrive here and camp on the outskirts of the village. Why they did so, no one knew, but all assumed it had something to do with an agreement between the two opposing clans.

She stopped and watched their slow approach, Warrick's men keeping close watch on them. The air having chilled considerably and tired from a busy day, Adara continued her pace to the keep, intending to rest when suddenly a battle cry ripped through the air.

The clan was under attack.

Chapter Twenty-one

Warrick's men were quick to defend against the marauding warriors, but it grew more difficult when another troop came pouring out of the woods on horse and headed for the village. They entered with force, some of them letting loose with their arrows as they did, taking down some of Warrick's men.

The MacVarish clan were quick to take up arms in defense. Women gathered the children and Adara went to help them. Two of Warrick's warriors rushed at Adara insisting she get to the safety of the keep.

She refused, wanting to help get the children to safety along with her. There was no time to argue with her. The two warriors helped herd the children along with a few of the mums while the other mums went to take up arms alongside their husbands.

The children ran quickly, running ahead of Adara to her relief. The two warriors remained by Adara, their task… to keep her safe. It was not long before one fell from an arrow to his leg while the other rushed behind Adara to shield her, urging her to run and not look back, to get to the keep.

She hoisted her garments, so the hems would not trip her, and ran so hard and fast she thought her increasingly pounding heartbeat would burst from her chest. The children were at the steps and she needed to get there and see them and her unborn bairn kept safe.

It was not long before she heard the warrior drop behind her, but she did not stop, she kept running. She caught flashes of dark shrouds as other warriors took their place doing their best to protect her, but it was up to her to get to the keep no matter what, and she kept running.

She cursed the rain that had fallen last night, the path to the keep heavy with mud in spots and she tried to avoid them, not wanting her feet to get mired in mud or for it to slow her down.

She was not far from the keep. Soon, very soon, she would reach the steps.

The sound of horses' hooves grew ever closer and she was terrified that at any moment an arrow would take her down. Two more of Warrick's men were suddenly behind her, keeping close on her footsteps. It was not long before both were hit, but this time when they went down, one fell into her, knocking her off her feet.

Instinct had her turning as she fell, so the bairn would not suffer the impact of the fall and she hit the ground with a hard bounce to her back. The rider was nearly on top of her and his bow was raised, an arrow ready to fly when one of Warrick's warriors launched himself at the man, knocking him off the horse and tumbling to the ground with him. The horse raised his hooves in protest and Adara rolled to avoid him, but his one hoof glanced the edge of her hand.

Pain shot up her arm and she wasted no time in scrambling to her feet. She was suddenly hoisted up off the ground, rushed into the keep, and deposited on a bench.

"Stay here, we will not let them breech the keep doors," the warrior said, "though it would not hurt to barricade the doors."

"Your name?" Adara asked as he turned to leave.

"Gavin, my lady."

"I know a warrior has probably already been sent to alert Warrick of the attack, but also send word to MacCara keep. It is closer and Craven will bring his warriors."

The young warrior smiled. "You think like Lord Warrick, my lady. His orders were the same if it should ever prove necessary. Word should have reached Lord Craven by now." He gave her a respectful nod and hurried off.

Wynn was at her side along with another servant while

the remaining servants helped the mums settle the children. Both women gasped when they looked upon her hand.

Adara feared what she would see, pain radiating up her arm. She winced when she glanced at it. Her two crooked fingers and down along her hand to her wrist was swelling and bruising before her eyes, and she feared her two crooked fingers had suffered even more damage.

Adara did the only thing she could think of, she ordered them not to touch her injury. Espy would come with Craven or follow quickly behind him if he refused to bring her. She would wait and trust Espy to tend it.

She quickly instructed the servants to do as Gavin had suggested and barricade the doors in the Great Hall and sent a servant to have the cook barricade the kitchen doors there as well. She had confidence that Warrick's warriors would be victorious, but it was wise not to take any chances. The servants, mums, and children were only too eager to do so and tables were pushed against the door and benches piled on top.

Adara sat with her right arm cradled in her left, the pain not as intense as it had been, though the bruising had grown worse.

Clashing swords could be heard outside along with screams of the injured and dying.

The children clung tightly to each other, the smaller ones gripping the mums' legs, some hiding beneath their tunics. It seemed like forever before a heavy pounding sounded at the doors and eyes, wide with fright, looked to Adara.

She did not hesitate, she got up and went to the door.

"Adara!"

Her legs grew weak with relief, recognizing the voice. "Craven!" she called out, then summoned everyone to move the barricade.

Craven and a few of Warrick's warriors entered the Great Hall.

"You are injured," Craven said as soon as he saw her hand. He looked to Gavin. "Go fetch my wife."

Adara silently thanked the heavens and her relief must have shown on her face.

"Did you think I would be able to keep Espy away?" Craven said with a shake of his head.

"How many will be in need of her skill? And how many will need burial?" Adara asked, worried for her clan and Warrick's warriors.

"Warrick's warriors are well trained in tending their own wounds as well of each other's wounds, though my wife will see if she approves of their skills. They are also trained to protect any and all belonging to Warrick. No one in your clan died. Some were injured but not badly. Warrick's warriors suffered many injuries and four of his warriors lost their lives, far less than the enemy did. God help those who attacked here today, for he will rain hell down on them."

Espy came rushing into the Great Hall as Adara gave orders for the children to be fed and looked after so the mums could go and see to their husbands. Only after the carnage was cleared would the children return home. Craven was quick to take his leave to assist Warrick's warriors in getting all done as soon as possible.

"This may be a bit painful," Espy said, probing Adara's injured hand after giving her a hug, relieved she had not been badly harmed.

Espy's touch was not as painful as she thought it would be, though Adara grimaced now and again.

"To my great relief, I do not believe any bones are broken," Espy said.

"The hoof barely glanced the edge of my hand."

"The blow bruised the flesh, but caught no bone. It will be tender and take weeks to heal. I will fashion a sling for you so that you may rest it. I will also show Wynn how to make a comfrey poultice to help with the bruising and healing."

"I know how to make a comfrey poultice," Wynn said, having remained close to Adara.

"That is wonderful, Wynn. You can make it now," Espy said.

"No," Adara said, "I want to go outside and see to my clan and Warrick's warriors."

"You need to rest this hand. There is nothing you can do for them," Espy cautioned.

"I can be there for them. Show them I care. Show them I am not hiding away in fear," Adara said.

"Aye, you can do that," Espy said, "but first let me fashion a sling so that your hand can rest and begin to heal."

"Send word, when my lady is near done and I will have the poultice ready," Wynn said, a tear in her eye as she looked upon Adara with pride.

Adara issued more orders, instructing the cook to see that food was provided for the clan and the warriors and left on the table for any who wandered into the Great Hall looking for sustenance.

It was not long after Adara's arm was placed in a sling that she and Espy left the keep and walked through the village, stopping to help those in need. Adara was amazed that there was less of a carnage than she had expected. The bodies of the fallen foe had been removed and those too badly injured to escape on their own had been left behind and were being tended by Warrick's warriors.

Adara may not have been able to give Espy a helping hand with the injured, but she lifted spirits with words of encouragement and praise for a victorious battle to both the clan and Warrick's warriors.

Adara also insisted on remaining with one of Warrick's warriors while Espy bandaged a gash in his leg. The young warrior, Brock, feared he would be left with a limp and not be able to continue as one of Warrick's warriors.

Adara leaned down and whispered near his ear. "Warrick would never desert one of his warriors who served him with honor as you have done."

Brock kept his voice to a whisper. "Please, my lady, do not tell anyone I allowed myself to fear."

Adara reiterated Wynn's words, but added a thought of her own along with them. "We all fear something, sometime, but it is whether we let that fear stop us that makes the difference."

Brock smiled gently. "I am grateful to you, my lady. You suffered a wound yourself and yet you tend others with your kind and encouraging words."

Adara acknowledged something then that had been growing ever stronger in her. "We are family, Brock. I will always tend my family."

It was night by the time Adara returned to the keep, exhausted, hungry, and her hand aching, Espy joining her against her wishes.

"I do not care, wife," Craven said. "You have done enough for the night. No one needs you now. You will eat and rest and tend to yourself." When Espy went to protest, Craven pressed his finger to her lips. "You would advise a woman in your condition to do the same."

Espy sighed. "You are right."

"Adara, you heard that, my wife says I am right," Craven said with a chuckle.

Adara laughed and looked on with envy as Craven smiled and took his wife in his large arms, Espy resting her head on his chest.

She was glad when Wynn appeared and diverted her attention, placing the comfrey poultice on her hand. It was not on her hand long when the Great Hall door burst open and in stormed Warrick.

Chapter Twenty-two

Silence reigned as all looked upon Warrick's dark eyes filled with such rage that many took quick steps back, though they were a distance away from him. His hands were fisted at his sides, his knuckles white, as if he was ready to deliver a deadly blow. His muscled chest heaved with a laborious breath and made one wonder if he had not already used his powerful fists on someone.

Adara saw none of that. She saw only her husband, the man whose arms she longed to be in.

She jumped up off the bench, the poultice falling off her injured hand, and ran to him.

Warrick caught her around the waist with his one arm, his eyes darkening even more when he caught sight of her bruised hand, she kept rested against her chest. He lowered his head as she stretched up on her toes to give his lips a quick kiss and her whispered words that followed shocked him, though he let no one see it.

"I have missed you so very much, husband."

Her heartfelt words wrapped around him and squeezed his heart and his worry had him saying, "You are injured. And the bairn?"

She was pleased to hear concern in his voice and see that he was unable to keep it from his eyes. "The bairn is safe and I suffered no more than a bruise that will heal. Unlike others who suffered far worse."

"My warriors did what they were trained to do and I in turn will see those responsible suffer for it." His voice lowered to a whisper. "Know that I have missed you too, wife, and as soon as I can I will show you just how much."

Happiness hugged Adara while desire tickled at her.

This had to be love she felt for her husband and the concern in his eyes at least let her know he cared for her.

Warrick ushered her over to the table where Espy and Craven sat, Craven standing at his approach.

Adara missed her husband's arm as soon as he released her to sit. She had been too long without his touch, without the feel of his strong hand in hers, and the strength of him wrapped around her.

Wynn returned the poultice to her injured hand and as she listened to her husband speak to Craven, fear creeped up to jab at her.

"I need your help. I need the Beast," Warrick said. "False words were given to me as a ruse to carry out this attack. How the fool ever thought to win against me, I do not know. But he will learn not only what his lies have cost him, but what happens when you attack my home."

"Whatever you need, Warrick," Craven said.

"We leave now. Slain is on his way to join us."

"I will gather my men," Craven said and turned to take his wife in his arms.

Warrick turned to Adara, leaning down over her.

"You will stay safe, husband," she said, feeling as if her heart was being torn from her chest. She did not want him to go. He had been gone far too long from her and what if he did not return? Fear crept up to poke at her.

"Heaven does not want me and either does the devil."

Adara rested her hand on his cheek. "I want you, husband, and that is all that matters."

"You are all that matters," he whispered and his kissed proved it.

She stared after him as he left the Great Hall, Craven walking alongside him and she prayed that both men returned safe and unharmed.

~~~

After Warrick and Craven had been gone three days,

213

Espy took her leave.

"I would not leave if this birth was not a difficult one, but Edrea has lost two bairns in childbirth years ago and when no bairns followed for many years she thought herself cursed or barren. This bairn is a miracle to her and her husband. I must be there to make sure all goes well."

"You are needed. You must go. I am good and all is well here," Adara said, not at all upset with her friend's necessary departure.

Espy took hold of Adara's uninjured hand. "I see good changes in you. Your fear has subsided and I am happy for you."

"In some ways I have changed, and though my fears still linger, I fight them. I never did that before. Never thought I had the strength to do it. You showed me that I did."

Espy smiled. "I gave you a taste of your strength. You are the one who drank fully of it."

The two women hugged and parted with promises of visiting soon and assurances that it would not be long before their husbands returned home.

Six of Warrick's warriors escorted Espy home and Adara went to keep herself busy and keep fear at bay.

She made a point of visiting those wounded in the attack, seeing if they needed anything and sitting and talking with those who were confined to bed. It was no chore to her. She actually looked forward to it each day. It helped greatly talking with Warrick's warriors. She was less fearful when she saw them in their black shrouds pulled down low over their faces.

Evening snuck up on her and she was glad for the day passing quickly. She took the evening meal alone in her room, not purposely avoiding those who supped in the Great Hall but unable to resist the urge for some time alone. She wondered if it was from years of spending more time alone than with others. She also wondered if Warrick were here would she feel the same.

She gave herself a quick wash, a difficult task with her injured hand, but she refused help from Wynn or any of the servants. She did not want them to see her scars. She knew they would talk, and talk spread, and her scars were personal, not for others to see and discuss.

She tried to hurry into her nightdress, the room holding a chill even with a strong fire burning in the hearth. Unfortunately, she got tangled in her nightdress, her injured hand paining her more today than usual and she got so frustrated, with her one good hand, she ripped the nightdress off from around her neck and one shoulder and tossed it to the ground.

The door swung open and Adara froze fearful of who would see her.

Warrick stood in the doorway, smudges of dirt and dried blood on his clothes, blood staining his knuckles and spots of grime on his handsome face. He had come straight from battle to her and the urgency on his face had her rushing forward in fear.

"Is everything all right? Is Craven—" She turned her head for a moment, fear and sorrow for Espy tightening her throat. When she turned to him again, she saw that her fright had seen it all wrong. He had rushed from the battlefield for one thing… her.

His chest heaved more rapidly than when he had first entered and his eyes sparked with passion. He wanted her with an urgency she had never seen before.

Adara reached out to touch him and he startled her when he backed away.

"Do not touch me," he warned.

She shook her head, not understanding and took a step toward him.

"I am warning you, Adara, if you touch me now—" A growl rumbled deep in his chest.

"But you came to me," she said confused.

"Too soon. Too soon from battle." He turned to go, turned so he would no longer see her body, slim, petit, and with a swell to her stomach, their child nestled safely there, and the soft triangle of blonde hair between her legs where he desperately ached to be. But it was too soon after battle, he would not be gentle, did not want to be gentle. He wanted to throw her down on the bed and plunge into her over and over and over.

He forced himself to step out of the room and it took all his willpower to walk to the stairs.

"I missed you, husband," he heard her say and he thought his rock-hard manhood would explode. He shut his eyes for a moment then forced himself to take step after step down the stairs. He would not treat her so wickedly. She was his wife. She deserved respect.

It had always been easy to assuage his need after battle. There were more than enough willing women in the camp who would spread their legs for him and his warriors. But his wedding night had changed everything. To his surprise, he found more pleasure with her than he ever had with any woman. Since that night he had thought of no other woman, wanted no other woman but his wife.

He stopped on the stairs, fisting his hands at his sides. Good Lord, but he ached for her. Had the whole ride here and when he swung the door open to their bedchamber and saw her standing there naked, he almost rushed at her so anxious was he to be inside her.

A glance at her injured hand and the swell of her belly reminded him he could not treat her like that. He could not. It would not be right.

I missed you, husband.

Her words rang in his head and in his heart. She missed him as much as he missed her. And had he not seen a want for him in her dark blue eyes, a want as strong as his?

I missed you, husband.

"No!" he commanded himself and went to resume his

steps down to the Great Hall where he would drink until he passed out, making sure he did not disturb her tonight.

I missed you, husband.

Her words were like a sea siren's call and he fought against them. But there was a demon inside him and when he made himself known there was no stopping him. The Demon never wavered, never tired in battle, and always took what he wanted. And he wanted…

He turned and vaulted up the stairs, a rumbling growl in his chest growing ever stronger. He burst into the room, went straight to his wife, fumbling with her nightdress, ripped it out of her hand, threw it aside, scooped her up, carried her to the bed to drop her bottom down on the edge, grabbed her legs and placed them over his shoulder, lifted his plaid and with one hard thrust entered her.

Adara's gasp filled the room, but it was not one of alarm, it was one of relief and pleasure. She had been devastated when she had told him she missed him and he had left her, walked away as if it mattered not to him. She almost followed him, then realized she was naked and tried once again to slip on her nightdress to no avail. She was giving it another try, fighting back tears as she did when he had entered the room again.

She groaned aloud as he drove in and out of her, grateful he had not waited, her need too great. All she wanted was him inside her, filling her with endless pleasure, joining with him as one, and… the satisfying moan burst from her lips as her husband gave her everything she ached for.

Warrick exploded with a roar, his climax ripping through him with a satisfaction like never before. What made it even more perfect was that he watched his wife toss her head back and yell out his name for the second time in a short few minutes.

He did not pull out of her until both their pleasures had faded, then he dropped on the bed beside her. He reached out and took her hand and released it with a curse when she yelped. He sat up. "Forgive me, I forgot about your injury."

Adara brought her bruised hand to rest on her chest. "It heals, though pains me at times."

"I never even—" He shook his head angry with himself.

"And glad I am you did not," she said softly and rested her good hand to his chest. "We ached for each other and I am grateful you let nothing interfere with that."

"He brushed off the grime that had fallen from his plaid onto her rounded stomach, then rested his hand upon the mound. "The bairn does well?"

"He is a busy one in there, forever moving, kicking, as if impatient to get out."

"While his da much prefers to be inside his mum."

Adara laughed softly. "A place his da is always welcome and where she prefers him to be."

He leaned down and kissed her gently. "We will do well together, wife."

"So you will keep me?" she asked playfully.

She might tease, but Warrick watched her smile falter and a hint of worry fill her eyes. "I told you, you are stuck with me whether you like it or not."

"I like it," she confirmed quickly.

"Good, for you are mine forever. I will let no one take you from me."

Adara pressed a finger to his lips. "I want no other. I want only your arms around me, your lips upon mine, your touch alone, and only you inside me."

Warrick kissed her finger, teasing the top of it with a nibble. "As I said, you are stuck with me... only me."

"A chore I favor," she chuckled.

"A chore am I?"

She caught the smile that tried to escape the one corner of his mouth. Soon, very soon he would smile. He would not be able to stop it. "Aye, a chore that needs tending. You need a bath and food."

"I could do with both," Warrick agreed. "And you will join me in the tub." He gave her no time to argue, he stood and disappeared out the door and Adara, fearing he would return with someone, rushed the blanket around her.

Warrick was not alone when he returned, Wynn followed on his heels along with two young lasses. They moved furniture around and when they finished two men carried a large round wooden tub into the room. Wynn instructed the two young lasses in how to drape the linen inside the tub and what seemed like an endless parade of servants began entering the room with buckets of steaming water.

Warrick began to disrobe, shedding his shirt and boots.

Wynn sat a small stool beside the tub and placed towels and soap on it and when the tub was filled to her satisfaction, she shooed the servants out and shut the door behind her.

Warrick hurried out of his plaid and went and scooped his wife up for the second time that night and lowered her gently into the water.

Adara couldn't stop the '*ahhhh*' that left her lips.

Warrick joined her, splashing the water over the side in his attempt to situate them both in the tub. It was good she was small or they would have never fit. She settled back against him where he had tucked her between his bent legs. She lay there enjoying the comfortably hot water, its heat soaking into the depths of her bones and warming her.

She knew from preparing baths for others that the heat would not last and she had no wont to feel chilled water after having enjoyed the delicious heat. With the soap on her right, she could not use her injured hand to fetch it.

"Please reach the soap for me, Warrick," she said and he did, though he did not give it to her.

"Your hand. You cannot do this yourself." He grabbed one of the buckets of water to the left of the tub and poured half of the water over her head, soaking her hair, then did the same to his. He lathered up her hair with soap and did the same to his hair.

Adara managed to turn around with her husband's help and with a smile she reached out with her good hand and began to scrub his hair and he did the same for her, though he used two hands.

"So tell me, wife, did you think on things that Maia told you?" he asked, forcing his thoughts anywhere but on her breasts that bobbed just above the surface of the water, tempting him. And he was glad the night was still young.

"I did," Adara said, trying to concentrate on her words but finding it extremely difficult. Never had someone ever washed her hair and it felt absolutely divine. His fingers dug firm against her scalp over and over and she did not want him to stop.

She fumbled with her words. Until finally she said, "The water will grow cold soon enough. We should wash and talk when we are done."

Warrick almost chuckled and it surprised him how often his wife almost had him smiling. He intended to stop her when she went to wash him. It had to be difficult for her using only one hand, but then she ran her soapy hand over his shoulder, scrubbing at a patch of grime settled there, and gently rinsed it with a handful of water and caressed it to make sure the spot was clean.

He enjoyed her touch far too much to stop her.

It was pleasure and torment they both suffered as they washed each other, Warrick finally snatching up another bucket of water to dump on each of their heads to rinse the soap from their hair.

A rap sounded at the door shortly after Warrick lifted her out of the tub and draped a towel around her and one around his waist.

He bid the person to enter and Wynn walked in.

"I have food and drink, my lord," Wynn said and Warrick gave a nod.

Soon the room smelled with the most delicious scents

and Adara realized she was hungry.

Wynn hurried the servants through their task and out of the room.

Adara went straight for the food almost tripping in her haste to get to it, her husband righting her with the strength of his hand.

"I am suddenly famished," she said, reaching for a piece of succulent meat.

"Just as you were on our wedding night," Warrick reminded.

"I remember, but then I had been too fearful of what lay ahead for me that night to eat any of the food that had been offered."

Warrick filled their tankards with wine. "No more fear of me, wife?"

"I cannot say I never fear you, for there are times I feel not fearing you would be foolish, but there are other times," —she smiled— "fear is the furthest thing from my mind."

Warrick turned his head toward the door with a scowl and Adara was not surprised when a knock was heard.

Roark entered after Warrick demanded to know who disturbed him.

"We caught the man who attempted to take your life."

Chapter Twenty-three

Adara paced about the room, circling it again and again, annoyed that Warrick refused to take her with him. She had wanted to hear for herself what the man would say and also see if in any way it was familiar with something Maia had said.

It continued to trouble her that she had been so wrong about Maia. Though, the more she considered it the more she realized it was her own gullibility that had been at fault. You think she would have been more cautious, having been disappointed so many times by people she thought had cared for her.

Should she be cautious of Warrick?

The thought brought her pacing to a halt and she sat down on the bed with a heavy sigh. Would she forever doubt and question? Or should she trust her heart and believe Warrick a good man, not the demon everyone claims him to be?

He killed his first wife.

She had battled with that knowledge since hearing it. She had betrayed her husband by releasing Maia and yet he had not harmed her. If betrayal did not have him taking his wife's life, what would? Supposedly, he killed her on their wedding night. What could he have possibly learned that would have had him take her life?

She had wondered if he had wed out of love or if it had been an arranged marriage. And if he had only met the woman shortly before they wed what possible reason could he have had to kill her?

Others might not think her husband kind and he certainly did not think of himself as kind, but Adara knew otherwise. He was a kind man… when he wanted to be. He could also show no mercy as he had with Maia.

Somehow she would learn more about Warrick's first wife and lay this mystery to rest.

A yawn had her stretching out on the bed, pulling the blanket over her and snuggling beneath it. She would wait for Warrick to return. He would tell her about the man and she would tell him what she recalled about Maia.

~~~

"We found him by accident," Roark explained as they walked through the village toward the contingent of Warrick's warriors camped on the outskirts of the village.

"How so?" Warrick asked.

"He was thought to be one of the injured MacNair warriors left behind after the attack, and another injured MacNair warrior informed one of our warriors that he was not of the MacNair Clan. The MacNair warrior wishes to pledge fealty to you."

"The taste of defeat will do that to you."

"He also told me that their chieftain ordered them not to harm your wife and when he saw that this particular warrior was going after your wife he followed after him, but one of your warriors got to the man first. He could not say enough about how your warrior vaulted in the air and threw himself at the man, sending them both crashing to the ground. Your warrior got up and ran to your wife and got her to the safety of the keep."

"Who was that?"

"Gavin."

"I will speak to him later and the MacNair warrior as well. How did you determine that this warrior is the one who tried to kill me?"

"He admitted it, but then he is close to death." Roark said.

"So he has nothing to lose. The only question is how much pain he is willing to suffer before he dies."

"His pain is already great. He may be more willing to talk if he is offered a quick death."

Warrick thought on that as he walked through the temporary camp his warriors had set up. Building had begun on permanent structures, the problem with the two opposing clans causing delays. The work would resume soon, since his warriors were well aware of the consequences of facing a winter without substantial structures to house them.

The camp was quiet, though not silent, it never was. His warriors were always on guard, always prepared. It was why there had been little loss of life and serious injuries sustained during the attack. He offered no praise to them and they expected none. Clan was family and in protecting each other the clan remained strong and they reaped the rewards of working together.

His warriors that were awake and those patrolling sent respectful nods to him as he walked through the camp and he acknowledged each one in kind.

Roark stopped a short distance from one of the campfires where a man lay on a blanket on the ground.

Warrick stopped beside him, looking down at the man. Roark had been right. The man was suffering and looked barely alive. His eyes were half opened and he moaned through labored breathing. The blanket covering him was wet with blood at his stomach. A gut wound… a painful way to die.

Warrick did not care that the man suffered, he deserved such a death for trying to kill Adara.

He kicked the man in the leg and his eyes shot open.

"Let the demon take me," the man begged, stumbling over his words.

"He prefers to see you suffer," Warrick said.

The man's words broke in pieces as he spoke. "Li-ke h-is fa-ther."

"The devil is no kin to me, but I am sure he will welcome you home soon," Warrick said, knowing he would get nothing from this man whose last breath was near.

The man sounded as if he choked on the words he fought to speak. "Yo-ur demon da."

Warrick dropped down on his haunches beside the man. "My father? You speak of my father?"

"Dea-th to th-e de-mon's son," the man said and his eyes bulged as he coughed and struggled for breath.

Warrick watched him die, no sympathy for the man who tried to kill his wife. What disturbed him was mention of his father. What had his father to do with anything?

"Strange that he should mention your father," Roark said as Warrick stood.

"My father was a victorious warrior, his love for battle renowned. He conquered many clans and lands, some for the King and others for his own pleasure. Many admired him, more feared him, and even more hated him."

"Perhaps the sins of the father return to punish the son," Roark suggested.

"If that is so, then many more will follow." Warrick looked down at the dead man, angry that death had taken him before he could learn more. "Dump his body in the woods for the animals to feed on and for his cohorts to see what happens when they go against the Demon Lord."

Warrick walked back to the keep alone, thinking about what he had said to Roark about his father and wondering if he had also described himself. But had that not been what his father wanted? For Warrick to exceed his father's reputation? For him to be even more admired, feared, and hated than his father?

His father cared or felt for no one and he had taught Warrick to do the same, to shield himself against everything and everyone. To let no one, interfere with what must be done, must be accomplished.

His father had given him everything he needed to be an

outstanding warrior, but both he and his mother had never given him an ounce of love. So through the years, he had given it no thought, until he met Adara.

She had touched something in him that had never been touched before and now that she had, he could not get enough of it. For the first time in his life, he believed he felt what just might be love and he feared losing it.

He took the stairs quickly, eager to return to his wife and when he entered the room and found her sleeping, he was disappointed. He wanted to make love to her slow and easy, tasting and touching all of her, joining with her as one—loving her.

He slipped into bed and settled himself around her warm, soft body that smelled of lavender from their recent bath. He almost smiled at the thought that he probably smelled as delightful as she did. He thought how wise that Roark had made no mention of it.

After laying there comfortably wrapped around his wife, she wiggled her way around in his arms and he was surprised to find her awake and more surprised at her words.

"I cannot believe you return to our bed to do nothing but sleep after making love to me only once after your lengthy absence." Adara said, poking playfully at his chest. She saw it then, a smile, not huge, not lasting long, but a smile none the less and she delighted in it.

Warrick caught his smile to late and after chasing it away, he was sorry he did. It had felt good to let it free and enjoy the intense pleasure it brought him.

"You are a hungry one, wife," he teased, taking hold of her poking finger.

"Famished," she said, her eyes bright with passion.

"Then a I better make sure you get all the sustenance you need."

"And then some," she whispered before bringing her lips down on his.

~~~

Warrick sat in the Great Hall with Adara the next morning enjoying the meal and their conversation. There was no talk of battle or pain and loss that came with it. Nor was there talk of future battles or clans that posed a threat. He could not ever remember when a discussion ever pleased him. There always seemed to be a problem he needed to settle. But at the moment, there was only the two of them and the possibility of a future filled with more than hate and greed.

"This one will need many brothers and sisters," Adara said, patting her stomach, then spooning some of the porridge that she had added honey to.

"You are a dutiful wife to give me many bairns," Warrick said but preferred it not be from duty that she did so.

Her cheeks flushed and she lowered her voice to a whisper as she brought her face close to his. "It is not out of duty I will give you many bairns, my lord."

Warrick felt a jolt to his heart. "If not duty, what?"

Her cheeks flushed a deeper red and she lowered her head not believing she had said what she did to him. Where had she gotten the courage. Or had it been foolishness that made her so bold?

Warrick slipped the back of his fingers beneath her chin and lifted it. "Tell me, wife."

With no demand in his voice and a spark of gentleness in his eyes, Adara whispered, "I love the intimacy we share."

Love.

No one had ever used that word with him and here she was admitting that she loved the intimacy between them. Her words were like a gift he had long wanted to open. Once, however, was not enough. He wanted to hear her say it again. Or was it that he wanted to make sure he had heard her correctly?

"I love how you make me feel," she whispered again not knowing where she got the courage to speak so brashly to him.

"How do I make you feel?" he asked, his voice a soft murmur.

Loved.

The word whispered softly in her head and she turned away, her chin slipping off his hand. She could never admit that to him. She barely was able to accept the possibility that she loved him. And what of the Demon Lord? Could he come to love her? Was he even capable of loving? But then no one would suspect that the Demon Lord could ever smile.

Adara turned her head to look at him and brought her lips near his to whisper, "Cared for. You make me feel that you care."

He felt a kick to his heart and gut this time. He was under attack and his shields were failing him. She was making her way past them and if he was not careful, she would see victory. He wondered if this was one battle he would not mind losing.

"Of course I care, you are my wife," he said, keeping his tone neutral.

She brushed her lips across his ever so lightly. "I am grateful, my lord, for no one has ever cared for me."

He felt his shield crack and shatter completely and she plunged forward and stole his heart. "No longer is that so," he said and was shocked when she threw her arm around his neck and hugged him tight.

"You are a good, kind husband," she said, after hugging him senseless.

"I am not kind," he said as if he commanded her to believe it and she shocked him again when she pressed a finger to her lips briefly before speaking.

"I will tell no one," she whispered as though promising to keep a secret.

He could not let her believe this falsehood about him.

He was not a good, kind man. He was ruthless like his father and like his father he had no heart, so while he hoped she loved him... was he even capable of loving her?

"I should tell you about Maia," she said.

He was glad for the change of subject. She did not need to know how cruel he could actually be. That had him wondering how she would feel about him when she learned that he had killed his first wife.

"Tell me what you remember," he encouraged and listened as she spoke.

Adara told him all she recalled and what she thought of the information she had remembered. "Maia was not born of this land and where she did come from she believed the women stronger than here. She was knowledgeable of many things and I believe fearless. I do not believe she was a woman who kept a hearth and home, though she was accustomed to chores, having brought garments to the stream to wash."

His wife was more observant than she realized. "How long did you know Maia?"

"A few short months, maybe six or less."

"What area of the Highlands was this?"

Adara scrunched her brow in concentration. "I believe the crofter family I served paid his share to the Clan Macomish." Adara saw the noticeable change in her husband's dark eyes. "You are familiar with the clan?"

That he had failed to keep that knowledge private irritated him. "The clan is not far from my ancestral home. How long ago was this?"

Adara appeared to concentrate. "Time was continuous for me, one season going into the next just as the days did until I thought of it no more. There was no marking of time for me. No birth date to celebrate or remember that a year had passed. That Maia had aged and I did not recognize her at first would have me believing it had been many years since I last had seen her." She shook her head. "But her face

229

was aged when I met her and her hair was beginning to gray so I would say maybe five or six years."

This time Warrick kept his surprise to himself. That Macomish land sat close to his land and that about five and half years ago was when he wed could not be a coincidence. Maia was in that area for a reason and that reason could have something to do with his first wife. He encouraged her to tell him more of her visits with Maia, anything of what she may have said to her.

Adara thought of some of the things she had discussed with the woman and she did not know if she would feel comfortable repeating the conversation with Warrick.

She was spared for the moment when Roark appeared and told Warrick he was needed.

"We will talk more later," Warrick said and left the Great Hall.

Adara gathered her cloak and made her way outside and to the kitchen garden, wanting to talk with Burchard. He had been here a long time and she was eager to find out if he knew anything about her mum.

She was making her way to the kitchen garden where Burchard was busy at work when she saw her husband approach the woods alone. If he was needed, why was he going into the woods alone? What could be there that required his attention.

A quick glance around had her wondering why she did not see any of Warrick's warriors. Why would that be? They were everywhere. Why not here? Had he ordered them away from this area? Curiosity poked at her, but good sense warned her not to follow her husband. The woods could hold danger. Maia and her group could be near. But what of her husband, he was alone. Who would protect him? What if something happened to him? What if he never returned to her?

Her thoughts so disturbed her that she lifted the hem of her garment and rushed off in pursuit of her husband.

Chapter Twenty-four

Adara feared she had lost her husband after entering the woods, seeing no sign of him. Then she heard voices. She thought better than to get too close since she was all too aware of her husband's uncanny ability to sense when someone approached.

She remained where she was able to hear snippets of the conversation.

"Tell me," she heard her husband demand impatiently.

"Found—" she strained to hear more, the voice low. "Not sure—"

"They kept hidden," she managed to hear her husband say though missed what followed then heard the last of it. "Secret."

"Difficult—" Once again she could not hear the man and turned her head to try and hear more. "Lead prom—" She barely caught the last of it, thinking she heard him say, promising.

She thought she heard the jingle of a purse heavy with coin and she recalled the night she had seen Warrick from the keep window handing something to a short man. Could this be the same man? Was he searching for something for Warrick?

Adara remained still, not wanting to make a sound and be discovered and she was glad she did since the man did not pass by far from her. He was short and covered in a dark cloak, and he snuck off deeper into the woods, his steps light and quick.

Only then did she give thought to Warrick finding her and she made a hasty decision. She sat on a fallen tree trunk and waited for her husband.

Warrick stopped abruptly when he saw her sitting there. How had he not heard her and what was she doing there? Concern battled with his annoyance and not trusting himself to speak since his tongue would lash out at her, he crossed his arms over his chest and, instead, glared at her. She spoke up quickly.

"I followed you when I saw you enter the woods."

He continued to glare at her.

"It was probably not wise of me to do, but I feared something might happen to you" she confessed. "But I did not disobey you."

His scowl deepened.

"You did not order me to stay in the keep." She tried a smile on him but it did not appease his scowl. She went to speak again and he raised his hand.

"No more. The only thing that saves you this time is that you speak the truth to me." He walked over to her. "What did you hear?"

"Little."

He tilted his head slightly and narrowed his brow, letting her know her response was questionable.

"Bits and pieces were all I could hear," she said.

"What did you surmise from those bits and pieces?" he asked, knowing she had enough wit about her to reach some type of conclusion.

"That the man searches for something for you. Something to do with a secret."

Warrick cursed beneath his breath, reached out and took hold of her hand, and pulled her to her feet. "You are to forget what you heard here today. You will never mention it again. You will not think on it. You will never question me about it. Do you understand, wife?"

She nodded, wondering if what she had come upon was more serious and perhaps more dangerous than she ever imagined possible.

"I mean it, Adara. I will have your word on it."

His commanding tone and the intense concern in his dark eyes had fear rising up to churn her stomach. What had she stumbled upon that was not for her to know? And how dangerous was this for her husband? Without hesitation, she said, "You have my word."

The village bell tolled, echoing into the woods and announcing that a troop approached the village.

Nothing more was said as they walked back to the village. It was as if she had seen nothing, heard nothing. That it had never happened. But it had and Adara wondered how she would ever completely forget it.

Adara walked close to her husband as they entered the village, his tall, powerful body a shield that protected her. The clans people did not seem bothered by the new arrivals and Adara saw why when she and Warrick reached the front of the village.

More of Warrick's warriors had arrived along with carts that Adara assumed were supplies. She smiled when she saw that, for why would Warrick send for more supplies if he did not intend to stay the winter here?

"Warrick!"

Adara turned at the sound of her husband's name being cried out and was shocked to see a woman a head taller than herself, pleasantly plump, with an abundance of red curly hair that fell down her back and over her shoulders, and a pretty face consumed by a large smile, run toward him.

Warrick muttered something and released his wife's hand just in time. The woman launched herself at him and he caught her up against him as she hugged him tight.

"I have told you time and again not to greet me like that, Callie," Warrick reprimanded.

"Have I ever obeyed you, Warrick?" Callie said with a laugh.

"She obeys no one," Roark said, approaching them.

He didn't get far. Callie let out a screech and ran into her husband's arms to hug and kiss him repeatedly.

"I have missed you so much. When word came that a troop of men were to return to MacVarish keep, I planned to hide in one of the carts. I was so relieved when I was told I was to accompany them."

Warrick shook his head. "I would have sent you back."

Callie's whole face lit in laughter. "No you would not have done that, especially since I have news from home you would want to hear."

"It would be easy to gather it from you and send you on your way," Warrick warned.

"Not if I deliver it sparingly," Callie teased.

"Roark," Warrick bellowed.

Roark kept his arm around his wife. "Go easy on him, my love. He is wed now and only beginning to know how to handle a wife."

Callie threw herself at Warrick again and he had no choice but to catch her. "So I heard. Heaven be praised! My prayers have been answered."

Adara stared in complete bewilderment. Never had she seen anyone treat Warrick as Callie did and that he did not threaten her with harm astounded her, and that she did not seem the least bit frightened of him shocked her even more.

Callie released Warrick and stepped around him to look at Adara. "You are a wee bit of a thing and beautiful." She gasped. "You are with child."

Adara was surprised to see tears fill her eyes and she noticed that Roark frowned.

"How wonderful," she said, reaching out and hugging Adara. "I am so happy for you and Warrick."

Yet Adara saw sadness in her eyes.

"Adara. My wife's name is Adara," Warrick said.

"We will be the best of friends, Adara," Callie said, taking Adara's hand and squeezing it. "You will tell me all about how you and Warrick came to wed." She stepped back. "But first I must have time with my husband. We have been separated far too long." She hurried over to Roark and slipped into his arms and turned a smile on Warrick.

"Go, we will speak tonight at supper," Warrick ordered.

Roark nodded his appreciation and Callie turned another huge smile on him, then they hurried off.

Adara stared at her husband when he turned to take her hand. He said nothing while they walked and he wore not a smile or scowl on his face. She finally had to ask, "How is it that she is so familiar with you?"

"I have known her since she was young and I tried to warn Roark not to wed her, but the fool had insisted he had lost his heart to her and life would be worthless without her."

Adara smiled. "How wonderful to have such a deep abiding love for each other, since it is obvious Callie feels the same."

"Aye, that she does," Warrick said with a touch of annoyance.

"It annoys you that she loves Roark? Had you once had feelings for her?"

"Good God no," Warrick snapped. "If she were my wife, I would have killed her by now."

Adara felt her whole body tense at his remark. Would he truly have done that? Had he done that? Had his wife irritated him so badly that he killed her?

"She has tried my patience since she has been young."

"How do you know her?"

Warrick walked Adara over to a large tree, the fallen leaves surrounding it crunching beneath their boots before they came to a stop beneath the bare branches. "Callie is my sister."

Adara's mouth dropped opened. She recalled Espy's words when she had asked if Warrick had siblings. *No one has claimed kinship to him.* Callie certainly showed her love for her brother, so why not claim him as such?

"No one but Roark knows that and now you. I feared she would be in harm's way if it was known that she is my sister."

235

"I will tell no one," she assured him, pleased he trusted her with this secret and for a second time that day gave her word. "You have my word on it."

"She does not help the matter with the way she throws herself at me, though I have repeatedly warned her not to. Not once has she ever listened to me. I have had to save her from nearly drowning several times before she learned how to swim. I have pulled endless splinters from her hands and feet and seen to endless other wounds she got while in the woods with me after I had ordered her repeatedly to go home and leave me alone."

Adara caught the way a light seemed to spark in his dark eyes and annoying memories did not spark such a light.

"But she never left you alone?"

"I believe it is why I demand obedience from everyone since she showed me none," Warrick said and the light in his eyes grew brighter.

"It must have been grand to have such a loving sister," Adara said.

"She was a pest." The light dimmed in his eyes. "It was good my parents sent her away to be properly trained. She did not want to go. She cried endlessly, begged me to help her. I did help her by handing her over to the nuns at the convent I delivered her to."

His voice held no warmth, no caring, yet somehow Adara felt the pain he kept buried.

"Callie remained there until I had her brought to my keep several years later. Where Roark foolishly fell in love with her and I learned that her time at the convent had taught her not an ounce of obedience. I gladly handed her over to Roark in marriage. She is his problem now."

Adara did not believe that at all. Warrick had handed his sister over to Roark because he knew he would protect her with his life. He cared more for his sister than he would admit and she was looking forward to talking with her and learning more about Warrick.

"I have some matters to see to, I will leave you in the keep to rest," Warrick said as they continued walking.

"I would prefer you left me with Burchard. I wanted to speak to him about the kitchen garden." That was not a lie she told her husband. She did intend to discuss the garden with him but she also wanted to see what he might know of her mum. A question slipped out that she had been meaning to ask him. "Why did your warriors show such interest in Burchard that day in the kitchen garden?"

"They not only watched him, they watched everyone. It was their duty to watch and report back to me anything they thought strange or could present a problem."

"Burchard presents no problem and he worries you will deprive him of his chore, thus his only family, those in the keep. He cannot lose them," Adara said in defense of the man.

"I have no intention of doing so and besides, the keep is your domain and since you have seen to your duties well, it is up to you what to do with Burchard."

"He remains where he is," Adara said with the same forceful command that her husband often used.

"Then Burchard has no worries. What will you do once you are finished talking with Burchard?"

"I plan on speaking with Emona the cook."

"Then I will leave you to see to your duties while I see to mine," he said, though found he did not like the thought of leaving her. He enjoyed her company. Whether they talked or silence fell between them, there was a comfort with her that he had not known before.

"I will miss you," Adara said and raised herself on her toes to kiss him.

His arm went around her and he lifted her so that her feet no longer touched the ground, but her lips could touch his. The delicate brush of her lips across his was not enough for him. He took charge and kissed her with an intensity that let her know he did not want to let her go. That he too would miss her.

When he lowered her to her feet, she leaned against him, weak from his kiss and not surprised by the arousal that tingled her senses.

"Rest when you are done with your chores," Warrick ordered, silently cursing himself for kissing her as he had, since it had his manhood aching and on the verge of swelling.

"You should rest with me," she hurried to say and her cheeks flushed red when she realized what she so audaciously implied. But it was worth it when she saw the small, wicked smile that lit his lips.

"You will get no rest if I join you. Now go see to your duties." He kissed her quick and whispered, "And I will see to satisfying your need tonight."

He turned and walked off and for some strange reason, there at that moment, watching his long strides, the way he stood so erect, his shoulders broad, his head high, Adara realized that she loved her husband. She did not know why she felt it so strongly at that moment, she only knew that she did. It was as if her heart and mind came together to let her know that this was love she felt for this man and she should accept it no matter how strange it seemed. And it did seem strange to love the Demon Lord, but then her life had changed completely that night he had taken her as his wife.

She wrapped her newfound love around her like a comforting shawl and smiled as she walked to the kitchen garden.

"You have done well, Burchard, the soil is ready to rest," Adara said approaching the old man. It had taken Warrick's arrival to stir things up and make her realize that her solitary existence had done her little good. She also realized the importance of all her uncle Owen had tried to teach her about the clan and the keep. How he had not grown frustrated with her for being such a poor pupil, she did not know. But then he had said time and again, "When you finally heal, you will have all this knowledge to help you."

He had been right. She had needed to heal, her heart and deep into her soul, but Warrick, surprisingly, was helping her with that, and she was grateful for his never-ending patience with her, and it pleased her that she finally was putting to use all her uncle had taught her.

"I hope it pleases Lord Warrick," Burchard said, brushing dirt from his aged hands.

"Do not worry, Burchard, your position in the keep is secure. Lord Warrick confirmed it," she said, knowing the man needed to know it came from Warrick himself.

Wrinkles deepened across his face as he smiled wide. "I am most pleased and relieved to hear that, my lady."

"I would be most pleased if you would take a few moments and talk with me."

"Of course, my lady. How may I help you?"

"This does not concern your chore here. It is about my parents. I was wondering what you knew of them."

"Your parents, my lady?" he asked as if not understanding.

"I know only what my uncle Owen told me about them and he mostly spoke of my mum, but I know little of my da. I was wondering if perhaps my da may have spoken to you. He was a crofter, a man of the land, so I thought he might have spent time talking with you."

"Odd that you should ask, my lady. Your da did speak with me." He shook his head. "Why a crofter would go so far north in the Highlands puzzled me. Your da knew the soil there could prove difficult to cultivate and some areas were too barren to even attempt to grow a crop." He scratched his head. "I do recall something your da said that seemed odd. He told me that the far north Highlands had a way of swallowing men up until they were never seen again. I asked him if you would be safe there. He told me you would be safer there than here." He scratched his head again. "It made no sense to me. You were a wee bit of a thing and safe here with your uncle. Why take you to a harsh untamed land where few went?"

That was a question Adara pondered while she asked, "I know nothing of my da's family. Did he ever speak of them to you?"

"I know nothing of his family, though I do recall your uncle's displeasure when your mum arrived here with a crofter for a husband. He had sent her to live with a titled family, having promised their dying mum he would see his sister taken care of, so that she could secure a good marriage that would provide well for her. He was disappointed when she returned home wed to a simple farmer. But Wynn would know much more about your mum and da than I would."

"How so?" Adara asked.

"She was the one who had looked after your mum since she was young and went with her when she went to live with the titled family. She also attended your birth. It devastated her when your mum refused to let her go to the Highlands with her. She claimed it was a too harsh of a place for an aging woman."

"I am grateful, Burchard," Adara said. "Every little bit I learn about my parents helps me to know them better."

"They loved you they did," Burchard said. "Always keeping you close, never out of their sight. They kept you safe they did."

Adara praised the old man once again for a job well done with the soil and for taking the time to speak with her before she took her leave. As she walked toward the kitchen, she wondered over what the old man had told her. Why had Wynn not told her she was present at her birth? Or how well she had known her mum? Though, the most disturbing question was why would her da say that the north Highlands had a way of swallowing men up until they were never seen again? Had he intentionally taken her and her mum to the Highlands to hide? And if he had, what had he been hiding from?

Chapter Twenty-five

Adara yawned herself awake and was disappointed to find her husband gone from their bed. She smiled and stretched her arms above her head and her feet out, waking her muscles and laughed softly when she winced, sore from her husband's intimate demands last night.

She laughed again since his demands had been in response to her own. Callie and Roark had not supped with them. A message had let Warrick know that the journey had exhausted her and she would see him in the morning along with her husband. Warrick had not believed it for a moment and was going to summon Roark when Adara had stopped him and pleaded with him to give the long separated couple time alone... just as she needed time with him.

That had convinced him quickly. They had supped in their bedchamber in between making love, the memories bringing a smile to her face.

She realized she had found herself smiling and laughing more since wed to Warrick than she had smiled or laughed in her entire life. She was content and fear suddenly began to poke at her. Would this contentment be brief? Would something rise up and steal it from her? Was she being a fool to even think she was content? Her questions peppered her fear and it kept rising and rising until she found it squeezing at her throat.

Warrick entered their bedchamber to find his wife sitting up in bed looking as if she was unable to catch her breath. He hurried to her side, rubbed her back, and spoke to her soothingly, seeing that fear had taken hold of her. Something that had not visited her of late.

As soon as Warrick lifted her into his arms and settled

with her in his lap on the bed, her fear began to subside. "What troubles you, wife?"

"I am content," she said on a heavy sigh.

His brow furrowed. "And this disturbs you?"

"Aye," she said, resting her head against his chest. She loved listening to his heart beat strong and steady or rapidly like it did after they made love. "Anytime I ever found the smallest bit of contentment, something terrible always followed it."

"Tell me of your small bits of contentment."

She raised her head off his chest. "You would probably find them foolish."

"If you treasured them so will I."

Where once his dark eyes intimidated her, having appeared cold and empty, now she saw a glimmer of warmth and concern. It had sparked in his eyes now and again, but lately it lingered when he looked at her. It brought her more comfort than he could possibly ever know.

"I enjoyed collecting my stones. They were the first things that was something of my own. I enjoyed the late nights, when my fatigue did not surrender to sleep immediately. When all was quiet and there were no chores to be done or no one yelling at me, poking me to move faster, or feeling the sting of a wooden spoon against my arm or hand. For just a short while, I felt free."

Warrick listened, her words stirring his own memories of similar nights and the freedom he had felt alone in the dark, free of his father's endless demands and his mother's cold heart. And there were those times his sister would sneak into bed with him, seeking safety and comfort from fear of her nightmares and what she would suffer if her father heard her scream in fright. That was the only time he never felt alone.

"The stolen moments I got when in the woods were favorites of mine, for I could imagine I was free, the day mine to run and explore." Adara smiled, recalling what he had told her of his time spent in the woods. "You know yourself. You had such days."

"There are things we share alike, you and I," he said, the thought pleasing him.

If that was so, could he come to love her as she did him? Adara could only hope and this time she held on tightly to that hope. She was beginning to believe that if she held hope close to her heart long enough, it made things possible.

Her stomach gurgled the same time the bairn gave a good kick, Warrick feeling it.

Adara stared in awe at the smile that lit her husband's face. She had thought he had fine features, but his features went far beyond fine when he truly smiled. And smile he did, broad and without hesitation.

"He is growing stronger," Warrick said with pride, resting his hand on his wife's stomach and feeling his child move. He could not, nor did he want, to stop from smiling. To know his child grew inside her was beyond magical. He had wanted a family, but he had wanted a wife that would love their bairns as much as he would, not a soulless wife and mum like his own mother. It had been the reason he had refused to wed after his first disastrous marriage. Now with Adara, it seemed possible.

"He is," Adara agreed, her own smile growing wide. "And he is hungry."

"Then we shall feed him." Warrick hoisted her off the bed along with himself and he set her on her feet and helped her to dress, her hand still painful.

Her soft skin, tempted him to touch her, run his hand down along her arm, her skin silky smooth. He was pleased she responded to his every touch, took pleasure in it, welcomed it, encouraged it. Never had he imagined he would have a wife so responsive to his every touch. Or smile at him as if she lo… he stopped the thought.

Adara did not love him. She did what was necessary as she had done her whole life. It had been the reason he had asked for a servant when he chose to wed. He had wanted someone accustomed to obeying every word. He almost laughed and that thought alone startled him. He had had no reason to laugh until Adara. Or to smile until Adara. Now he found himself struggling not to do both, to continue to be the heartless warrior his father had demanded of him, telling him again and again that to care or love anything or anyone weakened a warrior. The odd thing was that he never felt more alive or powerful since Adara had entered his life with her fears, lack of obedience, and her eagerness to couple with him.

He found he very much favored his wife and he did not want to think of life without her.

Her sharp gasp snapped him out of his musings and he saw that he had been the cause of her pain, not having paid attention as he slipped her injured hand through her sleeve.

His apology died on his lips, his father having beaten him every time he would say he was sorry until the words were not even a thought… until now.

"You are not to do anything that will bring your hand pain," he ordered in a way of an apology.

Adara smiled and raised her hand, the swelling near gone, but not the bruising. "It does better. Espy says that it will take time to heal and that even when the bruising disappears, pain will remain."

"A good reason to be gentle with it and let others do for you." He rushed a finger to her lips to stop her from responding. "I know that is a difficult task for you, but think how difficult it will be for you to hold our bairn when he is born if you do not give your hand time to heal."

"You are right," she said her eyes turning wide as she realized the wisdom of his words. "I cannot wait to hold our bairn. Having seen the joy a birth brings to a new mum has me eager to hold our bairn."

"You do not fear birthing our bairn?"

She smiled and shook her head. "Not at all. I know

there will be pain but I have known pain that consumed and tortured the soul. This pain brings joy and I will have no trouble enduring it."

Warrick kissed her gently. "You make me proud, wife."

Adara stared at him, her mouth agape until she managed to speak. "Truly?"

"I am proud of you and never forget it," he said and kissed her again. "Now come, let us feed that hungry bairn of ours."

"Wait," she said full of excitement and hurried over to a basket by the bed and retrieved something, returning to him with a wide smile. "I have been meaning to show these to you. Two stones with nature's designs on them to start my collection." She held them out to him.

Warrick took them and looked them over. "Most impressive, wife, especially the triangle shaped one. Where did you find these?" He held them out to her.

"They were a gift."

Warrick pulled his hand back, a scowl darkening his fine features. "Who gives my wife a gift?"

Adara saw her husband's anger surface and treaded lightly with her words. "Langdon. An old man who has been kind to me since my arrival here. He often joined me on late night walks after my uncle died and I found sleep difficult. He was kind to me, talked even when I remained silent until I finally began to talk with him. In a way, he helped me through my uncle's unexpected death."

Warrick should be pleased, but he found himself feeling jealous that not only had Langdon spent time with Adara, but that learning of her interest in collecting stones, the man had taken the time to find her two. While he had taken the one stone she had found and still had not returned it to her.

"He should have gotten permission from me first before giving you the stones," Warrick said, growing more annoyed at the man for doing something he should have done.

Adara took the stones from her husband. "Please,

Warrick, you will rob me of the pleasure of these stones, if you berate Langdon for his thoughtful gift."

"I mean the man no harm," he said and tried to convince himself of it, but jealousy kept nagging at him. "But he must learn to seek permission before giving a gift to my wife. Now, I will hear no more of it. The bairn needs feeding."

They left the room, Warrick set on finding Langdon before day's end and talking with the man.

~~~

They were just about to share the morning meal in the quiet of the Great Hall when the door burst open and Callie came rushing in, Roark hurrying in behind her.

"Wonderful," Callie said, clapping her hands together in delight as she approached. "I worried we missed the morning meal with you. Now we can share it together." She pulled her cloak off and tossed it on the table beside the one where Adara and Warrick sat. She rubbed her arms after sitting opposite the couple. "I am glad you sit close to the hearth and not at the dais. It is much warmer and more welcoming here."

Roark looked to Warrick.

"At least your husband has manners and waits to be invited to join us," Warrick scolded.

Callie reached out, grabbed her husband's arm, and tugged at him to sit beside her. "Do not be so stuffy, Warrick, we are family and I have missed you."

"I am pleased to have you here, Callie," Adara said and ignored the glare Warrick turned on her.

"I am delighted to be here and look forward to getting to know you better," Callie said with a warm smile.

"If she becomes too much of a pest, you will let me know," Warrick said to his wife.

"Be careful, Warrick, or I may deliver the news of

home sparingly to you," Callie said with a playful grin.

Warrick leaned his upper body across the table as he said, "Watch your words, Callie, or you will taste the wrath of our father."

Callie's smile vanished and she paled. "I meant no harm, Warrick."

Roark slipped his arm around his wife and pulled her close against him. "You know how her tongue speaks before she thinks."

"I am all too familiar," Warrick said and drew back until he sat erect beside Adara. "Tell me what news you bring."

Callie filled her husband's tankard with cider, then her own, and Adara saw how her hands quivered, the fright Warrick had given her having yet to diminish.

"The repairs to the dungeon are complete and Torrin does well training the guards who will work there. Many are surprised that torture will be used only with your approval."

Adara was also surprised and pleased to hear her husband was making changes to his dungeon. She would have preferred that he got rid of it completely, but she supposed to him it was a necessary evil.

"The fields have been expanded as you instructed and all of the building you ordered built before the winter sets in have been completed," Callie said and paused to take a drink of her cider. "A messenger from King James arrived and when he learned you were not there, he ordered the message be delivered to you."

"Then be done with it," Warrick ordered.

"I think it would be best if I delivered it privately to you," Callie said.

"I will hear it now," Warrick demanded.

Callie shrugged. "As you wish. King James says the legitimacy of your marriage depends on your success."

Fear rushed over Adara like never before. She knew it. She knew something would happen to steal her contentment.

King James would not sanction their marriage and why should he when she was nothing more than a servant.

Her hand rushed out beneath the table instinctively to take hold of Warrick's where his lay on his thigh. She was relieved to feel his strong fingers close tightly around her quivering hand and hold it as though he would never let it go and his response proved just that.

"No one will take my wife from me, not even King James," Warrick said and turned to his wife. "You are stuck with me, Adara, and always will be." He stood, releasing his wife's hand reluctantly. "Come, Roark, I want you to choose our fastest horse and rider. I have a message I want delivered to the King immediately."

Callie grabbed a chunk of bread and meat and shoved it in her husband's hand as he stood.

"I do not starve your husband, Callie," Warrick said.

Callie grinned. "He needs the food. I deplete his strength."

Warrick shook his head and walked away while Roark laughed and kissed his wife's cheek.

"Do nothing that will bring pain to your hand, wife," Warrick called out before reaching the door, and Adara smiled pleased by his departing words. To her, it showed he cared.

"You care for Warrick," Callie said as if not quite believing it.

"I do," Adara admitted freely. "He is kind to me."

Callie sighed as if in relief. "It is good to hear someone say that. No one would ever believe it, but I know that he is kind and I am relieved that his wife knows it as well."

Adara lowered her voice to a whisper. "He told me you were his sister."

Callie's pretty face lit with delight. "He trusts you. That is rare for Warrick."

Adara had not thought of that, but he had trusted her with the secret of his sister as he had trusted her when he told her not to tell anyone of what she had heard or seen in the woods. That knowledge brought her a sense of comfort.

"I want to be a good wife to him," Adara said.

"It would do Warrick well to have someone be good to him."

"You were good to him."

Callie's smile turned sad. "I was so hungry for attention, for love, and Warrick was the only one who did not push me away or ignore me. But then I was a pest. I never left him alone. I would have terrible nightmares and if I woke screaming my father would hit me and tell me I was a coward. My mother never came to comfort me. I was so frightened one night that I would have another nightmare and suffer my father's wrath that I hurried to Warrick's room and climbed into bed with him. He did not chase me. He wrapped his arm around me and held me. He did chase me in the morning, acting as if he just found me there. But I knew what he was doing. He was protecting me from our father discovering me there."

Adara listened. She had longed for loving parents, but she would have preferred to remain a servant than to have heartless parents like Warrick and Callie's. Her heart went out to the both of them for what they had suffered.

"There was a time I hated my brother and I regret that now, for I did not know that what he did, he did to protect me. He told my father all lies about me and convinced him I needed to spend time in a convent or I would never be able to secure a favorable marriage. He insisted on taking me there himself. He would not let Father's warriors escort me alone. I hated him for that. I called him foul names and told him I would never forgive him. I was so angry that I was a hellion at the convent. The one nun got so frustrated with my horrible behavior that she told me it was a good thing my father decided I was to spend time in a convent to prepare me for marriage and lucky that the chieftain my father had planned to marry me off to had wed someone else. When I learned the name of the chieftain, I realized that Warrick had saved me from a horrible fate. The man had been known to beat women unmercifully, his first wife dying from such a beaten. My brother saved my life."

Adara wiped a tear from her eye.

Callie did the same. "Warrick is the way he is, cold and uncaring, his kindness buried deep, because of our father, a brutal man, who trained his son to be like him."

"It was good he had you to help him," Adara said.

"I did nothing, though I wished time and again I could have."

"But you did help him. He learned how to care because of you," Adara said.

Callie shook her head.

"How else could he know what it is to care for someone if he had never known it himself? If he did not care, had not a bit of kindness in him, why would he have rescued you from that dreadful marriage arrangement?"

"I never thought of it that way. I only knew he saved me repeatedly from drowning, and from a hellish marriage." Callie smiled broadly. "It is because of him I met Roark and found true love. I met him when Warrick took me out of the convent and brought me to live with him shortly after our father's death." She continued grinning. "As soon as I laid eyes on Roark, I knew I loved him and that I would wed him." She laughed. "He did not have a chance." Her laughter faded along with her smile. "Though, I am thrilled you are with child, I am also envious. I fear I will never give Roark a child, though it is not for lack of trying."

"Did you talk about this with Espy when she was your brother's healer?"

Callie shook her head. "I was not in residence when Espy was there. I returned home just after the fire in the dungeon. I was with my mother. She was dying. When word came, I knew Warrick would not go and see her, but I felt obligated. He instructed me to close the keep and let what servants were left know that they were welcome to serve him if they so wished, though we both knew none would. There were only two servants left looking after my mum. She was a difficult and demanding woman." She paused as if the memories were too much for her. "The cleric and I were the only ones who stood over my mother's grave. The keep sits empty now, neither Warrick nor I wanting any part of it." Callie threw her hands up. "Enough with sadness. I was hoping you would show me around the village and perhaps introduce me to some of your clan."

"I would like that," Adara said, "and when Espy visits you must speak to her. She is a skilled healer and may be able to help you."

"Roark has said the same, so I look forward to meeting Espy."

"You will like her. She rescued me from your brother's dungeon."

Callie stared at her speechless, though only for a moment. "You were a prisoner in Warrick's dungeon. I did not know that. Tell me all about it."

Adara shared her story with Callie who asked endless questions and could not stop shaking her head, it seeming too unbelievable of a tale to be true. They walked through the village after that and Adara introduced her to some of the women she had gotten to know better. Adara was amazed at how easily Callie befriended others, but then a smile always lit her face and laughter came easily to her. Her happy nature was pleasant to be around.

When the temperature grew colder, Adara and Callie headed back to the keep and they settled in Adara's solar with hot brews, honey bread, and their shoeless feet stretched out to the heat of the fireplace.

Comfortable with Callie, Adara finally got the courage to ask her the one question she had been dying to ask her. "What can you tell me about Warrick's first wife?"

Chapter Twenty-six

Callie sighed and shook her head. "I wish I knew. No one dares speak of it. Even Roark will not discuss it with me. If I bring it up to anyone, they walk away from me. I have tried endlessly to find out what happened. I refuse to believe my brother killed his wife. He protects what belongs to him." She shook her head again. "He could not have done what some wagging tongues say he did."

"What did they say he did?" Adara asked fearful of what she might hear yet needing to hear it.

Callie shuddered. "They claim the room was awash with blood. It was everywhere. On Sondra, his wife, and on Warrick. They say he sliced her throat after having taken the knife to her body."

Adara stared at Callie, trying to digest her words. "That is not possible. He would not do such a thing."

"He has done such a thing. My father made sure he could take a knife to a man when necessary and not have it disturb him in the least. Warrick can be heartless when he wants to be and definitely when he needs to be. But I remember the words he whispered to me when he left me at the convent and I did not fully grasp until much later. He told me that we would never be like our mum and da. I realized later that he was trying to tell me to trust him. All would be well. And it was."

"I wish I knew the truth," Adara said.

"The only way you will ever know the truth is to ask him yourself," Callie said.

"I do not know if I have the courage to do that," Adara admitted to her own disappointment.

"Do you have the courage to live always wondering

what happened?"

"Why have you not asked him?"

"I did," Callie said, "and he told me never to ask him again. But you are his wife, he might answer you."

Adara was unsure if that would make a difference.

The bell tolled and it had Adara and Callie hurrying to the Great Hall. They were stopped before they could reach the keep doors.

It was the young warrior Gavin who told them they were to remain in the keep. A band of renegade warriors from the MacNair Clan were creating a problem, and Warrick and Roark had left to take care of it.

Adara wished she could have seen Warrick before he left and let him know he was to stay safe and return home to her. As the night wore on and he had not returned, her concern grew. It turned to a raging fear when he had yet to return the next day and two days later, though she fought not to show it, she was beside herself with worry for her husband's safety.

She tried to tell herself it was a foolish thought. He was a skilled warrior. He had fought many battles and had survived. But that was not the crux of her worry. She knew all too well what troubled her. She feared that if he never returned to her, he would never know how much she loved him, and she wanted him to know. She desperately wanted him to know.

It would take courage for her to admit it to him, but she needed him to know. She needed him to know that there was someone who loved him beyond measure. She simply could not deny it anymore, nor did she want to.

She loved Warrick and she did not want to question how or why or when it all happened. She did not care that many or most believed him heartless or ruthless, she knew differently. He had shown her differently. And he might not love her, but he cared for her, she could see it, feel in the many good and decent ways he treated her. He could dictate, demand, and threaten, but never ever had he raised a hand to her or harmed her. Never had he belittled her, made her feel less then as others had done. He was proud of her and he let her know it.

Adara paced in her bedchamber that night, the wind outside howling at the window as the rain slashed against it. Her worry for her husband grew and so did her fear. She kept it at bay, told herself all was well. Her husband was fine. He would be home soon. But as the night grew later, so did her fear.

She would lose him and never have gotten the chance to tell him she loved him.

The storm worsened, thunder crashing loudly, rain pounding viciously, a cold wind whipping at the windows and a sudden chill filling the bedchamber.

Adara could not help it. She could not hold back the tears. She wanted her husband. She needed him, needed to tell him how she felt, needed to feel his strong arms around her, the strength of him seeping into her. Needed to know this was all real, her husband, her bairn, her family.

The door opened quietly and Warrick entered the room, dressed only in his plaid, a sheen of dampness to his skin and his dark hair. She was so shocked to see him, she stood there staring at him, fearing he was not real that she had wished him there.

Warrick stilled, surprised to see her awake so late, but when he saw the tears streaming down her cheeks, he did not hesitate… he went to her. As soon as he moved, so did she. She flung herself into his arms.

"What is wrong? Is it the bairn?" he asked, keeping one arm snug around her while he wiped gently at her tears with his finger

"I was so afraid," she said, trying to control her weeping.

"There is nothing for you to fear, Adara. You are safe here. No one will ever take you from me. As I have told you repeatedly, we are stuck together you and I, forever and ever."

She shook her head.

"Aye," he insisted. "I claim it so and nothing will change that. You have my word."

She continued to shake her head, though more slowly. "I so feared—"

"No, wife, no fear, no more. There is no need for it. You are strong and courageous. There is nothing for you to fear."

His words gave her strength as did the strength of his loving arms. "I feared I would not get the chance to tell you how much I love you and always will."

Warrick was struck silent, her words settling in, swirling around him, grabbing hold of his senses and gripping his heart until he thought he would burst with joy. Never had he thought he would find a woman who loved him or that he could love. Adara had changed all that. She had captured his heart and settled in his soul. She was part of him and he was part of her.

Still, he could not bring himself to tell her how he felt, his father's words haunting him.

Love no one. It will ruin you.

Warrick chased his father from his mind and tried to speak, tried to tell her that he lov… he wanted to say it, needed to say it, needed her to know and yet the words would not leave his mouth.

Adara stretched up to gently kiss his lips. "You need say nothing, husband. I needed to say those words, needed you to know how I feel about you, how you have my heart, how I love you beyond reason. Nothing else matters to me as long as you know that."

Words would not come for Warrick so he did what he could to show her how he felt. He scooped her up in his arms and carried her to the bed. He stripped himself and her of their garments, then he stretched out beside her on the bed.

He touched her with a gentleness he rarely showed, running his fingers over her soft skin, turning it to gooseflesh.

"I love your touch," she whispered, her senses rising along with her flesh. "I love everything about you."

He took her lips then and not gently. It was a deep hunger he felt for her, one that he would continue to feel for her, since he believed he would never have enough of her. The more he tasted, the more he wanted. As hungry as he was to join with her, he took his time. He wanted to cherish this moment, keep it—her words—in his memory forever and in hers as well.

It was almost like making love to her for the first time and in a way it was, for this time it was love that brought them together.

His lips followed where his hands had touched and though no part of his wife was new to his touch or taste, it seemed as if it was. For the first time in his life, he was making love with someone who loved him, truly loved him, and it made all the difference in the world.

"I cannot wait, Warrick," Adara cried out. "I have gone too long without you."

He had not thought his manhood could grow any harder, his need any stronger, but knowing his wife thirsted unmercifully for him drove him over the edge and he entered her with an unrelenting need of his own.

He gripped her bottom, her legs resting over his shoulders, as he drove in and out of her, ever mindful to be careful of her rounded stomach and his bairn that rested within. He loved the feel of her tight around him and he tilted his head back and let himself get lost in the exquisite pleasure.

Adara had not thought she could enjoy making love with her husband more than she already did, but this joining proved her wrong. There was something different about it and she knew what it was, knew without Warrick saying a word, that he loved her.

She let loose all her fears, all her doubts, and let herself love him.

Warrick looked down at her, feeling the difference, feeling her give herself completely to him and he did the same.

They burst together in a climax that united them like never before, that pleasured them like never before, that felt them loved like never before.

Warrick took her in his arms as they lay in the aftermath of their lovemaking and pulled a blanket over them when their heated bodies cooled and felt the chill in the room.

"I like the way you greet me upon your return home," Adara said with a soft laugh.

It took Warrick a few moments before he could say, "I cherish the words you greeted me with, wife."

Adara snuggled closer to him, resting her rounded stomach against him and laying her leg over his. "Then I will greet you that way each time you return home."

Warrick felt the bairn move against him and her cool skin begin to warm against his and at that moment he knew true happiness, true love. "Promise me, wife."

Adara looked up at him. "Promise you what?"

"That you will always greet me as you did tonight."

Adara smiled. "You need no promise from me for that, for I shall tell you every day how much I love you and even more so when you return home after being away."

Warrick struggled to say the words he felt in his heart, but had been beaten into him never to be said, never to be felt, never to be known.

Adara saw the struggle on his face and while it hurt her heart to see it, it also pleased her, for he no longer hid his feelings from her. They were there for her to see.

She ran her finger over his lips gently and said what she knew he felt in his heart. "You need say nothing, husband. I know you love me."

He hugged her tight, pleased that she knew him so well.

"I am patient. I can wait, and one day you will tell me yourself." She yawned and settled her head on his chest and shortly after fell asleep.

He felt when she drifted off and hoped her words proved right. It had not been only his father who had beaten it into him about how useless love was, but his mother as well. She had told him love was for fools. Marriage was a duty that was meant to unite clans, forge stronger bonds, and produce heirs. His father also told him to stick his manhood into any woman he wanted to, but care nothing for her. Get his release and be done with it.

Through the years there had never been any woman he had ever cared for, but then he had been a cold lover, taking more than giving... until Adara. There had been something different about her. Something that had warmed him. He had not wanted to take from her. He had wanted to give to her, as she had given to him, and that had made all the difference.

He drifted off, thinking how much he loved his wife.

~~~

Adara sat in her solar a few days later with Callie, stitching garments for the bairn. They talked, Callie entertaining her with her time spent in the convent.

"How are you not scarred from beatings with how much you misbehaved?' Adara asked with a soft chuckle.

"I had wondered the very same thing. I had not cared about what consequences I would suffer when I got left there. When the nuns raised no hand to me, I was surprised and more embolden by their lack of punishment. They started locking me in my room, not much of a punishment since I was used to spending time alone. I learned after a while that it was the only punishment that I would suffer if I did something wrong. I realized then why they never took a hand to me."

"Warrick," Adara said.

Callie nodded. "I figured he had put the fear of God into them if they should ever leave a mark on me."

They both turned quiet.

Adara knew their thoughts were similar, the idea of Warrick threatening the nuns, making them both wonder if he would have ever raised a hand to them, and raising the question about what he might have done to his first wife.

"Did you ask Warrick?" Callie asked.

"Ask me what?" Warrick said, entering the room.

Both women jumped in their seats, but said not a word.

Warrick moved to stand in front of both of them, looking from one to other. "I expect an answer."

Callie went to get up. "I should go. Roark is probably looking for me."

"Stay where you are, Callie," Warrick warned, "since I suspect you have something to do with this question my wife has for me."

"It is my own question. Callie has nothing to do with it," Adara said.

Warrick looked to his sister.

"I may have told her to ask you," Callie admitted with no reluctance.

He turned back to Adara. "Ask me, wife."

Adara debated briefly, if she should think of something else to ask him, but she did not want to lie to him.

"The truth, wife," Warrick warned.

"The truth, husband," Adara said, demanding the same of him to her surprise.

He nodded.

"I know about your first wife, Sondra," Adara said and watched his face harden and his dark eyes turn cold.

"That is not a question. Ask your question, Adara," he demanded.

She found it much too difficult to ask and besides, she did not believe he killed his first wife, so the question was not necessary. "It is not important."

"Ask me," he commanded with such sternness that it had Callie shifting uncomfortably in her seat.

A twinge of fear rose in Adara as she asked, "Did you kill Sondra?" She felt as if Warrick's dark eyes grabbed hold of hers and held them captive, and she found herself holding her breath.

"Aye, I killed Sondra," Warrick said and turned and walked out of the room.

Chapter Twenty-seven

Adara hurried to her feet, the garment she was stitching falling off her lap, and rushed to the door.

"You should leave him be," Callie warned.

"No, he needs me," Adara snapped and went after her husband, knowing in her heart it was the right thing to do. She caught him on the stairs going down. "Warrick, wait," she called out and in her rush to catch up with him lost her balance and began to tumble.

Warrick flew up the stairs and caught his wife in his arms, his heart pounding in his chest at the fear of what could have happened to her.

Adara pressed her face to his chest and gripped his arm firmly, her own heart thundering as badly as her husband's, hearing it pound against her ear.

"You need to be careful, wife," he scolded.

"Of my steps or the words I say to you?" she asked, glancing up at him and before he could scold again she continued. "I should not fear speaking to you about anything, nor should we keep secrets from each other."

"You keep secrets from me, wife?" he asked, a warning note in his tone as he hoisted her up against him and, with one arm around her, carried her up the stairs.

"I have no secrets just some curious thoughts, which I will share with you once you tell me about your first wife," she said with a gentle smile.

"You bargain with me?" he asked with a scowl.

"I talk freely with you, husband, and I wish for you to do the same with me."

That she had had the courage to follow after him once he had admitted to killing his wife had amazed him. He had expected her to flee, run from him in fear, never to return. Never had he expected her to follow after him.

Her love for him was far stronger, she more courageous, than he had ever imagined, and he was not deserving of her. How had she been able to love him when she, like himself, had been deprived of love? Where had she found the strength?

"How can you love me?" he demanded as he entered their bedchamber.

She smiled and her words spilled out with a soft laughter. "How can I not? You are so loveable."

He lowered her to her feet. "Only a fool believes a demon loveable."

"Then I will gladly carry the title proudly, for loveable you are to me." She took his hand and walked him to the bed and tugged him down beside her.

He sat alongside her, his body rigid, not saying a word.

She spoke since he refused to. "Tell me what happened, husband, for I do not believe you capable of killing your wife... intentionally."

"That is your first mistake, I am capable of killing for any reason that suits me," he said, not turning to look at her.

Her body wisely responded to his cold tone and rigid façade, a tingle of fear crawling over, but she refused to give it credence. Was she a fool after all? Should she pay heed to his words? Should she continue to fear her husband?

Her answer came unbidden. "I grow tired of fearing you, husband. I much prefer loving you."

Warrick turned and looked at her.

"I was so frightened of you on our wedding night, then you touched me gently and continued to do so throughout the night. I had never been touched with such a gentle hand and what I believed was a caring heart. I felt a spark of happiness when I learned it was not you who sent me to your dungeons to be tortured. I wanted to believe that night meant something to us both. I think the fear of discovering that that might not be true kept me from returning to you. I wanted to believe our bairn was conceived out of love. I wanted to believe you cared for me." She squeezed his hand, she continued to hold, and her other hand she laid against his chest. "I love you and I know, somewhere deep inside, you love me. So, husband, I refuse to fear you any longer. Instead, I will give you all the love I have stored inside me, all the love I have so desperately wanted to give someone. I will love you when you scowl at me. I will love you when you demand things of me. I will love you when you threaten me with punishment. I will love you with my dying breath and far beyond that."

Warrick turned and with his thumb brushed away the single tear that ran down her cheek. He fought to free the words imprisoned in his heart, never to be felt, never to be spoken.

Adara's heart ached watching her husband struggle to speak and she smiled and brought her lips close to his and whispered, "Love me."

He captured her lips in a kiss that said more than any words could and they were soon shedding their garments, their naked bodies coming together and blending as one. Their touches were gentle yet demanding, their kisses tender yet urgent, their love strong and growing ever stronger.

It was their fastest joining ever, Adara's loving declaration having aroused them more than the most intimate touches, and their shared climax left them blissfully satisfied. They laid wrapped around each other in the aftermath of their lovemaking, a satisfied silence filling the room.

It was not until Adara shivered in his arms that Warrick realized that a chill in the room had settled over their naked bodies. He was quick to tuck a blanket around his wife before slipping out of bed.

"Do not go," Adara said, her small hands gripping his arm to tug him back in bed.

"A moment," he assured her and kissed her brow. He went to the hearth and added several logs, stirring the dying fire until it blazed with a strong flame. He returned to her, slipping beneath the warm wool blanket to scoop his wife up in his arms and settle her on his lap after sitting and bracing his back against the headboard. He pulled the blanket over them, tucking it around his wife.

Adara settled comfortably in his arms as she always did. It felt like coming home when his powerful arms slipped around her and held her close, and she cherished that feeling and always would.

"Time to talk, wife," Warrick said.

Adara looked at him and smiled softly.

Warrick loved her smile, especially when it was directed at him. He also loved the feel of her in his arms. He had felt she belonged there from the first time he had held her, and when she was not in his arms, he felt more empty, more alone than he ever did. He was grateful she belonged to him, grateful she loved him, but then he belonged to her as well and he loved her as well and that would never change.

"King James arranged a marriage for me," he began. "With all the land and power I was accumulating in the Highlands, he wanted a union of his choice that would prove beneficial to his rule. I agreed and Sondra was sent to me to wed. All I knew of her was that she was the daughter of a clan chieftain from one of the northern isles. We met on our wedding day—"

Adara remained silent as her husband paused in thought, though she rested a comforting hand on his chest his wife's warm, gentle touch released him from his captured thoughts and he continued. "She did not want to wed me. She made it clear with her first words to me. She told me I should die and rot in hell where I belonged. I told the King's courier there would be no wedding, but he made it clear that there was no changing what had been agreed upon. The woman had no choice. She would do her duty and wed me and I should do the same since the documents were binding.

"I intended to consummate our vows quickly and let her be." He shook his head. "She had other intentions. She made it seem that she surrendered to the inevitable and would do her duty when she drew a knife on me suddenly, and without the least provocation. I reacted instinctively. I grabbed her wrist as she lunged the knife at my throat, twisting it away with such a sharp force that the blade caught at her throat slicing part of it.

"I grabbed her neck, trying to stop the blood that poured from it, but I knew it was too late. Her last words were garbled but I managed to make sense of them. It seemed I gave her what she wanted most… death rather than be my wife."

Adara wondered over the woman's extreme reaction to the arranged marriage. The woman certainly had not feared Warrick if she turned a knife on him, so why not submit to her husband and be done with it?

"Naturally, gossip spread and tales flourished. Many believed Sondra's clan would demand I pay for her death with my own. How King James managed to avoid any retribution I do not know, but nothing came of it. I refused to wed after that until the King grew impatient and arranged another marriage for me. Before any documents could be signed—"

"You took me as your wife," Adara said.

"Aye," he said with a nod. "I wanted someone who was accustomed to obedience."

"Who better than a servant, though from the King's message it would seem he will not sanction our union unless," —she paused, her brow wrinkling— "the man in the woods, your mission, that is what the King eluded to in his message. Unless that mission proves successful, he will not sanction our marriage."

Adara's shiver of fear trickled across his skin and he hugged her tighter against him. "I will let no one, not even the King, take you from me."

"I believe you. I also believe you would die trying, if the King should send troops against you, and what good would that do if we could not be together?"

"You will not worry over this. I will make certain the mission is successful."

Adara nodded, praying it would prove so. "I am sorry about Sondra. I feared being wed to you at first, but she had to have been filled with tremendous hate for you to prefer death to being your wife. How could she hate you when she did not know you?"

"Reputation I suppose."

"Then should it not be fear she felt for you? Where did her hate come from?"

"I never gave it thought," he admitted. "It was over and done. There was nothing to think on."

Adara could understand that. There was harshness she experienced that was better left buried. Though something as horrible as what Warrick had dealt with, she could not imagine being buried so easily.

A knock sounded at the door.

"Who disturbs me?" Warrick called out gruffly.

"Come away from that door, Callie," Roark ordered.

"No. I want to make sure Adara is all right," Callie argued.

"Did I not forbid you to disturb Warrick," Roark snapped.

"Forbid? Wrong word, husband," Callie snapped back.

Adara laughed softly at the couple arguing on the other side of the door.

"You find it amusing, wife?" Warrick asked and found himself unable to stop from smiling.

"Aye, I do. Your sister has a caring heart and much strength that she would choose to face your wrath to see that I was all right."

"She should know I would never harm you."

"She was not worried you would harm me. She was concerned how I would feel after speaking with you about Sondra. She is a good friend to me."

"I am not leaving here until I talk to Adara," Callie said, though more shouted.

"Aye, you are," Roark said.

"Put me down! Put me down now!" Callie shouted.

Adara and Warrick both laughed, and Adara called out. "I am fine, Callie. Worry not."

"I am pleased to hear that. We will talk later. Now put me down, Roark," Callie demanded.

"No, not until I punish you for disobeying me," Roark said.

Callie gasped. "That is not fair, husband, I much prefer when I feel your hand slap my naked backside."

"Get her out of here, Roark!" Warrick shouted out with a roar and shook his head and squeezed his eyes shut for a moment. "I do not need to hear what he does to my sister."

Adara laughed, her stomach gurgled in hunger, and the bairn gave a kick.

Warrick's hand went to her rounded stomach as he shouted out, "Send a servant, Roark." He caressed her stomach, the bairn moving beneath his hand. "I should have known hunger would strike you. It always does after we make love."

"I think the bairn demands more nourishment as well. He is growing more active with each day."

"You mentioned something about secrets," he said, leaving the rest for her to say.

"Not so much secrets as thoughts that linger and make me question," Adara said.

"Question what?"

"Why my mum and da decided to journey to the north Highlands, a rugged place for sure. It was something Burchard said that got me thinking. He told me that my da said something about the far Highlands being a place where men go to disappear. He was a crofter. Why go someplace where the land was not welcoming for planting? I wondered if my da wanted to disappear and if so, why?"

"When crops fail, crofts fail. There may have been nothing left here for your da."

"But my uncle sent my mum to a titled family in hopes she would make a good marriage. How did a woman living with a family of influence end up marrying a crofter?"

Chapter Twenty-eight

A light snow greeted the onset of winter and Adara enjoyed an early morning walk through the village. With the bairn active, moving and kicking inside her, she decided a walk was needed to calm him. Often his da's firm touch would settle him, but she had found herself alone in bed this morning when she woke.

The last two months had been pure joy. There had been no more attempts on Warrick or her life and no sign of Maia or cohorts. She and Warrick spent much time together and when she was not with him, she was with Callie and, not one to sit idle, she kept Adara busy. Her friendly nature had her speaking to everyone and soon Adara found herself knowing those in her clan better than she ever had.

She felt something she never thought she would feel... blessed.

Her hand had healed nicely, though certain chores or movements did bring pain, as did the colder weather. At least it was healed enough where it would not pain her to hold the bairn when he was born. A time not far off.

She had rounded considerably, though she still was not as large as when she last saw Espy only about three weeks ago. It had been one of many visits in the weeks before winter had set in. Espy had made quick friends with Callie and had offered advice on improving her chances of getting with child.

As blessed as she felt, Adara could not help but worry something would come along and steal it all away from her. She tried to ignore the feeling of doom that drifted over her like a gray cloud, hovering for a time before drifting away again. Then there was the lingering question of why her mum and da chose to go so far north. She feared she would never learn the answer since she knew of no one who could tell her.

She had spoken to Wynn time and again, but the woman offered little that would help. More so than anything, she had painted a better picture of Adara's mum. Young, vibrant, curious, and so beautiful she had a bevy of fine young men after her.

Why wed a crofter?" Adara had asked Wynn.

"Your mum loved your da and your da worshiped your mum. I believe they were made for each other," Wynn had said.

Their love seemed to be established and Adara was pleased to know that. She only wished she could have seen it for herself.

"More snow will be coming our way today, my lady."

Adara turned with a smile. "How do you know that, Langdon."

"The crispness of the air and the scent warns one to prepare," he said. "May I offer my arm, my lady? There is ice in spots and you would not want to slip and fall."

Adara reached out and took his arm. "You are most gracious, Langdon, though I wish you would call me Adara as you once did."

"It is not proper, my lady."

"Perhaps when we are alone like now, so that I feel I speak with a friend not a servant." It was not until she had made an effort to talk more with clansmen that she realized she had failed to recognize many in the clan who had befriended her.

Langdon gave a quick look around and seeing the few people about were at a distance, he conceded. "Adara, I am pleased you call me a friend."

"I believe I felt a camaraderie with you upon meeting since you were as new to the Clan MacVarish as I was and though I did little to encourage friendship, you always had a

271

kind word for me."

"A new place, new people, it takes time to come to know one another."

"Even more so when one barely utters a word," Adara said with a hint of laughter.

"Wise ones know it is better to hold the tongue and listen than rattle on senselessly. I rattle on senselessly," he said with a grin and a nod.

"There were many times I enjoyed your rattling and still do."

"That is good to know, Adara."

"You address my wife disrespectfully?"

Warrick's sharp tone had both of them turning.

"And how dare you lay a hand upon her," Warrick said, taking quick strides toward Langdon.

Adara let go of Langdon's arm and stepped in front of him. "He did nothing wrong. He offered his arm to me so that I would not slip on the ice and snow, and he called me by my name by my request. Something he had done before I became your wife and something I have missed hearing."

"He should know better and so should you," Warrick said, his tongue scolding both like disobedient bairns.

Langdon stepped to Adara's side. "Please forgive my improper behavior, my lord. I meant no disrespect."

Warrick stared at the man, the deep lines between his eyes a mark of his angry scowl. That she found pleasure talking with the man annoyed him and had since the first time he had discovered they had talked often. He did not care if his wife spoke with other women, but it irritated him when she spoke more than a few words to another man. Or was it that Langdon continued to irritate him since learning he had given his wife the two stones?

He had spoken to the old man about it, feeling foolish upon seeing him. There had been nothing to be jealous and yet here he was again annoyed and jealous at finding the old man talking to Adara.

Warrick was quick to wrap his hand around his wife's when she reached out to him and just as hasty to tuck her snugly in the crook of his arm. "Langdon is a good man and serves you well."

"He would serve me better if he kept his hands off my wife," Warrick said, looking to the man with a threatening glint in his eye.

"Langdon—"

"The man can speak for himself, Adara," Warrick snapped.

"Aye, my lord, and I shall not be so disrespectful again," Langdon said and bobbed his head.

"Leave us," Warrick ordered and with a nod to both Adara and Warrick, Langdon took his leave.

"Not a word," Warrick warned. "You were wrong and so was he. Do not get him in trouble again."

Adara glared at him. "So it was all my fault?"

"Of course it was," Warrick said, keeping hold of her arm as he began walking. "You should not have been walking alone through the village when snow and ice cover the ground and you were wrong for telling him to refer to you by your name. If I had thought it was his fault, he would have felt my fist to his face."

Adara stopped abruptly, forcing Warrick to do the same. She turned a smile on him. "You are jealous."

"I am not jealous," he argued.

"You are jealous? Why are you jealous?"

Warrick rolled his eyes, hearing his sister behind him and grew more annoyed when he heard his wife's soft laughter. He turned, Adara turning along with him, to face his sister. "I am not jealous."

Callie stared at him, a wide grin on her full face, and her arms crossed over her chest.

Warrick snapped his finger at his sister. "Your husband needs to take a firmer hand with you."

"He did last night and I quite enjoyed it," Callie said,

her smile never wavering.

Warrick shook his head. "I have heard enough. Both of you into the keep now and stay there until I give you permission to leave."

Callie hooked her arm around Adara's. "You read my thoughts, Warrick. It is far too cold to be outside today. We will see you later."

Callie tugged Adara along with her and after a few steps, she turned her head to see her husband staring after them, his dark eyes still smoldering with anger. She slipped her arm out of Callie's, turned and hurried back to her husband. She raised herself on her toes once she was in front of him and before kissing his tightly closed lips, whispered, "I love you, husband."

Her words settled around his heart and squeezed tight just like they always did. He would never grow tired of hearing her say that to him, and his lips responded of their own accord. They loosened and his tongue slipped out to run across her closed ones, urging them to open for him, and they did.

Adara loved her husband's kisses. Whether gentle or firm, slow or eager, they never failed to tingle her senses and arouse her.

Warrick warned himself not to let the kiss go on or he would hoist her up in his arms and carry her to their bedchamber where they would spend the rest of the day, in bed and out, making love.

He silently cursed himself for listening to his own warning, but there were serious matters that needed his attention. He rested his brow to hers.

"I will wait in the keep as you say," Adara said, tracing his warm lips with her finger. "Do not keep me waiting long, husband." She kissed him when he went to speak, the kiss as hasty as the words that followed. "I have a hungry need for you." She turned and hurried to Callie, not looking back, worried if she did, she would not be able to leave him.

The two women hooked arms again and continued to the keep.

"I am so glad you love my brother as you do. I would often feel guilty that I found a good man to love me, show me the love that I craved so desperately, and Warrick had no one to do the same for him. Now he does and I am so happy for him. He deserves it after the hell my father put him through. Please do not ever stop loving him."

Adara squeezed Callie's arm. "Rest assured, Callie, that that would be impossible. My love for your brother grows stronger every day."

"Good. Now let us go eat, and after we will stitch more garments for the bairn."

"We have stitched many already."

Callie lowered her voice. "We may have need of more." She was quick to explain when Adara looked ready to cry out with joy. "I do not know for sure, but the possibility grows stronger with each passing day. I just hope it is so."

"Does Roark know?"

Callie laughed. "From the first day I thought it was possible I said something to him and he has shared each day with me, waiting and hoping that we will have a bairn of our own come this summer."

Adara offered what she could. "I will pray it is so."

With wide smiles, the two women entered the Great Hall. They ate and talked and talked some more after settling in Adara's solar.

A knock sounded at the door before a voice called out. "Roark requests that his wife meet him at their cottage."

Callie smiled. "If he requested that I meet him there, then things must be finished for the day, which means Warrick will return soon to you." Callie stood with a stretch. "I intend to enjoy my husband for the rest of the day. You do the same."

Adara smiled, planning to do just that.

The door opened not long after Callie left and Adara

turned with a smile. "What did you forg—" Her smile died on her lips when she did not recognize the servant standing there.

"I knew no one would know me."

Adara stared at the woman for several silent moments and then her eyes grew wide—it was Maia. She looked nothing as she once did. She was thin to the point of looking gravely ill, her eyes sunk deep in her face and her gray hair had been sheared off above her shoulders that were stooped as if age had taken quick hold of her.

Maia shut the door behind her. "I see by your look that you never expected to see me again. Your knife did enough damage to me, though it also saved me. By not pulling it from my wound it kept the blood from flowing out too strongly and my friends were able to save me, searing the wound, though healing took its toll on me."

"You will never get out of the keep alive," Adara warned, praying that Warrick would arrive soon.

Maia laughed. "I came here to meet death. I am not strong enough or foolish enough to think I can best the Demon Lord, but I can make him suffer by taking the life of his wife and bairn."

"Why? Why do you hate Warrick so much that you want him dead?"

"Sondra."

"His first wife."

"You know her name so you know what happened to her."

"I know she tried to kill him."

"Liar!" Maia spit out the word like venom. "He killed her for the joy of it. Demons do that."

Adara needed no convincing that that was a lie. Warrick had been taught to do nothing for joy only for gain. His marriage to Sondra had been arranged for just that. Warrick would have done nothing to jeopardize that.

"Sondra attacked him."

"She would not have been foolish enough to do such a thing. She knew well she did not have the skill or strength to best the Demon Lord," Maia argued, shaking her head. "I taught her well like I tried to teach you."

"You knew Sondra?" Adara asked, trying to make sense of what had happened.

"I raised her, took care of her, soothed her when she took ill and comforted her when she cried."

"You were her nursemaid?"

Maia did not acknowledge Adara's questions but her words answered for her. "Sondra was a precious child, beautiful, caring, giving, gentle... far too gentle for the Demon Lord and yet—" Maia shook her head. "It was my fault. I told her that she had a duty to do. That she had to obey her father and wed Warrick. I thought her love for Searle was nothing more than a young lass's fancy. I never realized how much she loved the young warrior or how much he loved her."

Adara remained silent, wanting to keep the woman talking, giving Warrick time to return to the keep.

"Sondra was the daughter of a Viking chieftain who had settled in one of the north isles. The King approached her father about a marriage that would benefit the chieftain and the King. Her father was all too eager to compile, the benefits substantial." Maia shook her head. "I never learned until later that her father had Searle killed when he learned of the young man's plan to rescue his beloved. Searle had learned of Warrick's father's brutality with women and feared what Sondra might suffer even before she wed the Demon Lord."

"Sondra told Warrick that he had given her what she wanted... death."

"So that she could be reunited with the man she loved," Maia said, tears filling her eyes. "When Searle's family learned about it, they promised revenge and I joined them in their quest. They returned home after Searle's brother took ill. They did not want to lose him as well. I, on the other hand, have nothing to lose. I lost it all when Sondra died."

"What had brought you to the area where I had first met you?" Adara asked.

"I arrived here with Sondra to help her learn about her soon-to-be new home, the land and its people, and to prepare her to wed Warrick. I returned with her two brothers and cousins to help them take revenge against the Demon Lord. We lost track of him for a while and was surprised to discover he had wed. I was shocked to see it was you he took as his wife—a mere servant. I knew you could prove beneficial for us and you did when you freed me. You will be my revenge against him. He will find you dead, his bairn cut from your stomach never to know life."

"You have no time to do such a horrid thing. Warrick will be here soon," Adara warned.

Maia laughed. "You are a foolish lass. Callie will wait at the cottage for Roark, but he is busy with Warrick. By the time the message is found to be false, it will be too late for you and your bairn."

Adara felt a catch to her heart. Her husband was not coming. It was up to her to save herself and their bairn.

Maia pulled a knife out of her boot. "You have grown larger with child and that will slow you down."

"And you are frail from your wound and that will give me an advantage," Adara said, placing doubt in Maia's mind as she tried to do to her. But it would not work. She intended to do whatever it took to keep her bairn safe.

Maia laughed again. "I admire you. You are far too courageous to be nothing more than a servant, but a demon grows inside you and you must die."

"The only thing that grows inside me is an innocent bairn."

"It is a demon seed and it will grow no more," Maia said and charged at Adara.

~~~

After waiting in the cottage for a while, Callie got annoyed that her husband had yet to arrive. She stepped outside and looked around. Seeing Langdon, she waved him over and asked, "Have you seen Roark?"

"Last I saw him he was with Warrick in the warrior camp on the outskirts of the village," Langdon said.

Callie, her anger mounting that her husband had sent for her then kept her waiting, set out for the camp. She met Roark and Warrick halfway to the camp.

"So you send for me, husband, then leave me waiting," Callie scolded.

Roark went to his wife and wrapped her in his arms. "Sent for you?"

"You requested I meet you in the cottage. The servant brought the message to Adara's stitching room and I hurried here eager to see you."

"I sent no message," Roark said and turned to Warrick who was already breaking into a run. "Alert the men."

The two men went opposite ways. Instinct had Callie following her brother.

Adara was in trouble.

Chapter Twenty-nine

Adara's mind worked quick, ruling out getting past
Maia to run for the door. The stairs would be no place to
fight the crazed woman. Instinct had her grabbing the
tankard on the table as she rushed out of the chair and
throwing it at Maia. It hit her in the head, stunning her for a
moment and giving Adara the time she needed to hurry and
grab a log from the pile by the hearth. It was not much of a
weapon, but it would serve as a shield against the knife.

Maia stumbled, almost falling, but caught herself.
Blood ran into her eye from the cut on her brow just above
it. She wiped it away with the back of her hand and glared at
Adara. "I will make sure that you are still alive when I cut
the child from your belly so you can watch it die along with
you."

Maia may have meant to frighten her, but Adara found
strength in her terrifying threat. "You are vile and I will see
you dead."

Maia laughed. "You will not best me this time." She
lunged again and Adara blocked the thrust of the knife with
the log and gave a shove, sending Maia stumbling back. As
she did, Adara hurled the log at the woman. It hit Maia in the
shoulder and sent her stumbling again only this time she
could not stop herself from falling, the knife slipping from
her hand as she did.

Adara rushed for the knife.

Maia was quick to roll and grab for it and as Adara's
hand reached the handle first, gripping it tight, Maia's hand
fell over hers, locking around it like an iron shackle and
yanking Adara, sending her to her knees.

Adara sent a punch to the woman's wound and Maia

sent a hard kick to Adara's one leg. Adara ignored the pain that shot through her leg, her only thought to keep her bairn safe. Maia raised her free hand and Adara grabbed her wrist and wrenched it back hard before the vicious blow could land on her stomach.

Maia let out a yell and let go of Adara's wrist to give her a quick punch to the jaw, stunning Adara for a moment but not enough to prevent her from raising the knife as Maia went to grab it from her. It sliced the palm of her hand and blood began to pour from it.

Pain and fury raged on Maia's face and in an instant her bloody hand grabbed Adara's neck, squeezing tight.

Adara plunged the knife into Maia's stomach.

The woman gave a cringing yell, then tightened her fingers at Adara's throat. "I'll choke the life from you before I die."

Adara struggled for air as she went to pull the knife out of Maia, knowing she had little time to get the next plunge where it would do the most good. Maia's free hand came up to stop her, but Adara grabbed her injured wrist and gave it a sudden, sharp snap.

The intense pain caused Maia to loosen her grip on Adara's throat, returning some breath and strength to her. It was enough to pull the knife from Maia just as her fingers dug into Adara's neck once again with a strength born of desperation to see her dead.

Adara did not waste a minute, she plunged the knife into Maia's neck with one good thrust. Blood spewed out, hitting Adara in the face and Maia's eyes widened for a second with what seemed like pleasure. The woman's hand loosened at her throat and Adara pushed it away, gasping for breath.

This time Adara took no chances, she pulled the knife out of Maia's throat and blood spewed out soaking her garment across her chest. She sat on the floor beside the dying woman and stared as her life drained away. "I gave you what you came for… death."

When the gurgling stopped and no breath came from Maia, Adara tried to stand, but she found she had no strength left. She crawled to the nearby corner and managed to sit up, bracing her back to the wall. She stared at the blood covering her hands, felt it wet on her face, smelled it on her garment.

With a hefty sigh, she rested her hand on her protruding stomach and closed her eyes. "You are safe, little one. You are safe."

The door burst open and the first thing Warrick saw was his wife, her eyes closed, blood covering her face, her hands, her garment, and he let out a furious roar that echoed through the entire keep and beyond.

Adara's eyes shot open and, seeing her husband, she smiled.

Warrick thought his heart would leap from his chest as he rushed to her and just before he dropped down beside her, he saw Maia, blood pooling around her, her mouth agape, and her eyes wide and lifeless. He turned his attention to his wife.

"This is Maia's blood," Adara said, seeing what she never thought she would ever see on her husband's face— fear.

"Are you hurt anywhere?" he asked, wanting nothing more than to take her in his arms and hold her tight.

She shook her head.

Warrick shut his eyes briefly and let out a breath, then he slipped his arms under his wife and lifted her gently into his arms and stood.

Roark waited by the door with his arm around his wife, tears streaming down her face.

"I want not a spot of blood left in this room," Warrick said to Roark. "Callie, please have the servants prepare a bath in my bedchambers."

She nodded.

"I am fine," Adara said, seeing the tears streaming

down Callie's face.

"We should send for Espy," Callie said.

"No," Adara said, "with the snow already on the ground and the feel in the air of more to come it is not good for her to travel in her condition. I suffered no serious harm. I do not need a healer."

Warrick thought otherwise. "Send for Cyra." He stopped his wife before she could object. "It is not for you to decide." He tucked her closer against him and walked out of the room and when they got to their bedchamber, he sat on the bed and rested her in his lap, his arms remaining firm around her.

"Warrick," Adara said with a soft worry when the silence grew too heavy.

"I thought you were dead," he said, resting his brow to hers. "I thought I had lost you." He raised his head his eyes settling on hers. "I have never known such fear, such helplessness… such rage at being powerless. I cannot lose you, Adara. You are a part of me. Without you my heart would not beat, I would not be able to breathe, my soul would not be free. You taught me what it is to love." He took a deep breath and said, "I love you, Adara. I love you with all my strength, all my heart. I love you forever and beyond."

Adara felt the tear trickle down her face. "Your words, your love, fill me with joy. I do so love you, husband."

The words spilled more easily from his lips. "And I love you, wife, more than I can express."

"You can show me." She grinned mischievously. "I love when you show me."

"I will show you often and tell you often."

"Every day," she teased with a soft laugh.

"Every day," he agreed with a whisper and went to kiss her.

Adara turned her head away. "Do not kiss me. I will not have her blood stain your lips."

Warrick took hold of her chin and turned her face to look at him.

"Please pay heed to my plea. I want it washed away, all of it, the blood from the past, the blood I wear now. I want us to start fresh, cleansed of all the evil we both have suffered."

"I will wash it away, wife, and when it is gone, I will kiss you for the first time."

Adara smiled. "I look forward to that kiss more than any kiss you have given me."

The servants began to enter the room, Wynn gasping when she looked at Adara.

"I am not injured," Wynn," she assured the old woman and slipped out of her husband's arms to stand and nearly collapsed from the pain that shot up her leg if she had not grabbed Warrick's arm.

He lifted her again in his arms and went to lay her on the bed.

Adara protested. "No, I am bloody and the bedding is clean."

"I do not care if the bedding gets bloody. The servants can change it," Warrick said and laid her on the bed. "You said you were not injured. What pains you?"

"My leg. Maia gave it a good kick."

Warrick pulled back the hem of her shift and shook his head at the dark bruise on the calf of her left leg. He was angry that he had failed to be there for her, failed to protect her, failed to keep her safe, and in their own home.

"It is not your fault," she whispered, knowing well his thoughts.

He lowered himself down on his haunches to look in her lovely dark blue eyes. "I told you I would keep you safe."

"And you did." She continued before he could argue. "You helped me conquer my fears and gave me the courage to defend myself. I am forever grateful you chose me as your wife."

"You tricked me into choosing you," he teased.

"However did I do that when I did not know you?" she asked with soft laughter.

"I chose a woman who appeared obedient, shy, fearful, and what did I get?" He smiled. "I got more than I bargained for. I got a woman stronger and more determined than any woman I have ever known and one that loves like I have never known. Now let me get you washed since I desperately want to kiss you."

When the servants left, Warrick stripped off her garments and cast them aside to be burned. He never wanted to see them on her again, no matter how clean they might be. He lifted her and gently placed her in the tub. He scrubbed her hair first, digging his fingers into her scalp, making sure he got rid of any blood that might be there. Then he scrubbed the blood from her body, watching as each part of her skin glistened and the smell of lavender began to drift off her. He worked quickly not wanting her to sit long in the water that had turned a putrid shade of red from the blood.

She was as eager as he to have the blood gone, to see it done and over with. She shivered when he lifted her out of the tub, a light chill greeting her.

He was quick to wrap a towel around her and stand her in front of the hearth as he dried her. The bairn had changed her body and he loved the more defined curves to her waist and hips, her fuller breasts, her rounder backside. He loved watching her stomach grow larger with their bairn. There would be many more bairns to follow, a given since they made love so often, and he looked forward to watching her stomach grow with each one, knowing their love had conceived another bairn.

"You are beautiful, wife," he said, his hand resting gently on her stomach.

Adara smiled. "For the first time in my life, I feel beautiful."

Warrick lowered his head. "You have always been beautiful."

Adara stretched her head up, eager to meet his lips as they came down on hers, eager to taste his kiss. It was no different than when he had kissed her before and yet it was different in every way. They were no longer strangers, no longer bound by a loveless union. They kissed because they loved and that was what made the kiss so different, so special in every way.

The kiss left Adara wanting more and she took his hand and tugged him toward the bed.

Warrick stopped her with a tug of his own. "We wait for Cyra, to be sure you are unharmed."

"That is not fair," Adara said with a pout.

"I agree, but until the healer confirms you are well, I will not touch you intimately." He rested his hand on her stomach. "I want to be sure you both are unharmed."

That he loved her enough to deny himself pleasure, stirred her heart, though it did not help the sensual stirrings in her.

Warrick quickly fetched her nightdress. He needed to cover her up or he feared he would not follow his own dictate. Afterwards, he settled her in bed and directed the servants to clear out the tub and to bring a hot brew.

He sat beside her on the bed as she sipped at the fragrant brew. "You were a brave warrior today, wife. You kept our bairn safe. I am proud of you."

Adara swelled with pride, something she had never felt in her life. "We have no more worry from them." Adara went on to explain what Maia had told her about Sondra and the man she loved, Searle, and how he feared for Sondra. "His own father having seen how brutal your da could be with women. He planned on rescuing her, but Sondra's da saw that that never happened."

Warrick assumed that was why the dying Viking warrior had referenced his da. He thought Warrick the same as his da, brutal and heartless. "The sad part is that I would have expected Sondra to do her duty as Maia had encouraged her to do. Now, though, after falling in love with you, I mourn the pain our arranged marriage cost her. I will see what can be done to make amends to Searle's family so they know I was not part of this."

"That is generous of you," Adara said.

"It is not generous. It is a wise thing for me to do."

Adara poked at her husband's arm. "Wise maybe, but definitely generous."

A knock sounded at the door and before Warrick could call out, Callie's voice rang clear. "It is Callie and Cyra is with me."

Warrick shook his head. "I will warn our sons about having a sister."

"What if we have all daughters?" Adara asked with a gentle laugh.

"Do not curse us, wife," he snapped and Adara laughed again as he shouted for Callie to enter.

Callie rushed in before Cyra and went straight to the bed. "Cyra was already on her way here from MacCara keep when the warriors came upon her. Espy asked her to check on you since Craven refuses to let her go anywhere, winter signs promising more snow."

Cyra smiled broadly as she approached the bed. "You have a lovely sister, Warrick."

"She is a pest," Warrick grumbled, it growing harder to keep Callie's identity a secret.

"And he loves me dearly," Callie announced as if she proclaimed it to be so.

Cyra held back her laugh. Adara did not.

"You should go and leave us women to tend Adara," Callie said with a smile to her brother.

"Where is your husband?" Warrick asked, not budging off the bed.

"I am right here to collect my wife," Roark said,

entering the room.

"I want to stay and see for myself that Adara is well," Callie protested.

"I am well, Callie. There is no need for worry. You can come visit me later and we will talk," Adara said.

"If Cyra gives permission," Warrick added.

"Of course," Callie said, "I will abide by anything Cyra says."

"Yet you have a difficult time following my orders," Warrick said.

"You are my brother," Callie said as if that in itself explained it.

"And your husband?" Warrick asked. "How do you not obey him?"

"I obey Roark," she said, turning a smile on her husband. "Sometimes. A few times. Every now and then."

"Like now," Roark said not able to keep a grin from his face. "Come, wife, we take our leave."

Callie looked to Adara. "I am glad you are well. I will see you later, hopefully. She hurried to her husband's side and out the door the couple went.

"Callie is a delightful pest," Cyra said, the soft laugh she had tried to stifle slipping out.

"Someone who agrees with me," Warrick said and stood. "I am grateful you came to tend my wife." He stepped aside, but he had no intentions of leaving the room.

"How have things been going with the bairn?" Cyra asked as she sat on the spot Warrick had vacated.

Warrick grew impatient after a while, Cyra seeming to ramble on about things that had nothing to do with what Adara had suffered. He was about to interrupt when her questions began to change. Warrick realized after a few more questions what the healer was doing. She was establishing a pattern to see if anything had interrupted it.

When she finally finished, having spent time examining Adara's leg thoroughly, Cyra said, "I will prepare a comfrey poultice for the bruise. It will help heal it and a comfrey soak will do your hand well."

"What is wrong with her hand?" Warrick demanded and saw that her right hand was tucked beneath the blanket.

Cyra stepped aside as he stepped forward.

He held his hand out to her. "Let me see it."

Adara could not very well refuse him, though she wished she could, since she knew it would hinder a chance for them to be intimate tonight. She slipped her hand from beneath the blanket.

Warrick cringed when he so how it had swelled. "Does it pain you?"

"It most certainly does," Cyra answered for her. "Espy asked me to see that Adara's hand continued to heal nicely. Today's altercation changed that."

"I did not notice it," Warrick said.

"The swelling started when she finally rested. The comfrey soak will help as will limited use of her hand until the swelling goes down and even for a while afterwards."

"I will see that she does," Warrick said, sending his wife a stern look and she returned a smile. "You will stay a few days to make sure she does well, Cyra?"

It may have been a request, but it was clear it was more of a demand.

"I have little choice with the snow that has started falling heavily," Cyra said, "though I do not mind. I was hoping to see if anyone else needed tending here."

"I am grateful for whatever healing you can provide for my clan," Warrick said.

"I will go see to having the poultice prepared while I partake of a hot brew. These old bones do not favor the cold."

"Thank you, Cyra," Adara said. "I am glad you are here."

"All is well, Adara. There is no cause for worry." Cyra closed the door behind her as she left the room.

Adara hurried to explain when Warrick sat on the edge of the bed. "I did not want you to worry or delay making love to me. That is why I said nothing about my hand."

He brushed the strands of her blonde hair away from her cheek, pleased that it now fell past her shoulders. He loved to run his fingers through the soft strands and watch the natural waves fall gracefully around her face. He also loved when she pinned it up and strands would fall free to tickle her cheeks or neck.

God, but he loved his wife.

"The future stretches in front us with endless days and nights to make love. As for worry, from this day on no worry shall be heaped on one and not the other. We share our worries."

She frowned. "That does not seem fair since mine is always greater than yours."

"And yours will be less when you share it with me."

He always sounded so assured and that always comforted Adara.

"If you say so, husband," she conceded.

"I say so, wife," he said and kissed her cheek. "Now tell me is there any worry you want to share with me?"

Adara could think of only one thing, but she had given her word she would not speak of it again to him. So how did she share her worry?

"Tell me what it is," Warrick urged, seeing that something kept her from voicing her concern.

"You told me never to speak of it again, but I worry— how can I not—when your mission is now tied with the sanction of our marriage?"

His brow narrowed and his jaw grew taut. "It would make matters worse if I shared that with you, but there is no need for worry. It will be done soon."

A knock sounded at the door and Roark called out, "A matter needing your attention."

Adara looked to her husband, unable to keep the worry

out of her eyes.

"No worries," Warrick commanded and gave her a hasty kiss. "Rest. I will return soon."

Adara lay there after he left, thinking on all that had happened. Was all good? Was there no reason to worry? Was her marriage secure?

Her thoughts were too jumbled to let her rest. She got out of bed and went to the window to look out on the cold, dreary day that seemed much like her thoughts. All was quiet, snow falling, the land a pristine white. All was well and she should not let worry trouble her.

Maia was gone. No one was out to kill her or Warrick. They were safe.

Her eyes caught movement at the edge of the woods. Someone was there.

Warrick suddenly came into view heading toward the woods and a short, cloak-draped figure darted out from beyond the trees and rushed toward her husband. The two talked and once again she watched as she did that night months ago as Warrick dropped a purse in the man's hand.

What secrets did they keep? What did the man search for?

Until she knew, her worries would not cease.

Chapter Thirty

The Great Hall was empty, no one about, the only sound the crackle of the roaring fire as Adara slipped on her cloak ready to take an early morning walk, the bairn restless since she woke. All had quieted in the month since Maia had attacked her and she was pleased that her leg healed quickly along with her hand. It pained her now and then, but mostly it had healed well.

She had another reason for a walk this early. She had woken to an empty bed and that was a rare occurrence. She wondered what had taken her husband from their bed and hoped her walk would uncover his whereabouts.

The cold stung her cheeks when she stepped outside and a light snow fell on her. There had been no heavy snow since a month ago, only a light spattering now and again, which allowed Adara the pleasure of her morning walks.

She had barely taken a few steps when powerful arms coiled around her waist, startling her, and she was turned around to settle in her husband's arms.

"What are you doing walking alone so early on this cold morning?" Warrick asked, keeping her close against him.

"The bairn was restless. I thought a walk would calm him and since my husband deserted our bed I had no choice but to seek a walk on my own."

"Out of necessity, never willingly do I leave you alone in our bed," Warrick said and kissed her cheek.

Adara turned her head along with her husband, hearing anxious footfalls. Roark rushed toward them and if his hurried footfalls did not alert to a problem, his expression did. There was worry in his blue eyes.

"A body has been found near the edge of the woods, not

far from the kitchen garden," Roark said. "You need to see it."

Warrick nodded. "After I return Adara safely to the keep."

Adara latched onto her husband's arm. "I am going with you and please do not argue with me on this. The bairn needs the walk and I want to see for myself who it is. Besides, it is not far." She tugged at her husband's arm as she stepped forward as though the decision had been made.

Warrick followed along with her, not bothering to argue. He preferred her with him anyway. He kept a firm hand on his wife, the light snow having turned to ice in some places., and he did not want her to suffer any fall especially with the birth so close.

The body lay just beyond the kitchen garden, a disturbing thought to Warrick. How had someone gotten that close without being spotted? His troubling thoughts turned to anger when he came upon the body.

"The man you met with in the woods," Adara whispered, staring at the short man, lying on his back, a deep gash in his temple.

Warrick stared at the dead man, Ronald. He had done business with the little man on various occasions, not that he liked him nor did he trust him, but he was a necessary evil. He had certain connections that he had acquired through years of dirty dealings. When Warrick's own attempts to find the man King James searched for had hit a stone wall, he had had no choice but to seek Ronald's help. At their last meeting, he had told Warrick that he was close to discovering the person's identity. Had Ronald succeeded and had he been followed here and murdered before he could give Warrick the information? Warrick had no way of knowing and no way of finding out what Ronald had come to tell him… unless he caught the person who murdered him.

What disturbed Warrick even more was that the person who killed Ronald had followed him here, which meant the culprit was aware that someone here was searching for the information.

"This does not bode well," Roark said.

Warrick nodded as he turned toward Roark and saw that his wife had turned deathly pale, staring down at the dead man. He slipped his arm around her. "You should not be looking upon this."

His words snapped her out of her fearful thoughts. "He is the man who helps you with your mission for the King. Any information he had died with him. King James will not sanction our marriage."

Warrick ran his warm finger along her chilled pale cheek, wanting desperately to have color return to it. "You are my wife and no one will take you from me. You have my word on that."

"The King *might* not take me from you, but with our marriage not sanctioned, it means our child will be considered a bastard and no heir to your land and holdings. I know what it feels like to have nothing, be considered nothing. I do not want that for our child."

"That is not going to happen. I will find the man who killed him and find out what he knew." He shook his head when she went to speak. "He is not dead long, which means the person cannot be far." He turned to Roark. "You have sent men?"

"They scour the area. He will be found," Roark assured him.

Warrick was relieved to see that a bit of color had returned to his wife's face when he turned to her. "I will see you safely to the keep where you will get warm, rest, and not worry."

Adara found anger suddenly replacing her fear. She had obeyed her husband and not questioned him about the meetings in the woods with the short man. Even when the King had threatened their marriage, she had not asked her husband about the mission. But now with the man dead and her child's future at stake, she could hold her tongue no more.

"You told me we would share our worries. This truly worries me," she said and surprised him by taking a step away from him. "You have kept me ignorant of this mission of yours for King James. I will know what goes on here."

"You make a demand of me, wife?" Warrick snapped and saw the sting of heat hit her cheeks though it was not because she was repentant, it was anger he watched flare in her eyes.

"Aye, I do," she returned to his side, placing her hand on his arm. "Being kept in the dark about this makes me worry all the more. Please, Warrick, I may be able to help, and I give you my word I will tell no one."

Warrick kept a silent tongue for a moment, then once again turned to Roark. "Have the body moved to one of the empty sheds. I will view it shortly and let me know as soon as you catch the culprit." His words left no room for failure. The culprit was to be caught. He turned to his wife, taking firm hold of her hand. "Come, we talk in my solar."

They were both silent on their return walk to the keep. Once in Warrick's solar nothing was discussed until the servants brought hot brews and Adara was snug in a chair near the fire with a warm wool blanket tucked around her.

Warrick stood at the edge of the hearth and spoke as soon as the door closed behind the servants. "I cannot impress on you enough the importance of no one knowing what I am about to tell you."

"I have given my word. I will say nothing," she assured him.

He continued, "The throne has gone through many kings through the years, some worthy, some not. Some true descendants, others not. There has been a claim in the last few years that a true descendant of the first King of Scotland, Kenneth Alpin, had been found and is rightful heir to the throne. King James was warned about him and supposedly was shown proof that he existed. My mission is to find that heir. I searched and hit a point where I could find out no more. The man murdered, Ronald The Wise as he called himself, since he could find things out few could, claimed to have knowledge of this heir. Ronald was a sly one, always alert, always listening and gathering information that could possibly someday, somehow prove beneficial to him. He would store the information away for later use. When he caught wind of an apparent true heir, he paid heed to the news and kept storing whatever he discovered. When you heard us in the woods that day, Ronald told me he was close to discovering the identity and whereabouts of the so-called true king. I can only assume that was the news he was bringing me and was killed for it. When my men find the person who killed Ronald, I will have the answers. I will find the person and complete my mission. It will be done and our marriage sanctioned."

"What if the culprit is not found? Or what if he has taken his life rather than chance being caught?" Adara asked.

"I will see this done, wife. There is no need for worry."

Her husband's confidence helped, but there was another worry. "This is a secret mission for King James?"

"Aye it is. His reign goes good and he needs no stain on it," Warrick confirmed.

"Once you find this man and see your mission done, what is to stop the King from seeing you dead since you know this secret?"

"You have a quick mind, wife," he said. "I believe I am more valuable to the King alive than dead. Besides, if he feared me knowing too much about him, I would be dead already."

"What of the true king? Would you not want to see him take the throne?"

Warrick's own words surprised him. "I grow tired of war and it would take a war to see this man sit the throne. Good men, women, and children would die, and who is to say this person is the true heir to the throne? And if he is, is he capable of ruling or will he be nothing more than a puppet king? Then what of those who rule him? Do they care for the people or only of wealth and power?"

"What if he is a good man?"

"You do not want to know the answer to that, wife," he warned and walked over to crouch down in front of her. "You have seen for yourself since you were young how cruel and uncaring people can be. I do what I must to protect my clan and keep them safe and I make no excuse for it. You will always be safe with me, Adara. I will do whatever it takes to make sure of it."

Adara leaned forward in the chair, her hand going to rest against her husband's warm cheek. "I never realized how much you sacrifice for others."

"A great warrior leader does not sacrifice, he does what he must."

Adara knew the words were not his own. "A lesson your father taught you?"

"One lesson that has served me well."

Adara turned a soft smile on him and leaned forward to brush a feather-like kiss to his lips. "I love you, husband. You are a good man." She kissed him again when he went to speak, sensing he would deny her claim. "Do not waste your words, nothing will change how I feel about you."

"Foolish woman," he scolded with a smile.

"Aye, that I am, husband," she said proudly. "Now go and do what you must. I am going to sit here and enjoy the warmth of the fire and my hot brew."

"I will have Wynn see that food is brought to you," Warrick said as he stood, then he kissed her brow.

"You will tell me about anything you find?" she asked.

"Aye, I will," he said and was gone.

Adara settled back in the chair, closing her eyes. There was something about the dead man that disturbed her. She allowed herself to recall the gruesome scene. What was it that she had seen that nagged at her? She could not place it no matter how hard she tried.

The servants further disturbed her thoughts when they entered the room and it was when one of the servants stepped in front of her to place a tray of food on the small table beside the chair that Adara realized what she had been trying so hard to recall.

She jumped up out of the chair, the blanket falling to the floor and ran from the room.

~~~

"What do you mean the tracker has found no tracks?" Warrick demanded, approaching the shed where Ronald had been taken.

"The only tracks he found leading to the keep were Ronald's and there were none leading away from the keep," Roark explained. "Though, the snowfall is light, it does not help."

"Have the men spotted anyone in the area?"

"Not a soul or a sign of one so far," Roark said, "and Ronald was still warm, the blood still flowing from him. The culprit should have been spotted by now. The men are spread out across the land. There was no way he could have slipped past them."

Warrick said what was obvious. "Which means the person is here in the village. The question is… was Ronald followed or did his search lead him here to the village? Something else has troubled me while searching for this apparent heir. Where is the support for this true king? Where are the warriors who would fight for him?"

"Perhaps many do not believe his claim," Roark suggested.

"Whatever the reason, it also helps keep his secret. Our only recourse is to find the man who killed Ronald and that should prove easy since he hides here among us."

The mourn of a distant horn caught both men's attention and had them taking quick steps to the front of the village.

~~~

The sound of the horn stopped Adara, forcing her to delay her search. She kept to the keep stairs, watching out over the village as many of the men wandered toward the front of the village while some remained behind, weapons in hand.

Callie hurried up the stairs to stand beside Adara. "Riders approach fast and strong."

Adara felt Callie tremble, the young woman having taken her hand.

"No attack bell sounds," Adara said, attempting to reassure her.

"No, but that does not mean that an attack does not take place elsewhere, which would mean my Roark would be sent off to handle it."

Warrick could go as well and the bairn's birth was not far off. Not that Adara needed Warrick to be there, though she preferred he was so that he could see the new bairn as soon as he was born.

"Perhaps it is nothing," Adara said, hoping to ease both of their concerns.

Adara's words proved wrong as soon as she caught sight of her husband walking toward her. His jaw was set tight, his brow deeply wrinkled, and his eyes sparking with anger.

"The damn fools pay me no heed. This time they will learn and quickly," Warrick said his declaration meant more for himself than those around him.

Adara went down the stairs to meet him.

Warrick took hold of her arm and hurried her back up the stairs and looked to Callie. "Go to your husband. We leave for battle."

Callie let out a cry and ran off.

Once in the Great Hall, Warrick took his wife in his arms. "The MacNair Clan are at it again and this time I am going to dispose of their nonsense quickly." He placed his hand on his wife's rounded stomach, spreading his fingers to feel as much of the bairn as he could." "I will be here for his birth." The bairn gave his da a good kick.

Adara smiled. "He is pleased to hear that." Her smile faded. "It is not that I need you here for me to give birth. It is that I would like you here. You give me strength." Her smile returned as she laid her hand over her husband's. "I may need more than I first thought since he is a determined one."

"I will be gone a day at the most. I will end this quick and the MacNair Clan will trouble me no more." He brushed his lips over hers. "I am glad Cyra did not return home and that Innis joined her here. Between a healer of old and a physician, I feel you will do well, and you will not be able to keep Espy away."

"I am pleased they will be here to help me, but—"

"I will be here, Adara, you have my word." He kissed her again and held her close.

She eased out of his arms. "The sooner you go, the sooner you will return to me."

"I love you, wife," he said and hurried away, his anger mounting that he was being forced to leave his wife when she needed him. He intended to make the MacNair Clan suffer for it.

Callie came running into the Great Hall shortly after Warrick left, tears streaming down her cheeks. "I warned my brother to bring my husband home safely. I will not be left a widow with a child on the way."

Adara recalled the joy on Callie's face when she told all that she was with child. She wore an endless smile until today.

"Warrick says he will be done fast with it. They will return soon and all will be well."

300

"I pray it will be so," Callie said.

It was not until later in the day when Callie returned to her cottage to nap that Adara got a chance to pursue her search. When she had looked upon one of the servant's hems, she had realized what had plagued her about the dead man. She had spotted a scrap of cloth on a bush not far from his body. It was the plain brown wool cloth the servants wore, but it was faded, which meant it was worn by a servant that had served many years here in the keep."

Adara went in search of Wynn, planning on asking her who, of the servants, wore the old faded garments. She found her in Warrick's solar, directing two servants. She smiled at the way Wynn admonished the young lasses for not doing their task correctly.

As Adara watched her demonstrate how to sweep the hearth thoroughly clean of ashes, her eyes caught the hem of her underdress and saw that it had been torn, a section missing. Her hand went to her stomach as an anxious flutter hit it.

"Wynn," Adara called out. "A word please."

Wynn nodded with a smile and ushered the lasses out with the bucket of ashes. After she shut the door behind them, Wynn turned to Adara. "What can I do for you, my lady?"

"You can tell me what you were doing in the woods with the man that was found dead."

Chapter Thirty-one

Adara sat by the fire in her bedchamber. It had been a long day with much happening. Espy had arrived by mid-afternoon, wanting to make certain she was there when Adara's time came. Callie had spent a good part of the evening talking with her and it was not until later when everyone began to retire that Espy had approached her.

"Something weighs heavily on your mind. Are you fearful of giving birth?" Espy had asked.

Adara had made excuse after excuse, but in the end she was sure Espy did not believe a one of them. Espy had been right about one thing… something weighed heavily on her mind.

Wynn had shocked her with what she had told her and she was still trying to digest it. She did not believe it possible and yet it had answered so many questions and had all made sense. After all these years, she had answers and yet those answers disturbed her more than she ever imagined possible.

She was relieved that Warrick was not there. She did not know how she would keep this from him, but she had no choice. She could not tell him. Not ever.

The night grew late, but Adara did not seek her bed. Sleep would not be something she would get tonight, and though she ached for her husband's return, she hoped it would be delayed at least a day. It would give her the time to… she wiped at the tear that threatened to fall.

How she would ever keep this from her husband, she did not know.

The door suddenly flung open and Adara jumped out of the chair, the blanket that had been wrapped around her falling to the floor.

Warrick stood there, his breathing harsh, his hand gripping the door handle, his knuckles scraped and bruised from battle. His dark eyes raged with the aftermath of battle and need... need for his wife.

Adara saw how he wrestled with his intense desire, her rounded stomach reminding him of the bairn, and knowing it was not a gentle lovemaking he wanted. But then Adara had a need to forget everything she had learned if only for a while, and she had a desperate need to feel loved, and her husband could give her that.

She stretched her arms out to him.

Warrick hesitated, his passion strong, and he feared his raging desire might bring harm to his wife and the bairn. He growled low in his chest, a warning to himself that he should leave, then his wife pulled her garment off and extended her arms once more.

Her invitation was too much to deny. He swung the door shut behind him and stripped off his garments as he walked toward her. He stopped a distance from her and warned, "I have no gentleness in me this night."

"Do you love me, husband?"

"More than you will ever know."

Adara stepped toward him and Warrick reached out and yanked her into his arms. His kiss was not gentle. It demanded with a hunger that Adara quickly fed. She was in his arms before she knew it, his lips refusing to leave hers as he walked them to the bed.

He lowered her next to the bed, but held her high enough off the floor so that he could tease her one nipple with his tongue before taking it in his mouth to nip at it.

Adara moaned, her hands going to grip her husband's arms taut with muscles. She dropped her head back when his tongue and mouth moved to her other breast, and when his lips moved to kiss her lips again, it stole her breath.

She barely caught her breath when he lowered her to her feet, spun her around, and bent her over the bed. She had little time to brace her hands on the bed when he thrust his hand between her legs to tease the small nub until it throbbed unmercifully. When she cried out from the pleasure building in her, his manhood drove into her hard and fast.

He gripped her backside as he pounded against her, a feral growl rumbling from him as he did. He needed her, he needed to bury himself deep inside her, feel her cocoon around him, hold him tight, know she loved him.

Adara's moans grew as did his growl and when she screamed out his name as she climaxed, he let loose with a roar, his own climax exploding with a fury.

Warrick dropped over her, his hands landing beside her own as she kept herself braced on the bed, her round stomach faintly brushing the bedding. She shuddered as the climax rippled through, enjoying every last ripple and she squeezed tight, keeping him inside her for a while longer.

He shuddered and groaned as he felt her clamp around him and he nipped at her shoulder, causing another shudder to run through her.

Adara wanted nothing more than to remain like this for a while, him buried deep inside her, feeling as if they were joined together as one. But with her breathing heavy, her arms growing tired, even though Warrick kept most of his weight off her, she did not know how long she could hold herself up.

She need not have worried, Warrick's arm slipped around her just below her breasts and he eased her down with him on the bed for her to rest back against him.

"I am too heavy against you," she warned, hearing his breathing rapid in her ear.

"You weigh little and it does not matter, for I would die an extremely satisfied and happy man right now."

"Do not say such a thing," Adara scolded as she struggled to get off him.

His arm tightened around her. "Still yourself, wife. You are not going anywhere. I rode hard to get home to you tonight and you will not be leaving my side."

She shivered, a chill rushing over her, her body having lost the heat of their lovemaking, and turning her skin to gooseflesh.

"Damn," Warrick muttered and eased his wife up on the bed, to rest her head on the pillows and hurrying her legs beneath the blanket. He pulled himself up beside her to tuck the blankets around both of them after settling her against him.

The bairn gave her a hard kick just as she cuddled against her husband and she let out a soft yelp and laid her hand on her stomach.

Warrick muttered several oaths, his hand going to slip under hers and caress the bairn that kept moving around and poking his mum.

"I should not have touched you," Warrick said, guilt stirring in him for causing her and the protesting bairn discomfort.

"You did nothing to disturb him. He has been busy on his own," she assured him. "Besides, he should know how much we love each other and know he will be loved as well."

The bairn moved again but more slowly as if his mum's words brought him comfort.

Adara could still feel the tension in her husband and hoped to ease it. "Espy is here."

"I am pleased to know that."

Adara smiled, feeling the tension in his body begin to wash away. "And with Cyra and Innis here there is nothing to worry about. Now tell me how things went with you."

"The MacNair Clan will trouble me no more. I left Benet and a troop of warriors to see to my orders. The fools lost far too many of their own and for no good reason. Now they are under my rule."

"Roark returned with you?"

"I would know no peace from Callie if I had left her

husband behind."

Adara laughed softly. "You love your sister."

"She is a pest," Warrick argued.

"A pest you love," Adara said on a yawn.

"You need to sleep, wife."

Another yawn followed. "I believe I do, but not before I tell you how very much I love you. No matter what, Warrick, I love you."

"And I love you, wife," Warrick said puzzled and a bit disturbed by her last few words.

No matter what.

~~~

The morning meal was a festive one with Warrick having returned victorious and though everyone was enjoying themselves, he could tell something troubled his wife. She smiled and talked with everyone and yet her thoughts seemed far off and he had noticed her gait was slower today as if something weighed heavily on her. It troubled him and he intended to speak to her about it when the meal was finished. Though he asked again as he had done twice before, "Are you sure you are feeling well?"

"A bit tired, that is all," she assured him.

"You should rest after the meal is done."

"My intentions," she said with a smile.

He knew his wife's smile well and the smile she had turned on him had been a forced one. Something was wrong and he intended to find out as soon as possible. Unfortunately, that was delayed, a message from Benet needing his attention.

He and Roark left the others, though not before ordering his wife once again to rest and for all to hear. He was glad to hear Espy question his wife as he took his leave.

"You are not feeling well?" Espy asked.

"A bit tired, nothing more," Adara assured her.

"Then you should rest. Your time grows near."

Cyra agreed. "Do rest, Adara, you will need your strength to birth the bairn."

"Begging your pardon, my lady, but you are needed in the kitchen," Wynn said.

Adara nodded and stood, the bairn turning hard in her stomach as she did. She stilled and rested her hand there.

"You should rest," Espy scolded.

"I will as soon as I see to this I will retire to my bedchamber for the day."

Espy appeared relieved. "Good, I will come see you there later."

The two women walked silently through the stone hallway that connected the kitchen to the keep. Before reaching the kitchen, they turned and went to the door that led them outside.

Wynn snatched a cloak off the peg by the door and draped it over Adara's shoulders. "He waits behind the large boulder just beyond the kitchen garden."

Adara nodded.

"God be with you, lass," Wynn said and hugged Adara.

Snow had fallen last night, leaving deep tracks for anyone to follow not that Adara paid mind to it. Her thoughts on one thing alone, and she found herself hurrying her steps.

~~~

Warrick could not get his thoughts off his wife. They had agreed on sharing their worries and something obviously was worrying her, yet she did not speak of it to him. He saw to the message from Benet, settling the matter quickly by letting Benet know that those who felt they need not obey their new chieftain would be sent to Warrick's castle to serve him.

He saw to a couple of other matters with haste as well,

wanting to return to his wife, but was once again delayed when Selwyn, one of is trackers, approached.

"I may have found something, my lord," Selwyn said.

Warrick nodded for him to continue.

"With the freshly fallen snow, I noticed two tracks similar to ones where the dead man was found. I followed the one and it brought me to another set that reminded me of a faint track that was also similar to another found not far from the dead man."

"You saw these similar tracks again today?"

"I did," Selwyn said. "I could not find where the one track originated from but it led me to the keep garden where I found the other one. The one returned inside the keep and the other went into the woods."

Warrick did not need to ask Selwyn if he followed the tracks into the woods. He was his best tracker and did his job well. "Where in the woods did the tracks take you and who do they belong to?"

"Langdon, my lord, and he waits behind the large boulder near the kitchen garden."

"The one who entered the keep, do you know who that track belongs to?"

Selwyn nodded. "I believe it to belong to Wynn, my lord, though I cannot be sure."

"Come with me," Warrick ordered and Selwyn hurried behind Warrick, Roark following along as well.

When they reached the kitchen garden Selwyn scurried past Warrick, calling out, "Wait." He dropped down and examined the imprint in the snow and turned to look in the distance. He hurried to his feet and went to Warrick. "Another track, my lord, and one I recognize since I am familiar with it, having seen it often... your wife."

"She goes alone?" Warrick asked, clinching his hand in anger while concern filled his thoughts.

"Aye, my lord," Selwyn confirmed.

"No one is to follow me," Warrick ordered Roark and

followed his wife's fresh tracks into the woods. His mind was in turmoil, fearing the worse. Had Ronald's search for the true king led him here? Had Wynn known something about the true king and Ronald confronted her on it? Had Wynn killed him? An unlikely possibility with her advanced age and lack of strength. Had Langdon defended Wynn against Ronald? Or had, in the end, the true king been hiding here in Clan MacVarish all this time? And if so why?

His wife's frantic voice broke through his disturbing thoughts.

"No! No, you will not!"

Warrick hurried around the massive stone, hearing her distraught plea and came to an abrupt stop. His wife stood in front of Langdon, her brow resting against his shoulder and the man's arms around her. He appeared far different than he usually did. His shoulders were not stooped, they were broad, his chest wide, his gray hair not hanging loose around his face, but gathered back with a strip of cloth at the nape of his neck, and his eyes did not squint as if he had difficulty seeing, they were wide and alert, and threatening as he glared at Warrick.

"Adara step away from him now," Warrick ordered, realizing Langdon stood with regal comportment.

Langdon kept his arms around Adara.

"Harm my wife and I will kill you and not slowly, which would please the King since I have no doubt you are the man I search for," Warrick warned, wanting to rush at the man and get his wife away from him. But a knife was tucked in the sheath on this belt and he would not take the chance that Langdon would harm her.

Adara turned then, raising her hand as if to stop him from stepping toward them and tears ran down her cheeks. "No! No, you cannot hurt him, I beg you. Please, please, Warrick, do not hurt him... he is my father."

Too stunned to respond, it took a moment for him say, "Your father?"

"Aye, he is my father. Wynn told me the truth when I confronted her with evidence of being at the scene of the dead man. I insisted on meeting him and now he tells me he is leaving. I do not want him to leave. I want him to stay so we can make up for all the years we have missed."

"That is not possible," Langdon said sorrow heavy in his voice.

"It is possible. Tell him, Warrick. Tell him you are no threat to him. Tell him you will not turn him over to the King."

Warrick remained silent. This could not have gotten any worse and yet it had.

"That is not what the King wants from Warrick," Langdon said, Adara turning a puzzled look on her father. "Warrick's mission is to kill me."

Adara snapped her head around, her eyes wide. "You will see my da dead?"

Warrick focused his scowl on Langdon. "What proof have I that he is your father?"

Adara was quick to explain. "Wynn. She attended my birth as did my da. She knew that my mum and da secretly wed."

Warrick wanted to roar with rage at that news, but his only response was his eyes narrowing in anger.

"You leave your husband with a dilemma, daughter," Langdon said.

"What dilemma?" Adara asked, innocently.

"Tell her, Warrick," Langdon challenged.

Warrick remained silent, though his dark eyes spoke loud enough for him. He was ready to kill.

"Let me answer for him," Langdon said. "If he kills me, he leaves you as the true Scottish heir to the throne, and King James will not have that."

Adara shook her head. "No. No, my husband loves me. He would never harm me and I care not about the throne. I love my husband and want only a life with him."

Warrick was stunned, that his wife would choose him over her rightful heritage. He was the only thing that mattered to her. Her words echoed in his mind. *I love you no matter what.* She had let him know then that nothing would come between their love... not even a throne.

Adara could not hold back her tears. They fell of their own accord. "This must stop. It must. Too much has been lost. I will not lose anymore." She gasped aloud from the sudden pain and her hand went to her stomach as she felt something gush down from between her legs. She looked down and the pristine snow under her feet spread red with blood.

Donna Fletcher

Chapter Thirty-two

"Warrick," Adara cried out, but before she finished his
name he had her up in his arms and was running to the keep.
She wrapped her arms around his neck tight and whispered,
"I love you, please, always remember that I love you."

"Do not speak like they are your last words. You will be
fine. Espy will see to it," Warrick said. "I command it. You
will not die."

Langdon ran past him. "I will alert them." He ran off
ahead of them."

"Warrick," Adara whispered.

"Not a word. Save your strength," he ordered, his fear
rising like a demon to devour him. This was his fault, all his
fault. "I should have never touched you last night."

"No, it is no one's fault. You will not blame yourself for
this." She rested her brow to his cheek. "I love you. I wanted
you. If you blame yourself, then you blame me too. You
blame our love and I do not want to think that."

"Think only on how much I love you," Warrick said,
angry with himself for heaping more worry on her.

Innis met them in the Great Hall. "Espy and Cyra wait
in your bedchamber."

Warrick flew up the stairs and his fear mounted when
he saw the dire looks on Espy, Cyra, Callie, and Wynn's
faces. The sorrowful looks on Craven and Roark's faces did
nothing to help as well.

"On the bed," Espy ordered.

Warrick placed his wife gently on the bed, the blankets
having been turned back in wait.

"Please leave us," Espy ordered gently.

"No! I will not leave her," Warrick said, taking his

312

wife's hand, so small and cold, and locking his fingers with hers.

"You cannot help her and you will only be in the way. Leave her to me and Cyra… it is her only chance," Espy pleaded.

"Go, my husband, I will do fine," Adara encouraged, though the lack of conviction in her voice said much more.

Warrick fought with his need to remain with her, keep her safe, protect her, but Espy could only do that now. "Do not let her die," he ordered, glaring at Espy.

"Espy will do her best, but if," —Adara fought to keep the quiver out of her voice— "if for some reason I do not survive, Warrick, I want Espy to save the bairn. You cannot be upset with her if she must do that."

"What do you mean?" Warrick demanded.

"I want her to cut the bairn from me if there is no other way."

Warrick's mighty roar echoed off the stone walls. "No! Never will I allow her to do that."

While everyone took a step back, fearing the Demon Lord, Craven stepped forward. "I thought that way once when Espy tried to save mine and Aubrey's bairn. If I had not been so foolish, the child might have lived. Pay heed to your wife's courageous words and give your bairn the chance I did not give mine."

Warrick could not fathom that happening to his wife. He did not even want to think about it. He could not lose her. He could not and yet it seemed as if everyone believed her already dead. No. No. He would not have it.

He leaned over his wife, kissed her cheek and whispered in her ear. "You will not die, wife. You will not leave me. I command it."

"I will do my best, husband," Adara whispered, a tear trickling down her cheek.

Warrick kissed her brow. "My love and strength stay with you." He reluctantly let go of her hand and as it slipped out of his, he feared she was slipping away from him forever. He walked over to Espy. "Save them both, I beg of you save them both."

The room went silent. No one had ever heard the Demon Lord beg anyone.

Craven and Roark followed Warrick out of the room and down to the Great Hall where Innis was instructing the servants to prepare hot water and to gather clean cloths and moldy bread.

"You will go help them," Warrick said as if it was an order.

"They are in more capable hands with Espy and Cyra, especially Espy. Her father was a great physician, traveling to other countries and learning methods physicians here thought barbaric. If anyone can save your wife and child's lives, it is Espy."

His words brought some comfort and hope to Warrick as he joined Craven and Roark at a table. He gave a glance around and was not surprised that Langdon was nowhere to be seen. He did not care at the moment. His wife and bairn were the only thing that mattered.

~~~

"Tell me the truth, Espy. Am I going to die?" Adara asked, feeling a trickle of blood run out of her now and again as Cyra and Wynn helped her out of her garments and into a nightdress.

Espy answered honestly. "I do not know. I will use all I know, all my father taught me, and everything Cyra taught me, to save you and the bairn."

Cyra walked over to Espy, leaving Wynn and Callie to settle Adara and whispered, "I have seen this and it does not bode well."

"I know, but Father taught me that it is due to the afterbirth coming first. If it blocks the birth canal completely

314

there is nothing I can do. If it only partially blocks the birth canal, then there is a chance the bairn can deliver safely. Adara can survive as long as the bleeding remains minimal and her labor is not long and strenuous." Espy looked to Adara. "Did anyone ever speak to you of when your mum delivered you?"

Wynn answered, "I was there and her mum delivered her with ease, barely a pain, and not a shout from her."

Espy was pleased to hear that, for it gave her hope.

Adara felt another pain and rubbed at her stomach, silently letting the bairn know all would go well. *Please, God, please let it be so.*

~~~

Warrick could not remain seated after a while. He paced the length of the Great Hall, fear refusing to leave him. He did not know what he would do without Adara. He had not known how empty his life had been until he met her. Now he could not imagine life without her. Or the bairn he had come to love, having felt him move within his wife or give a hardy kick. He had thought often on how if he had a son how differently he would teach his son compared to how his father had taught him. He would make him strong, courageous, though not through fear. He would teach him that love was not weakness but strength, and he would heap love upon him so that he could feel and know the truth of it himself.

He stopped pacing when he reached the front of the Great Hall and saw Langdon step out of the shadows.

"We should talk while you wait," Langdon offered.

Warrick nodded, realizing he wanted to know the truth, for his wife was now in danger of the crown.

The two men sat in a dark corner of the Great Hall, Craven and Roark making certain the two men maintained their privacy.

315

Langdon did not wait, he spoke up almost as if he were eager to share his story. "I stumbled into Faline, Adara's mum, in the woods." He smiled at the memory. "Actually stumbled right into her, my arms going around her as we tumbled to the ground together. I had not seen her as I sprinted recklessly past trees and bushes, over hills and down glens. It was something I had done since a child, run at great speeds. It gave me a sense of freedom. The instant I looked upon her dark blue eyes just like Adara's, I fell in love." He laughed. "I foolishly stole a kiss and though Faline got upset, I caught a hint of a smile on her lips. It was all I needed to encourage me.

"That spring into summer was the best time of my life. I fell deeply in love with a beautiful woman who returned my love tenfold. I did not care about anything but Faline and when she told me she was with child, I wanted only to take her someplace safe and build a life with her. Unfortunately, the King learned there was a possibility of a threat to his throne. Few knew of my identity, but it was enough that I feared for Faline and my bairn's life.

"My close friend since childhood, Gregory, agreed to pose as Faline's husband and take them both far north into the Highlands. I planned to meet them when it was safe and take Faline and our daughter away. We wed secretly before Faline left." Tears glistened in his eyes. "My last night with her was much too brief. I did not want to let her go, but I had to. My heart broke when I held and kissed her for the last time. She was so courageous, telling me not to worry, we would be together again."

Warrick watched the man choke back tears and his own heart ached for him. He would have done the same to protect Adara.

"I did all I could to make sure I buried my identity and even from those who thought I should make a bid for the crown. I knew the devastating possibilities that could bring and I wanted no more death and destruction for my country.

316

I left for the Highlands." Langdon turned silent and squeezed his eyes shut for a brief moment. "My heart shattered completely when I discovered that Faline had succumbed to fever shortly after Gregory lost his life to the same and that my daughter was nowhere to be found."

Warrick remained silent when Langdon paused for a moment, the painful memories difficult for him.

"I finally learned that Faline had begged a crofter family to take Adara to her uncle Owen and that they would be paid handsomely for it. They never did. I also discovered that an ally of mine discovered that Adara was my child and to keep her safe, so he thought, he saw to it that she was moved from family to family. I learned he died and with him all connection to my daughter. I continued to search endlessly for her to no avail and finally decided to return here to MacVarish keep and see if Owen had any knowledge of my daughter's whereabouts. I cannot tell you how shocked I was when I saw Adara. She looks exactly like her mum, dark blue eyes, pale skin, blonde hair, and petite. I stayed on here, wanting to be close to her, angry that she had suffered so much and wanting to keep her safe while I could, knowing that one day I would have to leave her just as I had to leave her mum." Langdon choked back his tears.

"Ronald found out who you were," Warrick said.

He shook his head. "He found out that the heir he searched for had an heir of his own and that Wynn knew who it was. He threatened to tell the King and detailed the torture she would suffer if she refused. But he promised that he could save her from it if she would confide in him the identity of the heir. He even offered to share the purse the King would bestow on him when he gave him the news. He planned on betraying you, and taking the news to the King himself."

"I thought he would, but that would have never happened. I have people in King James's court that would have informed me of his presence before he could have gotten to the King."

"You are a wise man."

"A cautious and untrusting man," Warrick corrected. "You killed Ronald when he met with Wynn."

"I did. He threatened my daughter's safety, her life, and Wynn was only too glad to help me protect Adara as she has done all this time, never revealing Adara's or my true identity. Listening and learning if anyone made mention of a true heir to the Scottish throne. She was delighted when Adara arrived here. She could watch over her and keep her safe... until you arrived and then she began to worry. Now you know all of it and it remains to be seen what you will do with it."

"You know damn well I will not have it known that Adara is your daughter and put her life at risk. You are far from blind. You know I love your daughter and would do anything to keep her safe. It is why you remained here when I arrived with her as my wife. You waited to see how I would treat her."

"Aye, I did, and at first I doubted you were good enough for her, but in time I saw in her eyes what I had seen in her mum's eyes... a love so strong it could not be denied. I saw the same in you and knew my daughter had found a good man despite your infamous reputation."

"We will handle this," Warrick said, "but you know you have no choice. You have to leave."

"I know, but not until after I know if my daughter survives this birth."

Warrick scowled. "She will survive."

"Even the Demon Lord cannot command it so. She is in God's hands."

"I hear no screams, nothing but silence," Warrick said unable to contain his fear.

"Her mum barely made a sound. She delivered Adara with ease, perhaps Adara does the same."

Warrick wanted to believe him, but all he could think

was that he was going to lose his wife and if he did life would not be worth living.

~~~

Adara's pain came quick and fast and Espy's words encouraged her.

"You do good. The bleeding is but a trickle," Espy said, rubbing her lower back that ached relentlessly while worried that at any moment Adara's bleeding could worsen. "We need to get this bairn born."

Another pain hit Adara and Espy was quick to position herself between Adara's legs. "Do not grow alarmed when you feel my touch, Adara." Espy looked to her grandmother and the woman stood close by ready to help. With gentle fingers, she felt the afterbirth that blocked the bairn from slipping out. It was thin and the bairn eager to be born, a good sign.

Espy encouraged Adara and in a matter of only a few minutes, the bairn slipped out as if in a rush, bloody and screaming at the top of his lungs. "A son," Espy called out and the room burst with joy. A rush of blood followed the bairn once he was fully out and fear gripped Espy, but it was a quick spurt, nothing more and Espy sighed with relief, though she took no chances. After giving the bairn to Cyra, she got to work making sure all of the afterbirth was cleaned away, then she packed Adara with moldy bread.

"Wise decision, granddaughter," Cyra said after she severed the cord and wiped the bairn clean some before handing the lad to his mum.

Tears filled Adara's eyes as she took her crying son in her arms and placed his red cheek next to hers. "I will love you always, son." The bairn stopped crying as if he recognized her voice and he settled against her.

"Let us get you and the bairn cleaned up, then we will fetch your husband," Cyra said.

The women worked together but when they were near

done, Callie ran toward the door. "I cannot wait any longer. My brother needs to know all is well." She hurried down the stairs, rushing into the Great Hall.

Warrick jumped up off the bench at the sight of his sister rushing into the room, and though tears streamed down her cheeks, she wore the widest smile he had ever seen and it vanquished his fear.

"You have a son, Warrick, and Adara is fine," she cried out as she continued to cry with joy.

Warrick rushed up the stairs, leaving Roark to hug his wife. Craven, Innis, and Langdon followed Warrick.

As soon as he entered the room, he went straight to his wife, laying prone on the bed, a bundle tucked in the crook of her arm. His wife was as pale as snow and her eyes heavy with exhaustion. He gave Espy a quick glance.

Espy did not hesitate to reassure him. "She needs bed rest and to eat hardy the next few days so she can grow strong again."

Warrick nodded, intending to see Adara did just that. He leaned over his wife and kissed her brow. "You are a courageous woman, wife."

Adara smiled and said proudly, "Meet your son. He is the image of you."

Warrick sat on the edge of the bed and stared at the tiny bundle. His wife was right. There was no denying the bairn was his, but then he never doubted he was and now no one else would either.

"He is a handsome one," Warrick boasted.

Adara's smile grew. "Like his father."

"Time to leave the new parents to themselves," Espy announced and let out a groan as she doubled over, grabbing her stomach.

Craven had his arm around his wife in an instant and demanded anxiously, "What is wrong?"

Espy straightened up with another groan. "The bairn can wait no longer."

"Have you been in labor all this time?" Cyra asked, worry in her aging eyes.

Craven glared at her. "Have you?"

"Most of the time," Espy confessed, "though that does not help me now. Now I need a bed so my grandmother can deliver her great-grandchild."

Craven scooped his wife up in his arms and rushed from the room, all following but Langdon.

He stepped over to Warrick and Adara and glanced down at his grandson. "He is a fine lad and your mum would be proud of you."

"You are not leaving, are you?" Adara asked anxiously.

"I am not going anywhere, daughter."

Warrick remained silent, both men knowing he failed to add *just yet*. Adara did not need to know that now.

Adara turned pleading eyes on her husband. "All is well between you and my da?"

"There is nothing for you to worry about. All is well."

"I will visit with you tomorrow, daughter," Langdon said and with a nod to Warrick left the room, closing the door behind him.

"Tell me you will not take my da from me," she demanded, her smile having faded.

"You have my word, I will not take your da from you," he said, not wanting to think of the day she would have to say good-bye to him.

"What of your mission?"

He did not like that worry filled her eyes on such a happy occasion, but he knew if he did not soothe her concern now it would linger and steal her happiness. "I will let the King know that the man he seeks is dead."

"What if he wants proof?" Adara questioned.

"I will provide him with a body." Warrick ran a gentle finger along her pale cheek. "King James will be satisfied when I get done with everything. This is no talk to have on the day our son is born." He touched his son's cheek and the tiny lad appeared to smile.

Warrick and Adara smiled along with their son.

"We are family and always will be," Warrick said. "Never would I have imagined that the day I chose a disheveled servant lass as my wife that she would change my life forever... in the best way possible."

"And never did I imagine that I could come to love the Demon Lord, but it was so easy, for he is such a good man."

"How many times must I remind you I am not a good man?" he said with a playful scowl.

"It would take forever," she said on a soft whisper.

Warrick brushed his lips over hers. "Then forever it is, wife."

Chapter Thirty-three

Three months later

"Lord Warrick wishes to see you in his solar," Wynn said, after entering Adara's stitching room.

"I will take my nephew," Callie offered, holding eager hands out to Adara. "May I take him to see Roark? He does not get enough time with him."

Adara handed her son over to Callie, the woman taking the sleeping bairn into her arms and cuddling him close. "You and Roark are going to spoil him. Take him, I am sure he will be pleased to see his uncle and he has just been fed so he has no need of me for a while."

Callie smiled and hurried to bundle the lad against the cold. "Go and take as long as you would like. Roark and I will look after him."

Adara left with Wynn and just before they reached the solar she stopped and with a gentle hand to the woman's arm asked, "Are you not feeling well, Wynn? You do not wear your usual smile."

"Tired, that is all, my lady," Wynn said and hurried off.

Adara wondered if she needed to lighten Wynn's duties again as she opened the door to the solar and when she saw her da standing there she knew what bothered Wynn.

Her da was leaving.

Adara remained at the open door unable to take another step. The last three months had been wonderful, the best in her entire life. Callie would deliver a bairn this summer and Espy had delivered a beautiful daughter, Astie, named after Cyra's mum, and Craven already had a small wooden sword made, ready to teach her how to use it. She had gotten to know her da, had learned more about her mum and his friend Gregory who had given so much to help her parents. She had loved spending time with her da and her heart had filled with joy every time he told her how much he loved her. He felt the same about his grandson, since he could not hold him enough, though now she knew why.

He had known he would not stay here and she had known it herself, though had not wanted to admit it. He would leave to make sure she remained safe.

Warrick walked over to her, his heart breaking for his wife. He rested his hand on her curved hip. Some of the changes their son had made to her body had remained, leaving her body even more alluring and inviting than before. She had healed well over the last few months and they had made love well and often. She had smiled more than he had ever seen her smile, spending time with her da and their son. He hated to see her smile disappear and her heart about to be shattered.

"I will wait outside the door," he said, wanting to give her time alone with her da, but wanting to be near if she should need him.

Adara shook her head. "No, do not leave me."

He leaned down to kiss her brow. "I will be right here for you."

Adara nodded and with limbs she feared would not support her, she walked over to her da. "You are leaving?" The words brought on tears that pooled in her eyes.

"Aye, I am. I have to," her da said, tears threatening his eyes as well.

"But Warrick took care of everything. The King searches for you no more."

"I must be sure. There is one who knows of me, a friend, and though there is talk he has died, I must make certain he told no one, for the safety of you and my grandson who carries my name—Langdon—a new name that takes me into my new life."

Adara threw her arms around her da, her tears falling freely unable to hold them back any longer.

Her da held her tight, his own tears falling. When she looked up at him, he was brought back those many years ago when he had said good-bye to Adara's mum, and his heart broke all over again.

"You will come back. Please, Da, come back to me," she begged.

"I made a promise to your mum that we would be together again and I failed to keep it. I make this promise now and I will not fail to keep it. I will return to you, daughter, and watch my grandson grow and all his brothers and sisters as well."

Adara hugged him tight again. "I love you, Da."

"And I love you, Adara, with all my heart." Her da eased her away from him, kissed her brow, and hurried to the door. As he passed Warrick, he said, choking back his tears, "Take care of her."

"Always," Warrick said.

Adara turned, tears streaming down her cheeks, and Warrick went to her and wrapped her in his strong arms, keeping her close, wishing in some way he could take her pain so she would suffer no more.

She hugged her husband tight, holding on to him, never wanting to let him go, fearful that somehow she would lose him too.

"I am not going anywhere, wife. I have told you time and again and will continue to tell you. You are stuck with me."

Adara turned a sad smile on him as she sniffled back her tears. "I am glad I am stuck with you."

"Do not worry over him. He will be fine and return when he is sure it is safe."

"So he promises, but I fear he will not keep his promise, though not through any fault of his own."

"That will not happen, wife."

He spoke with confidence she did not feel. "You cannot be sure of that."

"Aye, I can. I sent men to follow him. They will keep him safe for you and his grandson."

Adara's face broke into a wide grin. "Oh, Warrick, you could not have given me a better gift, and I will never be able to thank you enough."

"You need not thank me, wife. I love when you smile and I will do whatever it takes to keep that smile on your beautiful face."

Adara let her smile fade.

"My loving words chase your smile?" Warrick asked puzzled.

She tapped his chest, then ran her finger down to just below his waist. "I know what could put a smile back on my face."

Warrick brought his lips near hers. "As I said, wife, I will do whatever it takes to keep that smile on your face."

Adara brushed her lips over his. "You are going to be a busy husband."

"I am up to the task."

Her hand drifted further down, and her smile returned. "You definitely are."

Warrick scooped her up in his arms. "Where is our son, wife?"

"With Callie and Roark."

"Good, since his mum is going to be busy smiling for the next couple of hours."

THE END

Titles by Donna Fletcher

Highland Warriors Trilogy
To Love A Highlander
Embraced By A Highlander
Highlander The Demon Lord

The Pict King Series
The King's Executioner
The King's Warrior
The King and His Queen

Macinnes Sisters Trilogy
The Highlander's Stolen Heart
Highlander's Rebellious Love
Highlander: The Dark Dragon

Cree & Dawn Series
Highlander Unchained/Forbidden Highlander
Highlander's Captive
Cree & Dawn Short Stories
Highlander's True Love
Highlander's Promise
Highlander's Winter Tale
Highlander's Rescue

Warrior King Series
Bound To A Warrior
Loved By a Warrior
A Warrior's Promise
Wed To a Highland Warrior

Sinclare Brothers' Series
Return of the Rogue
Under the Highlander's Spell
The Angel & The Highlander

Donna Fletcher

Highlander's Forbidden Bride

The Irish Devil
Irish Hope

Isle of Lies
Love Me Forever

For a complete list of Donna's titles, visit her website.
www.donnafletcher.com

About the Author

It was her love of reading and daydreaming that started USA Today bestselling author Donna Fletcher's writing career. Besides gobbling up books, her mom generously bought for her, she spent a good portion of her time lost in daydreams that took her on grand adventures. She met heroes, villains, and heroines that, while usually in danger, always found the strength and courage to prevail. She traveled all over the world and through time in her dreams. Some places and times fascinated her more than others and she would rush to the library (no Internet at that time) and read all she could about that particular period and place. After a while, she simply could not ignore all the adventures swirling around in her head. She had no choice but to bring them more vividly to life, and so she started writing.

Donna enjoys living on the beautiful Jersey Shore surrounded by family and friends and a cat who thinks she's a princess, but what cat doesn't, and a dog named after a favorite hero…Cree.

Stop by and visit with Donna at her website www.donnafletcher.com and if you don't want to miss any of her new releases, subscribe to her newsletter.